Take Two

Other Life-Changing Fiction™ by Karen Kingsbury

9/11 Series
One Tuesday Morning
Beyond Tuesday Morning
Every Now and Then

Lost Love Series
Even Now
Ever After
Every Now and Then

Above the Line Series
Above the Line: Take One
Above the Line: Take Two
Above the Line: Take Three (spring 2010)
Above the Line: Final Cut (summer 2010)

Stand-Alone Titles
Oceans Apart
Between Sundays
This Side of Heaven
When Joy Came to Stay
On Every Side
Divine
Like Dandelion Dust
Where Yesterday Lives
Shades of Blue (fall 2009)

Redemption Series
Redemption
Remember
Return
Rejoice
Reunion

Firstborn Series
Fame
Forgiven
Found
Family
Forever

Sunrise Series
Sunrise
Summer
Someday
Sunset

Red Glove Series
Gideon's Gift
Maggie's Miracle
Sarah's Song
Hannah's Hope

Forever Faithful Series
Waiting for Morning
Moment of Weakness
Halfway to Forever

Women of Faith Fiction Series
A Time to Dance
A Time to Embrace

Cody Gunner Series
A Thousand Tomorrows
Just Beyond the Clouds

Children's Titles
Let Me Hold You Longer
Let's Go on a Mommy Date
We Believe in Christmas
Let's Go Have a Daddy Day (spring 2009)

Miracle Collections
A Treasury of Christmas Miracles
A Treasury of Miracles for Women
A Treasury of Miracles for Teens
A Treasury of Miracles for Friends
A Treasury of Adoption Miracles

Gift Books
Stay Close Little Girl
Be Safe Little Boy
Forever Young: Ten Gifts of Faith for the Graduate

www.KarenKingsbury.com

Karen Kingsbury

ABOVE THE LINE SERIES

Take Two

BOOK TWO

ZONDERVAN®

ZONDERVAN

Take Two

Requests for information should be addressed to:

Zondervan, *Grand Rapids, Michigan 49530*

ISBN-13: 978-1-61523-210-0

Published in association with the literary agency of Alive Communications, Inc., 7680 Goddard Street, Suite 200, Colorado Springs, CO 80920.

Interior design by Michelle Espinoza

Printed in the United States of America

Dedication

To Donald, my Prince Charming …

How I rejoice to see you coaching again, sharing your gift of teaching and your uncanny basketball ability with another generation of kids—and best yet, now our boys are part of the mix. Isn't this what we always dreamed of? I love sitting back this time and letting you and God figure it out. I'll always be here—cheering for you and the team from the bleachers. But God's taught me a thing or two about being a coach's wife. He's so good that way. It's fitting that you would find varsity coaching again now—after twenty years of marriage. Hard to believe that as you read this, our twentieth anniversary has come and gone. I look at you and I still see the blond, blue-eyed guy who would ride his bike to my house and read the Bible with me before a movie date. You stuck with me back then and you stand by me now—when I need you more than ever. I love you, my husband, my best friend, my Prince Charming. Stay with me, by my side, and let's watch our children take wing, savoring every memory and each day gone by. Always and always … The ride is breathtakingly beautiful, my love. I pray it lasts far into our twilight years. Until then, I'll enjoy not always knowing where I end and you begin. I love you always and forever.

To Kelsey, my precious daughter …

You are almost twenty and though I cringe even writing those words, I am blessed to be your mom and your friend. My heart soars with joy when I see all that you are, all you've become. This is a precious year for us because you're still home, attending junior college, and spending nearly every day in the dance studio. When you're not dancing, you're helping out with the business and ministry of Life-Changing Fiction™—so we have many precious hours together. I know this time is short and won't last, but I'm enjoying it so much—you, no longer the high school girl, a young woman and in every way my daughter, my friend. That part will always stay, but you, my sweet girl, will go where your dreams lead, soaring through the future doors God opens.

Honey, you grow more beautiful—inside and out—every day. And always I treasure the way you talk to me, telling me your hopes and dreams and everything in between. I can almost sense the plans God has for you, the very good plans. I pray you keep holding on to His hand as He walks you toward them. I love you, sweetheart.

To Tyler, my lasting song . . .

I can hardly wait to see what the next school year brings you, my precious son. Last year you were one of Joseph's brothers, and you were Troy Bolton, and Captain Hook—becoming a stronger singer and stage actor with every role. This year you began a new high school, where God has continued to shape you as the leader He wants you to be. I'll never forget the moment on the K-Love Cruise this past year when you were so deeply moved during worship. You told me, "Mom, I think God is leading me into a future of Christian music." Wow, Ty. What an amazing God we serve, that He is putting such a dream on your heart now, while you are not yet a junior in high school. I still love seeing you on a stage, but I sense that you want to spend more time on a different stage—the stage of life. I know it's hard realizing that time with your best friend, Kelsey, is running short. But you'll be fine, and no matter where God leads you in the future, the deep and lasting family relationships you've begun here in your childhood will remain.

Thank you for the hours of music and song. As you finish up your sophomore year, I am mindful that time is rushing past, and I make a point to stop and listen a little longer when I hear you singing. Your dad and I are proud of you, Ty, of the young man you've become. We're proud of your talent and your compassion for people and your place in our family. However your dreams unfold, I'll be in the front row to watch them happen. Hold on to Jesus, Ty. I love you.

To Sean, my happy sunshine …

What a scare we had this past year watching you go through encephalitis and mono. I'll never forget the way your faith shone in the emergency room that one terrible night. I told you that without a spinal tap, you might die. You only looked at me, confused, and said, "Well, then I'd be home with Jesus, and that would be better!" The staff at the hospital was amazed, and I stood in awe of your deep belief—even in the delirium of your sickness.

New things are just around the corner for you, Sean. I can hardly believe you start high school in the fall, taking on a host of new adventures in the process. Always remember who you are and whose you are as you venture into that next step. One of the things I love most about you, Sean, is your beautiful smile and the way your eyes light up when we're together as a family. Keep that always. You are a bright sunbeam, bringing warmth to everyone around you.

One thing that will stand out about this past year is your crazy ping-pong skills. I absolutely love playing against you, Sean. You're quick as lightning and it makes me a better player. Of course … I never really thought I'd be hoping for a win against my little boy. But then, you're not all that little anymore. I'm proud of you, Sean. I love you more than you know. I pray God will use your positive spirit to always make a difference in the lives around you. You're a precious gift, Son. Keep smiling and keep seeking God's best for your life.

To Josh, my tenderhearted perfectionist . . .

The weeks of this past school year have flown by, and you have grown right along with them, my precious son. So many memories will remind me of your eighth-grade year, but some will always stand out. The week, for instance, when you scored five touchdowns in your team's city championship—three rushing, two on interception returns. Then that same week you turned around and scored a total of eight goals in two intense soccer games against the top teams in our state. Amazing. No wonder I'm always seeking to make our devotions about staying humble! Seriously, sweetheart, God has given you tremendous talent in sports. I have no doubt that someday we will see your name in headlines and that—if God allows it—you'll make it to the pros. You're that good, and everyone around you says so.

Now, flash back to that single moment in a broken-down Haitian orphanage. There I was meeting Sean and EJ for the first time when you walked up, reached up with your small fingers and brushed back my bangs, and said, "Hi, Mommy. I love you." It might've taken six months, but I knew as you said those words that you belonged with us. The picture becomes clearer all the time.

Keep being a leader on the field and off. One day people will say, "Hmmm. Karen Kingsbury? Isn't she Josh's mom?" I can't wait for the day. You have an unlimited future ahead of you, Josh, and I'll forever be cheering on the sidelines. Keep God first in your life. I love you always.

To EJ, my chosen one . . .

Here you are in the last few months of seventh grade, and I can barely recognize the student athlete you've become. Those two years of homeschooling with Dad continue to reap a harvest a hundred times bigger than what was sown, and we couldn't be prouder of you. But even beyond your grades, we are blessed to have you in our family for so many reasons. You are wonderful with our pets—always the first to feed them and pet them and look out for them—and you are a willing worker when it comes to chores.

Besides all that, you make us laugh—oftentimes right out loud. I've always believed that getting through life's little difficulties and challenges requires a lot of laughter—and I thank you for bringing that to our home. You're a wonderful boy, Son, a child with such potential. Clearly, that's what you displayed the other day when you came out of nowhere in your soccer qualifiers and scored three goals.

I'm amazed because you're so talented in so many ways, but all of them pale in comparison to your desire to truly live for the Lord. I'm so excited about the future, EJ, because God has great plans for you, and we want to be the first to congratulate you as you work to discover those. Thanks for your giving heart, EJ. I love you so.

To Austin, my miracle boy . . .

Here it is, baseball season again, and once more I smile when I see you at bat. You take your sports so seriously, but even more than that, you take your role as our son seriously. The other day we were driving somewhere and you said that your friend Karter made an observation. "Austin," he said, "I think you're going to grow up to be just exactly like your dad." You shared that story proudly and beamed at us from the backseat. And up in the front seat, your dad had tears in his eyes.

Yes, Austin, you are growing up to be like your daddy. There could be no greater compliment, because your dad is the most amazing man. The bittersweetness of knowing that every morning you stand a little taller is juxtaposed with the joy of knowing Karter is right. You're a little more like your dad every day. I love your tender heart, Austin, the times late at night when you come to me, tears in your eyes, and tell me you're missing Papa. The other kids miss him, too, but I don't hear it from them as often as I hear it from you. Papa's still cheering for you, Son. As you soar toward your teenage years please don't forget that or him.

You're my youngest, my last, Austin. I'm holding on to every moment, for sure. Thanks for giving me so many wonderful reasons to treasure today. I thank God for you, for the miracle of your life. I love you, Austin.

And to God Almighty, the Author of Life, who has—for now—blessed me with these.

Acknowledgments

No book comes together without a great and talented team of people making it happen. For that reason, a special thanks to my friends at Zondervan who combined efforts to make *Above the Line: Take Two* all it could be. A special thanks to my dedicated editor, Sue Brower, and to my brilliant publicist Karen Campbell, and to Karwyn Bursma, whose creative marketing is unrivaled in the publishing business.

Also, thanks to my amazing agent, Rick Christian, president of Alive Communications. Rick, you've always believed only the best for me. When we talk about the highest possible goals, you see them as doable, reachable. You are a brilliant manager of my career, and I thank God for you. But even with all you do for my ministry of writing, I am doubly grateful for your encouragement and prayers. Every time I finish a book, you send me a letter that deserves to be framed, and when something big happens, yours is the first call I receive. Thank you for that. But even more, the fact that you and Debbie are praying for me and my family keeps me confident every morning that God will continue to breathe life into the stories in my heart. Thank you for being so much more than a brilliant agent.

A special thank you to my husband, who puts up with me on deadline and doesn't mind driving through Taco Bell after a basketball game if I've been editing all day. This wild ride wouldn't be possible without you, Donald. Your love keeps me writing; your prayers keep me believing that God has a plan in this ministry of fiction. And thanks for the hours you put in working with the guestbook entries on my website. It's a full-time job, and I am grateful for your concern for my reader friends. I look forward to that time every day when you read through them, sharing them with me and releasing them to the public, lifting up the prayer requests. Thank you, honey. And thanks to all my kids, who pull together, bring me iced green tea, and understand my sometimes crazy schedule. I love that you know you're still first, before any deadline.

Thank you also to my mom, Anne Kingsbury, and to my sisters, Tricia, Sue, and Lynne. Mom, you are amazing as my assistant—working day and night sorting through the mail from my readers. I appreciate you more than you'll ever know.

Tricia, you are the best executive assistant I could ever hope to have. I treasure your loyalty and honesty, the way you include me in every decision and the daily exciting website changes. My site has been a different place since you stepped in, and the hits have grown tenfold. Along the way, the readers have so much more to help them in their faith, so much more than a story with this Life-Changing Fiction™. Please know that I pray for God's blessings on you always, for your dedication to helping me in this season of writing, and for your wonderful son, Andrew. And aren't we having such a good time too? God works all things to the good!

Sue, I believe you should've been a counselor! From your home far from mine, you get batches of reader letters every day, and you diligently answer them using God's wisdom and His Word. When readers get a response from "Karen's sister Susan," I hope they know how carefully you've prayed for them and for the responses you give. Thank you for truly loving what you do, Sue. You're gifted with people, and I'm blessed to have you aboard.

A special thanks also to Will Montgomery, my road manager. I was terrified to venture into the business of selling my books at events for a couple of reasons. First, because I never wanted to profit from selling my books at speaking events, and second, because I would never have the time to handle such details. Monty, you came in and made it all come together. With a mission statement that reads, "To love and serve the readers," you have helped me supply books and free gifts to tens of thousands of readers at events across the country. More than that, you've become my friend, a very valuable part of the ministry of Life-Changing Fiction™. You are loyal and kind and fiercely protective of me, my family, and the work God has me doing. Thank you for everything you're doing and will continue to do.

Thanks, too, to Olga Kalachik, my office assistant, who helps organize my supplies and storage area, and who prepares our home for the marketing events and research gatherings that take place there on a regular basis. I appreciate all you're doing to make sure I have time to write. You're wonderful, Olga, and I pray God continues to bless you and your precious family.

I also want to thank my friends with Extraordinary Women —Roy Morgan, Tim and Julie Clinton, Beth Cleveland, Charles Billingsley, and so many others. Also my friends at Women of Joy, including Phil Waldrip. How wonderful to be a part of what God is doing through all of you. Thank you for making me part of your family.

Thanks also to my forever friends and family, the ones who have been there and continue to be there. Your love has been a tangible source of comfort, pulling us through the tough times and making us know how very blessed we are to have you in our lives.

And the greatest thanks to God. The gift is Yours. I pray I might use it for years to come in a way that will bring You honor and glory.

Forever in Fiction

Whenever I receive the completed paperwork for a Forever in Fiction winner, I read through the details of the life being honored in fiction—whether the person is alive or dead—and I am touched by the real-life stories that come my way.

That was especially true for Laurie Weeks, forty-five. I read the information sent in about Laurie, and I kept seeing all we had in common, how Laurie and I would've certainly been friends if we would've met. Our love of family and healthy living, board games and beaches ... Even our shared joy at documenting our family's activities in photographs. The similarities were striking.

Laurie was one of four siblings—three sisters and a brother. She married when she was twenty-two and had three children—Audrey, twenty-three; Lucas, nineteen; and Sam, seventeen. She loved the beach and the Bible and playing Apples to Apples when her family was gathered together. Trips to Atlantic Beach in North Carolina were always accompanied by a trip to her favorite Windmill Restaurant, walks on the beach, and fresh grilled salmon. She walked every day and never missed the sporting events and musical performances of her children.

Laurie was 5'5{dec63} and slender, with brown hair, green eyes, and a contagious smile. She rooted for the underdog, and people knew her as a peacemaker—confident and trustworthy. She played the handbells in her church bell choir and served as family photographer for the many special moments she helped create for those she loved. A spiritual high for Laurie was 2001, when she and Audrey took a mission trip to Nicaragua.

Laurie was diagnosed with multiple myeloma in June of 2005. Though she nearly died twice in the ensuing months, her family prayed for a miracle. Laurie lived long enough to attend the funeral of her ninety-six-year-old grandmother and long enough to share one last very beautiful Christmas with her family. She lived to see a final prom and her son's confirmation, along with one last season of football and musical performances. Throughout her illness, she endured much pain, but she never complained or let others see how she suffered. Though her family prayed for more time, God had other plans for Laurie. She loved Jesus very much and knew she would be well with her Savior—but she hated the thought of leaving her family. Laurie went home to heaven in March 2006—just nine months after her diagnosis. Those who love her miss her very much.

Laurie was placed Forever in Fiction by her sister—Cindy Jacks—who won the item at the Lafayette Christian School auction, a year after Laurie died. A special thanks to Cindy for honoring her sister this way. I chose to make Laurie the friend of my character Kelly Ryan—producer Chase Ryan's wife. Much as I believe Laurie would've been a friend of mine, her character will certainly be a friend to Kelly Ryan in this time of dramatic highs and uncertain lows. Cindy, I pray that your family will be blessed by the placement of Laurie in the pages of *Above the Line: Take Two* and that when you read this book you will always see some of Laurie here, where she will be Forever in Fiction.

For those of you who are not familiar with Forever in Fiction, it is my way of involving you, the readers, in my stories, while raising money for charities. To date, Forever in Fiction has raised more than one hundred thousand dollars at charity auctions across the country. Obviously I am only able to donate a limited number of these each year. For that reason, I have set a fairly high minimum bid on this package so that the maximum funds are raised for charities.

If you are interested in having a Forever in Fiction package donated to your auction, contact my assistant, Tricia Kingsbury, at Kingsburydesk@aol.com. Please write *Forever in Fiction* in the subject line.

Take Two

One

Kendall Adams sat across from her father in the executive boardroom of his Los Angeles high-rise and stared at the rolling hills of Hollywood in the distance. October was always like this—brilliant blue skies and air as clear as a summer day in Montana. Kendall breathed deep, stood, and sauntered to the window.

"I'm still amazed—" She glanced over her shoulder at her dad. "—that you're doing this."

"It's my passion too." Her father smiled, and the warmth in his eyes belied his cunning business sense and high-profile international-billionaire status. "I've been looking for an investment opportunity like this for years."

Kendall looked down from twenty-three stories at a busy Melrose Boulevard. What would this venture bring, this decision to team up with Chase Ryan and Keith Ellison? Was filmmaking where she would find healing for her broken heart?

She watched a breeze dance through the palm trees that framed the constant traffic below.

"You're thinking about him again." Her father was on his feet, coming toward her. "I can feel it."

"No." She linked her arm through his as he came up alongside her. "About the movies. And whether or not this is when life finds its way back to normal again."

A tight-lipped sigh hung briefly on her dad's lips. "I wish I never would've introduced you to that … that—"

"It's over." Her calm voice reflected none of the pain that still colored the edges of every moment. "I don't blame you or me. Or God. It's time for whatever's next."

A comfortable silence fell around them, tempered only by the distant sounds of telephones and office staff on the other side of the door.

"Will you tell them? The producers?"

"No." She didn't hesitate. "What happened was private. The media never really figured out the story, so no one else needs to."

Sympathy shadowed her father's expression. "Good call. You'll spend a lot of time with Chase and Keith, but it's better to ... well, you know, keep things on a business level."

Kendall studied her dad for a long moment. Times like this she still wondered if he merely offered fatherly advice or worried about saving face, about making sure no one knew how much she'd lost over the last year. How much they'd both lost.

A shiver ran down her spine. Maybe if she pretended it never happened, a time would come when she might go a whole day without feeling the pain.

The phone rang from the middle of the long table and her dad answered it. "Yes, fine. We're ready for them." He hung up and reached back to give her a hug. "It's a new day, Kendall. God's going to use this partnership. I have a great feeling about it."

Giving her father a smile, she ordered herself to set aside the memories of the past. Her dad was right. This was a new time for both of them.

She smoothed her blouse and stayed at her father's elbow as he moved to the door. His secretary knocked at about the same time and ushered in Chase and Keith. This was the first time the four of them had been together since the wrap party in Bloomington, Indiana, for *The Last Letter*, so the greetings between them took a little longer than usual.

As soon as they were seated at the table, Chase leaned back and gripped the armrests. "Keith and I truly appreciate you taking the time to meet with us." He looked at his friend and then back to Kendall and her father. "But with the economy the way it is, we don't want you to feel obligated to give us additional financial help. We wanted to get that out at the beginning."

Kendall felt like rushing around the table and giving the guy a hug. Did he know how rare his attitude was in Hollywood? The idea of looking out for someone else first?

She shared a smile with her dad and the look in his eyes told her to take the lead. She sat up a little straighter. "Actually, we're more committed to your movies now than ever."

"That's right. Kendall has great news about your next film—the one we talked about last time we were together." Her father looked elated. He had said once that his fortune brought him no joy whatsoever except when it could be used to share God's truth and light, and when it could help make other people's dreams come true. "And I'm certain you're needing more funds for the editing process, is that right?"

"Actually, we're okay." Keith opened a file he'd brought with him and handed copies of an accounting sheet to Kendall and her father. "The funds you provided at the end of the shoot have gone a long way. We'll get through the editing process okay. It's what happens after that."

"Publicity and advertising—or the P&A budget, as they call it." Kendall's father grinned. "Not a problem, guys. Count me in. We want this movie on the big screens."

Chase looked a little dizzy, and again something about him touched Kendall's heart. He was sincere and kind, genuine in his desire to make movies for the purpose of reaching people. With everything in her she hoped the movie business never changed him.

Once they moved past the initial budget issues for *The Last Letter*, Kendall took over. "The author of *Unlocked* is still very interested in giving you both the option for her book. It's been on the *New York Times* Best-Sellers List for ten weeks now."

"We know." Keith allowed the hint of a smile. "We figured she must've had a hundred offers by now."

"She has." Kendall felt her eyes begin to dance. Like her father, she loved this—watching the impossible become a reality for a couple of good guys like Keith and Chase. "But she wants to work with you." She pulled a notepad from her bag and checked the details. "Stephanie's on deadline for her next novel. She'll be busy the next month or so. Then she'd like to fly here and meet you. Get the option in ink." She looked up. "That should give you enough time to finish editing *The Last Letter* and submit the film to the festivals. Which I'd like to help with, by the way."

She could see Chase wrestling with a question. After a few seconds he lost the battle. "Brandon Paul? Is that still an option for *Unlocked*?"

Kendall laughed—the happy lighthearted laughter that had once marked her world. "He's more than an option. I talked to him yesterday. He's in. We only have to work out the details with his agent, pull together a screenplay and a director." She grinned at the men around her. "Monumental details like that."

Both Keith and Chase hesitated, but seeing Kendall and her father's confidence, they both chuckled and the mood relaxed. They spent the next few moments talking about their families, their wives and kids. Keith was worried about his college-aged daughter, Andi, away at school in Bloomington, and Chase was concerned his wife might get tired of running things back in San Jose. But for the most part, life was good for the producers, and Kendall was glad. They would need to be strong. If their experience was like hers, Hollywood life would test them sorely.

The meeting lasted another thirty minutes while they worked out specific details of the financing and repayment plan for *The Last Letter*. They discussed how Kendall would look for additional investors for *Unlocked* as well. The budget would be considerably higher because of Brandon Paul, but because of her father Kendall was very connected with Hollywood's wealthy elite—people looking for film projects to invest in. She knew she'd find someone.

When the guys left, everyone shared hugs. Kendall hugged Chase last, and not until she was in his arms did she realize with great alarm something that hadn't occurred to her before.

Chase's athletic build was the same as that of Kendall's ex-husband.

She drew back quickly, though not quickly enough to let on what she felt. Heat rushed to her cheeks, and she hurried through one last round of good-byes.

Even before the producers reached the end of the hall, Kendall's father kissed her cheek. "I have to check on another meeting down the hall. Will you be here?"

"No." She still felt flustered, dizzy almost. "I … I have an appointment in Laguna Beach with an investor."

She bid him good-bye and walked to the elevator, grateful no one else found their way into her car as she made her way down. Why hadn't she seen it before, the physical resemblance between Jay Randolph and Chase Ryan?

She hurried through the lobby and into the parking structure, and when she was alone in her car she leaned back against the headrest and closed her eyes. *God … let me get past this. Please.* She longed for a response. But there was none. And like that, the past played out again in her mind.

The car accident had been horrific, one of the worst in recent history. It had nearly killed Jay, and the details that followed had nearly killed Kendall. Jay had been driving Kendall's car. The head-on crash had taken place in a handful of seconds, long enough for a drunk driver in a work truck to cross the double yellow lines on Mulholland Drive and barrel head on into a speeding Jay. The mangled metal heaps that remained once the dust settled made it hard for rescue workers to know exactly how many victims they were working with.

At first media reports had it that Kendall had been killed in the wreck. But she was working with Compassion International in Costa Rica when the frantic text messages began popping up on her phone.

Are you alive?

Are you okay?

Thank God Jay's alive!

And dozens of promises to pray. She took a flight back that afternoon, and by the time her plane touched down everyone knew the truth.

The dead body in the passenger seat of Kendall's BMW was not Kendall, but rather the twenty-two-year-old model Jay had been secretly seeing. At almost the same time, another significant piece of information rose to the surface: the young woman had been eight months pregnant with Jay's son.

The story hit the news, of course, but to this day Kendall was grateful it hadn't blown up across the front pages. The media never made much of the fact that Jay was Ben Adams' son-in-law, and since the accident wasn't only Jay's fault, the media lost interest. The same couldn't be said for the lawyers in the case.

The parents of the dead pregnant model hired a team of attorneys days after her funeral. The victim had been the single mother of two little girls—neither fathered by Jay. But since the drunk driver had no insurance, and since Jay was cited with reckless driving for speeds in excess of eighty miles per hour, the lawyers came after Kendall's father—the registered owner of the BMW.

In court the truth about the woman came out. She had been a terrible mother, rarely visiting her children and leaving her own mother to raise them. At the time of the accident, the model hadn't spoken with her mother or her daughters for more than a year. Still, her mother contended that she could continue to raise her granddaughters, but she would need a great deal of money to pull it off. By the time the haggling and courtroom drama ended, the settlement for the woman's daughters had cost Kendall's father just under a million dollars.

The accident cost Kendall a lot more than that.

She talked to Jay just once afterwards, late at night during an unannounced visit to the hospital. She found him hooked to an IV, his legs in a pair of casts, bandages around his head. Even with that, he was watching TV as if he hadn't just been party to a fatal accident, as if his whole world hadn't fallen apart. She stood in the hospital doorway staring at him, seeing him the way he'd looked five years earlier, the night they met.

He must've heard her, because he turned his head, and when he saw her, his face fell. For a long while he held her gaze, then he turned off the TV and looked away. "I'm surprised you came."

"Me too." She moved slowly into his room, clutching her purse in front of her, as if keeping something between them might protect her heart from further damage. She reached the side of his bed and waited. Just waited, because she figured it wasn't her job to do the talking.

The silence quickly became unbearable and he rattled loose a long sigh. His eyes found hers again. "I was going to tell you." He brought his hand slowly to his face and pressed his fingers against his brow. "I just . . . I hadn't figured out how."

Kendall could voice just one question. "Did you . . . love her?"

He closed his eyes for a long time. When he opened them again he said something that had stayed with her ever since. "Everybody loves everybody in this business." His lips were dry and cracked. He ran his tongue over them, buying time. "It was my fault. I let it get out of hand."

"Out of hand?" She wanted to scream at him. His girlfriend had been about to deliver his baby. The baby Kendall hadn't been able to give him. "Were you planning to marry her?"

Again he hesitated. Then, "It doesn't matter."

Kendall thought of a dozen more questions, a hundred things she might say. But in the end she said nothing. The silence between them deafened her, the whir of machines and the sickly, antiseptic hospital smell filling her senses.

Finally he spoke. "My attorney is drawing up the papers. The divorce will be final before summer's over."

And like that, five years were finished.

The trouble was Kendall hadn't seen it coming. In the days since the accident she had relived every wonderful day of their relationship a thousand times. In all her life she'd never met anyone like Jay Randolph. He had a faith that made him larger than life, and a charisma that made him the center of attention wherever he went. Her father introduced them at an Academy Awards after-party. Kendall liked to say he swept her off her feet and stole her heart all in a single conversation.

Kendall credited the Lord with a pair of miracles in the months since that final meeting with Jay. First, she had survived with a determination to live—to truly live. Part of that came from her desire to help filmmakers like Keith and Chase make an impact in the entertainment industry.

The second miracle was this: her love for God lived still. She'd been tempted at first to walk away from her faith. That's what Jay had done. In Hollywood, Jay's beliefs had crumbled and fallen away until they were nothing more than a patch on his sleeve. They hadn't stopped him from having an affair, so why should Kendall think her faith could help her?

But that attitude had lasted only a few weeks before she literally felt herself wasting away inside.

Kendall grabbed a long breath and opened her eyes. The faith she'd seen in the eyes of Chase and Keith was real, genuine, and that was Kendall's greatest concern. She couldn't stand to see the movie business do to them what it had done to Jay. That's why she'd felt so alarmed by the strange feelings she'd had when she hugged Chase. She could never, ever develop feelings for him. Rather, the three of them needed to stick together, talk about their faith and their commitments, include God every step of the way.

Kendall's resolve grew as she started her car and pulled out of the parking complex. If they didn't keep God at the center of everything they did, the power of their films wouldn't really matter.

Because the next moral failure to hit Hollywood could be one of theirs.

Two

Bailey Flanigan pulled her jacket tight around her shoulders and pressed hard into the wind as she crossed the Indiana University campus. The rain beat against her lined hood and she picked up her pace, hurrying toward the theater building and her rehearsal for the upcoming musical, *Scrooge*. The old ornate brick building was in sight when she felt her phone vibrate. Andi or Tim, she figured. No one else would text her in the middle of the day.

She pulled her phone from the pocket of her rain jacket, and what she saw caught her breath. Cody Coleman? They hadn't talked in nearly a month.

Bailey stared at his name as she slowed her steps. He was more Andi's friend now, ever since the homecoming game when he'd walked past her and Tim without stopping. That same night Cody had spent an hour sitting in the parking lot talking with Andi. Now Cody and Andi texted and talked often.

Though the situation hurt, Bailey hadn't shared her feelings with anyone except her mom. When they talked about it they agreed: Cody had moved on. Sure, they'd seen each other on campus—from a distance, usually—and they sat in the same Campus Crusade meeting every Thursday night, but other than a polite wave or a quick hello, he hadn't talked to her.

Bailey scrolled down to the message. She felt her heart rate pick up as she read it.

MISS YOU ... MORE THAN YOU KNOW.

She read it again. And a third time. The message was short, but it spoke straight to her soul. She could tell herself whatever she wanted about Cody. Whether he'd moved on or not, she still had feelings for him.

"Does he ever mention me?" she had asked Andi just that morning as they left their dorm.

"Not really." Andi frowned. "It's weird, I agree with you. I think it's because of Tim."

Bailey's mom thought the same thing. Ever since Tim Reed had become Bailey's boyfriend, Cody had backed off. Never mind his promise of friendship, he'd cut her off completely. There were times when she wanted to make the first move, call him and ask why he was being so ridiculous, staying away from her and her family. But she always figured if he really wanted to reconnect, he'd call first. After all, he was the one who had walked past her at the Clear Creek High football game a month ago with barely a glance in her direction.

It was raining harder, so she used her body to shelter her phone. Her fingers flew across the small keyboard as she tapped her response.

YEAH, CODY … MISS YOU TOO.

She hit Send and slid her phone back into her pocket. Rehearsal for *Scrooge* was set to begin in half an hour, and she needed to go over her lines before things got started. She planned to find a quiet place in the auditorium and focus on her part. Andi and Tim were going to meet her there, since they also had lead parts in the upcoming show. This was no time to get into a conversation with Cody. She would need more than a few minutes to catch up with him, to find out why he'd been so distant.

She picked up her pace, adjusting her backpack a little higher on her shoulders, but before she walked another ten yards, her phone buzzed again. She released an audible sigh, and it hung in the cool, damp October air. "Don't do this, Cody," she whispered. "Don't mess with my heart."

She pulled out her phone once more. This time his message was much longer — so long it took two texts to get it across.

I KNOW … YOU DON'T THINK I CARE BECAUSE WE HAVEN'T TALKED. I GET THAT FEELING WHEN ANDI AND I TEXT. YOU NEED TO KNOW I'M JUST LOOKING OUT FOR YOU. WELL … OKAY, FOR BOTH OF US. YOU HAVE TIM, AND THINGS BETWEEN YOU TWO ARE MORE SERIOUS ALL THE TIME.

Bailey hated when he talked that way. She let her exasperation build as she scrolled to the second part of his message.

THERE'S NO ROOM IN YOUR LIFE FOR ME, AND THAT'S OKAY. I ACCEPT THE FACT. BUT PLEASE, BAILEY, DON'T THINK THIS IS THE WAY I WANT THINGS. LIKE I SAID, I MISS YOU MORE THAN YOU KNOW.

She read the messages once more, and tears stung her eyes. If he missed her, he should call her, maybe fight for their right to a friendship. Tim would understand. And besides, back before Cody went to Iraq, he'd had feelings for her that went beyond friendship. They both had.

Cody would be waiting for an answer. She started to tap out some of what she was feeling, but changed her mind. She was almost to the theater. Tim would pick up on her sad mood, and that wasn't fair. Besides, she was looking forward to rehearsal. Today they'd practice the scene all three of them were in — the scene from Scrooge's Christmas past.

She erased the few words she'd written and typed out a shorter message instead.

I WANNA TALK, BUT NOT NOW … CALL ME LATER.

As soon as she sent it she felt a sense of satisfaction. If he really missed her, he'd call.

She reached the theater door and put thoughts of Cody out of her mind. *Scrooge* opened in four weeks, and she wanted to give the rehearsal time her best effort. This was her first college musical. Much was riding on her performance.

Andi was already sitting in the auditorium, but as their eyes met, she didn't look like her happy, lighthearted self.

"How's your day?" Bailey walked to a seat a few spots from her roommate and dumped her wet backpack on the chair between them. "The rain got you down?"

Andi shrugged. "Rainy days and Mondays. Never a good combination, I guess."

"What happened?" After more than a month of sharing a dorm together, she could read Andi like a sister. She gave her a half smile. "You bombed your math midterm?"

The question was intended as a joke, and Andi allowed a small laugh. But the defeat in her eyes and the way she held her shoulders remained. "Remember the guy I met at that frat party?"

Bailey winced. "Ben, right? The guy in your math class."

"Yeah, well. He told his friends about me ... about that night." Shame shadowed her expression. "One of his buddies invited me to a party this weekend. He said there was always room for girls like me." She looked deeply hurt by the remark. "'Girls like me'? Is that really my reputation? After one stupid party?"

"For a few guys, maybe. But it's not like everyone on campus thinks that."

Bailey and Andi had talked about Andi's horrible experience at the frat party. She'd drunk more than she intended and walked with Ben across the street, where something worse would've happened if some couple hadn't come along and started asking questions. Ben left in a huff and Andi—too sick and drunk to walk home—had called Cody, of all people.

Every detail of Andi's terrible night had come out the next day, so Bailey knew the whole story. Even how Andi had tried to throw herself at Cody that night, and how mortified she'd been that Cody turned her down.

Bailey had been secretly relieved to learn Cody hadn't taken advantage of the situation. Still, it was hard for her to comment on her roommate's trouble that night when every action had been her own fault.

Andi stared at the auditorium floor, her brow lowered in deep concern. "Not just a couple guys. Their friends too. They probably think that."

"Okay, so six guys on a campus of forty thousand students." Bailey reached over and touched her roommate's knee. "I think there's still time to rebuild your reputation."

Andi leaned on the arm of her chair and held her head a little higher. "I guess. I just hate that anyone sees me that way. It's so weird, because ... well, you know that's not really me."

Bailey reached into her backpack and pulled out her script. "Think of it this way: every time you tell them you're not interested, you'll basically be telling them it was a one-time thing, a crazy night you still regret."

"True." Andi nodded slowly. "You always make me feel better, Bailey." She opened her own script. "I hate that I got drunk that night, but I don't know ... I'm not sure if drinking itself is really wrong. Like, the kids that do that all the time—as long as they're not hurting anyone, does that mean they're not good people? I'm still confused, I guess."

Bailey resisted the urge to sigh. This had been Andi's line of thought off and on since they'd met. She was the daughter of missionary parents, and she'd spent most of her life in Indonesia. But now her dad was a producer and had finished his first film, and Andi felt like she needed to rid herself of the good-girl image. As if she was ashamed of being too sheltered, too clean-cut.

Bailey flipped to her scene in the script and lifted a look to her friend. "You know how I feel."

A wary half-smile tugged at Andi's lips. "Just because a person thinks they're doing well doesn't mean they are."

"Right. The only measuring stick we have is the Bible." She tried to sound matter-of-fact, not overly critical. "We can mess up, but we have to keep getting back on our feet and turning to Him. That's what it means to be a Christian."

Andi thought about that for a few seconds. "I guess. It's just not as clear as it used to be." She was flipping through the pages of her script when her phone rang. Whatever name appeared in the window, Andi's smile was quick to reach her eyes. She snapped her phone open and settled back in her chair. "Hey! I thought you weren't calling until later."

Bailey wanted to ask who it was, but she didn't want to seem nosy. She focused her attention on her script and did her best not to listen to Andi's end of the conversation. But a minute into the talk, Andi laughed out loud. "Cody, you're so funny!"

That was all Bailey needed to hear. She stood and set the script down, motioning to Andi that she was going out to wait for Tim. Outside she fought the tears that tried to form. As far as she could tell there was nothing more than friendship between Andi and Cody, but still … They talked often, and whatever was happening between them seemed to be getting stronger. Even that would've been something Bailey could handle—if she and Cody were speaking to each other. In light of Andi's happy conversation, the pain of Bailey's lost friendship with Cody was more than she could take.

Not that she could talk about it with anyone but her mom. Tim wouldn't understand. If she was happy dating him—and she was—then why would it upset her so much that an old friend had lost touch with her? That would be his question and he'd have a right to it.

She would have no more answers for him than she had for herself.

The front steps of the auditorium were covered and dry, despite the damp air. She sat down and rested her elbows on her knees. At almost the same time she spotted Tim. He was walking toward her at his usual determined pace, red backpack slung over his shoulder. When he saw her, a smile filled his face and he waved. Bailey returned the wave and waited for him to walk up.

Dating Tim was easy, natural. The two of them had everything in common—their stage experience with Christian Kids Theater, their love for God, and the types of families they came from. Tim had no shady past, no troublesome background, no baggage. For years she had wanted nothing more than for Tim Reed to fall for her. And now he had.

He jogged up the stairs and took the spot beside her. "Hey." He put his arm around her shoulders and hugged her. "You look cute in a rain jacket."

"Thanks." She snuggled a little closer to him. "How were your classes?"

"Great." He reached for her hand and rubbed his thumb along her fingers. "You're cold. Here ..." In an act that was as thoughtful as it was romantic, he lifted her freezing hand close to his mouth and blew warm air against her skin. Once ... twice ... After the third time he rubbed her hand and grinned. "Better?"

"Better." She studied him, grateful. How many times had she dreamed of sharing a moment like this with him? "Tell me about your talk?" Tim was taking debate class and today they had staged a mock argument over Dr. Seuss's book *The Butter Battle*. Tim's side had argued in favor of buttering bread butter-side up.

He laughed and shook his head. "Craziest thing."

He launched into a story about how the other side came dressed with the backs of their shirts dyed yellow, and how his team had acted out a skit that ended up being mostly bloopers, especially after one of the girls got tongue-twisted and began fighting for the wrong side. Bailey enjoyed the story, loved the way it felt to sit here sheltered from the rain on the steps of the college theater with Tim warm beside her. She thought about the conversation Andi was having inside, and a pang of guilt pierced her heart. She had no right to be bothered by Cody's friendship with Andi. Neither of them meant to hurt anyone. Besides, for now it seemed possible that Tim was part of God's plans for her. That meant maybe Cody was part of God's plans for Andi. If that ended up being the case, Bailey could do nothing but embrace the situation. She was happy and content, and maybe this was only the beginning for her and Tim. Cody was simply a part of her past.

If she could only convince her heart.

Because no matter what logic said, she couldn't shake the hurt in her heart over losing him. Or the fear she lived with every day—that a part of her would always love Cody Coleman, the boy who'd played football for her father and lived with their family through his hardest years.

The once-in-a-lifetime guy she had fallen for when she was too young to know any better.

Three

The rented Santa Monica studio editing room was half the size of a single-wide trailer, with fewer frills. But that didn't matter to Keith. He and Chase sat in front of a computer control panel, their eyes glued to the spectacular images on the large screen overhead. Never mind the stuffy room. The picture drew them in so they were no longer in Santa Monica, but in Bloomington, Indiana, where *The Last Letter* had been filmed.

The editing equipment was state of the art, available for rent only in the Los Angeles area and provided by the earlier investment funds from Ben Adams. For the past few weeks Keith and Chase had spent Tuesday through Thursday working nearly around the clock to edit their film. Constantly during that time, they were reminded that a production team could capture tremendous acting on film, but the magic—the real magic—happened here.

In a ten-by-ten editing room.

"Mark that." Keith hit a button on the control panel, pushed back, and stood. He stretched and rubbed his weary eyes. "Dinner?"

Chase squinted up at the plastic black-and-white clock, the only decor in the room. "Seven thirty." He released a slow burst of stale air and hit another few buttons. The screen overhead went dark. "When did we eat lunch?"

"We didn't."

"Right." Chase chuckled, then yawned. "Late breakfast." He rose and rubbed the back of his neck. "The hours run together."

It was mid-November, and temperatures in Santa Monica hovered in the seventies, even at this hour. What little they'd seen of the day had been warm and blue and beautiful. Typical Southern California beach weather. Keith flipped off the light and locked the door behind them. Down a series of hallways and a flight of stairs and they were outside, a block away from Santa Monica's Third Street Promenade.

Keith drew a long breath. "The breeze feels good."

"It's called real life." Chase slipped his hands into his back pockets, his pace slow and thoughtful. "I keep forgetting it's out here."

They both laughed this time. Their editing hours were crazy—work through midnight, walk back to the Georgian Hotel on Ocean Boulevard, climb the stairs to the second-floor two-bedroom suite they were sharing, and crash for five, maybe six, hours. Then back at it by seven in the morning. With the price they were paying for the editing room, they had to keep this pace. Besides, they had a deadline. Kendall had entered the film in a number of independent film festivals, and if any of them bit, they'd need a finished product by the end of the year.

On top of that, they had a first-look deal with a major studio—something that guaranteed a DVD release, based on the actors the film had attracted. The problem with that deal was that the studio might not want a theatrical release. Putting a movie on the big screen cost millions, and rumor had it the studio was struggling. If the film didn't make it to the theaters, there was a chance Chase and Keith wouldn't recoup the money they'd spent making it. The investors would be repaid, but the producers would suffer the greatest financial loss.

So the pressure was on in a number of ways.

"The thing is—" Chase tilted his face toward the dusk sky overhead. "—even with all the madness, I love it." He looked straight at Keith. "I mean I absolutely love it."

Keith smiled. He loved that Chase shared his enthusiasm. "I never imagined …"

"I know." Chase stopped for a red light. "It's like we're sitting on this amazing movie, and no one has any idea."

They walked north. In this part of the city, Third Street was blocked off, allowing tourists and locals the chance to shop and ogle at the artists stationed up and down the Promenade. Up ahead a man stood in the middle of the street, a makeshift spotlight shining up on him. Head to toe the guy was silver. Tinfoil around his clothes, silver spray paint covering his arms, hands, and face. He played a flute. Next to him, a cheap portable table held a glass jar containing a handful of bills.

"Makes you wonder." Keith watched a few seconds longer. "The guy just woke up one day and decided he wasn't happy flipping burgers?"

"At least he's out here." Chase grinned and started walking again. "Doing something."

"Using his talent." Keith picked up his pace. "Pizza work for you?"

"Absolutely."

They ordered by the slice—two each—at a small dive just off Third and ate the first piece back out on Third Street at a tiny worn-out table with uneven legs. The breeze was cooler, the sidewalk fringed with street people, everything they owned on their backs or smashed into a shopping cart. The salty ocean air pulsed with heavy rap music from a couple street dancers at the other end of the block, the sound blending with the occasional honking horn and rumbling truck heading east on Santa Monica Boulevard.

Conversation was too hard against the noise, so they boxed up their second slices. Back in their rented editing room, they finished the pizza as Keith reviewed their notes from the earlier session. It was eight o'clock. Four hours until they could call it a night.

Keith grabbed two cans of Diet Coke from the small refrigerator in the back corner of the room and handed one to Chase. "Okay." He popped the top of his can and took a swig. "I want this scene less than two minutes total. We're still at five and change. I have an idea, but let's look at it again." He sat down in front of the console.

Chase took the chair next to him and hit the Play button. Three seconds from the front of a clip, two from the back, a camera angle deleted. A half hour disappeared, every cut piece saved in a digital file in case they needed it again. When the scene was down to two minutes, fifteen seconds, Chase rubbed his eyes. "That's better. Let's move on."

Before Keith could advance the film, his phone rang. He didn't recognize the caller ID. The area code was Los Angeles, otherwise he wouldn't have answered it. "Hello?"

"Keith Ellison? Barry Gaynor here. Los Angeles Film Festival."

"Yes, Mr. Gaynor." His heart slammed into double rhythm. The deadline for entering the LA Film Festival was December 5, weeks away. Entry in the competition was one of the reasons they were hurrying with the edit. "This is Keith. How can I help you?"

"Well," the man chuckled. "First off, call me Barry." He allowed a dramatic pause, then dropped his voice a notch. "Don't usually make these calls, but I had to this time."

Chase stopped fiddling with the control panel. He turned and watched the conversation, his brows raised. "LA Film Festival?" he mouthed.

Keith nodded.

"Anyway ..." The laughter faded from Barry's voice. "I hear from my good friend Kendall Adams you've got yourself a hit film."

"Kendall called them," Keith mouthed to Chase. He swallowed hard and tried to focus. "We were happy with it. Everyone gave it their best."

"That's what I hear. Kendall can't stop talking about it."

"We're editing now, my coproducer and I."

"Good. Think you'll be finished by the fifth?"

Keith allowed a smile. "That's the goal."

"So you're entering our festival, right? Kendall promised me."

"Yes. Definitely."

"When you submit it, send it to my attention." There was a smile in Barry's voice. "I'll be waiting."

"Definitely. Will do." They made small talk for another minute and the conversation was over.

Keith had cautioned himself not to get overly thrilled at any stage along the way of movie making. Too many things could go wrong. But as he set his phone down he had to work to keep from shouting out loud.

"What'd he say?"

"Kendall's the real deal. I guess she's friends with the guy who heads up the festival. You won't believe this." Keith stared at his friend and released a single laugh. "He called to make sure we were submitting."

"Because of Kendall?" Chase leaned back in his seat. "That could be huge. I mean, that doesn't happen."

Keith's heart settled down some. "Except with God. He might be using Kendall, but none of this happens without Him." He nodded at the oversized screen above them. "Let's get back at it."

They worked until after midnight, then walked back to the hotel. Fewer street people were out, but they were offered cocaine from a guy in a trench coat, and halfway to the Georgian they passed a pair of interested call girls. Keith and Chase never made eye contact.

"Have you thought about where this could go? I mean with Ben Adams behind us, and if we get picked up by a few of the festivals?" Keith tempered his voice. The wind off the ocean was stronger now, and he had to talk loud to be heard.

"I try not to." Chase shrugged. "I mean, it's exciting. But almost none of it's in ink."

The conversation faded until they'd climbed the green-painted steps to the hotel and walked up to their suite on the second floor. "You aren't convinced it's going to happen, are you?" Keith tossed his things on the small table near the television set.

"I believe in contracts." Chase flopped onto the sofa with a long sigh. "Look, I'm not trying to be difficult. Kendall's full of great ideas. The LA festival director wants us to submit our film. Stephanie Fitzgerald wants us to produce *Unlocked*. Brandon Paul wants to star in it. I'm having a blast, and everything sounds great ... but none of it's in ink. We still have a long road ahead."

"Reminds me of something I heard a director say once."

"What's that?"

Keith smiled. "'Movies very badly do not want to be made. It's the nature of the business.'"

"Exactly."

"Either way we have a great film."

Chase took a paperback from his bag and tossed it onto the coffee table. *Unlocked: A Novel*, by Stephanie Fitzgerald. "See?" He grinned at Keith. "I think it could happen. With God all things are possible, right?"

"You're gonna love the book." *Unlocked* centered around an autistic boy miraculously changed by the power of music, a boy whose life changed everyone around him—especially his older teenaged brother. It was a story destined for the big screen. Keith had finished the book a week ago. "The whole time, I could see Brandon Paul as the boy's older brother."

"It'd be huge." Chase smiled, but he didn't look excited. "All we need is an option from the author, an A-list screenplay, a meeting with Brandon Paul's agent—vice president of the top talent agency in town—and about ten million in the bank."

"Right."

"Makes teaching jungle tribes about Jesus look like a picnic."

Keith laughed and fell into a chair adjacent to the sofa. "Same God."

He took the remote and flipped on the TV. On the way to ESPN a news story caught his eye and he stopped clicking. Ten high school kids caught on camera playing drinking games.

"This one's for YouTube," one of them shouted out as the shots were poured.

"Yeah, YouTube!" One of the guys grabbed a glass and raised it high. "Winner's gonna be famous."

The anchor cut in and explained that before the end of that night one of the kids had died, and another stopped breathing and suffered brain damage. When the first two teens passed out—with one kid's video camera still rolling—the other teens merely laughed and clanked their shot glasses toward the forms on the floor.

Keith pictured Andi, his precious daughter, getting drunk at a frat party last quarter, and he felt suddenly sick to his stomach. He clicked the Power button and turned to Chase. "Knocks the wind out of you."

Chase was still staring at the dark TV screen. After a few seconds he leaned back in his seat and exhaled hard. "Saddest story I've seen in a long time."

"Makes me think of Andi." Silence fell heavy between them, the story, the reality of it, hitting its mark. Andi still hadn't shared all the details of her drunken night, but what if that had been her? Stepping up to the challenge of her peers, downing one shot glass after another? The boys who had fallen to the floor didn't look like particularly bad kids. Just kids. Teens giving in to the culture around them.

"Sometimes I need to remember—" Chase leaned forward, his elbows on his knees. There was an intensity in his eyes that hadn't been there before. "—that's our audience, those kids. That's why we're doing this."

"It's why we'll be back at it tomorrow, why we have to stay with it and believe God's doing something big."

"You're right." The clouds of doubt cleared from Chase's eyes. "It's why we believe in Kendall Adams and Brandon Paul and every other detail along the way."

"Exactly." They were quiet again, and Keith turned his eyes to the window and the sheer curtains dancing in the ocean breeze. The pictures wouldn't leave his head. The teens gathered around someone's kitchen, the vodka bottles lining the counter. The shot glasses and the laughter. All the laughter, as if they were bullet proof. As if they wouldn't be attending a funeral a few days later.

What about the parents? How helpless had they felt seeing the video, watching their kids pass out, watching them collapse to the floor, desperately wanting a second chance to somehow be there, to call for an ambulance? How did any of them feel now?

Suddenly the images in Keith's mind changed, and he wasn't seeing the shot glasses or the liquor bottles or the dying teenagers.

He was seeing his daughter, bright-eyed and innocent, telling a circle of jungle women about the love of Jesus Christ. And he was seeing her as she was now—experimenting with drinking and guys and choices that went far outside the realms of her upbringing and faith.

That was it, really. The kids in the video were no different from Andi and every other young person. They faced temptations that came at them from every side. Pornography and homosexuality, drinking and drugs, and anything goes. A disdain for faith, and an overall hedonistic lure that had a way of changing even the most grounded kids. That's where the power of film could make a difference. The right movie could give a generation of young people a reason to stand firm, to believe again in the rewards of living right and holding fast to God's truth. That's all Andi needed right now. It's all any kids in this generation needed.

A reason to stand.

Keith could hardly wait for morning.

Four

Kelly Ryan shut the bedroom door where her girls were finally napping and walked silently down the hallway of their small ranch house to the kitchen. The girls had been up late last night, hoping for a call from their daddy.

A call that never came.

Two weeks remained before Thanksgiving, and again Chase and Keith were off in Los Angeles editing, working practically around the clock to finish the movie before the festival deadlines.

Kelly entered the kitchen and grabbed a handful of M&Ms from a bowl on the counter. She popped a couple in her mouth, and then a few more, so they'd last. Then she gave up and finished off the rest all at once.

Lately she'd been more overwhelmed than she wanted to admit. The M&Ms were proof. It was only two o'clock and she'd nearly finished off half a bag. Between that, the overdue electric bill, and the laundry piled taller than Macy on the living room sofa, rest was nowhere in sight.

Back in Indonesia, Kelly had eaten fish and vegetables, whole grains and beans, and little else. She'd been lean and full of energy, ready to handle whatever crisis or task the day brought. But with Chase gone, she felt frustrated and forgotten. Last night was like so many of those before it. She and the girls ate leftover macaroni and cheese and then stayed up waiting for Chase's call. When contact didn't come, Kelly faced a barrage of questions.

"But why, Mommy?" Molly's brow lowered. Not much slipped past her. "Doesn't he have his cell phone?"

"Yes, baby." Kelly had felt so weary she thought about crawling into bed next to her oldest daughter and forgetting the work that waited for her in the kitchen. "I'm sure he wanted to call."

Macy listened to every word, and the combination of the late night and the ache of missing her father finally caused her to burst into tears.

"I want my Daaaaddy."

"Okay, okay." Kelly lifted the covers up over Molly and then moved to Macy and did the same. She sat on the edge of Macy's bed. "Let's quiet down. Everything's going to be all right." She rubbed her hand over Macy's back, comforting her. "Let's pray and ask God to help Daddy get his work done quickly."

Kelly prayed out loud and sang songs about Jesus and God's promises until both girls fell asleep. Then she trudged back to the kitchen to a sink overflowing with dishes that hadn't been washed since breakfast. The old house didn't have a dishwasher, so when every last dish and pan was scrubbed clean and dripping dry, Kelly found the Baskin Robbins Rocky Road in the garage freezer and dished up a bowl. Companionship for a round of laundry and late-night infomercials. She didn't cut the lights in her bedroom until just before one a.m., setting herself up for another rushed morning with Molly and Macy scrambling into her room and jumping on her bed sometime before eight.

Molly was four, and Macy two, and neither of them attended preschool. Kelly taught them letters and numbers and a few times each week the three of them sat around their wobbly kitchen table and colored princess pictures or made crafts with bright card stock and water paints. But the rushed morning changed everything about the hours that followed, and today was no exception.

Kelly moved into the living room and grabbed the first threadbare towel from the mountain of laundry. When Chase was here, they'd have the girls in bed by eight-thirty and work on the laundry or bills together. Strange how in his absence the workload seemed to quadruple.

A sigh slipped from deep inside her. "I'm sorry, Lord. I hate this. I should have a better attitude."

If only she wasn't so tired. Her days as a missionary had been equally hard, but in a different way. There was manual labor—threshing wheat, grinding flour, baking with the village women, cleaning. She'd learned to sew and repair basic functional household items and cook, and every night at dusk activity wound down. Sleep came easily in Indonesia, the way it rarely did in San Jose—at least with Chase away.

She sighed and checked her reflection in the microwave hood above her gas stove. No shower, but she had at least brushed her hair and put on a light foundation. She had to at least look decent with company coming over. Today was the second Thursday of the month, which meant Laurie Weeks would be here any minute.

Laurie headed up the Monday-morning Bible study at San Jose Community Church. She had three kids, a constant stream of family photos on her Facebook, and a love for the beach—same as Kelly. A few months back when Bible study let out, Laurie asked if they could have lunch together. Over Caesar salads Laurie noted that Chase had been gone a lot. Kelly explained about the movie, about the mission of her husband and Keith, and over the next hour the two became fast friends. Kelly was grateful. She needed friends now more than ever.

Kelly grabbed another handful of M&Ms and slid them into her mouth. She hated this new habit, getting by on junk food. But when she was running on empty, the candy helped. The trouble was she was gaining weight because of it, which meant that any junk food in the house had to be hidden from Chase. The last thing she wanted was his scrutiny, him wondering why she wasn't eating right and taking note of her slightly bigger size. She wasn't hungry, of course. She was overwhelmed. Treading water in an endless sea of menial tasks and impossible debt, struggling to grab even a breath of air so she could keep at it one more day.

But not Chase. He couldn't see how she was drowning because his own happiness didn't allow it. He came home from the editing trips overflowing with excitement about the movie. What did he know about her life these days? The lawn mower was sputtering along on its last leg, and the vacuum needed replacing. Most of the time, Kelly felt like just one more broken-down machine, completely cut off from Chase's work and his exciting movie life.

When he was home, Kelly had a dozen questions, but the one that rose to the surface most often lately was about the movie's theatrical release. She had believed from the beginning that if they actually finished the film, if they found enough investor money to complete the project, then it would take only a matter of months before the picture hit the big screen. Especially now that the guys had connected with glamorous Kendall Adams and her father. Because of them, money for their film projects was much less of a concern.

But Keith and Chase had an attorney now—Dayne Matthews' brother, Luke Baxter. Luke had read Chase and Keith's contract and warned them that a theatrical release wasn't a guarantee—even with the right funding.

According to Luke, the contract with the studio was ironclad. Either the studio executives would view the final cut of the movie and give the okay for a theatrical release, or they wouldn't. The problem was this: even with the P&A budget covered, the studio would face a financial risk by putting the film in theaters. Very simply, it was a risk the execs might not want to take.

And if the film didn't make it to theaters, the guys would likely not make back their money.

Kelly had been horrified when she first understood the situation Chase and Keith faced. She talked to Keith's wife, Lisa, and the two agreed they needed to pray. Without a theatrical release, Keith and Chase could face bankruptcy and a complete loss of credibility as filmmakers. All their efforts could amount to little more than nothing.

Kelly filled the kettle with water, slipped it onto the front burner, and turned the flame up high. Laurie loved tea at their twice-monthly get-togethers. It would be the healthiest thing Kelly had placed in her mouth since Chase left for LA four days ago.

She leaned against the counter and stared at the dull linoleum floor. *Remember the fireflies*, she told herself. *Don't forget about the fireflies.* Years ago when Chase learned fireflies really existed, he determined anything was possible. It was a mantra they lived by. But Kelly was lonely and depressed. Money was tight, and there was no end in sight to the long days without her husband. She still wanted to believe in his movie career, but week after week without him had sapped her of every bit of excitement and enthusiasm.

"Stay positive," Chase told her two days ago, the last time they talked. "God's brought us this far. He'll work out the details."

Kelly wanted to believe him.

There was a light knock from the front room. She slid the bowl of M&Ms to the back edge of the counter and hurried to get the door.

An unusual rain had hit San Jose that morning, and the storm was blowing hard outside. Laurie shook the water from her windbreaker and stepped quickly inside. "It's nasty out there." She was breathless as Kelly shut the door behind them. "Feels like it could snow."

"Another ten degrees and it could."

The water had begun to boil in the other room. Kelly led the two of them into the kitchen, where she poured the tea. Apple-cinnamon, a reminder of the holidays right around the corner.

They sat at the table and Laurie caught her breath talking about her kids. Audrey wanted to take another mission trip, and Lucas was switching his major at San Jose State. Sam had won senior honors on his football team, and life was good. Good and fast and full.

A comfortable quiet filled in the spaces between them, and they sipped their tea, listening to the wind howl through the trees outside.

Laurie put her cup down. “Chase is still in Santa Monica?”

“He is.” Kelly’s face fell before she could stop herself.

“That’s what I thought.” Something in Laurie’s eyes changed. “You look tired.”

Tears came from nowhere. Kelly blinked them back and studied the teabag in her cup.

Laurie waited, patient and kind as ever. “Wanna talk about it?”

A sound more sob than laugh came from Kelly and she brought her fingers to her lips. “It’s nothing, really. I mean … things are okay with us.”

“The movie?”

“I guess.” A teardrop fell onto the table. Kelly dabbed at it, and then at her eyes. “The guys might not get a theatrical release for *The Last Letter*. If they don’t … the film could lose money, and … Well, the actors will think the movie was a mistake.” She found control again. “It could be their last picture.”

Confusion clouded Laurie’s eyes. “I thought they got some kind of good news a while back.”

“They found funding, otherwise they wouldn’t have had the money to finish the film. But now their attorney is telling them they’re in an unbreakable deal with the studio, and the studio is struggling like everyone else. The theatrical release of an independent film is a risk, and so without a miracle, the movie will only release on DVD."

The rain picked up and pounded a steady rhythm on the roof and windows of the Ryan's three-bedroom ranch. Wind howled and a tree outside bent almost to breaking. When the gust let up, Laurie took another drink of her tea. "Is that it, then? The movie?"

Kelly didn't have to ask what she meant. "It gets old, I guess. Chase gone all the time." Frustration tightened her throat, and she whispered her next words. "We've maxed out our credit cards and taken out loans. We're living on barely anything. All this … for what? How's the culture affected if the movie never makes it to theaters?"

"Honestly?" Laurie set her cup down. Her eyes radiated kindness. "I'm more worried about you and Chase than the movie. When's the last time you went out?"

"Alone?" Kelly tried to remember. "I can't remember."

"Okay, how about this. I'll take Molly and Macy one night this weekend so you and Chase can go to dinner."

"Really?"

"Of course. My kids love your girls." Laurie sat a little straighter, enthused about her idea. "We can play croquet out front. Sam's been into that lately. You and Chase pick a nice restaurant and take your time. Let's make it Saturday, so he won't be drained from the drive back."

Kelly didn't want to admit they didn't have enough money for dinner at a restaurant. Besides, she had no idea what she'd wear. Most of her clothes were too tight to look good. But so what? Chase loved her, anyway. Maybe they could eat at home and take a walk around the track at Mount Pleasant High School down the street. Just to get out together. The idea sounded better than any of the weekends they'd had lately. Chase coming home tired, desperate for sleep, and spending his waking hours watching football or on the phone with people connected to the movie.

"Saturday?"

"Saturday." Laurie laughed, her smile easy. "Say yes."

"Well …" Suddenly the idea sounded wonderful. "Okay." She reached across the table and took hold of Laurie's hands. "Thanks, Laurie. We'd love it."

The conversation moved to matters at church—the current women's Bible study, which was nearly finished with Thessalonians. "Something in the middle of chapter 5 keeps staying with me." Laurie folded her hands around her mug. "'Be joyful always; pray continually; give thanks in all circumstances, for this is God's will for you in Christ Jesus.'"

Kelly looked outside. The wind and rain were just as bad as before, with no signs of letting up. *Be joyful always. Pray continually. Give thanks in all circumstances.* She hadn't done any of that lately. But then … when she was on a downturn like this, she never did. Between the kids and keeping the house running, she didn't have a minute to herself. Besides, she couldn't spend the day grazing from one snack to another and praising God at the same time. With her, it was one or the other.

Laurie stayed until Molly padded down the hallway, holding her worn blanky and rubbing her blue eyes. She stopped short when she saw Kelly wasn't alone. "Hi, Miss Laurie."

"Hi, Molly." Laurie's eyes immediately softened. "You look just like my little girl did when she was your age."

Molly smiled, not sure what to say. She went to Kelly. "Time to get up?" She yawned.

"Yes, sweetie." Kelly held out her arms and Molly came to her, sliding up easily on her lap. Kelly kissed her blonde head. "Is Macy still sleeping?"

"Mm-hmm. She's more tired than me." Molly jumped down and shuffled to the sofa a few feet away in the den. She curled up at one end and brought her blanket to her face.

Laurie helped carry the mugs into the kitchen, and then hugged Kelly good-bye. "Call me if something changes. But really, Kelly. Saturday. I'm planning on it."

When her friend was gone, Kelly took the spot beside Molly and patted her lap. Molly climbed up and laid her head down on Kelly's shoulder. "I miss Daddy," she muttered into Kelly's sweatshirt.

"Me too." She stroked Molly's long hair. "He'll be home tomorrow."

From the other room, soft tired cries told them both that Macy was awake. "Sissy!" Molly was on her feet again, scrambling toward the bedroom she shared with her sister. She looked over her shoulder as she ran. "Let's do something fun, Mommy."

Kelly pulled herself up and caught a glimpse of her reflection in the mirror that hung on the wall next to the TV. She looked heavy and old and worn out. The rain was bringing her down, and she agreed with Molly. They needed something fun. Something to take the edge off the loneliness and uncertainty, the fears about the movie, and the long stretches of days without a call from Chase.

She grabbed another handful of M&Ms on the way to helping Macy up onto the toilet. Her youngest was dry, at least. A victory.

Back in the kitchen, Kelly took out a large mixing bowl and the bag of Nestlé chocolate chips she'd bought the day before. "I have an idea." She found a grin for her girls.

"Mmmm!" Molly jumped around and patted Macy on the head. "Yay, Macy, look! We're gonna make cookies!"

"Cookie!" Macy put her hands straight up and danced in a circle with her sister.

That's right, Kelly told herself. *Chocolate-chip cookies. Something to make us feel good.*

Rejoicing and praying could come later.

Today she would bake.

Five

The Thanksgiving dinner party took place at Katy and Dayne Matthew's house high above the shores of Lake Monroe in Bloomington, Indiana. Bailey was home for a few days—no classes or rehearsals—and Andi had used her parents' frequent flyer miles to fly to California and be with her parents. So at three o'clock on Thanksgiving Day Bailey found herself in the backseat of her family's Suburban headed for the lake. A light snow swirled through the air, and a layer of threatening clouds hung over the afternoon. Something by Carrie Underwood played in the background, but Bailey wasn't listening. She was working too hard trying to shake the loneliness that hung around her heart.

"Don't you think it's kinda weird?" Ricky was in the third seat, belted between Justin and Shawn.

"What's that, honey?" Their mom shifted so she could see Ricky from the front passenger seat.

"Having Thanksgiving dinner somewhere else? It feels weird."

"It does." Shawn nodded, and Justin and BJ agreed.

"I mean, it'll be fun," Ricky grinned. "I love looking for eagles off their back porch, especially in the snow. But still ..."

Bailey agreed. She missed the routine and tradition of Thanksgiving at home, but she knew the reason.

"Like I told everyone a week ago ... Dad has a game tomorrow." Mom smiled. "Your father and I agreed we'd rather not spend the day cooking." She gave their dad a quick kiss on the cheek. "I think it was a great call."

"Nice of the Matthews to ask us." Dad looked in his rearview mirror at the six kids. "It'll be a good change."

"Yeah, except ..." Ricky shrugged. "It wasn't the same this morning without the turkey smell and the liver and neck and everything."

The other boys laughed, and after a few seconds Ricky did too. They were still laughing when they turned into the Matthews' long driveway. Bailey stared at the house and remembered a few years back when Dayne had been in the terrible car accident in Los Angeles. Back then he was the biggest movie star in Hollywood, and with paparazzi chasing him, he'd lost control and nearly been killed. During his recovery, Bailey and her family and everyone involved in Christian Kids Theater had come together and completely made over this lake house. When Katy and Dayne returned to Bloomington, the house and yard were filled with everyone who'd taken part in the work. The makeover had brought people together, and kids in CKT still talked about it.

They parked and piled out. Bailey took two of the four pumpkin pies—their contribution to the meal. Those and the bag of rolls Ricky carried. With the entire Baxter family expected for dinner, Bailey figured there would be thirty-four people eating turkey.

"Good thing the girls are bringing extra turkeys." Her mom stepped aside and let Shawn rush ahead to get the door. "We'll need them for this group."

"Yeah, for our group alone!" Ricky rubbed his stomach. "I could eat a whole drumstick."

"You usually do." Justin giggled and elbowed his younger brother.

"Okay, that's enough." Their dad came alongside Shawn as they knocked at the door. "No roughhousing today. Be Flanigans, and be helpful." He winked at them amid a host of "Yes, Dad" responses.

Now that she was older, Bailey loved watching her parents, the way they snuck kisses and hugs and still laughed every day, and the way they set a high bar for her and her brothers. It was the sort of marriage and family life she wanted someday down the road.

"The Flanigans!" Katy was the first to the door. She hugged Bailey's mom and welcomed everyone else. "The football game's on in the den!"

"Can we go out back and look for eagles?" Ricky was already one step in that direction. "And watch football after?"

"Of course." Katy laughed and led Ricky toward the back door.

"But don't track snow into the house." Their dad followed and lightly roughed up Ricky's blond hair. "And don't stay out too long. It's getting colder."

Dayne entered from the other room and grinned at the group. "It's not a party till the Flanigans are here, that's what I always say!" He gave their dad a solid hug with one arm. In the other he held a sleeping baby Sophie, who at five months was the perfect mix of Katy and Dayne. Bailey took in the sight of him and smiled to herself. Dayne Matthews might've been brilliant in the roles he played on the big screen. But no role had ever suited him as well as this one: husband and father.

Would that be her someday, married to an actor years after the two of them had lived out their onscreen dreams? Or would the man holding her baby be a former football player, like her daddy? Bailey couldn't picture what the future held, only the present. She and Tim were still seeing each other. He was supposed to stop by for dessert later—an invitation Katy had personally given him.

Bailey walked the pies into the kitchen where Ashley was placing potato pieces into a pot of boiling water. "Hey!" She looked up and blew at a wisp of her bangs. "Happy Thanksgiving!"

"You too." She set the pies down and moved closer. Out of all the Baxter sisters, Bailey was easily closest to Ashley. She babysat for her, and back during her CKT days, Ashley had been at many rehearsals painting backdrops and pitching in with the sets. "Where are the kids?"

"With Landon." Ashley took another handful of potatoes and set them into the water. "He's convinced Janessa loves football."

Bailey laughed. In the other room she could hear her parents talking to Kari and Ryan, and beyond them there were other voices. Luke and John Baxter's and the rest of them. She noticed the frozen bags of peas sitting alongside the kitchen sink. "Need help?"

"Not just yet. But stick around. I'm sure we'll think of something."

They talked for a few minutes about Ashley's painting schedule and Bailey's rehearsals. "I'll be pretty busy until the show closes mid-December."

"I love *Scrooge* as a musical." Ashley finished her job and put a lid on the pot. She turned to Bailey and wiped the back of her hand across her forehead. "We're all going. I think on opening night."

Bailey felt a wave of nervousness, but it quickly passed. She'd played to full houses at every CKT opening night. This wouldn't be much different. "Tim's doing great. I mean, sometimes I think he *is* Scrooge."

Ashley's eyes were kind, but they looked at her a little deeper than before. "How are things? You and Tim?"

"Good." Her answer came a little too quick. She could tell from her expression that Ashley wanted a different answer from the expected one. "It really is. I just wish …"

"You could stop thinking about Cody?"

Bailey felt something sad fill her eyes. "Yeah. I haven't talked to him in weeks."

"Your mom was telling me that." A knowing look crossed her face. "You know why, right?"

"'Cause of Tim." She took in a slow breath. "Love's so complicated."

"Well said." Ashley's quiet laugh was that of someone who had been there. "Only by God's grace did Landon and I find our way together."

"I can't picture you two apart."

"We almost let it go." She looked out the window. Snow was falling harder now. "We would've regretted that the rest of our lives. But even still we almost didn't make it." She looked at Bailey again. "Sometimes the most difficult path is the very one we're supposed to be on."

"Hmmm." She could've been talking about Bailey and Cody, for sure. "I keep praying, asking God to show me."

"He will." Ashley put her hand on Bailey's shoulder. "In His time He'll show you just what you need to know. I would only add one piece of advice."

"What?"

"Be looking. Because the kind of love God wants for us, the kind I have with Landon … That sort of love rarely happens twice."

Bailey's mom, Katy, and Ashley's three sisters entered the kitchen ready to do their part to move the dinner along. Their chatter ended the quiet moment between Bailey and Ashley.

Bailey opened the cans of black olives and poured them into one of the serving dishes. She was tossing the cans into the garage recycling bin when from her back pocket she felt her cell phone buzz. Probably Tim texting her about what time he should stop by. She paused on the steps of the garage and checked.

But the text wasn't from Tim. Once again it was from Cody. Bailey felt her breath catch a little as she stared at the message on her screen.

HAVEN'T TALKED TO YOU IN A WHILE ... JUST WANTED TO WISH YOU AND YOUR FAMILY A HAPPY THANKSGIVING.

She hesitated, looking from his name to the message and back again. Andi had been talking to Cody almost daily, and she'd told Bailey that Cody was spending Thanksgiving with his mom. Just the two of them. Andi might be Cody's new friend, but Bailey knew him better. She understood how difficult spending time with his mother was for him. His father hadn't been in the picture since he was a baby, and his mom had introduced him to drinking games when he was just fourteen. By the time he reached his senior year in high school she was in prison on drug charges. She'd been out for several years now, deeply sorry for how she'd let Cody down during his growing-up years and clean from drugs and alcohol as far as Bailey knew. But it was still difficult. In the past Cody—and then in later years both he and his mom—had spent Thanksgiving with Bailey's family. Cody had less of a problem being with his mom when they were in a big group.

He had to feel lonely today, same as Bailey.

She exhaled and realized something: this must be the reason she'd felt down on the way to the Matthews' house. She was missing Cody. Whether she wanted to admit it or not, whether they had spoken only hours ago or not for the past few weeks ... she missed him.

The happy mix of voices continued on the other side of the garage door, but where Bailey was standing, a few feet from the trash and recycling bins, it was cold and quiet. She tapped out a quick response.

HAPPY THANKSGIVING TO YOU AND YOUR MOM TOO. WE MISS YOU.

She leaned against the cool garage wall and waited, reading his message and hers twice more before the next text came through.

HOW'S TIM?

Anger stirred the muddy waters in Bailey's soul. Couldn't he at least tell her he felt the same way, that he missed her as much as she missed him? The way he'd told her that day when she was on her way to rehearsal? He did miss her—he had to, otherwise he wouldn't have texted her.

She slid her phone shut in a rush and slipped it back into her pocket. They wouldn't have any friendship at all until he could see past her relationship with Tim. Cody had been her friend long before she started dating Tim. The fact that he continued to let Tim come between them meant only one thing.

He was okay with letting their friendship slip away.

Everyone was setting the table when she returned to the kitchen, and the dining area was a joyful chaos of little kids being seated at one of three tables and highchairs sliding into place. Bailey pitched in, setting bowls of sweet potatoes on the various tables and finally taking the place between her mom and Ricky. All around the dining room people talked and laughed, celebrating the time together and remarking about the look and smell of the food spread out before them.

But Bailey felt no hunger. She wanted to call Cody and tell him to quit being so distant, to get in his car and come over so they could walk down to the lake in the snow and find what they'd lost these last few months. The idea was ridiculous for a lot of reasons, not the least of which was that Tim would be here in an hour.

When everyone was seated, Dayne stood and prayed. "Father, we come to You this Thanksgiving Day with full hearts. Thank You for giving us eternal life, and for the people around this table. Thank You for long-lasting relationships, and for new life—" He paused, his voice rich and full. "—like baby Sophie and baby Janessa. We have so much to be grateful for, dear God. Bless this food to our bodies, and thank You for providing it. We love You, Lord. In Jesus' name, amen."

A round of amens echoed from around the room.

After everyone served their plates, Dayne asked them to share what they were most thankful for.

"One rule." Katy smiled at the group. "An answer can only be given once."

"I'm first!" Cole, Ashley's son, jumped up and raised his hand. Landon helped him back to his seat.

"Cole will go last." He put his arm around Cole.

"Ahh, Dad." Cole wasn't really that upset, because his eyes still danced. "All the good answers will be taken."

"You can be thankful for me, Coley!" Maddie, Brooke's oldest, cast a teasing look across the table at her cousin. "Unless that one's already taken."

Everyone laughed, and the round of thanks began. Bailey was glad for the distraction. People quickly moved from being thankful for God and family and friends and food to specific things—the success of the local crisis pregnancy center, the way the Colts were coming together for Bailey's dad, and her brother Shawn's *A* on a recent biology test. Bailey felt her phone receive another text message just as her turn arrived. She ignored it. "I'm thankful for my roommate, Andi. She's sort of like a sister, and I'm grateful for that."

Finally it was Cole's turn. He thought for a long moment, clearly struggling to think of an answer. Finally he threw his hands in the air. "Okay, fine. I'm thankful for Maddie."

"Thank you, Coley." Maddie folded her hands on the table and gave her cousin a satisfied smile. "I'm thankful for you too."

Again everyone laughed, and conversations broke out all around. Bailey poked her fork around in her peas and mashed potatoes, but all she could think about was the text waiting for her. Even during a regular dinner, her parents didn't like them texting. Today that would be especially true. She ate a few bites of turkey and set her fork down.

"You okay?" Her mom's smile was full of compassion.

As usual, she could read Bailey's heart and mind even though nothing had been said about the text messages. Bailey shrugged one shoulder. "Cody texted me."

"And?" With so many people talking around the room no one listened to them.

"Wished me a Happy Thanksgiving." She sighed. "I told him I missed him, and instead of saying he missed me, too, he just asked me how Tim was."

Her mom gave her a sympathetic smile. "Maybe he's being smart."

"How?"

"He's making you think about your decisions." She put her arm around Bailey's shoulders and gave her a gentle squeeze. "Look who you're sitting here thinking about."

Her mom had a point. But was Cody's silence really deliberate? With all the time he spent talking to Andi, it seemed like only a slight possibility. "Maybe he's interested in Andi. He doesn't want me missing him, when I'm supposed to be thinking about Tim. You know …" She met her mom's eyes. "So I don't do something stupid like start liking him again."

"I don't think so." Her mom picked up her knife and fork and cut a bite of turkey.

"You seem so sure."

"I am sure." Confidence shone in her eyes. "I saw how he looked at you that day at our house. He adores you, Bailey. No matter what you decide, I think maybe he always will."

Bailey hung onto that thought.

When dinner was over, everyone worked together clearing the tables and loading Katy and Dayne's two dishwashers. Bailey was helping her mom and Ashley place ten pies along the granite kitchen bar when the doorbell rang. Dayne answered it, and Bailey watched from where she worked as Tim Reed stepped inside. He and Dayne talked for a minute, the way they always did when they saw each other. Tim had been one of the first CKT kids Dayne met, and the two shared a special friendship. Dayne was a sort of mentor for Tim, which was a great situation for a lot of reasons.

Their conversation gave Bailey the chance to watch Tim from a distance. He was taller than back in his CKT days, and handsome in a polished sort of way. He loved God and he fit in well with Bailey's friends and family. *Why, then*, she asked herself as she pulled three pie servers from a drawer and set them on a napkin, *aren't you head over heels for that guy?*

She had no answers.

Tim finished talking with Dayne and crossed the room to the kitchen. He smiled when he saw her, but she wasn't sure his eyes actually lit up. Not the way she would've liked. "Hey ... Happy Thanksgiving." He gave Bailey a quick hug as he studied the pies. "Looks like I got here just in time."

They compared notes about the day and ate pie and played a new board game—Eye to Eye—and when the night was over sometime after ten o'clock, he hugged her again and they went their separate ways. The ride back was quiet, with Ricky and BJ nodding off before they had gone far. The trip gave Bailey time to review her evening with Tim. They'd had fun, for sure. They laughed and enjoyed being together. But if she was painfully honest with herself, something was missing. Something in the way Tim looked at her.

She remembered her mom's words. *"I saw how he looked at you ... He adores you."*

Maybe that was it. Tim looked at her on a surface level. He smiled and seemed happy to see her. But when Cody looked at her, there were no layers left, nothing he didn't reveal, nothing he couldn't see. He didn't really look at her so much as he looked into her. To the deepest, most real, places in her heart and soul.

Her mom seemed to sense she needed alone time, so she didn't ask about Tim or how Bailey had felt seeing him. Good thing. Bailey didn't have an answer for herself, let alone her mother. Not until she was changing out of her jeans did she remember her phone and the text message she'd never read. She pulled it from her pocket and clicked a few buttons.

I MISS YOU TOO.

She was drawn into those four simple words as if he was standing right here beside her. Again her breath caught. Tears stung her eyes, and she blinked them back. She wasn't crying because she was sad. The tears were because maybe her mother was right. He must care more than he let on or he wouldn't have sent this text a full hour after his last one. Maybe he'd analyzed his message about Tim and how Bailey hadn't answered, and finally—after a very long time—he'd texted how he felt. How he really felt.

He missed her too.

As she finished getting ready for bed, her thoughts moved from the text message to her conversation with Ashley earlier that day. Love was complicated. That was true with Tim, and it was true with Cody—whatever sort of love she had for the two of them. Landon had been the difficult path for Ashley, and right now Cody was the difficult path for Bailey. So maybe Cody would be a bigger part of her life again someday. Or maybe they'd only be friends. Even that was more than they now shared.

She thought about Ashley's advice: to pray about Cody and Tim, of course, but also to look for the answers. "*That sort of love rarely happens twice.*" Yes, that's what Ashley had said.

Bailey climbed into bed and lay still on her pillow, the darkness around her. *I'm looking, God. I want to hear Y ou, but nothing seems very clear.*

I am here, my daughter. All things work to the good for those who love me. Remember that.

The answer came quickly and easily, the way it rarely did. The response was part of a Bible verse from Romans chapter 8. Something she'd read yesterday morning before class. But still . . . it was sort of surreal to think God loved her enough to speak peace to her like that. That He loved her whether she heard His responses or not. He was here, with her, regardless.

She closed her eyes, wrapped in the Lord's arms, loved and cared for. Only one thought from the day remained as she drifted to sleep, and it made her smile, lying there in the darkness.

Cody missed her.

One more thing to be thankful for.

Six

THE DEADLINE TO FINISH EDITING THEIR movie was a living, breathing being, hounding them through every day and crawling into bed with them at night. Even still, Chase and Keith took Thanksgiving off. Their families deserved that much. Chase had pushed for dinner at their house, since that way they could put the girls to bed after dessert. But now the meal was behind them, he wondered if he'd made the wrong choice. Maybe pulling off a big dinner had been too much for Kelly, or maybe she was still upset with his schedule. Whatever it was, Chase hadn't been able to lighten her mood all day. It was late now, and they sat around the room with the Ellisons and their daughter, Andi, talking about the week ahead.

"You really think you'll finish before the fifth?" Lisa sat next to Keith, but the question was directed to Chase. He was the director, the one with the skill in the editing room.

"We have to do color correction and sound mixing. The principles are scheduled to meet us at the studio early next week for voice touch-ups. And we've hired someone to work on color. The guy's amazing."

"Is there money for that?" Kelly's question came out sharp, pointed. She sat across the room in a worn-out chair they'd gotten at a garage sale. One more sacrifice in the quest to make movies.

"We're still working with money Ben invested at the close of filming." Chase dug deep for an extra dose of understanding. He'd told her this before. "We can definitely get through the editing process."

"But if there's no theatrical release?" Kelly looked tired and anxious, the lines between her eyes deeper than usual. She didn't have to spell out the dire financial consequences. Not with Andi in the room.

"No one'll take you seriously if you go direct to DVD." Andi sat on the other side of her father. She'd been a great help with Molly and Macy today, and now they were asleep she seemed glad to be part of the adult conversation.

Andi was right. If she hadn't said it, Chase would have. The financial concerns were only part of the trouble they faced. They had to wrap up editing and submit to the film festivals Kendall had lined up. Then they needed to pray for a favorable response from the festival committees. If that happened, they'd have a good argument for a theatrical release when the studio screened the film. Not only so people would take them seriously, but so they would have a chance to earn back the money they'd spent.

"Luke Baxter is working on the studio contract, looking for a loophole. But he agrees that we need to pray. God's the great Counselor, after all."

Kelly raised a wary brow. "Lawyers don't work for free. It all costs so much."

"We've accounted for that, Kelly. Obviously." Chase immediately regretted his tone. Kelly had a right to feel nervous.

"I was just asking." Kelly tried to hide her hurt, but her eyes gave her away. She stood and headed for the kitchen, glancing first at Keith's wife. "More coffee?"

"Definitely." Lisa joined her, and they rounded the corner into the kitchen.

At the same time, Andi stood and headed to the back room to work on a paper for her English class. Once they were gone, Chase heard Kelly's defeated laugh. "This thing is going to break us all—you ever feel that way?"

Chase couldn't hear Lisa's answer, but his wife's lack of confidence made him feel suddenly tired—too tired to continue the conversation. He looked at Keith and saw his friend had also heard Kelly. He kept his voice low so the wives and Andi wouldn't hear him. "I thought we were past this. A few months ago she was nothing but supportive."

Keith was within arm's reach, and he put his hand on Chase's shoulder. "You can't blame her for being worried."

"Lisa's not."

"Of course she is." Keith's smile was layered with wisdom. "She doesn't talk about it the way Kelly does, but if we don't make our money back on this movie, we'll lose our house."

The news hit Chase with a cold wave of reality. "That bad?"

"Yes." Keith clasped his hands and stared for a moment at the place between his feet. "We took out a second mortgage on the house, and the payments are way beyond our comfort zone. Same as you."

Chase nodded, his mind drifting. He and Kelly rented the house they were in, so as long as he drew a salary from their work they wouldn't be homeless. But their credit cards were maxed out. If the money ran dry, and if the studio waited too long for a DVD release, Chase and Keith could reach a point where there would be no money even for a meager paycheck. He pictured himself talking to Kelly, explaining that she would need to get a job so they could pay their bills, and he shuddered. He'd quit making movies and clean toilets at a gas station before he'd ask Kelly to get a job. Especially if it was to support him while he followed his dreams. The sobering reality of that made him understand a little of what had Kelly feeling down.

After the next round of coffee, Keith, Lisa, and Andi went home. Keith promised to pick up Chase for the drive to LA first thing Sunday morning. They wanted half a day to discuss their plans and meet with Ben Adams one more time before they returned to the editing room to begin their most intense week yet.

When they were gone, Chase leaned against the closed door and locked eyes with his wife. "Is it the money? Is that what's eating you?"

"I'm not the problem." Kelly touched her fingers to her chest, her expression anchored in disbelief. "We can't walk around pretending we aren't in trouble." She paused, and raw fear flashed in her eyes. "What if the film doesn't break even?"

Chase didn't want to fight. He folded his arms and leaned his head against the cool wood door. His tone was quietly resigned. "It's Thanksgiving, Kelly. We're supposed to thankful."

"I am. But I'm also realistic." She tossed her hands and exhaled her frustration. "We're running out of money, Chase. You've got a movie almost done, and that's great. But where do we go from here?"

"Do we have to know?" His anger rose a level. "Whatever happened to trusting God? Believing He has a plan for us?"

"Don't start with that." Kelly let her hands fall to her sides. The girls were asleep down the hall, and he watched her fight to keep her voice in check. "Of course God has a plan. That doesn't mean the plan is for you to make movies, right? Or did you get a memo from God and forget to tell me?"

Chase hated when she was sarcastic. Her eyebrows lowered and the lines deepened across her forehead. In moments like this she seemed a different person from the girl he'd married. As if the two of them had never laughed or loved at all.

He thought of all the responses he might give her. He could tell her sarcasm didn't become her, and he could remind her that before they left the mission field they had agreed God wanted them here, in California ... making movies. But again he was too tired for the battle. He brushed his hand in her direction. "Never mind."

"Wait …"

He didn't want to. Without looking back, he walked to the kitchen and surveyed the dishes still crowded around the sink. He rolled up his shirt sleeves and began scrubbing the sweet potatoes and dried-on stuffing. Four of the plates were already washed when Kelly came to him. She studied him for a minute, and then joined in, wrapping up the leftover pie and putting away spices and whipped cream left out from dessert. From the corner of his eye, Chase watched her linger near the spice cupboard, searching for something.

Then, almost abruptly, she straightened and with only the slightest hesitation she told him good night and she was gone. As she walked away, he saw something he hadn't noticed before. She was wearing stretch pants—the kind she wore when she struggled with her weight. He'd noticed she was a little heavier than usual, but the pants were a sure sign.

He dried his hands and stooped down near the spice cupboard. Far in the back, where he would never have otherwise noticed it, was a wadded-up plastic grocery bag. He reached back and pulled it out. Even before he opened it, he had an idea of what he'd found. This was Kelly's weakness—hiding food. Sneaking chocolate and cookies so that no one would know she struggled. He opened the bag and there was the proof. It held at least fifty Hershey's Kisses, and just as many empty wrappers.

Anger rattled his nerves once more. He stood and moved to the trashcan beneath the sink, but he stopped before slamming the bag into the trash. Instead he set the bag out on the counter in plain sight. If she wanted to eat candy, she could eat it. He would love her no matter what.

"Why, God?" The prayer felt as worn out as he did. Did their money troubles really have her that depressed?

He massaged his thumb and fingers into his temples and willed the tension there to ease. Compassion tempered his frustration. Kelly didn't want to eat like this. She was worried and discouraged, afraid of their money troubles and Chase's future as a filmmaker. He looked out the window again.

What can I do, God? How can I love her so that I'm all she needs?

Almost as soon as he'd laid the question before God, Chase knew the answer. He would never satisfy all Kelly's needs. Only the Lord could do that. And until she learned to turn to Him when she felt overwhelmed, the struggle would continue.

How long had she been discouraged this time? She'd come to the shoot and together they'd shared alone time—something rare for them. She'd been supportive and loving and sure that God would see them through. But after his second LA editing trip, he'd noticed something different about her. She seemed distant and short. Now he understood just how hopeless she must be feeling.

Please, God ... give her strength. I'm not sure how much I can help her.

No matter how he approached the subject, he couldn't win, couldn't help her. He finished the dishes, praying for her the entire time. Clearly the answer was the one God had placed on his heart moments ago: she needed Christ—His satisfaction, His fulfillment, His strength.

As he turned off the lights he no longer felt angry. Instead he was determined to do the one thing he could do: pray for her without ceasing, that she might find the strength to do the same.

Before her discouragement grew any worse.

SHE'D BEEN FOUND OUT.

Kelly knew it early Friday morning as soon as she saw the bag of candy on the counter. Her heart slid into a fast and frantic rhythm, because if Chase knew ... If he knew, then she wasn't sure how she could face him. He and the girls were asleep, but they'd wake up soon. Chase would give her that look, the one that said he was aware of her struggles and that he was disappointed in her. She would be forced to come clean about her eating, and she would feel like a fat failure in front of her husband. Too depressed to find her way to daylight.

Her heart found its regular beat again. Defiance muddied the stagnant water of her heart. If Chase knew, there was no point hiding the candy. She moved the bag back to the spice cupboard, right up front. She could eat what she wanted to eat, and if she gained weight, then so be it. She had to keep the house and yard up, pay the bills, and keep the family going on almost no money. She would find control later, after the New Year. Chase was never home anyway, gone running after a dream that seemed less and less likely.

The pans were still soaking in the sink. She studied them, defeated, and caught her reflection in the mirror. She stopped short and stared at herself, hating what she saw. The weight was piling on, and she could do nothing to hide the fact. Her face looked pasty and puffy, creased with concern and deceit.

She took a step closer. Rebelliousness didn't become her. When had her eyes lost the shine that marked them a few months ago when she went to Bloomington, Indiana, and declared to Chase her absolute support? Punch drunk, that's how she looked, battered by the abuse she wielded on her own body. Her blank eyes reminded her of someone lost somewhere in the middle rounds of a boxing match against depression. A match she was destined to lose.

A realization began to take root, and she felt conviction taking hold of her, shaking her and ordering her out of the ring. Life wasn't meant to be a web of lies, and only one reason could explain why Chase had found out about her recent mindless eating.

God wanted him to find out.

She hung her head and didn't try to stop the gathering tears. A long, slow sigh made its way from her, taking with it every argument she'd ever made in favor of hiding food and falling prey to a diet of chocolate and McDonald's. None of this was Chase's fault; it was her own. Chase loved her and cared for her and the girls in a way too great for words. His time away was a necessary part of the commitment of filmmaking—an adventure she'd agreed to and supported even as recently as her trip to Indiana.

Footsteps sounded in the hallway, and Kelly ran her fingertips beneath her eyes. She sniffed and looked at herself once more. *God, I need You. I can't do this without You.* The next few minutes were going to be humiliating, but if they were God's way of taking her out of the fight, then she had no choice but to go along. However awful she felt.

"Kelly?" Chase came up behind her and stopped a few feet away. "I didn't hear you get up."

"Sorry." She wasn't willing to look at her husband yet. She knew exactly what she'd find in his eyes. Disapproval, disgust, and disappointment. The three *D*s. "The pans needed washing."

She held her breath and turned, facing him. But as they looked at each other, Kelly found she could barely exhale. Chase's expression wasn't angry or suspicious. His light-brown eyes showed a vulnerability, a love and concern that melted Kelly and shattered her defenses.

"Can you come here?" His words were kind and without accusation. He made no attempt to come to her, almost as if he could sense her vulnerability and he wanted her to know he wasn't on the attack.

She came to him, her eyes never leaving his. He wasn't her accuser, he was her friend, the one who had stood by her regardless of her highs and lows. As she reached him, he held out his hands and she wove her fingers between his. The touch of his skin felt intoxicating, lightening her spirit more than anything hidden in the cupboards—as if the unspoken honesty between them resurrected an intimacy long buried in layers of guilt.

Her body came up against his and she rested her head on his chest. "I'm sorry." Looking at him was still too painful. "About the candy."

He kissed the top of her head, their hands still linked. "You don't have to hide from me, Kelly. You're under a lot of pressure here. I know that."

"But …" She lifted her eyes to his again. "I'm turning to all the wrong things."

There was no need for him to say anything about that. "I'm here, Kel. If you need help, I'm here. I love you no matter what you eat, or how you look. I just want you to be happy."

The reference to her looks cut, and she winced a little. He'd have to be blind not to notice the weight she'd put on these past few months. At the same time, she believed he meant what he said—that he loved her whatever her size. But meaning it and living it out were two very different realities. If she didn't want their marriage to suffer, she had to find her way out of the darkness. "I've been so down, running everything here by myself."

"I'm sorry." His words were deeply sincere. "I hate being gone."

She released his hands and slid her arms around his waist. "I wish you weren't leaving so soon." If only he could stay this next week, take walks with her and shop with her, help her have a normal week. Maybe then she could make things right with herself and him, and even God.

"I love you, do you know that?" He leaned back enough to see her, study her. "You couldn't do anything to change that, Kel. I mean it. But don't hide things from me."

"I won't. Never again." Kelly laid her head against his chest once more and heard his heartbeat. The heartbeat of a man who loved her unconditionally. She tried to imagine telling Chase about surviving on candy and macaroni so she could find the energy to drag herself through a day of mowing the lawn and clipping coupons, washing dishes and doing laundry. All while trying to be both mother and father to their girls. No wonder she hid her stash of junk food. It was proof she was beyond discouraged and relying on all the wrong sources to survive.

Verses flooded her mind, Scriptures that ordered God's people to keep their deeds in the light, to avoid all darkness where sin could grow unchecked. Rather than flinch away from them, she embraced them, accepted them as truth. For another five minutes they stood there, clinging to each other, breathing to the beat of each other's heart, and believing that Kelly's secret, mindless eating was behind them. She would move ahead in honesty and light. She would tell him when she was tempted to spend an entire day eating ice cream bars and chocolate chip cookies. She wanted a fresh start now, so she could enjoy Christmas without the feelings of stomach pains and indigestion, without the oppressive guilt and weight gain. She was finished with it, once and for all. As soon as the moment passed, before anything could deter or distract her, Kelly would visit her hiding places and gather the garbage, taking it directly to the trashcan in the garage. And that would be that.

But before she could make a move, the girls woke up. They came down the hall holding hands, their flannel nightgowns covering all but their bare feet and fingers. When they reached the place where their parents stood hugging each other, the girls began to giggle.

The moment was suddenly over, and the girls clamored for breakfast and a trip to the park and piggy-back rides on Chase. There were eggs to make and dishes to wash and laundry to start, and in the mix of laughter and chaos that was their morning, Kelly never got around to throwing out the junk food, never made her way to her hiding spots.

She still intended to, of course. She would toss everything as soon as she had a chance, as soon as the morning allowed.

And for at least half the day, she actually believed that.

By noon, a compromise began to take shape. She wouldn't toss the food just yet, because what if the girls wanted a sweet snack? Money was tight, so it was practically sinful to throw out perfectly good cookies and candy. She could put them out when company came, the next time Laurie Weeks stopped by, maybe.

The compromise grew and swelled, and by nightfall she was already planning a trip to McDonald's with the girls as soon as Chase left for LA. They could eat cheaper from the dollar menu than anything she could cook, and at least she'd get one night without dishes. As for the other junk food, she wouldn't eat it now. She'd merely keep it around for a pick-me-up.

Just in case.

Seven

Andi met Bailey for lunch the day *Scrooge* opened at Indiana University's performance auditorium. She'd never been in a musical, and her stomach hadn't been right all day. She took a table in the midst of the confusion of the cafeteria and scanned the doorway for her roommate. She was still looking when a guy from her science class walked up.

He was biracial—white and Middle Eastern, maybe. Tall with a nice smile. Once in a while he'd asked her about lecture notes, but his name escaped her. "Waiting for someone?"

"My friend." Andi was careful not to seem interested. The guy was nice looking, and he seemed charming in his own way. But she'd already gotten into too much trouble with guys she didn't know. She smiled, but kept the walls up behind her eyes. "She'll be here any minute."

"That's okay." He sat down and put his backpack on the table. "I'm Taz. You've seen me in science class, but I'm also a film student. You're an actress, right?"

An actress. "I am." She liked the sound of it, even if so far she'd only been an extra in her dad's movie. "How'd you know?"

"You're gorgeous. Your dad's a producer—I saw you as an extra when he was filming on campus. And you're starring in *Scrooge*, which opens tonight." He winked at her. "I'll be there, by the way. Me and my roommates. They're film students too."

He pulled an envelope from a pocket in his backpack and slid it across the table. "This is for you. I didn't want to give it to you in class."

Andi's nerves were already on edge because in six hours she'd be slipping into the flowing gown that made up her costume for *Scrooge*, hoping she could still breathe when the curtain went up. She stared at the guy, now sitting in Bailey's seat. *A little pushy*, she thought. But something about his approach appealed to her. "You wrote me a letter?"

"Sort of. It's more of an offer." He leaned back and smiled, definitely satisfied with himself.

"Hmmm." Andi ignored the slight wave of anxiety his mention of opening night caused her. She felt her defenses fall. The film student stuff piqued her interest. "You're making a film? Is that what you're saying?"

"A short film. It's for a class, but I have connections. If I get the right people to star in it, we might win some awards." He stood, his eyes dancing. "It'd look great on your résumé."

A hint of a thrill ran down her spine. A short film with her as the star? That would be way better experience than extra work. Maybe then her dad would take her dreams of an acting career seriously. At least she would have something to show an agent or a director. She tossed her blonde hair over her shoulder and took the letter. "Thanks for thinking of me."

He laughed. "Are you kidding? You would be amazing."

The flattery felt good.

In the distance she saw Bailey make her way toward the table, so she hurried her next words. "How do I reach you?"

"Everything's in there," Taz nodded at the envelope. His smile was friendly, confident bordering on cocky. He gave her shoulder a quick, light touch, and his eyes connected with something in hers. "See you tonight." With that he was gone, moving through the crowd in the direction he'd come.

A few seconds later, Bailey reached the table and sat down, breathless from the cold air outside. Six inches of snow covered the Indiana campus, and another foot was forecast for the weekend. The perfect backdrop for *Scrooge*.

Bailey looked at Taz as he reached the cafeteria door. "Who was that?"

"Some guy in my science class." Andi still had the envelope in her hand. "I guess he's a film student." She lifted the envelope. "He gave me this."

"What is it?"

"An offer to star in a movie he's making."

"Really?" Bailey took off her coat and gloves and settled in closer to the table. Her eyes sparkled and she looked relaxed and comfortable. Not even a little nervous about opening night. "Well … come on! Open it."

Andi shared everything with Bailey. Whatever the offer inside the envelope, she was glad her roommate was excited for her. She slipped her finger beneath the sealed flap and pulled out a single piece of paper, then slid her chair around the side of the table so she and Bailey could read it together.

"'Dear Andi,'" she read aloud. "'My name is Taz Bazzi, and I'm in your science class. I'm making a movie—a short film, really—and I'd like you to consider starring in it.'"

"Andi!" Bailey grabbed hold of Andi's wrist. "That's fantastic. Lots of actresses get their start in short films."

"Seriously?"

"Yes. For sure." Bailey looked back at the paper. "How'd he know you could act?"

"He saw me working on *The Last Letter* and he knows my dad's a producer. At least that's what he said." Andi continued reading. "'I've been looking for the perfect girl for the role, and for awhile now I've known it was you. So here's a little bit about my film. It's sort of a docudrama about a conflicted girl trapped by her parents' outdated rules and understanding.'"

Andi gave a nervous laugh. "That's a little close to home."

"Keep reading."

She found her place. "'The girl's parents think she's at college, but she takes a quarter off and finds her way to the streets. She tries a lot of dangerous and edgy things before realizing that her place is here, back on campus.'" That was the end of the summary. The rest was Taz's contact information.

"Does she ever work things out with her mom and dad?" Bailey sounded less enthusiastic than before.

"Doesn't say." Andi turned the paper over, but it was blank on the back. She flipped it again and found his contact information, and then for the first time saw a few lines in small print at the bottom of the page. It told her they could set up a screening time and that the shooting schedule could be worked around her availability. The very last line was something Andi couldn't bring herself to read out loud.

Some partial nudity required.

Bailey peered over Andi's shoulder and read the fine print at the same time. "Partial nudity?" Bailey pushed back from table. "Creepy guy. Probably not even a film student. Just a porn freak."

Andi was bothered by the partial nudity thing, but she wasn't as upset as Bailey. Partial meant a few shots in her bra and underwear. Something like that. Besides, film was art. Wasn't that what the actors on her father's set had talked about? Sometimes compromise was necessary in order to get a message across …

Her eyes moved to the bottom of the page where a website was listed. She folded the paper and put it back in the envelope. "At least he was upfront."

"Yeah." Bailey's laugh was filled with disbelief. "Because he wants a look at *your* front. Don't you get it? The guy's probably making a soft porn film and somehow I get the feeling you're flattered."

She was, but she didn't want to say so to Bailey. Her roommate had connections like megastar Dayne Matthews and his actress wife, Katy Hart Matthews. What did Andi have? A dad who was more missionary than moviemaker and whose first film might never find its way out of DVD Land. If she wanted to be an actress, Taz was right. She needed all the experience she could get.

She slipped the envelope through the opening at the top of her backpack and smiled at Bailey. "I'm scared to death about tonight."

"Wait." Bailey leaned forward, more intense than before. "You're not considering that? Tell me you'll throw it in the first trashcan."

"I wanna check out his website." Andi kept her tone even, as if her calmness might make Bailey see that she was overreacting. "I owe him that much."

Bailey's eyes flashed. "You don't owe him anything. Come on, Andi. Show up to read for a guy like that and you could be raped."

"Please." Andi managed a light-hearted laugh. "If I was going to do it, I wouldn't meet with just him. There'd be other people and it would have to be somewhere on campus."

Another shocked sound came from Bailey. "You can't be serious? You're actually considering this? Even with the nudity?"

"Partial nudity. Like in a bikini or bra or something."

"So you're going to do it?"

"Well ..." Andi hesitated. Only one right answer remained. "Of course not. I'm just saying I should respond to him. Let's drop it, okay?"

"Tell him no."

"All right, all right." Andi wanted to say that she'd tell him whatever she wanted and Bailey could just get used to the idea.

But she was pretty sure she wouldn't take the job, anyway, so it didn't matter. "Talk about tonight. Are you scared?"

"No." Bailey looked like she was struggling to transition from her disapproval to the play they were about to star in. She busied herself with her gloves and then stopped and found the beginning of a smile. "You'll be great, Andi. You don't have to be afraid."

"So you're really not?"

"Not at all." Gradually Bailey softened, and the smile returned to her eyes. "There's nothing like opening night. The packed house, the buzz of anticipation backstage, the orchestra warming up for the first performance."

Andi felt her stomach tighten again. "What if I get out there and forget my lines?"

"You won't." Bailey laughed. "The adrenaline rush actually makes you think more clearly. Remember your audition?"

The two of them and Tim Reed had auditioned in a group, each performing in front of the creative team separately. "I was scared then too."

"And you were brilliant." Bailey shrugged. "You'll be brilliant tonight too."

Bailey's confidence was contagious. By the time they left the cafeteria, two things had happened. First, Andi's nervousness had faded to nothing more than excited energy. And second, Bailey had forgotten about Taz and his offer. At least it seemed that way. But after classes when Andi reached the dorm, Bailey was already there, sitting cross-legged on her bed reading her Bible.

"Hey." Andi tossed her backpack on the floor near her dresser. It was snowing again, and she dusted off the shoulders of her coat as she peeled it off and threw it on the end of her bed.

"Hey." Bailey looked up, but only briefly.

"What're you reading?"

"Romans 12. 'Do not conform any longer to the pattern of this world, but be transformed by the renewing of your mind.'"

She closed the Bible and anchored her elbows on her knees. "That section."

Andi knew it well. "Why that?"

"I don't know." Bailey sighed. "Just thinking about that Taz guy and his crazy offer. It's weird how people think they can do anything as long as they label it 'art.' Anything at all."

The sentiment was something Andi's father had said in the weeks leading up to his decision to leave the mission field for a career as a producer. He wanted to redefine art, take things way above the line from where they were. Andi wasn't so sure. She could see merit in some of the movies her parents disliked. She was pretty sure she and Bailey wouldn't see eye to eye on this, so she said nothing. Instead she busied herself with removing her gloves and scarf and setting them on the edge of her desk.

Bailey watched her. After this long as roommates and friends, they kept few secrets from each other. "You're thinking about it, aren't you?"

"About what?" Andi forced herself to look innocent.

"You know what." Bailey hugged her knees. "The film. The one with the nudity."

"Partial nudity." Andi had run out of busy work. She dropped to the edge of her bed, her shoulders a notch lower than before. "I think maybe I disagree a little."

"Disagree?"

"About the whole 'art' thing." Andi had been honest about her unconventional feelings before. She couldn't stop now if she wanted to stay close with Bailey. "Sometimes partial nudity might be valid for the sake of art, don't you think?"

"Not at all." There was no anger in Bailey's voice. The intensity from earlier in the day was gone, and in its place was a peace, a glow that seemed to come from deep inside her soul. But there was no hesitation, either. "Our bodies are sacred to God, the temple of the Holy Spirit. We're supposed to treat them with respect."

The truth came straight from the Bible. Andi knew that much. She pushed her fingers through her hair and tried to find an explanation that would make sense. "The body is a beautiful thing. Maybe it's honoring it to put the body in a more visible light." She stretched out on her side and leaned up on one elbow. "Or maybe if a film shows the terrible things that can happen to someone who makes bad decisions, and if that film requires partial nudity to get the point across, then maybe that's honoring. Because maybe it'll teach some teenaged girl not to make those same bad choices."

"Come on, Andi." Bailey raised one eyebrow. "You must be kidding."

That was the trouble. She wasn't kidding. Not that she was ready to sign up as the lead in Taz's film. She needed more information, like where the film would be shot and who would be there and whether it was truly a class project and how much nudity and whether it was in full light or only silhouetted.

"See, that's what I thought. You're seriously considering it." Bailey sounded worried. "Andi, you know better than that. I could give you a hundred Bible verses that would prove making that film would be a mistake. Romans is a good place to start."

"That's just it." Andi sat up again. "The pattern of the world interests me. I'm just being honest. I'm not saying I don't want to be a Christian, but ... I don't know. I want to experience life. Not avoid it."

For a long while Bailey didn't say anything. Then she stood, crossed the room, and sat down next to Andi. They both turned so they were facing each other. "I'm not going to judge you, Andi. But let's at least pray, okay? There's a lot going on."

"Sure." Andi didn't mind praying. She still liked the idea that God was there, that He cared about what she did or didn't do. But that didn't change her desire to experience life—in a safe manner, anyway. All of life. Maybe not by getting drunk at frat parties or by putting herself in dangerous situations. But acting in the short film of a student at Indiana University? Actually starring in it? The idea sounded more attractive with every passing hour.

Bailey seemed to sense Andi had made up her mind, but she said nothing about it. Instead she took hold of Andi's hands and began talking to God in a way that was familiar and comforting. She prayed about their opening night, that they would remember the words, and that the audience would be packed with people. "Let them see the meaning in the story, Lord," she added. "The message of regret for people who don't make the most of every day they've been given."

Her prayer moved on then to the movie offer from Taz. "The world will always have what looks like a better offer." Her voice was kinder still, without a drop of accusation. "Help us see life through Your eyes, Father. So that we know when the world is trying to mislead us. We need Your help, or we'll be ... Well, we'll be like people without faith. And that would be a very sad loss, Lord. Thank You for listening. In Jesus' name, amen."

Andi appreciated the prayer and the way moments like this made her and Bailey closer. But she still wondered if Taz was serious, if he and his roommates were really going to be at the show tonight. And if they were, she wondered if they would wait for her afterward. If so, then maybe she could ask him her questions in person. At least then she'd have all the information.

They both turned their attention to getting ready. Their characters needed long, curled hair—so they stood in front of the small mirror and shared Bailey's curling iron, passing it back and forth and spritzing hairspray as they went. They were just putting on their coats and gloves again when Andi got a text. Her first thought was Taz. Maybe he'd gotten her number and now he was texting her, looking for her answer. But as she reached for her phone, she saw she was wrong. The text was from Cody.

HEY, ANDI. WANTED YOU TO KNOW I'LL BE THERE TONIGHT. I'M TAKING MY MOM. CAN'T WAIT TO SEE IT. BREAK A LEG!

She grinned at the phone and her heart soared. She hurried with her response.

YAY! I'M GLAD YOU'RE GOING, BUT DON'T LOOK AT ME DURING MY SONG. LOL. I MIGHT FORGET THE WORDS AND RUN DOWN TO JOIN YOU IN THE AUDIENCE.

Andi couldn't figure out Cody Coleman. Times like this she was almost certain he had feelings for her, which would be amazing. There was no one she'd rather date than Cody. He was the hottest guy she knew, but more than that he had a wisdom, a faith that was borne of real-life experience and a genuine need for God. The kind of faith Andi wished she had.

"Who're you texting?" Bailey wrapped her thick wool scarf around her neck and chin. The air temperature outside was already in the low teens.

"Cody." Andi tried not to feel guilty, but she did. Whenever she and Cody texted, things felt a little awkward with Bailey. "He'll be at the show."

Bailey's eyes flickered, proof that the news clearly registered somewhere inside her. But nothing in her expression told whether she felt grateful or upset by the fact. Bailey grabbed her bag and headed for the door. "Did he say anything else?"

"Yeah. He's coming with his mom."

For a second, Bailey stopped and looked over her shoulder. "You know Cody's mom?"

"No." Andi wrinkled her nose, confused by the question. "Why would I know her?"

Bailey shrugged. "Just seemed like he wouldn't tell you that unless you knew her."

"I know she's had a rough life. Been in prison, drugs, that sort of thing. Cody says he's trying to build a new relationship with her."

This time there was no mistaking the hurt in Bailey's eyes. "Great." She checked her watch. "We better go."

They decided to drive because the theater was on the other side of campus and even a five-minute walk wouldn't be easy in the freezing-cold snow and wind. On the way to the car, and then to the theater, Bailey talked about her costume and Tim's nervousness about playing Scrooge. She touched on how she might take a break from theater after this quarter and the struggle she was having in her harder classes. But Cody's name didn't come up again.

Andi tried to assess Bailey's response to Cody, her seeming lack of interest. All along she had told herself that Cody had feelings for Bailey, that the two of them were only kidding each other by keeping their distance and maintaining that they'd never seen each other as more than friends. Anyone around the two of them could feel the chemistry there. But watching her now, Andi wondered if she might have read Bailey wrong. Maybe Bailey really didn't have feelings for Cody. She was still dating Tim, after all.

They ran into the theater, using their backpacks to shield their curly hair from the snow, and Andi was suddenly overcome with a rush of joy and exhilaration. Life was actually going right for her. She was truly living—living in a way that she wished her friend Rachel Baugher might've lived. Rachel, who died in a car accident without ever realizing her dreams. That wouldn't be Andi. She was going to live here and now, without reservations.

She ran through the list of all that was right in her life. She was about to star in her first musical, and she was being asked to star in her first movie—and it was a movie. Short film or not. On top of all that, maybe Cody did like her after all. The possibility seemed so real she could almost see the two of them together, holding hands and laughing. Bailey wouldn't care. At least it seemed that way.

And for the first time every dream she'd ever had seemed within reach.

She could hardly wait for the curtain to go up.

Eight

Bailey couldn't explain the hurt consuming her heart.

This was opening night, and she wanted everything about it to be a celebration. She was sharing the stage with Tim, a guy she admired and respected. In the audience would be her parents and brothers, along with some of their friends. Katy and Dayne had bought a block of tickets in the center orchestra section, so they'd be there, along with Ashley and Landon and the boys and a few of the other Baxter sisters and their families. Everyone Bailey loved.

Even Cody Coleman.

She and Andi helped each other into their costumes and then moved into the greenroom where all cast members did their own stage makeup. They sat next to each other at a long row of tables. Each spot had a stand-up mirror, and as Bailey began applying her makeup, she was struck again by the sadness consuming her. Or was it jealousy?

This is all because of Cody, she told herself. *Dear God, I know he's not interested in me as anything more than friend. Help me stop thinking about him*. But the moment the quick prayer was over, his face was back in her mind again. Smiling at her, haunting her.

"You okay?" Andi dabbed white powder over her foundation. For the part of Isabelle, she needed to look paler than usual.

"Sure." She gave Andi an instant smile, almost too instant. "Just thinking about my lines."

"Oh." Andi resumed her dabbing. "Okay. You seem kinda quiet."

"Sorry. I'm like this before the first show." She smiled again at her friend. "I'm fine. Really."

Her hurt was something she would only share with God, at least until she had some alone time with her mom. Figuring out her feelings for Cody was hard enough without involving her roommate.

She took a cotton pad and lightly applied thick foundation across her cheeks. Why didn't he at least ask about her? Cody knew she was in the show, so he could have dropped her a quick text as easily as he'd texted Andi. The occasional random text, like on Thanksgiving, wasn't enough. Or was he really avoiding her because of Tim?

She began moving too fast, and her foundation streaked. *Slow down*, she told herself. So what if Cody's here tonight. The way he'd treated her lately, he was just another guy on a campus of tens of thousands of guys. But even so, she couldn't shake his image.

She applied another layer of makeup. She needed paler skin for the show. The Ghost of Christmas Past was supposed to have an otherworldly, ethereal look. When she finished, she stepped back. "Definitely ghostlike," she muttered.

"You look great." Andi put the finishing touches on her eye shadow. She was pale, but striking. The way Isabelle was supposed to look.

Bailey hadn't been jealous of her friend's part since the cast list went up, but here, knowing Cody would be in the audience ... For a brief moment she wished she could take the stage in the dress Andi was wearing instead of the velvet cloak assigned to the Ghost of Christmas Past.

They were both studying themselves when she saw Tim enter the room. At least she assumed the guy was Tim. The transformation was that dramatic. He had reported to the theater half an hour earlier to meet with a professional makeup artist, and now he looked sixty years old. His hair was streaked mostly gray and his face looked haggard and wrinkled.

She turned to face him. "That's amazing. You look totally different."

"I even talk different." A few of the other cast members stared at him as he crossed the greenroom. "They put some kind of tightening gel near my mouth so that I'll sound like an old man."

"It's working." Bailey took a step closer and studied his face. "Seriously, I almost didn't recognize you."

"I hope not." He tried to laugh, but it sounded strained with his tight mouth. "This isn't really the look I'm going for offstage."

Bailey giggled as Andi faced Tim too. "Definitely Scrooge." She put her hands on her hips and did a slow twirl. Her dress was pale blue with small white lines of satin. It clung to her upper body, while below her waist it billowed out in soft folds of blue that gracefully hit just below her ankles. With her blonde hair hanging down her back in curls, she was stunning. Any of them could've seen that. She grinned at Tim. "What do you think?"

Tim watched her. "Wow." His stage makeup couldn't hide the appreciation in his eyes. "Scrooge would've been a fool to walk away from you."

The compliment made Andi blush even through her pale powder. "Why, thank you, Ebenezer."

Bailey pulled her red velvet cloak around her shoulders and tried not to be bothered by the exchange. She couldn't blame Tim. His character was motivated largely by the regret he felt in walking away from the woman he'd loved as a young man. Scrooge needed an attraction to Isabelle for the audience to believe the story.

Still, the comment made her feel thick and unattractive. Her cloak came in tight around the neck, but otherwise she would remain shapeless on stage. The only thing that would make her performance stand out was the slight bit of sarcastic humor written into the script. Their director had told her to milk it for all it was worth.

But nothing about the role made her feel pretty.

Tim seemed to realize he hadn't shown her the same attention he'd shown Andi. He came to her and put his hands on her shoulders. "I like your hair that way, curled." He touched his fingers to the side of her face. "You're beautiful, Bailey. A vision."

"In a red velvet cloak?" She made a silly face. "That's okay. Thanks about my hair though. I like it this way too."

He gave her a side hug just as the director bounded into the room. "Okay, people. We've got a full house." He chuckled. "Oh, and Dayne Matthews is in the fourth row. This will be a first for my career directing plays at Indiana U." He made eye contact with Tim and a handful of the other leads. "Let's give it our best tonight."

They circled up and he gave them a few reminders. "All right." He sounded as nervous as any of them. "Everyone take their places."

Only Tim and the kid playing Bob Cratchet were needed for the first scene, but before he walked onto the stage, Tim looked into her eyes. "All day I kept thinking about you, how this was like CKT and ... I guess just how special it is that you're here." He kept his voice to a whisper. "That we're in this together."

"I guess I hadn't thought about that." For the first time since she'd met Andi for lunch, Bailey felt her mood lighten. She'd been consumed with Andi and the shady film offer, confused by how a girl raised by missionary parents could actually consider starring in a movie with nudity. Then there'd been the lack of texts from Cody. And the way her costume hung like heavy drapes.

But now, with Tim gazing at her—even though his eyes sagged with artificial wrinkles—she suddenly felt like a princess. A montage of memories from a dozen CKT shows played in her mind. From days when she had dreamed of dating Tim Reed.

And now here she was, Tim's girlfriend, the two of them about to take the stage at Indiana University for the first time. "You'll be amazing … just like always."

"You too." He looked like he wanted to kiss her, but it wasn't the time or place. Instead he gave her hand a quick squeeze and walked onstage. The orchestra was silent, ready for the cue from the conductor. He gave it and the music began in a beautiful rush of strings and horns, and like that, the air was filled with Christmas.

The opening scene was flawless. Tim was so believable that Bailey and the others couldn't help but watch from the wings. Bailey had to keep reminding herself that the guy in the counting shop on stage was her nineteen-year-old boyfriend and not the crotchety mean old man he pretended to be. He was that convincing. Tim seemed to pick up steam, getting better still as he was warned by his dead business partner that he would be visited by three additional ghosts.

Bailey and Andi stood in the wings and squeezed hands. "You'll be great," Bailey whispered.

"I think I'm sick." Andi's eyes were wide.

"You're not." Bailey heard her cue but suddenly all she could think about was Cody—where he was sitting and what he was thinking. Whether she would be able to see him from the stage. She pushed his image from her mind. "Gotta go."

She adjusted her cloak and walked on stage with a sort of floating, waltz-like step. Tim was on his knees looking under the bed for any sign of a ghost, grumbling about the warning being a bunch of nonsense. Before he could stand, Bailey tapped him on the shoulder.

His dramatic reaction received a loud bit of laughter from the audience. Bailey remained stoic, straight faced. She had to work to keep herself from listening for Cody's voice.

"Who are you?" Tim scowled at her, stood, and dusted himself off.

Bailey lifted her chin, proper and poised. "The ghost whose presence was foretold to you."

Their exchange was brief and well rehearsed. They'd worked on stage together too long to be anything but professional in a moment like this. She led Tim across the stage to where he could watch a scene from his childhood. After that, she ushered in another moment from Scrooge's past—the dance at Fezziweg's where Scrooge first falls in love with Isabelle. Andi entered the stage and there was almost a collective gasp at the vision she made. Truly she was stunning.

Andi danced with young Scrooge, and together they sang a perfect duet. Whatever anxiety Andi had felt about this scene, she was in her element now.

After watching the dance come to an end, Tim reached out toward Isabelle, who of course could not see him. Tim's expression, the longing in his body language, told everyone in the theater he wanted nothing more than a chance to go back in time, back to that moment with Isabelle. Just once more.

The way I feel about Cody, Bailey thought. Again she forced herself back into the scene. But distraction came easily. Bailey's part required her only to stand alongside Tim and watch the past play out. She had only a handful of words left before the end of her scene. Was Cody mesmerized by Andi the way the rest of the audience must be? She blinked. *Focus, Bailey ... God, please help me focus.*

Tim looked ready to cry as he watched young Scrooge bend on one knee, pull out an engagement ring, and hand it up to a thrilled Isabelle. At the same time, Tim slowly took hold of that same ring, now on a chain around his neck.

"Come." Bailey took his hand and led him to yet another spot on the stage. This time the scene was far sadder. The saddest in the entire play. Young Scrooge was in the counting house as Andi walked up, dressed the same but with a bonnet and a shawl over her shoulders.

"I'm leaving, Ebenezer." She delivered her lines like a pro.

For the first few seconds, young Scrooge barely looked up, still counting. But when Andi insisted that where she was going he would not see her anymore, he stopped. "Why? You were going to marry me."

Tim took a step closer to the action, desperate to stop the younger version of himself. "Don't let her leave … you fool!"

But Andi tossed the engagement ring onto his counting scale, and with a final few words, she left. Again Bailey caught a glimpse of Tim as he reached out, longing for a way back to yesterday. Anyone would've believed he'd been in love with Andi, and that he'd never gotten over her.

The scene ended with another song—a duet between the two Scrooges, one where Andi returned to the stage in a lyrical dance intended to represent her moving farther from his life. Again she was graceful, a vision as she moved across the stage.

Bailey watched her, but she was thinking about Cody again. *He's probably falling in love with her right now*, she told herself. What guy wouldn't be? Her red cloak felt heavier, thicker than before. She must've looked like a set piece compared to Andi. A coat rack, maybe.

Tim glanced back at her, as if she could do something to undo the passing of time. Then he turned to Andi once more and launched into his final verse of the song. As it ended, as Andi danced offstage, Tim turned, anguished, to Bailey and took her hand. "Spirit, remove me from this place. I can bear it no more." The handhold was a plea, an urging from Scrooge, but Tim held her fingers a little longer than they'd rehearsed. His eyes locked onto hers, and though no one from the audience—not even the director—could've told he was breaking character in any way, he did. For a flicker in time, the longing in his eyes was as intense as it had been when he stared at Isabelle. Only this was real, Bailey had no doubt. And it was aimed at her.

The incident was over almost as soon as it began, but it left Bailey breathless. She wanted to smile, but she couldn't, because the Ghost of Christmas Past certainly did not smile. But inside she was giddy. Tim might as well have stopped the action and announced to all the room that Andi couldn't turn his head. Not when he was in love with Bailey.

She felt herself stand a little taller as the scene wound down and as she delivered her final lines—lines that warned Scrooge to love today, while time still allowed. "There is never enough time to say or do the things you want in this life, never enough time to love the way you want to love," she told him. "We are only here for a little while, Scrooge, and then we are gone."

With that, she took the same slow, otherworldly steps off the stage, ignoring Tim's pleas that she stay with him, that she allow him to live a little longer in the past. As soon as she stepped into the wings, she fell against the wall and remembered the moment with Tim again. Suddenly her own lines came back to her. "*Never enough time to love the way you want to love...*" So why was she wasting her time thinking about Cody? She was dating an amazing guy, one she'd looked up to all her life. He had none of Cody's crazy past. He'd never been drunk or slept with a girl, and on top of all that he cared enough to know exactly how she felt in the midst of their scene.

Whatever her feelings for Cody, however she'd been frustrated by him, none of that mattered. Tim was a great guy, and he'd proved that out there on the stage, not caring if anyone caught what he was doing or not. Her heart felt lighter than it had all day.

She removed her red cloak and listened as Tim and the Ghost of Christmas Present sang one of Bailey's favorite songs from the show. "I like life ... life likes me ... life and I fairly fully agree ..."

Bailey couldn't agree more. She worried about Andi's choices, and yes, if Cody fell for her there would be times when Bailey would hurt. But she had Tim, and in light of that sweet moment on stage, she couldn't be happier.

Tim was wonderful in the final scene of the first act, and Bailey watched his every move, silently cheering for him. As the curtain fell at the beginning of intermission, Bailey waited for him in the shadows.

He started to pass by, the area too dark to make out shapes or people. "Tim," she whispered as loud as she could without being heard on the other side of the curtain.

"Bailey?" He was out of breath, adrenaline and exhilaration no doubt racing through his veins.

"Here." She reached out and touched his arm. "You were amazing."

"You too."

They couldn't hang out in the wings for long. The director would expect them to report to the greenroom to hear his notes on the first act and to receive any last-minute direction for the second half of the show. But they had a few minutes at least.

"I mean, I kept believing you were really Scrooge."

He came nearer, facing her. Even this close and as their eyes adjusted to the darkness, he looked like an old man.

"I love this. I could perform in New York, you know?"

"You could."

"You too. Seriously, Bailey, you should've been Isabelle. You're so good."

She should've been Isabelle? Bailey opened her mouth to thank him, to tell him that was the exact thing she needed to hear, but the words got jumbled on the way up from her heart. Instead she slipped her arms around his neck and hugged him. Finally, when she was sure of her voice, she pulled back and searched his eyes. "Thank you."

Here was further proof that something was building between them, something that hadn't been there before. Tim didn't ask what Bailey was thanking him for. He didn't have to. Instead his voice softened. "I wanted you to know that my character might desire Isabelle—" He brushed his cheek against hers. "But I want you, Bailey. Only you."

Her heart responded by pounding in her chest, and she wanted more than anything to kiss him. A quick kiss wouldn't have violated any university theater rule, but again this wasn't the time. So she eased from his arms and grinned at him. "Come on. We need to get back."

Bailey played a townsperson in the second act, and everyone in the cast gave their all as the show ran down. In the final scene, when Tim sang about being ready to begin again, Bailey wanted to join him. If ever she'd been ready to truly move on it was here, tonight. Not until she was back on stage and staring at a standing ovation did she realize perhaps the most important thing about the night—something that hadn't happened since the moment Tim looked at her that way in the middle of their scene.

She hadn't thought about Cody once.

Nine

From his place in the back of the theater, Cody watched the actors take the stage for their curtain call. He could've been wrong, but he sensed a change in Bailey, something he couldn't pinpoint or put into words. Up until now, on the rare times when he and Bailey shared a few words or a conversation, he sensed she still had feelings for him.

Just not enough feelings to walk away from Tim Reed.

But now? There seemed to be some new and stronger chemistry between Bailey and Tim, and as the applause began to die down and the houselights came up, Cody watched Tim sling his arm around Bailey's shoulders, both of them laughing as they walked offstage with the cast.

He looked away. At the other side of the theater near the front were Bailey's parents and brothers, people who just a year or so ago had been his family. He thought about crossing the theater to say hello, but they would be looking for Tim now. Not him.

"I see you." His mother leaned in close. She was still clapping, but she made sure he could hear her voice over the noise of the audience.

Cody turned to her, his expression blank. "See what?"

"How you look at her."

"Andi?" Cody shifted and watched Andi saunter toward the edge of the stage. She was still waving at the crowd. He had told his mom that he and Andi were becoming better friends and that she'd asked him to her opening night. He nodded as his eyes found his mom's again. "She was beautiful. Perfect."

His mother had been absent for so much of his life, trapped by her demons and addictions. She had missed much, but not anymore. These days she was going to church with a few friends from her alcohol recovery class, and she'd been sober longer than he could ever remember. They were actually building a relationship for the first time.

She looked at him and raised a brow. "Not Andi." She held up her copy of the *Scrooge* program and pointed to a photo just inside the front cover. "Bailey Flanigan. You couldn't take your eyes off her."

With everything in him, Cody wanted her to be wrong. Bailey wasn't interested. She was dating Tim, and that was that. Especially tonight, when something very special seemed to linger between the two of them. Andi was striking, gorgeous as Isabelle. In his high school days, back when he was a jerk to just about every girl he came across, Cody wouldn't have had the ability to see past Andi Ellison.

His mom was still looking at him, and he felt something crack in his resistance. Finally he drew a long breath and admitted just enough. "I've cared about her longer." The crowd was filing out, moving past them, and Cody was in a hurry to talk about the play or where they were going afterwards for coffee. Anything else. Bailey and he were a thing of the past for lots of reasons. He wasn't comfortable having his mom look straight into his heart, not when he hadn't quite given her viewing privileges.

But they were at the end of their row, and before they could file out, she touched his arm and waited until he looked at her again. "It's okay, Cody. I've known for a long time."

"Known what?" He tried to sound neutral rather than frustrated.

Her voice grew nostalgic. "How you feel about that girl. How you've always felt."

"Mom." He forced an exhale. "No offense, but you weren't around when Bailey and I were friends. And that's all we were. We've never been anything more."

"I wasn't around much." Her eyes were heavy with the pain from years lost. "But when I got out, when I came home … I saw the way you looked when you talked about her. I knew then." She had to look up to him, but she put her hand on his cheek. "And I know now."

"Mom." He didn't want to talk about Bailey. Not with his mom, anyway. He was trying to build something new with her, which meant he didn't want to look backward. Not regarding his mom, and certainly not regarding Bailey. When it came to the ins and outs of his heart, she was hardly a qualified expert. He smiled at her. "Can we talk about something else?"

"It's just—" She let her hand fall back to her side. Her face grew concerned, almost worried. "Cody … I like the Flanigan family, but … I don't want you to get hurt. You've been hurt enough."

He was suddenly aware of his prosthetic lower leg and his lonely afternoons and a lifetime of not knowing his mother—and, mixed together, he hated how it made him feel. "Mom, please." He was not a victim. Not because of his war injury or his past, or anything Bailey might mean to him. "I'm not hurt. I'm fine."

She ceded with a slight nod, and her eyes shifted to the sticky floor between them. "I'm sorry. I just … I worry about you."

"Don't. I can take care of myself." He couldn't get angry with her. It was too late for that. He put his arm around her shoulders and gradually walked her down the aisle toward the door. She was trying, something he'd prayed for. His frustration gave way to kindness, confidence. In this, their new relationship, he was the leader, the stronger one. He had almost forgotten that. "So … what'd you think of the show?"

"Good." Her smile was tentative, but she understood. The conversation about Bailey was over. "Very good, really. The guy playing Scrooge was amazing."

Tim Reed. Cody narrowed his eyes. "He's been acting for awhile. Just a freshman too."

"Really?" His mom seemed ready to move on, too, glad that Cody wasn't upset anymore. She put her arm around his waist and gave him a hug. "The show put me in a Christmas mood." She looked up at him. "I think we should put lights up this year. What do you think?"

The conversation felt easy again, the way Cody liked it. They were still talking about decorating for the holidays when they walked into the far end of the lobby. The crowd was spread throughout the space, and the cast mingled among them, everyone laughing and talking and taking pictures. His mom gave him a gentle elbow in the ribs. "There's your friend. She played Isabelle. What's her name?"

"Andi." He followed his mother's gaze, and there she was, looking as beautiful as she had on stage. "Andi Ellison." Cody watched her, the way she tilted her head and tossed her hair. She was talking to a couple of guys and clearly enjoying the attention. Andi knew she was beautiful. She would always know it.

"I like that girl." Her mom took a few steps. "I'll be in the restroom." She dropped her voice, as if anyone would hear her with the commotion around them. "Go talk to her. I saw her look over here."

"Thanks, Mom." He kept his tone light. When she was gone, he leaned against the far wall and slid his hands into his jean pockets. He wished he had feelings for Andi, wanted to be interested in her. His mom was right. Andi was into him. Cody had known that for a long time. Especially after she'd made a play for him that night when he'd helped her home after she got drunk at the frat party. But there were ten quick reasons why he wasn't interested. The biggest: Bailey Flanigan. He could hear her laugh from across the room. He sighed, and it felt like it came from the basement of his soul.

Cody studied the architecture along the windows and doorways. He read the posters that lined the wall leading into the theater. Anything so he wouldn't give in to his desire to find Bailey and at least stare into her eyes, tell her she'd done a great job. *Don't look for her*, he told himself. *She's with Tim. She'll be with him now.*

A minute passed before he lost the battle. Without being too obvious, he made a casual sweep of the room and saw her in the middle of a large group—her parents and brothers, three of the Baxter sisters and their families. She had her red cape slung over one arm, and even from this far away the sight of her took his breath.

Cody shifted a few inches for a better look, and Tim came into view. From the opposite end of the long room, he looked like an old man, still in costume like the rest of the cast.

His eyes easily found their way back to Bailey. Her long, light brown hair falling around her shoulders in layers of curls, her fine features and infectious laugh. How had he let her slip away? Their story was almost like the one that had played out on the stage. A story of lost chances and useless regret. If he could will it, he wouldn't be standing here alone, watching her live her life with some other guy. He would be back in her entryway, Fourth of July, holding her and telling her how much he'd missed her while he was gone. God could've taken him home after his capture, and he would've been okay with it except for one thing.

The memory and hope of Bailey Flanigan.

But instead of telling her exactly how he felt, instead of admitting he was in love with her, he'd done the opposite. He'd praised her for dating someone more her type, and he'd assured her that he wanted only to be her friend. For her sake. Because she deserved better.

But now … now he wasn't the drunk guy who played with girls' hearts. He was a different person, a guy who loved God and wanted a future based on faith and family. He was the right kind of guy for her now. And no one would ever love her more.

Cody stood a little straighter and filled his lungs with a determined breath. All his life he'd been a fighter. He'd scrapped and scrounged to survive as a latchkey grade school kid when his mother's drinking left him without supervision, and he'd fought hard to find his place with the Flanigans—his only way of getting through high school. No one had worked harder on the football field, and when he was a prisoner of war, he had never, not once, given up.

So why had he given up so easily on Bailey?

The muscles in his jaw tightened, and he forced himself to look away. Maybe he was supposed to take to heart the message of the musical. It was almost the New Year, so this could be the time in his life when he stopped hiding in the shadows and actually tried a different tactic. Like talking to her and texting her, being the friend he'd promised to be. She wasn't married. Unless she asked him to stay away, he could certainly make himself more of a presence in her life.

The change of heart coming over him was so strong, he didn't see Andi until she was standing directly in front of him. She giggled and ran her hand along his forearm. "Hey … you look like you're in another world."

He was. "Oh, hey, sorry. I didn't see you." He felt his guard go up. "You did great."

"Thanks." She crossed her arms in front of her and shivered a little. "I was scared to death. You have no idea."

"We couldn't tell."

Andi hesitated. "Oh ... your mom!" She glanced around. "Where is she?"

"Restroom. She'll be right back." Cody peered in the direction his mom had walked off in, and for the first time he realized she was taking a long time. He turned back to Andi. "How many shows in the run?"

"All this weekend—five shows—and then three midweek and another five next weekend. Thirteen altogether."

"That's a lot." He didn't want a long conversation with Andi. She was a nice girl, but he didn't want to lead her on. He pressed his back against the wall behind him again. "You and Bailey weren't at Cru this week." Cru was the Campus Crusade meeting each Thursday on campus. At the beginning of the semester they'd all gone together.

"Dress rehearsals." Andi wrinkled her nose in a cute girly sort of way. "This week we have a show, and then Christmas break. I guess we'll start up again in January."

"I guess." He looked down the hallway again for his mom. Maybe he should go after her, in case she'd fallen or something. He gave Andi a distracted glance. "You ready for finals?"

"Pretty much." She gasped. "I almost forgot to tell you. This guy in my science class is a film student. He's making an independent movie and he wants me to star in it! I was just talking to him! Isn't that great?"

"Yeah, great." Cody didn't want to be rude, but he was finished here. "Hey, listen. I gotta go find my mom." He hugged her. "Seriously. You were great tonight."

"Thanks." She seemed flustered, a little confused by his early exit. "I sorta thought maybe we could go out for coffee, you and your mom and me. I guess I could hang out with the film guy." She gave a disappointed shrug. "He asked, but ... I don't know. I wanted to hang out with you."

"Oh." He hesitated. She was sincere and kind, and a girl whose shaky faith could use all the right people surrounding her. What would it hurt if they included her for coffee? Bailey was obviously busy tonight. "Okay, sure. Let me go find my mom."

He held back from taking another look at Bailey as he walked the opposite direction down a hall toward the bathrooms. He wasn't sure whether to be worried about his mom or not. He'd lost track of time watching Bailey, so he wasn't sure how long she'd been gone. A few minutes? Five … ten? He picked up his pace.

Just as he was about to turn the corner, she stepped into view, fiddling with something in her purse. She stopped short when she saw him. "Cody. What are you doing?"

"Looking for you." He dropped his gaze from her eyes down to her purse and back up again. Why was she acting guilty? Like she was hiding something? "What took so long?"

"I got a phone call." She slipped her purse up onto her shoulder and smoothed her coat, more confident than a few seconds ago. "Someone from my Bible study."

Cody hesitated. He'd seen his mother crash hard too many times to count, seen her spiral into the evil, clutching hands of her addiction and each time fall lower than the last. He studied her eyes and searched for a hint of deceit, for even the beginnings of the telltale signs—the shaking hands and slightly wild-eyed look. But there was nothing, no reason to doubt her. He breathed out. "Okay." He turned and fell in beside her. He wanted to believe her with everything in him. This was their time, their chance to be mother and son, like they'd never been before. He allowed his nerves to settle and again found a smile. "I ran into Andi. I told her she could join us for coffee."

"That's wonderful." She grinned at him, maybe a little too big. Maybe not. "Introduce me!"

They reached the foyer again and Andi was still there where he'd left her, talking to a few of her fellow cast mates. He couldn't tell if Bailey was still in the group at the far end of the room or not.

His mom leaned in as they drew nearer to Andi. "She's so pretty."

"Yes, Mom." Cody chuckled. He wasn't used to spending time with his mother, and her persistent efforts to set him up were almost comical. As if in these past few months she wanted badly—almost desperately—to become his friend and confidante.

They reached Andi, and Cody put his hand on her arm. "Mom, meet my friend Andi."

"Andi! Why you're absolutely adorable!" His mom still didn't have strong social graces. She was nervous, having spent so many years behind bars of one kind or another, and sometimes she made up for it by being a little overly dramatic, a little over the top. This was one of those times.

"Mrs. Coleman, ma'am." Andi nodded. "Nice to meet you."

"Aren't you sweet." She laughed awkwardly. "Call me Cassie. That's what my friends call me." She gave Andi an impulsive hug. "You're a perfect Isabelle."

"Thank you, ma'am." Andi's eyes danced. Awkward or not, she was eating up the attention.

Cody was ready to leave. Across the room, he noticed Bailey separate herself from the group and jog lightly toward them. He willed her to stay away, because already Bailey suspected he had feelings for Andi. And with his mom certain Bailey was going to break his heart, everything about the coming moment screamed disaster.

His mom didn't notice Bailey. She was still gushing over Andi in a way that was borderline embarrassing. "I'm sure Cody told you we thought you were brilliant tonight, just brilliant. Brilliant."

She was at the last "brilliant" when Bailey reached them. Bailey seemed to register that this might be a special moment and that maybe she shouldn't interrupt. Her last few steps were slower, tentative. "Hi. Sorry ... I don't want to interrupt." She nodded at Cody and his mom and finally turned her attention to Andi. She was already taking a step back, retreating. "We're getting pizza. Wanna come?"

"Um ..." Andi smiled at Cody. "I'm having coffee with Cody and his mom."

"Right." Bailey seemed to realize she might've been rude. "Hi, Mrs. Coleman, Cody. Thanks for being here."

"I was just telling Andi that she was brilliant tonight." His mom linked arms with Andi. If Andi thought the move was strange, she didn't act like it. His mom grinned widely. "The perfect Isabelle."

"Yes." Bailey seemed flustered, unsure of what to say. "Well, just wanted to see if you had plans. See you later."

"Okay." His mom waved good-bye to Bailey in a way that seemed almost sarcastic.

Cody was furious with his mother. She had intentionally lavished praise on Andi at Bailey's expense. Bailey had already turned around and was walking away. Cody's mind raced, looking for a way to salvage the moment. "Bailey ... wait." He took a few hurried steps in her direction and then walked slowly beside her until they were out of earshot of his mom and Andi. He touched her elbow and she stopped and faced him.

"You better go." Her eyes were ice cold. "Don't want to make them wait."

"Bailey, please ... don't be like this." He wanted to tell her she would've made a more believable Isabelle and that he'd had a revelation and he was going to be a much more present part of her life. But Andi and his mom were waiting, and there wasn't enough time to explain himself. "You were wonderful tonight."

She looked at him a little longer than necessary, but still the walls were up. “Thanks.” She took another step away. “You and Andi . . . have fun tonight.” With that she was gone, hurrying back to her family and Tim—none of whom seemed to have noticed the two of them talking, or even that Cody was there.

Cody wanted to put the entire last ten minutes into reverse. He should’ve gone to Bailey and complimented her sooner. Tim or no Tim. The trouble was he had a habit of keeping his distance. This new determination, this change of heart God had given him wasn’t something he could act on immediately. He had to think things through first. But still—now he’d made things worse than before. Or his mom had.

He walked back slowly. His mom no longer had her arm linked with Andi’s, but she was speaking with a great deal of animation, talking with her hands and telling Andi some long story about who knew what. Their coffee break brought more of the same. His mother dominated the conversation, talking fast and laughing at times that weren’t always appropriate. Cody tried not to imagine that maybe she’d taken something in the bathroom, an upper of some kind. She was just making up for lost time, trying to be the best mother possible. That’s what he told himself.

But more than that, as the night wore on and after he’d dropped off his mom and walked Andi home, after he’d given her a quick hug good night and told her once more how great she’d done in the play, and after he ignored her slightly wounded look because he didn’t go with her into the common area of her dorm and talk for another hour, he became more convinced than ever about his next step, what the near future was going to hold. He was a fighter, and he had no reason to stop fighting now. He was going to do what he should’ve done a long time ago.

Fight for Bailey Flanigan as if his life depended on it.

Ten

The Last Letter was done. They'd made their editing deadline with a few hours to spare and Chase could barely sort through the emotions consuming him. Exhaustion, relief, anticipation, and full-out heart-stopping exhilaration. He and Keith had looked forward to this day since they set out to be filmmakers. It was Friday, December 5, and they'd just sent off the first copy of their movie by courier service to arrive at the office of the Los Angeles Film Festival committee sometime before midnight. They'd called their wives with the great news, and now they were catching their breath, still hanging out in the rented Santa Monica editing room.

Chase leaned back in his chair and stretched his legs. "It's like a different movie—with the color fix and sound correction. The editing." His voice couldn't contain his enthusiasm. "Much better than I ever thought it would be. Even with the performances we got on set."

"Don't get too excited." Keith was standing, leaning against the console that contained the editing equipment. He wore old jeans, a rumpled T-shirt, and a weary smile. "We're not done yet."

"Ah, come on." Chase allowed a whine to color his voice. He didn't want to talk about the studio screening coming up or the possibility they wouldn't get a theatrical release. He couldn't stand to think of the meetings with Ben and Kendall or the work to be done in order to submit to Kendall's list of additional film festivals. Keith was right. The road ahead was long and precarious, but Chase didn't want to think about a single minute of it.

Not yet. He closed his eyes. "Can't we have a day to just be done?" He blinked his eyes open and sat up a little more. "Like maybe we could do something really unconventional and go celebrate. Get a couple Cokes and walk down to the pier."

"At nine-thirty?" Keith laughed. "I guess. You know what I want to do first?"

"Take a nap?" A yawn caught Chase mid-sentence.

"No. I want to pray." Keith moved to the chair opposite Chase.

"Yeah. I like that." Prayer. Because they never would've arrived at this place without the miraculous leading of God. Chase's mood was suddenly sober. "Go ahead."

Keith put his hand on Chase's shoulder and bowed his head. He waited for a few seconds. "Lord ..." His voice trembled. He sucked in a quick breath. They'd worked nonstop since five that morning to finish on time, and the moment was overwhelming for both of them. He tried again. "Lord God, we asked You to take us to Los Angeles and give us the chance to make movies for You. Well, here we are, one movie finished, and we are nothing short of awed. This editing room feels like hallowed ground, Father, because You met us here. None of this—" He took another quick breath, steadying himself. "None of it would be possible without Your provision, Your leading. So before we move from this place we wanted to say thanks. Thank You, dear God. For what You've done and what You'll yet do. Thank You. In Jesus' name, amen."

Chase was just adding his own amen when he felt his phone vibrate. He pulled it from his pocket as Keith slid his chair back in place and turned his attention to the editing console. They wanted at least ten master copies of the movie before they left the room. Eight were already made, and the ninth was ready to be popped out of the machine. Chase opened his phone and stared at the small screen. The text was from Kendall. She'd promised a meeting with Stephanie Fitzgerald and Brandon Paul, but so far nothing had come together. Chase smiled. They thanked God for what He was about to do and almost before they finished praying Kendall contacted them.

He held up his phone. "You won't believe this. Kendall's texting me."

Keith uttered a tired, knowing laugh. "I love how God works."

The message was brief.

SORRY WE'VE BEEN OUT OF TOUCH FOR AWHILE. MY DAD AND I HAD BUSINESS IN PORTUGAL. WE'RE BACK NOW AND I'M IN TOWN. ARE YOU IN SAN JOSE OR HERE?

Chase quickly texted back.

IN SANTA MONICA. JUST FINISHED EDITING THE LAST LETTER HALF AN HOUR AGO.

Her response was almost instantaneous.

CONGRATULATIONS. PERFECT TIMING, THEN. I'M CLOSE. THERE'S AN ALL-NIGHT DINER ON THIRD AND WILSHIRE. MEET ME THERE IN THIRTY MINUTES? WE NEED TO TALK.

"She wants to meet in half an hour." Chase was on his feet, his energy returning at a rapid rate. "Will we be done?"

"Should be." Keith checked the console again. "The last DVD will be ready in about ten minutes. That'll give us time to clean up and drop off the keys."

Chase began tapping on his phone's tiny keyboard again.

WE'LL BE THERE.

Her response was upbeat.

GOOD. CAN'T WAIT TO SEE YOU BOTH.

He closed his phone and slipped it back into his pocket. Then he raked his fingers through his hair and paced the length of the room. "The timing of this?" A single laugh came from him, a sound that was more grateful disbelief than mirth. "I mean, come on." He stopped and stared at his friend. "We've been calling them, what? Five times a day for a few weeks?"

Keith checked a few of the controls. "You sound surprised."

"I am." He laughed again. "I'm surprised I'm standing."

A calm filled Keith's eyes. "Aren't you the guy who worked beside me in the jungles of Indonesia? Didn't you see flood waters recede before our eyes without any explanation, and disease leave people who'd been sick for years?" His smile was warm. "Don't tell me you're surprised at this. God's got everything under control."

"Right." Chase allowed himself to relax a little. "Of course." In that instant he felt foolish for ever worrying, ever doubting they'd survive the process of making this first film—or that they'd connect with Kendall about the next one. He tried to imprint the moment upon his memory, how it felt knowing with absolute certainty that God was in control. He had a feeling he would need it as a reference point in the journey ahead.

The last DVD was ready, and they carefully loaded the original and ten master copies into a locked briefcase. Chase took a last look as they left. "I might even miss this place. It was starting to feel like home."

They both laughed as Chase hit the lights and they locked the doors behind them. Ten minutes later they walked through the door of the diner and scanned the place for Kendall. The smell of french fries and something sweet mixed in the warm air, and even in the somewhat dim light it didn't take long to see her. She was sitting with another woman, someone Chase recognized as the author of *Unlocked*. Her face had been on the cover of magazines and on talk shows since the book took off. He elbowed Keith, but his friend had clearly already noted the same thing. Kendall and the author here together could only mean one thing.

God was adding one more miracle to the list.

KEITH DIDN'T GET AS EMOTIONAL AS Chase, but still, he was working hard not to feel overwhelmed by what he saw.

"Two?" A teenage hostess approached them, bright pink hair and a pierced lip. She smacked her gum and grabbed a couple menus, waiting for their answer.

"Uh ..." Keith saw Kendall notice them. "Actually, we're meeting someone."

"Fine." She handed them the menus. "Seat yourself. Your server'll be by in a minute."

Keith and Chase made their way to the table, and the women stood as they walked up. The author was black with stunning eyes, much prettier in person. Clearly she and Kendall were friends.

"Guys!" Kendall came around the table and shook first Keith's hand, then Chase's. "I'm so glad this worked out." She turned. "This is Stephanie Fitzgerald, author of *Unlocked*. She's a friend."

Introductions were made all around, and Keith marveled at the energy the two women shared. Stephanie had a glow about her. She had to be in her early forties, but she was tall and slender, and in her black dress pants and pale-blue silk blouse she didn't look a day over thirty.

They took their seats around the booth, and Stephanie leaned forward on her forearms, practically bursting. "Did Kendall tell you?" She looked at Keith. "I'm a huge fan of your work."

Keith resisted the urge to look over his shoulder, as if maybe she was talking to someone else. He took a sip of the water in front of him and stifled a nervous laugh. "She said something about it ... a few months ago."

"I know." Stephanie shared a frustrated look with Kendall. She talked fast, with a lyrical tone to her voice. "We're both so busy. I was on deadline for my next book, two of my six kids had birthdays. My husband and I celebrated twenty years. Just your average couple o' months at the Fitzgerald house." She grabbed a quick breath and launched into a story about how she'd stumbled onto a short film he'd made back in his college days and how she loved his sensitivity and the undeniable elements of faith.

"Everyone in town's asking for the rights to *Unlocked*." Kendall raised her brow in Keith and Chase's direction. "But Steph wants to work with you guys."

"Absolutely." Stephanie grinned at Chase. "I can't wait to see *The Last Letter*. There's buzz all over town." She included Keith. "Something special's happening with you two, and we know what it is." Her eyes shone with a light so genuine it warmed the space between them. "It's your faith in Christ. Same as it is for Kendall and me."

Keith couldn't have asked for a better start to the meeting if he'd scripted it himself. Stephanie Fitzgerald's books were mainstream—number one *New York Times* bestsellers. But they were gripping and inspirational, and Keith had heard that she was a Christian.

"Finally today I called Kendall and said if she couldn't set up a meeting tonight, I'd find you myself."

They all laughed, and Kendall patted Stephanie's hand. "Good thing I was in town. I didn't like thinking about her knocking on studio doors up and down Santa Monica Boulevard."

Keith didn't want to sound ignorant, especially after the praise and confidence Stephanie had just heaped on them. But he wanted to move things ahead. "An option, then, right? Isn't that what happens next?"

"Exactly." Stephanie pulled a two-page document from an oversized bag next to her. "I had my agent draw this up a week ago. He said it's pretty standard." She pointed to a line halfway down the first page. "Options usually cost around five thousand, sometimes more."

"But I told her you two hadn't made any money yet and you were working off investor funds." Kendall's smile filled her face as she turned to Stephanie. "So ..."

"So I asked my agent if we could take a zero off. Give you the option for five hundred instead." She looked completely at peace with the decision. Thrilled about it, even.

Under the table, Chase kicked his foot. Keith swallowed, not sure what to say. "That's … that's amazing."

"I want this to work for all of us." She leaned back, satisfied. "God's already told me it'll be bigger than any of us can imagine. Plenty of time for zeroes. It's all God's anyway."

"Yes." *Plenty of time for zeroes.* The author's faith seemed rock solid, and Keith silently breathed a prayer of thanks. Teamed up with Stephanie and Kendall, possibilities would become realities in a hurry.

"I want to tell you, Ms. Fitzgerald, *Unlocked* was amazing." Chase had been quiet until now. Probably trying not to pass out. "I couldn't put it down."

"Thank you. And call me Stephanie." She smiled at the group of them. "I think we'll make a wonderful team."

Kendall added to that. "Stephanie doesn't have time to be a part of every step of the process. She has two books to write next year, and she speaks at writer's conferences around the country. She wants a final look at the screenplay and a week or so on the set, but otherwise she's trusting us."

"I'm assuming Kendall will join you on the production team?" Stephanie's eyes were hopeful.

"Absolutely." Keith and Chase had talked about this at the last meeting with Ben and Kendall. She had experience at almost every level of filmmaking. They would be fortunate to have her on their team. "It's already a plan."

"She's the best." Stephanie gave Kendall a heartfelt hug. The waitress appeared then and they ordered a plate of nachos and four iced teas. When she left the table, Stephanie nudged Kendall. "Well, tell them already. I can't stand the suspense."

Kendall laughed. "I already did."

Next to him, Keith could feel Chase holding his breath again.

"But tell them about the phone call earlier today."

"Okay, okay." Kendall personified joy and optimism. She practically glowed as she continued. "Brandon Paul called me today. He's been filming his series with NTM Studios and finally came up for air today. He told me he's talked to his agent and he wants the lead in *Unlocked*. It's very important to him. So we're a step closer."

Keith wanted to ask why the picture mattered to the young megastar, but that would come later. The dizzy feeling had returned, and he steadied himself discreetly against the edge of the table. "I wasn't sure ... We didn't know if he was still interested."

"More than ever." Stephanie looked satisfied. "Brandon and I are friends. We met on the set of his series a year ago. I was doing research." Her smile dropped off just a bit. "He's not a believer, but I'm working on him. I think the faith element of *Unlocked* intrigues him."

"That and the fact that it's a brilliant story." Kendall's smile faded, and her tone became more serious. "God has a reason for bringing Brandon Paul our way. I've known him for a few years. He's a great kid with more demands on him than most people will know in a lifetime."

Keith could only imagine. Like most NTM stars through the decades, the guy's face was everywhere. Everything from billboards to pop cans, tween jewelry and pillowcases to Blockbuster gift cards. He could only imagine the headiness of such fame, and the difficulty navigating it. "We shot *The Last Letter* in Bloomington, Indiana. Dayne Matthews lives there now with his wife and baby daughter."

"That's right." Stephanie nodded. "I knew he'd pulled out of the Hollywood scene. I wasn't sure where he'd settled."

"Chase and I had dinner with him and his family while we were there. He's got a lot of wisdom about handling fame. You know about his car accident right?"

"The whole world knew." Kendall frowned. "Paparazzi will kill someone before something's done about the insanity."

"He might be a help to Brandon at some point." Chase exchanged a look with Keith. "He's a great guy. Strong in his faith. Not many other people know what Brandon's going through."

"That's important." Kendall exchanged a look with Stephanie. "We'll keep that in mind as we move into this project."

Stephanie pulled another copy of the option from her purse and slid both across the table. "Take these. I don't expect you to sign them here, but read them over. Have your attorney take a look."

The waitress brought their food, and while they ate they talked about the book Stephanie was working on and a few of the stories she was planning for the future.

"How do you keep it all straight?" Chase took a long swig of his iced tea. "Don't the characters get mixed up in your mind?"

"Never." Stephanie laughed again. "My books are like movies in my mind. Very separate and distinct from each other. When I sit down to write, I see the film, like I'm in it somehow. I never feel like I'm making the stuff up. It's more like taking dictation, trying to capture everything I'm seeing and hearing and feeling."

"Amazing." Keith always marveled at the vastly differing ways God dished out talent. Back in college, he'd struggled to write his fifteen-page senior paper. A whole novel? It would've been an impossibility. "What made you write *Unlocked*?"

The question seemed to hit a painful nerve. The subtle way she dropped her gaze to her plate for a few seconds told them that much. "My sister, Jasmine. She was autistic."

Keith noted the way Stephanie used the past tense, but he didn't want to ask.

"Steph's sister was hit by a car when she was nineteen." Kendall's voice softened appropriately. "She and their mom were shopping, and something frightened Jasmine. She panicked and ran straight into traffic before her mom could stop her. She died at the hospital that night."

Stephanie's eyes teared up. "Twenty-two years ago. Doesn't get any easier."

"I'm sorry." Keith reached across the table and covered the author's hand with his own for a moment. As he withdrew it he looked at Chase. "We saw the dedication to Jasmine and wondered."

"We shared a room." Stephanie's eyes were bright again, dimmed only by the strength of the memory. "The doctors used to tell us she was unreachable, that she lived alone in her own little world." She shook her head. "But I knew otherwise. When we were alone, I'd put on music ... Diana Ross or the Temptations. Lionel Richie, even Elvis. I would start dancing, and after a minute, she'd smile at me and join in. Music gave us a bridge. We danced across it often."

Keith was breathless from the word picture. "The same way it happens in *Unlocked*."

"Yes." A love both bright and intense burned in her eyes. "We need to rethink the way we view autistic people. They can be reached if we try."

Kendall gave her friend a sad smile. "Steph and I have talked about it. In some ways—until we find that life-saving faith in Christ—we're all autistic. Living in our own world, trapped by the smallness of our existence and needing something, anything, to pierce the silence and open our eyes to the reality around us. Music can be that for us too. Music can introduce people to God."

Suddenly the passion Keith felt for this future project magnified a hundred times. This was what they'd asked for, right? Films that could touch and change the world. He tried to imagine the power in a picture like *Unlocked.* The power in the movie's soundtrack. A chill ran down his arms and he swapped a look with Chase. His friend was feeling the same way, he was sure. "I have a feeling God's going to use this movie in amazing ways."

Stephanie smiled, and again her eyes grew watery. "That's why I'm here." She studied Keith and then Chase. "I believe you two can touch the world with this movie. The way Jasmine's life, her joy and light, so deeply touched me."

The woman was both beautiful and poetic. Keith hoped they had lots of time together during the process—even with her busy schedule.

They talked a little while longer, and then Stephanie had to get going. "My honey's waiting up for me." She held out her hand toward Keith and then laughed at herself. "What am I doing? Come around here and give me a hug. We're already family—we have the same Father."

Keith and Chase moved out from behind the table and took turns hugging Stephanie good-bye. She was still smiling when she left, her steps light and full of the same energy that had come from her throughout the meeting.

When she was gone, Keith and Chase sat back down with Kendall. Keith felt breathless from the brilliance of all that lay ahead. "She's wonderful."

"Isn't she?" Kendall grinned. "I knew you'd love her."

"She's mesmerizing." Chase leaned forward on his forearms. "Something very special's happening here."

"And getting there will be the ride of a lifetime." She pulled out a notebook. "Okay, we have a lot to cover in a short time." She started by bringing up the idea of the three of them forming an official production team. "I wanted to talk about that sooner, but there wasn't time."

"Chase and I love your enthusiasm and vision. The people you're bringing into this."

"Absolutely." Chase finished his iced tea, his eyes never leaving Kendall's. "God put us together for a reason."

"I think we need a new name, at least for this film. Oak River is good—but we need something that shows the world your vision."

Keith appreciated how she called it their vision. She wasn't taking over, just coming alongside them—helping out in whatever way she could. "We haven't thought about a new name. But I'm open to the idea."

Chase was too, and after a few minutes they came up with a name they all liked better: Jeremiah Productions. The name came from the Scripture from Jeremiah 29:11: *"For I know the plans I have for you," declares the Lord, "plans to prosper you and not to harm you."*

"The goal," Keith said, "has always been that the world would find hope in Christ as a result of the movies we make. So the name is perfect."

Once they had that detail established, Kendall flipped open her planner and tapped her pen on one of the squares. "I've set up a meeting with Brandon Paul for this Monday morning. Ten o'clock, here at the diner. It's an easy meeting place, and they serve a great breakfast. Legend in this town. Then I'd like you to meet his agent in Studio City the next day around four. My dad wants to catch up with you too."

Keith winced. They had planned to drive home in the morning, and then he and Lisa had tickets to fly to Indiana on Monday. They'd planned to spend the week with Andi and see several performances of *Scrooge*.

"You're busy?" Kendall picked up on his hesitation.

"We aren't, are we?" Chase turned to him. He seemed anxious to make the meetings work.

Keith understood. In this business, a month could easily go by before everyone had a clear date on their calendars again. "We have Andi's play this week." He studied the calendar page. "I guess we could head out at the end of the week instead. Catch the weekend shows."

"Right." Chase nodded. "That would work."

"You're sure?" She looked cautious. "Family commitments are a priority. I understand that."

"No. It's okay, really." Keith was already imagining how he'd tell Lisa, and then Andi. Chase would have to talk to Kelly too. But she would understand. Everything would work out. The meetings were crucial if they were going to push ahead with the production of *Unlocked*. "Let's plan it."

Kendall wrapped up their meeting telling them that she had a feeling things were going to get pretty crazy for them and their families. "You've got the film festivals and the screenings for *The Last Letter*. Everyone's going to be talking about you, your vision and talent, and the fact that you snared a coup with the acquisition of *Unlocked*." She paused, her expression more sober than it had been all night. "We need to pray for your families, for your faith and your sanity. For all of us, that we'll keep our feet on the ground."

Agreement came from Keith and Chase, and before they parted ways, they held hands and thanked God for the amazing situation He'd placed them in, begging Him to go before them, to protect them and their families, and to keep them grounded in His truth along the way.

As they left the restaurant, Keith stopped cold and stared at Chase. "Did that just happen?" He uttered a disbelieving chuckle. "I mean, really? Did it seriously just happen?"

Chase laughed too. "I have a feeling we'll be reminding each other often — that this is really happening."

They talked about all that had transpired in the past hour. The meeting with Stephanie Fitzgerald and her passion for this project. Kendall's enthusiasm, the vision she had for the future. The involvement of Brandon Paul. They decided to wait until tomorrow to call their wives, and as they reached the Georgian Hotel Keith thought again how grateful he was for the prayer at the end—that they stay grounded throughout the process.

Because even now he could barely feel the street beneath his feet.

Eleven

The Saturday matinee was over, another memorable performance by the *Scrooge* cast, and Andi was about to head into the lobby to meet the audience when she saw noticed a voicemail message from her parents. She pushed a few buttons and listened.

"Hey, Andi, it's Dad. We're stuck at the Denver airport. They're clearing ice off the runway." He paused. "I'm sorry, baby. We'll get there as soon as we can. Sometime tonight for sure."

Andi snapped her phone shut and tried not to feel hurt. Her parents could do nothing about an ice storm, but still . . . they were supposed to be here all week. Her dad's LA meetings had made that impossible, so now they only had this weekend to see her show. As it was they were going to miss tonight's performance, which meant they'd only see tomorrow's matinee, since the night show was sold out.

Fine, Andi thought. If her dad could make filmmaking a priority, so could she. The offer from Taz looked better all the time.

She had a text waiting too, and she checked it. Cody's name popped onto the screen.

HEY, ANDI. I TOLD YOU I MIGHT BE THERE TODAY, BUT I HAVE TOO MUCH HOMEWORK. I'M SURE YOU'LL DO GREAT. SEE YOU LATER.

Disappointment painted heavy brush strokes across her heart. Cody was pulling away, she could feel it, and she didn't know why or what she'd done. He didn't have to want her to be his girlfriend, but still it was nice talking to him. This past week they'd barely even done that. And now he was too busy to show up.

"Everything okay?" Bailey sat next to her, checking her makeup.

"My parents." Andi slipped her phone back in her bag. "They're stuck in an ice storm."

"Oh. I'm sorry." Bailey looked like she understood. "My parents'll be here tonight. If yours don't make it, come over afterwards. We're playing Pictionary."

"Okay." Andi smiled. Bailey's invitation took the edge off her loneliness. She really wanted her parents to be here, but at least she didn't have to be by herself. She hugged her friend. "Thanks. That'd be great."

They walked out to the lobby with several other cast members. The director liked them to mingle with the audience for fifteen minutes before changing out of their costumes and taking their dinner break. Andi loved this part of performing, hearing the praise from complete strangers, realizing how deeply they'd been touched by the show. Mixing with the public was one of the most fun parts of being in the show.

The local newspaper had run a review on the musical in Monday's paper, and the writer singled her out. "Andi Ellison is a breath of fresh air in this old, often stodgy, story of a grouchy man and his transformation. If Scrooge could walk away from the beautiful, talented Ellison, then he must need a serious fix." She hadn't told her parents about the review because she wanted them to see it in person. But they'd had one delay after another.

Out in the lobby, people noticed them immediately. Bailey was called over by a group of kids from Cru, and Andi was called in another direction by people waving programs. She smiled and walked toward them, and for the next ten minutes she signed autographs, answered questions about the stage process, and smiled for two dozen pictures. Only then did she recognize Taz and his friend—the one she'd met on opening night. From the corner of her eye she watched the two guys discuss something, and then the friend smiled and waved and walked away, leaving Taz by himself.

As soon as he was alone, Taz turned toward her. He hung back, watching her, aware of the people still gathered around her. When her eyes met his, he smiled at her, and the connection between them was almost physical. Andi looked back at the little girl holding out a program for her to sign. She hoped no one could see the sudden heat in her cheeks.

What was she feeling? An attraction to Taz? She blinked, fighting a sudden weakness in her knees. Taz's offer of a starring role had caught her attention, of course. She was anxious to talk to him about the dates for shooting his independent film. But until now she hadn't felt a connection between them. She tried to focus, but it was impossible. From twenty feet away, she could feel his eyes on her as strongly as if he were touching her.

When the audience goers had moved on, Taz slowly walked up, his confidence a tangible force around him. He smiled, and again she felt his eyes looking deep into her soul. "Can we talk?"

She felt flustered, and it bothered her. She smoothed out the layers of her blue dress and gathered her composure. "I have to change. And we have another show in a few hours."

"I'll get you a coffee. We can talk outside when you're ready."

Andi's heart picked up speed. He wasn't exactly asking, and that bugged her too. But a thrill of attraction ran through her veins at breakneck speed. An attraction like she'd never felt before. She heard herself telling him that she'd take a grande soy latte and that she'd be out in fifteen minutes.

His grin was slow and lazy, and his eyes danced. "I'll be waiting."

Back in the dressing room, the director spent ten minutes talking to the cast about the townspeople scenes. "You're getting a little out of control." He frowned. "Too much milling about and animated conversations. It's distracting us from the main characters."

When the director was finished, Bailey came up to her, brows raised. "I saw you."

"What?" Andi didn't want to answer for what she was about to do. She hadn't done anything wrong, and Taz was different, interesting.

"You know what." Her tone wasn't condemning or unkind, but she sounded worried. "The film student. I don't like the way he looks at you."

"He's fine." Andi busied herself with her costume, unbuttoning the back and slipping out of the dress. What did Bailey know about meeting guys at school? She had Tim. And now that Cody was losing interest … "I like him." Andi tossed her hair. "We have a lot in common. Besides, we need to talk about the movie."

Instant disappointment colored Bailey's expression. "Andi, no. You're not taking the role."

"I might." She worked to sound confident and controlled. Like she had thought through this.

Bailey's face mirrored her skepticism.

"I know—the partial nudity." Andi lifted her hands and let them fall back to her sides. "The way I see it, sacrifices need to be made for the sake of art." She thought about her parents' trip delay. "That's true with everyone in filmmaking."

"Don't compromise." Bailey released an exasperated sigh. "Please, Andi. Be smart. You don't even know this guy."

"I don't need to. It's not like I'm interested in him," she lied. "He wants me to star in his film. He's intriguing. It's that simple."

Bailey hesitated, like she wanted to say more. "Tim's waiting for me. We're getting lunch and sitting on the wall out back. You should join us."

"Maybe later." Andi hung up her dress, removed her character dance shoes, and slipped into her jeans and turtleneck sweater. "Taz is getting me a coffee."

Another sigh. "Be careful."

"Thanks." Andi looked up long enough to give Bailey a hurried smile. "I will."

With Bailey gone, Andi slowed her frenzied pace. Just once she wished her roommate could be a little adventurous. They were in college, after all. What other time of their lives would an offer like this come along, the chance to star in a student film? This was what college was about.

She regained the calm she'd lost in the last five minutes. She wasn't going to sit in her dorm fearing the world or the God who'd made it. Life was nothing but an accumulation of experiences, and this would be one she remembered always.

She fixed her hair and checked her makeup. It was a little heavy, but she didn't want to reapply it before the next show. She put her jacket on, snatched her purse from the floor, and made sure she had her phone. Then, with a final look at herself, she walked back into the lobby. She wasn't sure Taz was serious, or—if he was—that he'd be back yet. But he was there, leaning against the door frame of the main entrance, a coffee cup in each hand. He locked eyes with her from the moment he saw her, and didn't break the connection once as she walked up.

"You're even better this weekend than last." He handed her a hot white cup. "One soy latte."

"Thank you." Her heart was doing it again, pounding like crazy, and she wished she'd asked for something without caffeine. This was crazy, this breathless way he made her feel. She'd seen him in her science class every day since school started. Why the attraction now? She stared at her coffee and tried not to look flustered. "Where should we go?"

"There's a bench out there a little ways. It's more private than staying here." He held open the door and walked beside her as they headed down the path. The cold air hit them like a freezing wall and took her breath away. At least she hoped it was the cold air.

Taz wore a nice jacket, something from Abercrombie, and mixed with the ice cold air she could smell his cologne. His pace was slow and easy, like his smile. "Do you always have the biggest crowd after a show?"

"No." She giggled and felt the compliment to her core. Especially today, with Cody canceling on her and her parents delayed in Denver. "Tim Reed barely has enough time to sign all the programs that come his way. He's been brilliant as Scrooge."

"Because his greatest regret was losing you." He looked down, and their eyes met again. "That would make any guy crazy."

Andi didn't know what to say, so she smiled at him and then faced straight ahead again. Snow was gathered a foot high on either side of the path, but the cement was cleared. They reached the bench and she sat down first. He took the opposite side, leaving ample space between them. Andi felt herself relax. Bailey didn't have to worry. The guy wasn't making a move on her. He was making a movie. There was a difference.

They sat in silence for nearly a minute, sipping their coffee and watching their breath make wispy shapes in the air between them. Finally he lowered his drink and narrowed his eyes, looking into hers with a kindness and depth she hadn't noticed before. "I've wanted to make movies as far back as I can remember."

He didn't seem to be looking for a response, so she stayed with her drink, watching him, waiting.

"Film is a special medium, powerful, encompassing." He shifted his look to the barren trees not far from where they sat. "Only through film can a person vicariously experience the thrill of espionage or the pain of prison bars, the satisfaction of revenge or the power of taking another life." He paused and his eyes found hers again. "Film can make a person know what love should be, what sexual love feels like. The experience can be that real." He drew a slow breath. "It's a medium bigger than ourselves."

Andi wanted to feel embarrassed by his blunt description, but she was drawn by it instead. He was right in many ways. Wasn't that why people went to the movies? So they could live the lives of the actors on screen, if only for a few hours from the dark privacy of their theater seats? She lowered her coffee to her lap. "Acting's that way too. Crawling into someone else's skin and bringing something to life you otherwise wouldn't have known."

He seemed pleasantly surprised by her description. "Hmmm. A girl who's as deep as she is beautiful." He tipped his head in her direction, and his eyes flirted mercilessly with her. "You're a rare find, Andi Ellison. How come some guy hasn't snatched you up and made you his?"

"I don't know." Her cheeks were hot again. "I've been out of the country most of my life."

"Tell me." He was in no hurry. It was a part of his charm.

For the first time she wished her story was more exotic, that she'd been the daughter of a great and powerful archaeologist and together her family had spent more than a decade on the site of a world-famous dig in Africa somewhere. But she had to be honest. No matter what his belief system, she was what she was. "My parents were missionaries." She gave him a weak smile. "I grew up in Indonesia."

"Christian missionaries?" He seemed interested, if maybe slightly amused. "I admire missionaries."

"You do?"

"Yes. They are committed to their dreams and beliefs. To live a life of service toward another people is admirable. Like anything else that resonates in the soul."

"Resonates in the soul?" Yes, that was it. The new ideas and thoughts she'd been feeling were ones that resonated in her soul. Andi felt her head begin to spin. This was the sort of conversation she'd longed to have with Bailey or Cody—anyone who would talk to her. But whenever the conversation veered out of the box

of biblical truth, her friends took a hard stance. Things were either right or wrong. Andi had a feeling that wasn't the case for Taz.

He looked at her in a way that made it feel like he'd known her forever, like no one would ever know her better. "My parents were Muslims, but they sort of lost their fervor for the dogma when they moved to the U.S." He took a slow sip from his coffee. "I'm agnostic. A skeptic, I guess. I believe people are entitled to believe. Whatever their beliefs." He chuckled and put his arm along the back of the bench. His shoulder muscles showed through his coat. "How's that?"

She laughed too. "I like it."

They talked for half an hour about politics and peace, raving radicals and religion before he paused for a long moment. "About the film." He angled his head, and she fell into his eyes. "Have you thought about it?"

Her attraction to him was growing stronger with every passing minute. He was interesting and intelligent, and so far a perfect gentlemen. But somehow Andi felt stripped bare in his presence. Like he had a gift of seeing past the layers of formality and pretense. "I have. I'd like to see the script." She cupped her hands around her drink and hoped he couldn't read the truth—that her mind was made up. She was taking the role. She could hardly wait to work under his direction.

"I have a copy in my car. How much time do you have?"

She pulled her phone from her purse and checked it. "Ten minutes, maybe fifteen. We have an extra dance rehearsal before tonight's call. It's a full company number."

He looked at her a long time, and she felt herself react. His stare was like a physical caress, and after several seconds she looked down at her drink. *What is this feeling,* she asked herself. *I've never experienced this in all my life.*

"Andi." His voice was velvet.

She looked up again.

"I love watching you on stage. You act with your whole body, heart, and soul. That's important." He leaned forward and rested his elbows on his knees. "In the art of acting, our bodies are the colors. Our hearts the canvas. This sort of artwork is expressed through the soul—if we're gifted at it, anyway." He patted her knee. "You're gifted, Andi. When you act, you work your magic straight through me. No doubt about that." He stood. "I'll get the script." With an easy, loping jog he was off, headed for the parking lot.

Andi exhaled and sank into the back of the wooden bench. It was like he has some supernatural power, something that rendered her captive, caught in his spell. She sipped her coffee and tried to understand why she hadn't felt this way before around him. Now there was something about him that made her breath catch in her throat, her heart race out of control.

She steadied herself. *Get a grip, Andi. You're being ridiculous.* But even as she handed out instructions to herself, she could smell his cologne hanging in the frozen air, hear his voice. "*I love watching you on stage ... You're gifted ... You work your magic straight through me ...*"

She closed her eyes. This was crazy. She barely knew the guy. The script did matter, even if she hadn't thought so a minute ago. She would approach the next conversation with him differently, with her head in charge.

She sat straighter and took a few deep breaths, willing her head to clear. He jogged back up the path a moment later and sat beside her again, a little closer than before. Had he given himself another spritz of cologne, or were her senses really that aware of him? She blinked twice, focusing.

"Here." He handed her a thin, stapled document. It couldn't have been more than thirty, forty pages.

As the papers moved from his hand to hers, their fingers touched and a jolt of electric attraction ran through her veins, dropping her stomach to her knees and making her fight for her next breath. Her mouth went dry, and she ran her tongue along her lower lip. "Thank you."

Taz was sitting sideways, facing her straight on. "The entire film won't be longer than half an hour. But I'm looking for a tremendous amount of energy in that time, a very powerful message."

Andi wasn't sure she should ask, but her curiosity got the better of her. "You told me a little about the plot, but … what's the theme?"

"It's about pushing limits, taking chances and being willing to experience the consequences." He looked away. "Consequences aren't always to be suffered, but to be experienced. Wholly—body and mind, heart and soul." He found her eyes again. "If we are willing to experience anything in honesty, then we can become more than ourselves." He grinned, and the philosopher was gone. "Besides … whatever the message, it'll be unforgettable if you're the lead."

"Thank you." The wind was picking up, and Andi started to shiver. "I'll read it." She tucked her chin in and felt her look turn shy. "When do you need to know?"

"Take a week. You'll need time after the show wraps tomorrow."

She was flattered that he knew her schedule. "A week it is."

He angled his head, flirting with her for all he was worth. "But you know … I was thinking something."

"What's that?" The chemistry between them made her forget being cold.

"I might need to add a line or two in the script. You know, since I'm the producer and director. And I'd have to ask your thoughts on it."

"True."

"So ..." His eyes became puppy-dog hopeful. "I was thinking —for the sake of the film—maybe I should get your number."

She tried to keep a straight face, but she couldn't. Laughter tickled her throat. She held out her hand. "Give me your phone."

He did, and she entered herself and her number as a new contact. "There." She gave it back to him. "In case you come up with an extra line or two."

"Right." He stood and helped her to her feet. Again the touch of his hand against hers spread an intoxicating sensation throughout her body. She let her fingers stay in his a few seconds longer than necessary, the whole time looking straight into his eyes.

"I hope you like the script." His voice was soft, his face just inches from hers.

"Me too." She didn't blink, didn't dare break the connection between them.

He gave her hand a final squeeze and then released it. "This could be interesting."

"Yes."

"Complicated, but interesting." He was so close he could've leaned down and kissed her. But instead he took a step back and led the way as they walked the path back to the theater. At the lobby doors, he stuck his hands into his pockets and shrugged, his eyes full of depth and kindness, and a power she didn't fully understand. "See you around, Andi."

"Yeah." She gave a slight wave. "See ya 'round."

She had five minutes to report for dance rehearsal, and after that the night show passed in a blur. Her parents didn't show up, but they left another message. Their plane would arrive sometime around midnight, and they'd see her in the morning—before the Sunday matinee. But even with that disappointment, as she and Bailey headed back to the Flanigan house for Pictionary, Andi was beyond happy. On the drive, Bailey asked about Taz, but she kept her answers short and evasive. She didn't want to talk about him, didn't want anyone judging her. "It's no big deal," she lied. "I probably won't do the film anyway."

"What'd you guys talk about?" Bailey's eyes were shadowed in suspicion. "You were out there a long time."

"Mostly filmmaking. A little bit about the script." She shrugged. "It was nothing."

Bailey dropped the subject, which was good for both of them. They played on the same Pictionary team with Bailey's mom, and they won easily.

"It's not fair." Bailey's brother Shawn slumped back in his chair after the game. "Girls just know each other better."

Everyone laughed, and the girls won another round before calling it a night. On the way back to the dorm, Andi was grateful Bailey didn't bring up Taz again. Instead they listened to Rascal Flatts, which was perfect. The break in conversation gave Andi the chance to privately relive the time with Taz. Enough so that as she got ready for bed, for the first time she didn't think once about grabbing her Bible or Rachel's journal. She had no conflicting thoughts or pangs of guilt. Only memories of Taz. His smile and his eyes, the way he thought differently than the other kids she knew. The way he made her feel. And as she fell asleep she realized she was not just intrigued by the film student from her science class.

She was head over heels.

Twelve

Bailey watched the clock on the wall in her Advanced Algebra class and willed the last five minutes to pass quickly. She was meeting Tim for lunch, and she could hardly wait to see him. Since Christmas, both their schedules had been too busy to spend much time together. Bailey had been so focused on her grades it was already late January, and the two of them hadn't been on a date in weeks. Not only that, but life was about to get busier. Tim and Andi had auditioned for the university's upcoming musical—*Robin Hood*. Bailey's current class schedule was too intense for theater, but she was taking private voice lessons with Katy Matthews, Dayne's wife, and dance classes at night on campus.

On top of that Bailey wanted to be more involved with Campus Crusade, which was organizing a late-summer mission trip to Costa Rica. The Cru meetings had taken on a pattern. She and Tim would sit near the front, while Cody sat in the back. Most Thursdays Andi found a reason not to go. As for Cody, Bailey felt so distant around him, it was like they'd never known each other. But rather than focus on Cody, Bailey was getting more involved with the ministry aspects of the group. She and several other Cru girls had started meeting once a week in the common area of Bailey's dorm, and she was grateful for the interaction. They'd met twice so far, and both times Andi had been too busy with schoolwork to join them.

Bailey had a feeling there was more to it than that. Her roommate was splitting her time between schoolwork and Taz, but whenever Bailey asked about the filmmaker, her roommate shut down. As difficult as it had been for Bailey to imagine Cody and Andi together, certainly Cody would have been better for her than Taz.

"What about his faith?" Bailey had asked a few weeks ago.

Andi had given her a tired look. "He thinks everyone should have a right to believe what they wish."

Bailey wanted to ask her what Bible verse that came from, but she didn't want to be sarcastic. Cynicism would only turn Andi further from the truth. Instead she nodded thoughtfully. "And what about him? What does he believe?"

"He's agnostic. A skeptic, as he likes to say." Andi was quick to follow up on the fact. "Which is why it's good he has someone like me in his life."

Bailey tapped her pencil on her math book and tried to focus. The professor droned on about integers and absolute values within the context of a proof. Bailey let her eyes wander to the window and the snow outside. She missed Tim, but the time apart for them wasn't all bad. Bailey and her family had been together more often, which gave her the chance to hang out with her youngest brother, Ricky. He'd been sick with winter colds lately—coughing a lot and feeling tired. When she was home, Bailey could play backgammon or the Wii with him—so he wouldn't notice the cough so much. Not that she was worried about him. Ricky had had successful heart surgery as a baby, and he was very healthy now. But every winter was a struggle.

At the front of the classroom, the professor checked the clock and smiled at the auditorium full of students. "That'll be all. Tomorrow's Friday. Come prepared for a quiz on chapter 2."

Bailey slung her backpack over her right shoulder and hurried out the back door. She scanned the distance from the math building to the cafeteria and saw Tim walk into view. This was their meeting spot on Thursdays, when their schedules allowed them time to share lunch. She smiled and waved, and he jogged to meet her, his backpack pulled tight around his shoulders. "Hey." He gave her a quick hug as they walked. "I can't believe how cold it is."

They'd had a record-breaking winter so far, more snow than any of the locals could remember. Classes had even been cancelled a few days last week. One of the students had tacked a note on the Math Building: "School closed—due to global warming."

Bailey pulled her coat more tightly around her shoulders. "I can't wait for warmer weather." She felt her eyes light up. "I almost forgot. My mom's taking us to New York City for spring break. She wants to meet up with one of her old friends." She grinned at him. "She said you could come with us."

"Really?" He stopped and dropped his backpack on the cement pathway. "Are you serious?"

Her laughter was light and easy. "Yes, I'm serious!"

"We're going to New York City!" He let out a celebratory hoot, picked her up, and swung her in a full circle. When he set her down he did another solo circle. "I can't believe this." He put his hand on his head, his expression dazed. "That's the most amazing thing ever!"

"I know." She laughed again. "Come on. We're making a scene." She linked arms with him and snuggled close to his side. "If we're going to live there someday and star on Broadway, you better at least learn your way around."

"I still can't believe it." He stopped again. "I better double my hours at the bookstore."

"Nah, silly." She gave him a gentle tug and they kept walking. "My mom's treating. You'll go as our guest."

"Now I'm really in shock." He ran ahead of her a few steps, turned and faced her, walking backwards. "You're serious?"

"Tim." She shook her head. "You're acting crazy."

"Okay, okay." He exhaled. "I'll try to believe I'm not dreaming."

Inside the cafeteria they got their lunches and found seats together in a quiet back corner. This time Tim controlled himself. "Will we see shows and everything?"

"Of course." Bailey giggled. She realized something that had been more obvious lately: Tim made her laugh. Everything about being with him was wonderful and getting better all the time. "Going to plays? That's the whole point."

"So … I mean, I haven't ever really researched Broadway. What's playing there?"

"My mom said something about seeing *Mary Poppins*—which is amazing, because we've seen it before. Then maybe *Shrek, the Musical*—which would be funny and stars Sutton Foster, who is, like, the best Broadway actress ever."

They talked about the brilliant set design and music of *The Lion King*, and a new show called *In the Heights*, about life in the barrios of New York City.

"Too bad we don't have more time." Tim was eating a cheeseburger. A blob of ketchup smeared onto his cheek, but he didn't notice it. "We'll be there just a week."

Bailey pointed to her cheek, and Tim caught the message. He swiped a napkin over his face and grinned at her. "I'm too frozen to feel anything."

"Yeah, but anyway, the shows are every night except Monday. Two on Wednesday and two on the weekend days. We could pretty much see whatever we want. My mom loves Broadway plays."

"Wow." He seemed speechless. "Tell your parents thanks. I can't wait."

The topic changed and they talked about *Robin Hood*. "We'll find out tomorrow if we got cast."

"Of course you will." She rested her forearms on the table and leaned closer to him. "You're unbelievable on stage, Tim. You'll be Robin Hood, for sure. You and Andi will have a great time." She no longer worried about Tim being attracted to her friend. Andi was different these days, and she spent much of her time with Taz. The time away had hurt their friendship. At least it seemed that way. She said she hadn't committed to Taz's film. But Bailey thought her roommate might be lying to her. She actually hoped Andi would get a part opposite Tim, so he could help talk some sense into her.

"There was more competition this time." Tim glanced at her, but only as he hurried to finish his burger. "You glad you didn't try out?"

"Definitely. I need a break. Katy Matthews is giving me voice lessons and I added a few night dance classes. That'll help me more than being in a play right now." Bailey's strength was dance, but it didn't hurt to brush up. Especially if she was serious about getting an audition in New York City. "One more thing about New York. My mom's friend knows the casting director of *Wicked*. I guess he's going to introduce us to some people while we're there."

"That's crazy." Tim looked beyond thrilled. "That's so great. I mean, picture it. You and me performing on Broadway together! Living the dream."

"One day." She gave him a full-faced grin. "But for now ... we better eat. Class starts in ten."

They finished and said good-bye just outside the cafeteria and walked separate ways to their next class. Tim was fun, Bailey thought as she trudged down the sidewalk. Never mind that sometimes she wished he were a little more romantic, a little more like the guy who had held her hand on stage during *Scrooge* opening night. Since then she'd longed for those moments, but they rarely came. Tim didn't look at her long enough to give her a window to his soul. But that could come later, if the two of them stayed together. For now it was nice to have a great guy in her life, someone who shared her faith and wasn't about to let her down.

The way she'd been let down before.

Snow began to fall as she reached the English building, and after she'd walked down the hall and up a flight of stairs, she saw the note. English 102 was cancelled. The instructor was ill and not expected back until Monday. Bailey adjusted her backpack and pulled her coat tighter. The walk from English to her dorm was the longest of the day. As she stepped back outside, her hood helped take the edge off the biting wind, but it only allowed her a limited window of sight. She was halfway to her dorm when she felt someone come up beside her.

"Bailey." The voice was Cody's. No amount of time could remove the sound of it from her heart. "Didn't you hear me?"

"What?" Her heart pounded so loud she was sure he could hear it. She pulled her hood down so she could see him. The campus was quiet this time of day, only a few people out of class walking across the outdoor mall.

Cody's eyes were intense, full of questions. "I had to run to catch you."

"Oh." Her mouth went suddenly dry, and she wondered if her heart might burst from her chest. "My hood … I can't hear anything with it up."

Snow fell softly around them, and Cody tried to catch his breath. "Did you get a new phone?"

"No." Bailey looked down and kicked at the loose snow gathering near their feet. She lifted her eyes to him. "I've been busy."

He looked like he was trying to process that. "Okay." He shrugged and for a long moment he seemed at a loss. The muscles in his jaw tightened and he exhaled hard. "I've called a bunch of times. You know that, right?"

"I guess I'm not sure why." She took a step back and folded her arms across her chest. A chill cut through her, one that came more from being so close to Cody than because of the winter wind. "You went months without calling, and now … Now I don't get it."

"That's why I've been calling." He moved like he was going to take a step closer, but then changed his mind. He buried his fists in his coat pockets and held his ground. "During your show, it was like—" He hesitated, struggling, his eyes lifting to the slate-gray sky. After a few seconds he looked at her again, his eyes bathed in emotion. "I can't let you go, Bailey. It was my fault. I talked about being your friend, but I didn't act like one."

Bailey thought of all the times Cody had blatantly ignored her, the times when he'd talked to Andi but couldn't be bothered to call her. Tears poked at the corners of her eyes, but she held them back. "I was so mad at you." Her voice caught between heartbreaking sorrow and fighting mad. "You had Andi and it was like … I didn't matter at all."

"You did." He released a frustrated breath. "You do. I wish you could know how much I miss you."

"You miss what we used to have." She took another half step back from him. A talk like this would get them nowhere. They had their own lives now. "You're all about Andi. She can be your friend."

"No!" His answer was sharp, and it caught them both by surprise. He worked to calm himself. "She and I are nothing."

"Okay." Bailey, too, fought for composure. "Then I'm in love with Tim."

"Are you?" He was breathing harder now, leaning toward her, his eyes intense. A couple of kids passed on a nearby sidewalk, and again he lowered his voice. "Are you really, Bailey? 'Cause I see you with him, and all I'm saying is other than on stage, I've never seen you look at him, the way …"

"The way what?" She practically spat the words, and in that moment she didn't care if they hurt him. She almost wanted them to hurt, so he'd give up and walk away. She didn't need him to play with her heart now.

Tears blurred her vision and she couldn't tell where her anger stopped and her hurt began. "The way *I* looked at you? Back when I thought you had feelings for me?" She looked over her shoulder, planning her escape. "I was wrong, okay. I was younger then and ridiculous. You never saw me that way." She backed up again. "It's too late now. We've moved on."

He came a few steps closer. "Don't leave." But before he could say anything else her cell phone went off.

She pressed her fingers to her eyes and pulled the phone from her pocket. It was her parents. "It's home." She held up one finger and took the call. "Hello?"

"Honey, it's Mom. We're at the hospital. Ricky's having trouble with his heart." She sounded controlled but scared. "His doctor's not sure what's happening. They're trying to stabilize him."

"Mom, no ..." She put her hand to her face and turned from Cody. "He's okay, right? I mean, he's not in real danger?"

"The doctor isn't sure." There were tears in her mom's voice. "Can you please come?"

"I'll be right there." She snapped her phone shut.

"What happened?" Cody was at her side again, his eyes filled with concern.

"Ricky. His heart." She looked up at him, and fear paralyzed her for a moment. "He's in the hospital." She took a step in one direction, and then changed her mind and started in another. Her car was in the parking lot outside her dorm, but she couldn't remember which way to get there. "I need to go."

"Come on." He took hold of her hand and started running. "My car's close. I'll drive."

Bailey tried not to think about the feel of his hand around hers as she ran beside him, the discussion from seconds ago forgotten. Cody had lived with them, and he loved all the Flanigan boys as if they were his own brothers.

Cody didn't release her hand until they were in his car. On the way to the hospital they talked about Ricky's recent cold. "He's been more tired than usual." Bailey had knots in her stomach. "We all figured he was just growing or something."

"We need to pray." Again Cody reached for her hand, and he begged God to be with Ricky and to give the doctors wisdom to get him out of danger. When the prayer was over, Bailey pulled her hand back. Her mind was racing in a million different directions. What was happening with Ricky, and how come his heart was having trouble so many years after his heart surgery? And why ... why was her whole body trembling because of a single touch from Cody?

They reached the hospital and raced inside and up the elevator to the fifth floor—the cardiac unit. As soon as the elevator doors opened Bailey spotted her parents down the hall talking to a doctor. Her mom broke off from the group and met her halfway down the hallway. "He's stable." She pulled Bailey into a long hug. "Thank God, he's stable." She drew back and kissed Bailey's forehead. "You got here fast."

"Cody brought me." Bailey's knees shook and she shivered. "What happened?"

"Thank you." Her mom hugged Cody and then rested against the hospital wall. She looked pale and exhausted. "He was playing outside, shooting baskets."

"It's freezing out." Bailey felt faint. She leaned her shoulder into the wall, facing her mother.

"You know Ricky. He's never cold."

"I remember that." Cody moved in close to them, his voice low. "You couldn't get the kid to wear long pants even in the dead of winter."

Bailey wasn't sure why, but Cody's presence made her feel safe and warm and protected. She couldn't analyze the reasons right now. "Then what?"

"He came in and he was white as a sheet. He said his chest felt funny, so I checked his pulse." Her mom closed her eyes. When she opened them, there were tears in her lashes. "It was racing so fast, Bailey. So fast I couldn't count it."

"You brought him in?"

"I was about to, but he fainted." She gulped and a stream of tears slid down her cheeks. "I called 9–1–1 and I went with him in the ambulance. Your dad followed behind with the boys — they're in the waiting room."

Bailey's head spun. Her little brother passed out? Did that mean he'd come close to ... to ... She couldn't think about the horrible possibilities. "What was it? Do they know?"

Her mom nodded. "His heart went into an abnormal rhythm. Maybe from the cold or from his exertion, or maybe because something's wrong with the electrical part of his heart."

"Meaning it could happen again?"

"It could. They'll check a few things while we're here, and then Monday we'll go to Children's Hospital in Indianapolis. They can run the rest of the tests there."

"What's the worst case?" Bailey wasn't sure she wanted to ask. She pictured her blond little brother shooting free throws in the front yard near the family garage this past weekend. If he had to cut back on sports, he'd be devastated.

"He might need a pacemaker. Something to help make sure it doesn't happen again."

The idea sounded horrific. "He's so young."

"It's only a possibility. He's on a medicine for now, to keep his heartbeat controlled." Her mom straightened and put her arm around Bailey. With her free hand she wiped at her tears again, then reached out and put that arm around Cody's shoulders. "It was so scary."

"Is he awake?" Now that they weren't outside in the freezing air, Bailey could smell Cody's cologne. She hated how easily she responded to his presence, falling for him as if she didn't have a boyfriend, as if he'd never ignored her, never chosen to be friends with Andi over her. She bit her lip. "Can we see him?"

She drew a long breath and released the hold she had on them. "He's tired, but he'd love to see you." She looked at Cody. "You too." She paused, sincerity in her tone. "It's been a long time."

"Too long." Cody didn't break eye contact.

Her dad was still talking to the doctor, but as Bailey and Cody walked up he stopped and hugged them both. His eyes told them that he was as concerned about Ricky as her mom had been. "Things were very bad for a little while there."

"We prayed on the way here." Bailey kept her arm around her dad's waist. "I'm sure everyone was praying."

"At church too. I called on the way here. And the Colts team chaplain rallied the guys."

"I could feel the prayers the whole ride here." Her mom steadied herself against her dad.

Bailey felt herself relax a little. "At least he's okay."

"For now. They want to watch him tonight, and then he can come home in the morning if his heart rate stays steady." Her dad frowned. "The tests next week will tell us a lot."

"Jenny said something about a pacemaker." Cody shifted so that he was a little closer to Bailey.

"He could end up with another open-heart surgery."

A sick feeling ran through Bailey. She couldn't stand the thought of her brother having that kind of surgery. She shuddered slightly and moved toward the door of Ricky's room. "We wanna see him, okay?"

"Go ahead." Her dad gave them a weary smile.

Her parents stayed out in the hall, talking in hushed tones while Bailey and Cody went in to be with Ricky. He looked tired but happy, unaware of the danger he'd survived in the past few hours. "Hey, Cody, how'd you get here?"

"I brought your sister." Cody took the spot on one side of the bed, and Bailey moved to the other. "We were together when she heard about this."

"Yeah, kinda weird, huh?" Ricky made a face. "I think I just got a little too cold."

"It's definitely cold out there." Bailey ran her hand over his now matted pale hair. "How you feeling, bud?"

"Tired." He yawned. "But I can breathe better."

They talked for awhile, and eventually Bailey's parents and brothers joined them. After half an hour, Bailey and Cody had to get going. Both of them had homework, and Cru was that night. With Ricky out of immediate danger, there was no reason to stay longer. They said their good-byes, and her brother Connor gave Bailey an extra-long hug. "It was really bad," he whispered. "God saved him, Bailey. Seriously."

Again Bailey felt a sick feeling pass over her. *God, thank You for helping him.* She uttered the silent prayer as easily as she drew her next breath. "Text me if anything gets worse."

Connor agreed. "You're home for the weekend, right?"

"Definitely."

"Good." Connor was in the latest CKT play, but he didn't have practice this weekend, so they could have time together. Time to catch up and laugh about the latest funny videos on YouTube or the news at Clear Creek High, where Connor was a sophomore.

Before they parted, Connor raised an eyebrow. "What's with Cody?"

Bailey's heart fell flat. "Nothing. He was there when I got the call. That's it." She drew back and waved once more to Ricky and the others.

"Hey!" Ricky made an effort to sit up, but he seemed too tired to pull off the move. "Cody, you gotta come around more. I can throw a football thirty yards now."

Cody chuckled. He and Ricky had always shared a special connection because of football. "I definitely have to see that."

Exhaustion and relief made Bailey feel tired as she and Cody walked back to his car. His elbow brushed against her arm a few times, and she tried not to enjoy the sensation. This whole crazy afternoon was like something from a dream, like it had never happened. They were quiet on the ride home, but the time gave Bailey a chance to collect her thoughts, to find solid ground again.

When Cody dropped her off at the front door of her dorm, he got out and stood facing her. The awkwardness was back, now that they no longer had a reason to be together. The wind chaffed at their cheeks and the barren branches in the trees overhead clacked together with every light gust.

Cody found her eyes and held them. He had a way of looking straight to her heart, and this late afternoon was no different. Finally he took a slow breath. "I meant what I said."

"About?"

"Being friends. I'm not giving up." He seemed to gather himself, his frustrations from earlier in check. "I'll keep calling and texting until you trust me again."

Bailey felt like the air had been sucked from her lungs. Until she trusted him again? Did he really know her that well? After so much time had passed since they'd talked, could he be so exactly spot on about how she felt? She wasn't sure what to say, so she looked down again and studied the snow.

"That's it, right? I pulled a disappearing act, and now you don't trust me."

She wanted to tell him to stop, that he had no right reading her thoughts. But she was too touched by how well he still knew her. Even so, she had to be honest. "I have Tim, now … and you … you need to move on too."

He started to say something, but again he changed his mind. "I can't do that."

Bailey felt the sadness build and grow inside her. Because this was where he was wrong. "You can."

"I wanna talk about you and me, what we could—"

"There is no you and me, Cody." She steeled her heart against him, protecting herself. "You wanted me to date Tim, and that's what I'm doing."

"You're in love with him?"

"Yes." She couldn't help the hesitation that followed. "Sometimes I think I am."

For a few seconds she thought he was going to note that a person in love would think so all the time. Not sometimes. But instead he seemed to lose the will to fight her. His shoulders sank a little. "Okay, then." He drew her tenderly into a long hug. "I'm glad Ricky's okay."

"For now." She could barely draw a breath, her heart racing from the feel of his arms around her. She couldn't remember feeling this way in Tim's arms even once.

"Yes, for now." He was still hugging her. "It was good seeing you today. Nothing's felt so right in a long time."

She exhaled, and tried not to cry. "Thanks." She spoke the words against his neck. "For being there today." When she couldn't stand another moment being so close to him, she pulled back. She wanted to tell him how wonderful it felt seeing him, and how he'd made her feel safe and protected at a time when she was scared to death. But there was no point. She took a step toward her dorm. "See you at Cru."

A subtle disappointment shaded his eyes, but he smiled anyway. "Okay. See ya."

Bailey turned and took quick steps up the walkway and into the dorm. She didn't turn around and wave one last time even though a part of her wanted to steal one more look. The fact was she couldn't turn around. Not because she was afraid he'd see the tears finally streaming down her face, but because she didn't want him to see something far worse. Her eyes would no doubt give away the fact that no matter how she lied to him or to herself, the truth remained—Tim or no Tim.

She was still in love with Cody Coleman.

Thirteen

KELLY WANTED TO BE HAPPY FOR Chase, but no matter how hard she tried she couldn't work up anything but the familiar feeling of despair. She sat on the edge of their bed and watched her husband buzz around the room, packing his bag and practically bursting with the thrill of all the week held.

"I mean, really, Kelly, I was beginning to wonder if the whole *Unlocked* things was really going to happen, like maybe Kendall was just being optimistic, you know?"

Kelly's stomach hurt from the waffles she'd eaten that morning. She crossed her arms and nodded. "I wondered too."

"But this is just like God. Four weeks with nothing, not a hint that Kendall's news was going to pan out. I mean, Brandon Paul might've changed his mind or maybe the studios weren't as interested as before. And then—" He snapped his fingers. "Out of the blue a call like this. I mean, Kendall's the real deal. She can make things happen, I'll say that."

Kelly wondered if her husband could hear himself. "She must be really something."

"She is." Chase stopped, as if for the first time in the last five minutes he grasped how he was coming across. "As far as the industry goes."

They were at the end of February and the call had come in yesterday morning. Kendall had been working behind the scenes, apparently, and now she wanted Chase and Kevin to come to LA for a week of meetings. Talk about making things happen. Kelly had never known jealousy before, but she understood it completely now. Her husband could barely stop talking about Kendall and the magic she could work in Hollywood.

The first meeting this week would be a private screening of *The Last Letter* at Kendall's house Monday evening. In attendance would be Kendall; her father, Ben; Stephanie; and NTM's very own Brandon Paul—teen sensation and easily one of America's most well-known superstars. She could understand Chase's excitement. If only Kendall didn't have to be such an integral part of it.

"I can't believe it." Chase's smile seemed permanently etched into his face. His tone hadn't come down once since Kendall's call. "All those powerful people in one room just to watch our movie."

"They have to see if you're legit." Kelly meant the comment to sound positive, but it felt flat as it left her lips. Again she pressed her arms hard against her aching stomach.

"Legit?" His smile faded a little. "They already know we're legit or they wouldn't come out for a screening." He gave a quick laugh, as if he had no time to waste being negative or distracted. A stack of shirts sat on one side of the bed. He lifted it and placed it into his open suitcase. "This is about Kendall showing off our work and getting everyone else excited so that we can start getting things lined up for *Unlocked*."

"That's what I meant." Kelly stood and sighed. She watched Chase put a stack of socks and then a few pairs of dark jeans into the suitcase, then she walked to the bedroom window and stared out at the house next to theirs. Times like this the houses felt so close together she could practically reach out and shake hands with the neighbors. She closed her eyes and thought about how lonely she would be once Chase was gone. Let him go and show off his movie to a bunch of Hollywood types. Where did that leave her?

Chase stopped and stared at her. "You okay?" He was still smiling, his eyes still lit up. But for the first time that evening concern flickered in his expression.

"It's hard when you're away."

"Babe." Chase came to her and put his hands on her shoulders. "This is temporary. God's opening so many doors. Kendall says it's only a matter of time before we can buy something closer to LA. Then I can be home every night."

"Kendall probably knows." A tired smile tugged at her lips. She didn't want to sound bitter or jaded. "I'd like that."

"I'd like it too." He leaned in and kissed her lips—one tender, lingering kiss. "We all would."

"What am I supposed to do until then?" She looked out the window. "You keep leaving me to take care of the girls, handle the finances, run the house." She turned to him again. "All by myself."

Chase still had his hand on her back, but he let it fall to his side. "I've been home most of February."

"I know." Again she gathered up the hint of a smile. "I'm sorry. It's just ... I feel removed from it, Chase."

"From what?"

"Everything you're doing. The excitement and the meetings, the connections with people in the industry. The screening at Kendall's house, the socializing with the likes of Stephanie Fitzgerald and Brandon Paul." She faced him. "Doesn't it ever feel a little surreal?"

Chase thought about that for a long moment. "Not really." He met her eyes. "We prayed for this, all of us. Remember that? Day after day, months at a time. Now that God's answering us, I guess I only feel grateful."

She nodded, but she could feel her smile drop off. He returned to packing, talking about the conversation he'd had with Kendall and Brandon Paul's agent and how excited the young actor was to star in *Unlocked*, and how Stephanie Fitzgerald had texted him. Actually texted him! And how she was thrilled for the chance to preview his work Monday night at Kendall's.

Kelly studied him as he talked and packed, moving about the room with the energy of someone setting off for a once-in-a-lifetime trip. Something about him seemed different, more confident maybe. Better than having him down and discouraged, wallowing in fear of defeat, she supposed. But still, there were moments when she felt like she was watching someone else's husband get ready to leave. The energy in his face, the speed in his steps, the enthusiasm in his voice. And the realization that she had no real part in his excitement.

Suddenly a handful of scenarios ran through her head. Chase arriving in Los Angeles and being seduced by the Hollywood lifestyle, wanting to stay longer than a week, and maybe renting a place so he wouldn't have to commute. She pictured him coming home and telling her that he was going to stay at Stephanie's house, or maybe Kendall's. He would call and tell her he'd had it with her discouragement and that he was frustrated at her weight gain. Maybe he and Brandon Paul would hit it off and Chase's photo would be in the next round of gossip rags.

"Kelly?" Chase was standing there, his lips slightly parted, a baffled look on his face. "I was talking to you."

"Sorry." She took another deep breath and found the energy to cross the room again. She dropped once more on the edge of the bed and looked at him. "What'd you say?"

"I asked if the girls had anything special going on this week."

Kelly stared at him, not sure if he was serious or not. "Other than Molly's fifth birthday on Friday, you mean?"

"Uh …" Chase blinked and stuttered a bit. "Exactly. Other than that."

"You forgot."

"I did not." He turned back to the suitcase and sifted through what he'd already packed. "I was distracted, that's all."

"You forgot about your daughter's birthday, Chase. Just admit it." The anger building inside her was the first strong emotion she'd felt all day. It made her feel better, like she at least had control over this.

"I'm busy, okay." His happiness took a momentary backseat to his impatience. "Of course I know when Molly's birthday is. I just forgot it was already coming up this week, that's all."

"Well, it is." Kelly's enthusiasm for an argument died a quick death. "You'll be home by then. Don't worry about it, Chase. I'll make sure everything's set up. A few presents, balloons, a cake and ice cream. The works. All you have to do is be home from Hollywood."

"Thanks." He maintained his frown, clearly concerned with himself for losing track of the weeks. But after a few seconds, he motioned to the bedroom door. "I need a few things from the kitchen. I'll be right back."

For a panicky instant, she wondered if he'd find her cookie dough, but then she relaxed. Not where she hid it in the back of the refrigerator. No one would look there. She stood and walked to the mirror atop their secondhand bedroom dresser. One side of the oak-wood frame was scratched, but otherwise it served its purpose. Kelly could get a look at herself coming and going, marking each day how she got a little farther from her normal weight, a little more out of control. She stared at herself, at the way her sides had filled out and her hips had rounded from her waist.

Why am I doing this to myself, God? She looked into her own eyes and waited. But she heard no divine answers, nothing but the roar of shame and guilt that came with every day she delayed the turnaround. The strange thing was she really didn't want to eat the junk. Honestly, nothing she'd slipped into her mouth had tasted good enough to swap out her health and appearance. But she ate, regardless. Ate almost as if she wanted to kill herself with the food. Or at least kill something about herself. Because when she was bent on eating like this, there was never enough chocolate, enough cookie dough or ice cream bars to fill whatever cavernous hole she was trying to fill. She wasn't hungry, she was broken. Too discouraged to see the sunshine outside.

She heard Chase's returning, and she stepped away from the mirror. Better not to let him catch her looking. The moment might give him pause to reflect on how she'd changed. The lie she told herself was this: if she didn't attract attention to herself, then maybe he wouldn't notice what was happening. In a moment like this it was a lie she believed, so she moved away from the mirror just before he reached the bedroom door.

"Vitamins!" He held up a bottle of One A Days and then tossed it in his open suitcase. "Can't forget these!" He hummed as he grabbed a bag of deodorant and toothpaste from the bathroom.

How is he so happy? she asked herself. *Doesn't he see I'm falling apart?* She watched him, but he was again bouncing-off-the-ceiling happy, looking forward to seeing where God would take their filmmaking, thrilled about spending a week with Keith and Kendall and his new friends. Kelly and her insecurities, her doubts and discouragement, were nowhere on his radar. For that matter, neither were the girls.

Molly and Macy ran into the room, Macy chasing after her older sister and screaming for the doll in Molly's hands. "Mine!" Her voice pierced the air. "My baby!"

"It is not!" Molly held it high, just out of Macy's reach. "It's mine, Mommy. Everyone knows she's mine."

Chase seemed oblivious, packing his shaver into a carry case. Kelly sighed and stooped down to Macy's eye level. "You have the baby with the blue dress. Remember?"

Macy stuck out her lip. "I want that one!"

Kelly thought about how much she was like her youngest daughter, wanting the junk food she couldn't have. It was a problem as old as the Garden of Eden. She pulled Macy close and smoothed her blonde hair. "The pink baby belongs to Molly." She kept her voice calm, something she was working on with the girls. "Now let's go get your dolly, okay?"

With her options dwindling, Macy hesitated for only a few seconds. Then she slipped her hand in Kelly's and stuck out her chin at her sister. "I have Mommy."

Molly looked concerned until Kelly sighed. "You both have me, and I have both of you." She smiled at the girls and then walked Macy to their bedroom and found the blue baby doll. "See?" She held it out for Macy. "This one's best for you, because she's yours."

Macy clung to the doll and pressed it against her face. "Mine."

Kelly dropped to her daughter's bed and closed her eyes. These days her body rode a wild rollercoaster, full of energy one minute, followed by a crash so low she barely had energy to walk through the house. This was one of those moments. Molly skipped into the room, her doll clutched tight to her middle. "See, Macy, that baby's yours."

No longer intent on arguing, Macy only clung to her doll more tightly. "Mine," she said again.

"Girls." Kelly's eyes were open now. "Let's remember that we love each other. You girls are best friends, so let's treat each other that way. That's what Jesus would want." Kelly felt like a hypocrite even as the words passed between her lips. What Jesus would want? Had she even thought about such a thing these past few months? The real issue was her relationship with Chase. What if things did work out for the guys? The risk would shift from a financial struggle to a moral one. What if Chase became too friendly with the beautiful Kendall Adams? Or what if they were suddenly rolling in the money? How could they live a high-end Hollywood lifestyle and still care about the souls of people?

All of it scared Kelly, and drove her to bury her feelings rather than take her doubts to Chase, or even to God.

"Honey? I gotta go," Chase called to her from the kitchen.

"Come on, girls." Kelly felt a hundred years old as she rose to her feet. "Let's say good-bye to Daddy."

"But . . ." Molly's eyes grew wide with concern. "He can't leave. This week is my birthday."

"He'll be back by then." Kelly hoped her smile brought Molly the assurance she needed.

The three of them walked to the kitchen and exchanged a round of hugs with Chase. The buzz of excitement still emanated from him, as if he couldn't wait to get on the road.

"What's the plan for tonight?" Kelly faced him, her arms folded in front of her.

"We're going over the first draft of the screenplay for *Unlocked*. We won't get through it all, but we have most of tomorrow too. Then tomorrow night's the screening at Kendall's."

Kelly nodded slowly. She'd never met Kendall, but she'd googled her and seen pictures. The girl was young, blonde, and stunning—full of the enthusiasm Kelly couldn't quite muster. Everything about her seemed to represent the glitz of Hollywood and the lure of filmmaking. Kelly sighed and tentatively eased her arms around Chase's waist. "Drive safely."

"We will." He lifted her chin with his forefinger. "You okay?"

"Fine." She found the practiced smile, the one that always seemed to make him stop asking questions. "I'm happy for you."

"I want you to be happy for *us*. Me *and* you. If things keep going like this, a year from now we could be in LA. None of these trips."

Kelly tried to picture fitting in with the Hollywood set, starving herself into size-5 jeans and dying her hair blonde like

Kendall's. She would never fit in, and then what? How could she and Chase continue if he wanted that world and she felt alienated by it? She maintained her smile. "Whatever you want, Chase."

"Not me." He leaned in and kissed her softly. "It's what God wants. Every prayer we've lifted to Him, He's answering for us. You watch." His eyes shone. "We're going to do this, baby. We're going to change the world with the power of film. God's letting it happen."

"Then … I'll keep praying." It was the one thing she could do, even when she didn't feel like talking to God. She would pray. And maybe tomorrow she would toss the junk and try to eat better — salmon and broccoli, egg whites and vegetables, yogurt and flaxseed. She knew the drill. Now she only had to want it badly enough to change.

Chase pulled his suitcase to the front door and gave them all another round of good-byes. "I'll call when we get in tonight."

"You're staying at the Georgian again?" Kelly swung Macy up onto her hip.

"Yes. Same place, same room. Our home away from home."

Turned out Ben Adams knew the owner of the Georgian, so now the guys were getting a much lower rate. A good thing, since their savings were gone and they still had another few months of screenings before a studio might reimburse them for the money they'd invested in *The Last Letter*. Chase hoped that if Brandon Paul liked the movie well enough, they'd get a screening with NTM's home entertainment division, and maybe the film giant would pick up the movie. It was one more area they were praying about.

Kelly, Molly, and Macy stood on the front step and waved as Chase drove away in his used four-door. The girls then wanted to go out back and play on the swings. "Push us, Mommy! Please!" Kelly opened the door for them and promised to be out in a few minutes. When she was alone, she pulled a bowl of M&Ms from the cupboard and set it on the counter. She needed energy if she was going to handle another week of single parenting. She grabbed a small handful of the candies and popped them in her mouth.

"Mommy!" Her girls squealed with delight as she came into view. The yard was small and boxy, the swing set a rusted leftover from the last tenant. But the girls didn't care. For them it was paradise, a playground within a few running steps of the back door. "Push us, Mommy!" Molly was trying to pump her little legs, but she wasn't getting very high.

"Push!" Macy was sitting in the swing next to her sister, clinging to the chains so she wouldn't fall off.

"Hey, not fair. It's my turn!" Molly whined and stuck out her lower lip.

"You'll each get turns." Kelly gave her oldest daughter a look. "You have to be patient with your sister." Kelly pushed Macy a minute or so, and then stepped to the side and pushed Molly. "See ... you each get turns."

While she pushed the girls, Kelly noticed that the yard was overgrown again. But the mower needed new blades or a tune-up. One more thing they couldn't afford. That, and both girls had dentist appointments tomorrow—which meant a fifteen-dollar copay each. She blinked back tears as she kept pushing. *Dear God, I feel so overwhelmed. Please, help me get through this. I can't do this by myself.*

Precious daughter, you're not alone. I am with you always.

The reminder rang clear and true across the lonely places in her heart. On the mission field she'd heard God's voice constantly. But here He was easily drowned out by the noise of merely living. Fresh peace cast light across the moment. *Thank You, Lord ... for seeing me here, for caring.*

"I'm swinging higher than you, Macy." Molly stuck her chin out and kicked her feet high into the air.

"Nah-uh! I'm higher too!"

"Time for a break." Kelly straightened and pressed her hand to her lower back. She hoped for another gentle whisper, but not over the bickering of her little daughters. "Let's go inside and color."

The girls hesitated, but then they grinned at each other, slid down off the swings, and ran laughing into the house, their petty arguments forgotten. Kelly raked her fingers through her shoulder-length dark hair and followed them.

Inside, Molly raced into the kitchen and immediately found the bowl of candy. "Hey!" She pointed to the bowl. "It's M-a-Ms." She giggled. "That's better than coloring, don't you think so?"

Heat rushed to Kelly's cheeks, but she recovered quickly. Molly didn't understand the idea of hiding food, so she wouldn't connect the fact that candy was out now that Daddy was gone. "Candy's for special times." She slid the bowl toward the back of the counter, partly behind a plant and definitely out of sight from the girls' heights. She wanted her girls to eat healthy, to grow up avoiding the junk food that had so often trapped Kelly. "Maybe a few pieces after lunch."

"Mommm." Molly's whine was quick and incessant. "Please, can we have some now?"

"Later." She put her hands on her hips. "And never if you keep whining like that."

Molly took a few seconds to transition, but then she found her happiest, sweetest smile. "Okay, Mommy. Sorry about the whining."

A half an hour of coloring and Kelly was settling the girls down in front of a rerun episode of *Bear in the Big Blue House* when the phone rang. Kelly spotted Chase's phone number on the caller ID, and she smiled. Of course. He would be calling to apologize for not realizing the sacrifices she was making. He was having all the fun, and she was doing the work. Certainly an hour on the road would've been long enough to realize his mistake.

"Hello?" Her voice was pleasant, understanding. "Chase?"

"I'm sorry, babe." He sounded more frustrated than repentant. "Kendall just called. She's arranged a meeting with Brandon and his agent for Friday—it's the only day they're both available."

Her blood ran cold. "Molly's birthday?"

"Yes." His sigh rattled across the phone line. "I'm so sorry. Let's celebrate it Sunday, after I get home."

"She's not two, Chase. She knows what day she turns five, and she'll know you missed it."

"What can I do?" His tone held an edge, as if he didn't expect an argument. "I'd be there if I could, you know that. It's not like—"

"What?"

"Come on, Kelly." A softness crept back into his voice. "I hate this as much as you do. It's a sacrifice we need to make."

"*We*?" The week ahead loomed like a series of cloudy, gray afternoons without the slightest chance of sunshine. "Fine, Chase. Whatever you have to do."

For a long while he didn't say anything. She could hear the rush of wind and traffic in the background, and finally he groaned quietly. "I'm doing my best, baby. You gotta believe that."

Molly and Macy were sitting in the living room, their arms around each other's necks, glued to the TV. The three of them would get through the week, and Kelly would have to come out whole on the other end. What choice did she have? She closed her eyes and pinched the bridge of her nose. "I believe you."

"Okay, then." He sounded relieved. "Let's talk later tonight."

The conversation ended, and Kelly felt the beginning of tears. How could she explain that she didn't want to run their home by herself, that she was tired of being a single mom so much of the time. With all the great news about *The Last Letter* and *Unlocked*, there were still no guarantees. And every step of the way seemed to take Chase further from her, further from the simple missionary life they'd once shared.

God ... are You there? Really? She sniffed and listened, but this time there was nothing. No response, no Bible verses to lend her wisdom or comfort or peace. Suddenly she felt like running—fast and far, somewhere away from the aging little house. She wanted to open up to Chase, but she wouldn't think of telling him about her spiraling battle with discouragement. Depression, even. He wouldn't want to come home at all. But that meant she had little to say. Not to him, and not to herself. She grabbed another fistful of M&Ms and downed them in a single motion. Then she walked to the back of the house, stared out the window, and cried. Not just because of the dark place she'd worked her way into.

But because she no longer knew how to find her way to the light.

KEITH WATCHED HIS FRIEND CLICK HIS cell phone shut and drop it back down on the console between the two seats. A ripple of alarm wrapped around his heart and tightened a little. "How's she doing?" Keith was driving this first leg of the trip. He glanced at Chase, studying his frustration.

"Not happy." Chase anchored his elbow on the window frame and let his head fall into his hands. "Sometimes I think she doesn't understand. The time away's hard on me too."

For a while, neither of them said anything. Then Keith took a long breath and stared at the road straight ahead. "My dad used to tell me life was like an uncooked pizza crust."

Chase gave him a side glance.

"Think about it." Keith sat back in his seat, one hand on the wheel. There was no traffic, and this far out of San Jose the afternoon was blue skies and mid-seventies. He adjusted his sunglasses. "You get one ball of dough for life, and you spend your days rolling it out, making it go as far as it can possibly go." He caught another look at Chase. "As you roll the dough, little cracks develop along the edges. Fix them right away, and there's no problem. But let them go and they'll rip right through the center of the crust."

"That's what your dad used to say?" Chase sounded tired.

"Smart man. Used to make homemade pizza for us once a week. Told the story just about every time." Keith pictured his father, rolling out the crust and stopping every minute or so to fix the edges. "Cracks are like that in pizza and in life. Catch them early, or lose everything you worked for."

Chase dropped his hands to his lap and narrowed his eyes. "Cracks." He angled himself so he could see Keith better. "Like the one between Kelly and me?"

"Exactly." Keith didn't want to make the moment too dramatic. Chase had been struggling in his relationship with Kelly for a while now, and always they seemed to work things out. But if a crack was developing, now was the time to fix it. His expression grew more serious. "Whatever you have to do, Chase, whatever it is, take care of the crack. You and Kelly, your marriage, your family. It's more important than the whole ball of dough. Know what I mean?"

Slowly, Chase nodded. He turned and looked out the side window and again there was quiet in the car. Keith was fine with the lack of conversation. Maybe God was giving Chase a picture in his mind: the pizza maker, rolling out the dough and stopping along the way to smooth out the cracks.

God, speak to him. Give him wisdom where Kelly is concerned. We've come too far to let this movie-making hurt things at home for either of us. Please, God.

I am with you, Son. I am the strong tower you can run to in troubled times. I am here.

The silent answer resonated in Keith's heart, the way it often did. He didn't care if Chase thought the analogy about the pizza crust a little hokey. It was a visual that worked, one that had stayed with Keith since his boyhood days. Keith wasn't truly worried about Chase's marriage. Not now. But that was the beauty of saying something early. Trouble had been splintering the edges for Chase and Kelly long enough. The time had come to do some mending, or watch something far worse develop.

A split that neither of them could repair.

Fourteen

Chase hardly breathed during the screening. He could barely take in what was happening around him. He'd never been anywhere like Kendall's house—a plush, expansive tri-level with entire walls of glass, built into the Hollywood Hills. And sitting with him around the room were people he'd once only read about. Kendall and her father, Ben; Stephanie Fitzgerald; and Brandon Paul. Even Luke Baxter had flown in for the week of meetings, confident he could help on a number of levels.

Kelly had asked Chase if he ever felt like his life had become surreal. He'd told her no, that he wasn't overwhelmed by the glitz and glamour of everything happening around him. But here, every few seconds, Chase asked himself what in the world he was doing rubbing elbows with some of the most powerful people in the industry.

The Last Letter seemed to take twice as long to finish, and more than once Chase and Keith exchanged a look that said neither of them could wait for feedback from the people watching. Everything about their future with *Unlocked* hinged on the next few hours.

Chase tried to relax and enjoy the film, but it was impossible. *God, it's in Your hands. Let them love it, and give us success here. Please ...*

In response, Chase remembered one of his favorite Bible verses, something from Philippians chapter 4. "*Present your requests to God. And the peace of God, which transcends all understanding, will guard your hearts and your minds in Christ Jesus.*"

Yes, that was it. He needed to place all his questions and fears in the hands of Christ, so that the peace of God would rule over not only this moment but whatever other moments the night held. Success or not.

When the film finally ended, Chase noticed something he hadn't before. Stephanie was crying. She wiped her fingers beneath her eyes and for a long while the group sat in the dark, watching the credits and saying nothing. Stephanie found a tissue from the coffee table and blew her nose. Then she turned to Chase and Keith and grinned bigger than anything she'd given at their first meeting. "That—" She motioned with her elbow toward the large screen, "—was beautiful. Absolutely beautiful." She stood and went to Keith first, and then to Chase, hugging each of them and practically lifting them off the ground. "That's what I'm talking about! I knew you were the right guys. Everything I'd seen and read told me that—your skill and determination, your talent and your faith." She stepped back and let out a loud victory cry. "Thank you, Jesus! We got nothing but sunshine and clear skies ahead. *Unlocked* is going to be amazing!"

The others in the room chuckled at her excitement.

"Hey!" Stephanie spun around and pointed at Brandon. "Don't laugh at me!" She was teasing him, enjoying the moment. "Tell me you didn't get tears all backed up in those beautiful eyes of yours!"

"Okay, okay." Brandon breathed in deeply through his nose. "You're right. It was good."

"I was crying like a baby." Luke tossed his hands and grabbed a tissue.

The sight of their attorney acting as emotional as Stephanie made them laugh and added to the feeling of celebration. Chase listened to the exchange and prayed he wouldn't wake up, prayed he was really hearing this sort of feedback and not lost in the middle of a dream. Keith popped him on the shoulder and grinned. It wasn't a dream. The people gathered in Kendall's screening room loved *The Last Letter*.

"It's everything I knew it would be." Kendall stood and flipped on a light. "What do you think, Dad?"

"Amazing." He pulled himself to his feet and gave first Keith, then Chase a hearty handshake. "You've got my support. Like I said, I'll fund the P&A for a theatrical release on this film, and I'm good for half the money on *Unlocked*."

Chase couldn't breathe. He pressed his leg against the sofa behind him so he wouldn't fall to the floor. The P&A budget was five million dollars, and though Ben had hinted about footing the cost, this was an actual promise. Chase had the feeling he was going to whip out a legal document over chips and salsa later that night. Sure, they still needed to convince the studio executives that *The Last Letter* was worth the financial risk for a theatrical release. But with this sort of reaction, Chase suddenly wasn't worried.

But more than that, Ben's offer to fund half the Brandon Paul movie meant two things. First, they were ready to talk to a studio about the project. And second, they could retain creative control—since providing half the budget would give them that privilege.

Chase could hear people talking around him, but all he could think about was Kelly, how she'd doubted whether they could make movies at this level, at the Brandon Paul level. And how God had proved to all of them that they could.

They moved into the kitchen and then on to the formal dining room, where a housekeeper had set the table with a Mexican dinner. Once they were seated and the food served, Chase and Keith talked at length with the others. Luke Baxter was showing himself to be a skilled professional, an up-and-coming legend in entertainment law. He had already drawn up paperwork for the financials.

"I understand you're available tomorrow also?" Ben took three *taquitos* from the closest platter. "We need something in writing to add to the investment money I've already put in for *The Last Letter*, and of course we need to spell out our deal with Brandon."

"Absolutely." Luke was quick to answer. "I'm in town all week."

Brandon set his fork down. "My agent and attorney want to be in on that. I think we're meeting Friday." He scooped a blob of avocado dip onto his plate. "My agent's going to want a polished screenplay before we commit to anything with a studio."

So many pieces to the puzzle. Chase felt dizzy, and not the least bit hungry even as everyone around him dove into their meals. The conversation didn't turn back to movies again until after dinner.

"Brandon." Kendall was sitting on Chase's other side. "Why don't you tell the producers your story. The one most people don't know."

Chase was dying to know more about the kid. They were about to invest millions of dollars into the guy—that and their futures as filmmakers. He and Keith knew little about the actor, only what was common knowledge in the magazines. Brandon was twenty-two, but he could convincingly play a high school kid. He'd come onto the scene as part of an NTM series about a high school jock who was really the son of a European king. *Prince Jake* was the series, and it had blown away the expectations of NTM. Prince Jake's image was on everything from pop cans to pizza boxes, T-shirts to bath towels. Brandon Paul could sing, dance, and act, and he was a teen heartthrob like the country hadn't seen in three decades. The only black mark was Brandon's younger sister, Paisley, who was also in show business but who had occasional drug trouble, according to the tabloids. But Chase had never found out more than that.

Brandon's eyes revealed little emotion. He was comfortable with this story, but clearly he didn't enjoy telling it. "My parents don't agree with my acting career. They homeschooled us and hoped that my sister and I would attend Harvard, get doctorate degrees, and find a cure for cancer. I call and tell them how things are going, but they don't watch my stuff, and they don't take it seriously." He gave a single shrug. "It is what it is."

"Tell them about your sister." Kendall's tone was soft.

"Right." He exhaled slowly. "We used to be very close. My parents didn't approve of our acting, but at least we had each other. But that wasn't enough for Paisley. She wanted my parents' acceptance so badly." He exhaled and stared at his lap for a long minute. When he looked up, the pain was there for all of them to see. "She's a drug user. Heroin. She'll surface for a few months, stay clean, and get a commercial or an extra role in a movie. But then she's gone again. Living on the streets, sharing needles with strangers. She goes by a different last name. The press doesn't know the half of it."

Chase's heart broke for the guy, and all he and his sister had lost because of their parents' narrow-minded attitude.

Brandon squinted as if he could keep out some of the pain. "Funny how people think money's the answer. I'll never live long enough to spend mine, but it can't help Paisley. Not until she wants the help. Every job, every day I'm on set, I feel like I'm living for both of us. Like I owe it to her."

Chase thought for a moment. In some ways Brandon's story reminded him of Dayne Matthews. A young guy without the support of his parents. The only difference was that Dayne's adoptive parents had been killed when he was eighteen in a single-engine plane crash. Still, the two actors would have common ground. Brandon might really benefit from the strength and faith of someone like Dayne.

Kendall was explaining that Brandon wasn't actually a Christian. "Not yet, anyway." She patted Brandon's hand. "I'm working on him."

"I'm open. It's just ..." His eyes grew distant. "I'm not quite sure God believes in me. You know?"

There was a general sense of acknowledgment about how Brandon felt, and Keith admitted that he had been through a time like that during his final years of high school. "I'd been taught about God all my life, but those few years, I wasn't sure what I believed."

"Exactly." Brandon gave a slow nod. "I guess you could say I'm searching."

"For now." Kendall's smile toward Brandon was kind and full of warmth.

"Yes." He chuckled. "For now."

Keith took over the conversation, engaging both Brandon and Ben about the themes of *Unlocked* and how they would play out on the screen. But before the talk could get too serious, too focused, Ben stood and smiled at the group. "You know what we need?"

Chase had no idea.

"A good old-fashioned ping-pong tournament." He grinned at Kendall. "My daughter's just about unbeatable. And I find nothing gets the imagination going better than a few rounds of table tennis."

They all laughed, and Chase and Keith joined the others on a walk out back and down a sidewalk to an outbuilding—this one holding two ping-pong tables and a half a dozen sofas anchored to the perimeter of the room. "It used to be a storage place for my father's boats." Kendall smiled as they went inside. "A few years ago we turned it into a ping-pong room."

Chase had never seen anything like it. A dry-erase board hung on the wall near the closest table, and scribbled across it was a tally sheet of some kind. Kendall laughed again. "My dad's pretty competitive. We keep track of the games we play in a year."

"Because one of these years I'm gonna beat her, by golly." Ben searched a shelf near the entrance to the room and grabbed a red paddle. "This is my baby. I call it The Blade."

Chase loved this. Who would've thought that movie people at this level would spend their evenings playing ping-pong?

Stephanie grabbed a paddle similar to Ben's. "I'm not so bad myself." She twirled the paddle in her hand and aimed it at Kendall. "Let's see who's queen of this palace."

"We'll sit out the first round." Keith nodded at Chase and the two of them took the nearest sofa. "So we can size up the competition."

That left Kendall and Stephanie on one table and Ben and Brandon on the other. Kendall seemed to go easy on Stephanie, and halfway through the game, the author was up by two points. But then it was like Kendall found another gear. She began using a spin-type serve and slamming the ball instead of returning it.

"Oooh, girlfriend's got game." Stephanie raised her hands and did a little victory dance on behalf of Kendall's play. "I don't mind losing to someone with skill, no, sir."

On the other table, Ben was giving Brandon a fight. But youth had its advantage, and the game was leaning hard in Brandon's favor. Chase liked Brandon's style—all offense and risk. It was the way they'd been forced to play the game of movie-making.

But even still, he kept finding his attention turning to Kendall. She laughed as easily as she breathed, and besides being a skilled player she had an infectious confidence about her. As if she never really doubted the fact that she'd win the game, any more than she doubted the fact that the movies she wanted to make with Chase and Keith would be successful beyond their wildest dreams.

If only Kelly could be like that, Lord—confident and convinced. Believing in the work we have ahead of us.

As soon as the thought passed through his mind, Chase roped it back and chastised himself. He couldn't compare Kendall and Kelly, not now or ever. Kendall had been born into the world of wealth and movies, so of course she was calmer about the risks ahead, more certain. Kelly knew only that they'd run up their credit cards and borrowed money they couldn't afford to repay to help fund *The Last Letter*. She was alone with the girls too often, and she wasn't happy about it. That much was obvious from the strain between them.

If they were going to work with Kendall and her father, Chase couldn't for one minute nurture a growing interest in anything about Kendall. Period.

Keith worked in on the next round, taking on Brandon, while Ben matched up against Stephanie. That left Chase and Kendall.

"I'm thirsty." She motioned for Chase to follow her. "Help me bring in a flat of water bottles."

Once they were outside, Kendall's pace slowed. Her eyes danced in the moonlight as she looked at him. "You're the real deal, Chase Ryan. I admire you."

He tried not to feel overly flattered. "Why?"

"Because." Their conversation was easy, comfortable. "Your ambitions and dreams, your mission for making movies that will change lives." She breathed in slowly and gazed at the stars overhead. "It's all going to happen. I've prayed about this for a long time, and I can feel it."

Chase tried not to focus on her pretty face, her confidence. For a moment he looked straight ahead toward the house. But then his eyes met hers again. "Sometimes it's hard to believe."

"Well, believe it." Her smile worked its way through him. "One day soon all of Hollywood will want a part of this, of what you and Keith are starting right here."

Their pace slowed almost to a standstill. Chase had been curious about her, but there'd never been a time to ask until now. "What about you, Miss Kendall? What drives you to be a part of all this?"

She thought for a second, her long blonde hair blowing gently in the night breeze. "Redemption, I guess. I've seen a lot of heartache in this town." Her smile was laced with sorrow, an expression that seemed to hold more than she was willing to reveal. "I want my days in this business to matter, I guess. Just like you."

They reached the house, and Kendall punched in a code near the third garage door, causing it to open. She moved toward a stack of water pallets. Chase tried to reach it before her, so she wouldn't think about carrying it. But as he bent to take hold of the top box, his right hand touched hers.

"I've … I've got it."

"I can help." She looked at him, locked eyes, and for the flicker of an instant Chase felt it. An attraction between them that terrified him. He adjusted his grip on the box and heaved it into his arms. "Don't be silly."

Kendall seemed to try to hide her alarm, but it was there. She moved quickly back to the open garage door. "Thanks. I … didn't mean for you to carry it by yourself."

The walk back to the rec building passed much quicker. They talked about ping-pong and her father's determination to beat her. But not once then or at any time during the rest of the night did he see the vulnerability she'd revealed to him on their earlier walk.

When they were finished playing and after they'd all downed a number of water bottles, they went outside and looked at the lights from the Hollywood Hills. Chase stood next to Keith, but Kendall had positioned herself on his other side—some distance away. "It's pretty, isn't it?"

"Mmmm. Yes." Chase looked from her to his friend. He wanted to ask Kendall more about her earlier comments, about all she'd seen in Hollywood. But this wasn't the place. "What do you think, Keith? Beautiful up here, huh?"

"Definitely. The perfect Hollywood home."

After a few minutes, Brandon and Stephanie announced that they had to get going.

"Well, then ..." Ben held his arms out. "Let's pray." He waited while the others circled up around him.

By the time Chase realized who he was standing next to and what was about to happen, it was too late. He kept his gaze away from Kendall's as they linked hands, and once more he tried not to think about the way her fingers felt against his.

Ben bowed his head. "We have much to be thankful for, much to ask of our Mighty God. We never imagined we'd be here, on the verge of a making a movie that the world will want to see, a movie that has the power to bring new life to everyone who sees it."

His prayer went on another minute and it ended with Stephanie adding a few heartfelt words. "*Unlocked* is a movie that could change the way people think. It could send them running into Your arms if we do things right." She spent a few seconds thanking God, praising Him. "We come before You, ready to hear Your voice. Whatever You ask. In Jesus' name."

"Amen." Kendall clapped, immediately releasing Chase's hand. She grinned at the others. "The glory of God. That's the only reason we're all here."

Chase tried to forget the attraction he'd felt earlier. There could be nothing more than friendship and business between him and Kendall. They were going to do what they'd set out to do, taking Hollywood by storm. And along the way they would accomplish the only goal that really mattered.

The goal to change lives with the power of film.

THE NIGHT HAD GONE BETTER THAN Kendall ever imagined—with the exception of one thing. Her attraction to Chase. She'd already warned herself about him, but she had to be more careful. Not that there was any real danger. He was happily married, and she wouldn't consider crossing the line of friendship. Her faith and her past wouldn't allow even the hint of that. But still she needed to watch herself.

The movie had been amazing, of course, as she'd known it would be.

After Brandon and Stephanie left, Kendall's father took off too. That left Kendall, Keith, and Chase. Kendall wasn't ready to call it a night. They still had the first draft of the screenplay to look over. She led them into a softly lit den and produced three copies of the script, one for each of them. Before they got started, Keith excused himself so he could call home. Kendall thought about telling Chase that maybe he should call home too. After all, this was exactly the sort of alone moment with Chase she needed to avoid. But she didn't want to seem too personal, so she took the farthest seat from Chase.

As he looked over the script, Kendall studied him and realized again that he was very attractive. He would stand out in the industry once he and Keith made a name for themselves. His athletic build and chiseled face would become recognizable in no time, and there would be offers to stray. Dramatic offers. She knew because they'd come her way more than once. She bit her lip and felt compelled to pray for him.

Please, God, help him be strong when temptation comes. Help me too. We need to stay close to You.

She leaned on the arm of the sofa. "Tell me about your wife. She must be wonderful, holding down things at home while you're out here following your dream."

"She is." Chase hesitated, but only briefly. "She's my best friend. I hope someday soon we can move down here. Then she can come to meetings like this, and at the end of the day we can be home together." He looked more composed than earlier, when they went for the water in the garage. "I think you'd like her."

"Me too." Kendall ignored the hint of envy. "It's rare, being married to your best friend." Kendall wasn't sure now was the time to tell Chase about her own sad past. Maybe later, when Keith was with them. The guys would both benefit from hearing the story at some point. For now she only wanted Chase to know she supported his marriage. "Don't ever let this business get in the way of what matters. It happens too often."

He smiled, and determination resonated in his expression. "Keith calls it the pizza-crust philosophy. Fix the small breaks along the edges so you don't get a crack straight down the middle."

She laughed out loud and nodded. "Exactly."

Keith joined them again, and they reviewed the highlights of the screenplay. They talked another hour about the pacing of *Unlocked* and how crazy things were bound to get. But long after the guys left, Kendall continued to pray for them. She went outside and sat on her patio deck, staring at the stars overhead and begging God to protect them against the devil's schemes. They were playing with high stakes and there were bound to be pitfalls along the way. Disappointments and discouragement, distraction and temptations.

She peered up at the vast sky and felt the closeness of the Lord. "God, please help me make this experience one that glorifies You," she whispered. "Help me do my part to keep all of us walking the narrow path." Her own personal life might not have been a shining example of God's love and commitment. But she couldn't help that. What she could do was help her new friends stay the course.

Because it would do no good to win the world through the message of a movie only to lose themselves in the process.

Fifteen

ANOTHER MONTH HAD PASSED AND STILL Cody was getting nowhere with Bailey. He was stuck in the middle of a debate in his sociology class, and his leg ached where the prosthetic piece fit up against his flesh—a sign the weather was about to change. Last week's warm temperatures had dropped so that here, at the end of March, winter felt like it had never given an inch in its tug-of-war with spring.

"What I'm saying is I can't support our troops in a situation like the war in Iraq. Our nation is practically fascist the way it attacks other nations without reason." The student speaker was a wiry guy with glasses and a loud voice. He had short hair and a clean-cut look that defied his views. "It's not about patriotism, it's about common sense." He was on his feet, staring down anyone who dared differ with him. "No one forced those men and women to enlist. They knew what they were getting into when they signed up. A losing conflict, and an ill-fated attempt at tearing down a society because of nothing more than fear."

Cody rolled his eyes. Since the spring quarter had begun, the professor had little control of the class. Days that were earmarked for lectures often became all-out debates, typically on topics involving war or terrorism or the rights of Americans to express their dislike of the United States. The professor was a woman who liked to point out that half of Hollywood would've left the country if the wrong president had won the recent election. Nearly every debate was sparked by the guy with the glasses. Peter something. Cody couldn't remember his name.

"How about that, class?" The professor's political viewpoint could swing either way. She sat behind her desk, her hands folded. Outside a chill wind whistled against the windows of the classroom. "Anyone have a differing viewpoint?"

Cody preferred to think about Bailey, about finding a way to connect with her again. He didn't want the task of facing off with the radical kid in his class, but someone had to do it. He hadn't gone to Iraq and lost his leg so that he could take a backseat when his country's freedom was being discussed. "I was one of those guys who enlisted in the army after high school."

A hush fell over the class. Across the room, Peter slowly took his seat, one eyebrow raised suspiciously in Cody's direction. The professor nodded. "Go on, Cody."

"I enlisted because I believe in the United States of America, in her freedoms for all people, and in her strength as a nation of peace, prosperity, and human dignity." His voice took on a strength that built as he continued. "I enlisted because I was then, and I am now, willing to risk my life to defend this nation. Because this country will fall into enemy hands if our generation is not willing to take a stand."

"Rhetoric," Peter mumbled under his breath.

"No." Cody's voice sharpened. He stood and took a step toward his fellow classmate. "Not rhetoric. The battle for freedom is real, one that requires people to act on what's right."

"War in Iraq?" The kid didn't seem as sure of himself as before. "That's what you think is right?"

"No war is right, but sometimes ..." Cody shifted to take some of the pressure off his prosthetic leg. "Sometimes war is necessary. In order to defend the privileges and freedoms we have as Americans."

He paused, not sure if he should go on. Finally he decided he'd said enough, but even as he lowered himself to his seat, a few guys at the far end of the classroom stood and began to clap. A girl and another guy joined them, and then most of the front two rows. Ten seconds passed while one student after another rose to their feet and joined in the applause. Finally only Cody and Peter and the professor remained seated.

The outpouring was more than Cody had imagined, and it touched him deeply. Even so, by the time the class was over, Cody felt exhausted, drained from the emotional battle of defending himself and his decision to serve. He was finished with his classes for the day, and he needed fresh air to clear his head. Snow still clung to the ground in patches, but the grass showed through along the campus mall. He took the long way around, purposefully walking past the football stadium and the practice field. A group of guys dressed in sweats were throwing the ball, working with a couple of coaches near the fifty yardline.

Cody stopped and watched.

Wasn't it just yesterday that he'd been the guy throwing the ball? Before Iraq, before he lost his leg? Back then he and Bailey had been more like brother and sister, and he'd known for sure he'd play football at the college level somewhere. But the offers didn't come the way Cody had imagined, and with his home life a mess, enlisting seemed like the best option. It still seemed that way.

While he was in Iraq his existence had centered around surviving one day to the next. But now that he was home ... his ideas about the future had shifted with every quarter. He'd thought about being a doctor, and then maybe a firefighter or a paramedic—if they'd take him with his prosthetic lower leg. He even considered going into law so he could help defend freedom in a different way.

But standing here facing the football field, he felt a certain familiarity, one that had filled him and consumed him more often lately. He wanted to be a football coach. Like Jim Flanigan, he wanted to spend his days around the game he loved, influencing kids so that a generation of young men would grow up understanding sacrifice, hard work, and dedication. The sorts of things that came through in the game of football.

Yes, that's what he wanted to do. He would teach high school history and coach football, and he would pray to be an influence for generations of kids like himself. Kids drawn to drinking and partying, kids with little or no family influence who would be lost without the coaches and role models in their lives.

His vision blurred and he could almost see himself working with the quarterbacks and receivers, teaching them how to look for the open man and throw a ball downfield.

Teaching them about life.

He kept walking and as he turned away from the football field, another image came to mind. The face of Bailey Flanigan. She had to be part of this future too. But she was still dating Tim, still barely returning his text messages, and rarely answering his calls. She had a wall up around her heart, and he didn't know how to tear it down. If he could convince her to trust him again, then he could figure out her relationship with Tim, whether she was really in love with him. A thought that terrified him.

He kept his eyes down as he walked the path to the parking lot and found his car. He needed time away from campus, away from his constant search for Bailey between classes. He had a new job at the grocery store in Clear Creek, bagging food and helping people out to their cars. It paid more than the last one and helped him keep up his end of the rent. But today he had four hours before his shift, so he took the turn to Lake Monroe.

The leaves were just starting to bud out on the trees that lined the two-lane highway. Spring wanted a chance, if only the cold temperatures would let up. He reached the water and parked in his favorite lot, the one near the footpath that circled the lake. For five minutes he walked hard and fast over the trail, ignoring the pain in his leg, until he reached an outcropping of rock, a place where he'd come before to think and talk to God. He walked out onto it and sat down on a smooth, flat area. A breeze blew across the water and stung at his eyes, but he didn't care.

God, I have so many questions. So many unknowns about tomorrow. He squinted against the wind and lifted his eyes to the clear blue beyond the lake. *Your Word says You have great plans for me, to give me a future and hope and not to harm me. But how do I know which way to turn?*

My son, do not be troubled ... Do not be afraid ...

The words whispered to him in the rustling of tree branches on either side of the rocky point. As if God were indeed here with him, holding him up and encouraging him.

Sometimes he wanted a new start, a new university a thousand miles away from Bailey and his life in Bloomington. A place where people wouldn't know him as the GI who came home without his lower left leg. Where he wouldn't have to look for Bailey every time he walked out of class. But then, he'd only miss her more.

She belongs to someone else, God. Why can't I get her out of my head?

Wait on me, my son. Remember the fruits of the Spirit.

Cody closed his eyes and the words came back to him, words Jenny Flanigan had drilled into the minds of her kids, including him when he lived with them. *Love, joy, peace, patience, goodness, kindness, gentleness, thoughtfulness, and self control.* "If you truly seek God's plans for your life," she would tell them every day or so, "then your life will show fruit." And she'd go into the list again. *Love, joy, peace ...*

Patience was one of the fruits, but Cody was tired of being patient. He had a few friends, guys he'd played football with at Clear Creek High, but most of the old team was into heavy partying now. He'd rather stay home and study. But today—today he wanted the friendship of Bailey and her family so intensely he could feel the ache with every breath.

Show me, God. I want to be her friend. I can't lose her now.

Again the fruits of the spirit flashed in his mind. *Love and joy, peace and patience, goodness and kindness* ... Maybe that was it. If he was going to show those fruits to the world, then he needed to stop avoiding the Flanigans. He'd turned his back on the family as surely as he'd turned his back on Bailey. Regret surrounded him. Ricky's tests had shown he didn't need another open heart surgery. Not yet. But he might someday soon. How could Cody justify staying away when tomorrow wasn't guaranteed to any of them?

He stood and breathed in deeply. God was here with him; Cody could feel His presence. And at least now he had a plan. Bailey could be busy with Tim, but that didn't mean he had to stay away from her family.

They were his family, too, and they always would be.

He walked with determination back to his car and made just one stop on the way out to the Flanigans'—his mother's house. He parked out front and stood on the porch, knocking, waiting.

"Mom?" The door was unlocked, and when she didn't answer it he went inside. "You home?" He heard something in the back bedroom, but she still didn't answer. "Mom?"

He'd made a point of spending more time with her—especially since Christmas. Their trip to see *Scrooge* had been sort of a new beginning, but every time he came to see her he had his doubts that maybe she was using drugs again. She was an addict, same as him. That meant the temptation would always be there.

He walked past the kitchen and there on the counter was something that stopped him cold.

A small mirror, and in the stream of light from the window he could see the hint of white dust on it. He didn't want to think so, but the mirror had the distinct look of something someone had used for cocaine. He grabbed hold of it and glanced around the counter for a razor blade—which would pretty much guarantee his suspicions. But there was nothing. He carried the mirror toward the bedroom. "Mom?"

"Yes!" She sounded too cheerful. "I'm in here."

He followed her voice into the bedroom and found her bustling about, making her bed and straightening her pillows. "Sorry." She stopped and put her hands on her hips, breathing deeply. "I didn't hear you. Today's cleaning day."

The last thing he wanted was to ask about the mirror, but he had to. She needed to know that he was watching, checking her behavior. He held it out to her. "I found this on the counter."

She hesitated for half a second. "Oh, that. It goes in my bathroom. I set my perfumes on it." She took it from him. "I was going to spray it with Windex, and I got distracted."

He released it to her and studied her for another half a minute. "I never noticed it before."

"I've had it forever." She hustled the mirror into her bathroom and came back empty handed, brushing her palms against her jeans. "So much to do. The place was a mess."

Cody wanted to believe her. A mirror, in and of itself, was not proof that his mother was doing cocaine or any other drug. But he had reason to wonder. Every other time she'd been released from prison she went back to using. He had prayed this time would be different, and so far he believed it was. But she needed the strength of Christ, same as he did. "You going to church with me this weekend?"

"Of course." She laughed easily. "Church and Sunday school." She'd found one for recovering addicts, and combined with her midweek drug classes, she seemed more grounded than before.

But still Cody worried. "Okay, then." He came to her and kissed her cheek. "I was just driving by. Thought I'd check on you."

"I'm fine, silly, but thanks for stopping." She didn't mention the drugs. Neither of them liked talking about the possibility. "My neighbor Linda invited me for dinner, so I have to get my cleaning done before then. She's a widow, you know. The two of us keep each other company."

Cody hung around another few minutes before leaving. His mother's quick actions and rattling conversation worried him, but he hoped she was telling the truth.

As he left he checked the clock on his dashboard. He still had more than two hours before his work shift, and only one place he really wanted to go.

He pulled into the Flanigans' driveway ten minutes later, parked his car in the familiar place, and walked the length of the covered porch to the front door. Jim met him and the two hugged. "I've stayed away too long," Cody said as he stepped inside.

"Way too long." Jim welcomed him in. "Can you stay for dinner?"

"Maybe this weekend." He looked Jim straight into the eyes. "I miss you guys a lot."

Jenny met up with them in the kitchen. "Cody! I can't believe you're here."

At the sound of his name, the five Flanigan boys hurried into the kitchen and surrounded Cody with pats on the back and challenges for a football game or a square off in a game of 21 on the basketball court. Ricky looked happy and healthy, and a sense of deep gratitude filled Cody's heart.

They played a round of Wii Mario Kart, and when Ricky had soundly beaten all of them, they went out front and played three-on-three on the basketball court. Cody found his place among them as easily as he had the first time he set foot in their home. The Flanigans loved him. No matter how much time passed, they always would.

Not until he was on his way out the door to his work shift did Jenny ask if he'd talked to Bailey. Jenny, more than the others, seemed to understand the feelings Cody had for the only Flanigan daughter.

"She doesn't talk to me much." He smiled, but he could feel the sadness in his eyes. "I made the mistake of ignoring her for a while, trying to give her and Tim space." He made a face. "It backfired, though. Now she doesn't trust me."

Jenny was quiet for a moment. Finally she put her hand on Cody's shoulder and gave him an understanding smile. "I know my daughter, and I know how much she cares for you." She tilted her head, weighing her next words. "Be patient. You and Bailey are young. Don't give up on her friendship just yet."

Her words resonated deep inside his soul. On the way to work, he couldn't get past the theme of the afternoon. *Patience.* He wasn't sure how that would play out in the weeks and months ahead, but he was sure of one thing: if God wanted him to be patient, he would be patient because Bailey was worth the wait.

Even if all he had to look forward to was her friendship.

Sixteen

Andi had kept her conversations with her parents to a minimum. Dad was so busy and her mom had too many questions about whether she was going to church and what she was reading in her Bible and whether she was dating or not. How could she break it to her parents that she hadn't opened her Bible once since Christmas?

But this was the last day of March, her father's birthday, and as she sat in her dorm room alone she suddenly missed him more than she had in a long time. She called him and smiled when he picked up on the first ring. "Daddy!" She wasn't the girl she'd once been, but in this moment she sounded the same, like nothing had changed. "Happy birthday!"

"Andi! Thanks, sweetheart. I wondered if I'd hear from you today."

"Where are you?"

"At home. We've been back and forth to LA almost every week, taking meetings around town, making plans and getting details in place for the next film."

"So it's really going to happen?" Andi felt a thrill run down her spine. "Brandon Paul and the whole deal?"

Her dad laughed. "We're meeting with him and NTM tomorrow."

"What?" Andi was on her feet, pacing the small floor of her dorm room. "I wanna be there! Who's starring opposite him?"

He rattled off a list of NTM stars, girls with years of experience. "It'll be a known name, for sure."

Andi felt the disappointment. She'd read the book *Unlocked* twice, and she loved the storyline. Two brothers—one a high school football star, the other a young autistic boy who couldn't connect with anyone until his brother's friend—involved in musical theater—reached out. With the power of music, the doors of autism were unlocked and a bridge built between the two brothers. "Can I at least read for the part?"

"Honey." There was no budging in her father's voice. "This is an NTM film, with NTM stars. Everyone will be a household name."

"But how do you become a household name if no one gives you a break?" She didn't want to sound whiny, but what good was it for her father to make movies if she didn't at least get a try when it came to casting?

"You wait your turn. And in your case, you finish school first." He lightened his tone. "How's the quarter going?"

"Great. Rehearsals are about to begin for *Robin Hood.*" She was Maid Marian—a bigger part even than her role as Isabelle in *Scrooge*. But Tim hadn't gotten the part of *Robin Hood*. He was one of the merry men instead, so she was working mostly with kids she didn't know. "My grades are good and I'm caught up."

"What about your social life? You told your mom you were sort of seeing someone?" Her dad sounded awkward now, as if he really didn't want to know.

"His name is Taz. He's a film student." She wasn't ready to be fully honest about Taz or her feelings for him. She definitely wasn't going to tell her dad about the student film she was about to shoot. "He's interesting. I like hanging out with him. Nothing serious."

The conversation lasted a little longer, and Andi wished him happy birthday again before hanging up. Only then did she exhale and sink back onto her bed. It was a lot of work, keeping up even this much of a facade for her parents. But she had no choice. If they knew about Taz's strange way of thinking or the role she was about to take in his film, they'd be on the first plane to Indianapolis. They'd probably pull her from school. No need to worry them. She was entitled to explore a little. That's what college was about.

She glanced at Bailey's side of the room and wondered what her friend was doing. It was Friday midday, and that evening in a small classroom on campus Andi would film her first few scenes for Taz. Bailey was probably out with Tim, talking about the book of Romans or sharing a latte at the coffee shop off campus. Later tonight Tim would probably take her to a movie or hang out with her at the Flanigan house. Good and wholesome, her sweet friend Bailey.

Andi wanted more out of life.

She'd thought Cody might be the guy for her. Following his lead would've been one way she could've stayed on the straight and narrow, believing in God and His plans and the same old lines she'd believed all her life. But Cody wasn't interested and she certainly wasn't going to stay in her room alone, reading her Bible.

She finished her homework in two hours and checked the time on her phone. She was supposed to meet Taz and his team in less than an hour. She changed her outfit and slipped into her tightest jeans, a tank top, and a pull-over sweater. The scene called for her to look rebellious, so she darkened her eye makeup and added three extra layers of mascara. Even when she was satisfied with her makeup, she put her cosmetics in a travel bag and slipped them into her backpack. Taz had said to bring them, just in case they needed more.

Her decision to make the film was an easy one, especially after she read the screenplay. Her character was a good girl who only wanted to experience more of life. More than her parents were willing to let her experience. If Andi could relate to any character right now it was the teenaged girl Taz had dreamed up for his student film. If that wasn't enough, Taz had shown her three of his previous student films, and Andi was blown away. The quality and depth of his movie-making was on the level of some of the top independent films around. She was honored to take the role, and Taz had promised her the partial nudity was nothing. A quick shot, necessary for the integrity of the film. Bra and jeans—so hardly any real nudity at all.

"You'd show more skin in a bathing suit," he'd told her.

Andi stared at the mirror. Her father's words came back to her. Wait her turn. Wait for the very chance he held in his hands—the chance to star opposite Brandon Paul. She felt the bitterness of her disappointment. Her own father wasn't willing to help her. Fine.

Details of the night ahead played in her mind. "Tonight's for me," she whispered at her reflection. "I'll show everyone."

What better way than to star in Taz's film. She could make a name for herself and get the recognition she obviously needed. Then maybe it would be her turn. She'd show NTM and the film industry and her father—all at the same time. She wanted to be like the real-life NTM princesses, the girls who snagged all the roles and were idolized by little girls all over the country.

Andi studied her features. She had the looks, right? But NTM stars had been auditioning in Hollywood since they were old enough to walk. Andi? She'd been stuck in the jungles. She felt her determination double. Never mind her late start. College would give her the chance to show the world she was a skilled actress even without the experience.

On her way out the door, Rachel Baugher's journal caught her eye. How long had it been since she'd flipped through the pages of her friend's final words? She hesitated and walked to her dresser. For a long time she stared at Rachel's photo on the front, the same one that hung on her wall. Poor Rachel, who'd never lived long enough to experience life. Andi felt the loss of her friend like she hadn't felt it in months. She opened the spiral-bound book to someplace in the middle and began to read.

"As a camel kneels before his master to have him remove his burden at the end of the day, so kneel each night and let the Master take your burden." The quote was written in Rachel's painstakingly neat printing, surrounded by white space above and below so that the words stuck out on the page. The idea was nice, and a few years ago Andi would've agreed. Kneel before God and He'll take your burdens.

But Andi's burdens were different now. She wanted to be a movie star. Most days she couldn't understand how college was getting her any closer to her goal, with the exception of one thing—the movie she was going to make with Taz. Film projects like that would give her experience and open doors that simple prayer could never open.

Andi was sure of it.

She closed Rachel's journal and set it back down on her dresser. But after a few seconds she slid it to the back of her top drawer, along with the framed photo of her friend. Rachel was gone. Looking at her face each day only confused her. And with the opportunity Taz was giving her, she couldn't afford to feel confused. She shut the drawer and hurried from her dorm out across campus to the theater building.

When she reached the door of the classroom Taz had reserved for the film project, she saw there was dark paper taped across the small window. She smiled. Taz had promised her privacy. She knocked, and he opened the door after only a few seconds. His smile warmed her heart. "You're early."

"In case you needed me." She felt suddenly breathless, excited about what lay ahead. The screenplay was truly cutting edge, relevant and honest. This would be her biggest role yet, and she wanted to prove she was up to the task.

Taz touched his fingers to her cheeks. "I always need you, Andi." His voice was low and smooth, for her alone. "Make no mistake about that." He ushered her into the room where several other people worked to set up the shoot. Two college kids assembled oversized lights near a quasi-set consisting of a bed, a nightstand, and a mirrored dresser. In another corner of the room a student worked on a sound panel, testing a wireless microphone.

Relief washed over Andi. In the back of her mind she hadn't quite dismissed Bailey's warning—that maybe Taz wasn't legitimate, that he was some kind of weirdo, wanting her to strip in a student film. Now Andi could see Bailey would've approved. Nothing shady about the shoot whatsoever.

"You feeling it?" Taz turned to her. He touched his fingers to her shoulders and ran them lightly down the length of her arms.

She felt her cheeks grow hot. She felt his presence like a physical force—if that's what he meant.

He grinned. "The character, I mean? Are you feeling the character?"

Again she relaxed. "Of course. I've studied the script ten times this week."

"Good." He came closer, looking her over. "A little more eyeliner." He walked around her, looking over her outfit. "I'd like to tease out your hair a little. It looks too clean-cut the way it is."

She nodded, quick to agree. "I wasn't sure how to change that."

"I can take care of it." He called to a female student working over a clipboard in another part of the room. "Norma, can you do some touch-up?"

"Of course." The girl gave Taz a flirty smile.

A sense of pride came over Andi as she watched Taz. He wasn't interested in the girl or anyone else. He only had eyes for her.

When Norma was satisfied with Andi's hair and makeup, the two of them returned to the classroom. The lighting guys notified Taz that they were ready and then hung back, lost in their own quiet dialogue. A sound-proof observing area adjoined the room, and Taz ordered the crew into that space. "Places." His voice was confident, methodical. Not a bark like most directors. "Quiet on the set."

Other scenes would be shot on campus in daylight. Two were set to be filmed in a Bloomington diner. But tonight's scenes would be the most intense, where Andi's character was melting down and making choices about leaving home. Andi could relate to the character a little more each day.

"Andi ..." Taz came to her and again touched his fingers to her cheek. His gentle caress sent electricity down her arms and legs. "You ready, love?"

She swallowed. "I am." This was her break. She'd show everyone.

"Okay, take your place."

Andi stood and smoothed the wrinkles in her shirt. She caught her reflection in the mirror and held it for a moment. What was that look in her eyes? Guilt? Anger took the lead in her emotions. Guilt should be the last thing she was feeling. She wasn't doing anything wrong. She blinked and tried to work herself into character .

Only one other student remained in the room where the filming was taking place—the cameraman, already positioned behind the enormous lens.

"Now remember ..." Taz stood a few feet away, his eyes locked on hers. "You've just had a falling out with your mother, and you're sick of her rules, sick of your life. You want to run away." Taz's words were slow and melodic, mesmerizing. "You're angry, trapped, ranting at your fate. But then slowly, gradually, you focus on your image in the mirror. For the first time you see that you're beautiful, and that maybe your body is your ticket out. You could model or act. As you study your reflection, you slowly start to remove your clothes. First the pullover, then the tank top … until all that remains is your bra. Hold that pose until I cut."

Andi knew her lines and her character's motivation. She had read the part too many times to count, wrestling with whether she should do it before realizing she had no choice. These were the stepping stones actresses had to take if they were going to reach the top. Besides, the film was sensual, and the storyline demanded this scene. At least from an artsy point of view.

Taz took a few steps back, "Okay, tell us when you're ready."

Andi thought about the teenaged girl, the struggle she felt against her parents. They couldn't tell her how to live or when to be home. She wanted to make her own rules for once, to be someone of her own creating. She waited as the character came to life inside her, and she gave a nod to the camera.

"Quiet!" Taz held up his hand. "Three, two, one … rolling. Action."

Andi stormed into her room and flopped down on her bed, her arm crooked over her eyes. After a few seconds she sat up, angry, trapped. She exhaled hard and looked around the room, searching for a way out. The corkboard with school photos tacked to it, the simplicity of the bedspread across the foot of her bed. Same old thing, every day. She stood and made a face at the walls around her, at the familiarity of it. Slowly she moved to the window and grabbed the faux windowsill. "I hate this," she seethed through clenched teeth. "I hate it more every day."

Like a caged animal, she paced back to her bed and picked up a notebook on her dresser. A few seconds of staring at it, and she threw it down on the bed. "I want out!" Her words were hard and sharp. She loved this, loved her character.

Then, from the corner of her eye, she caught her reflection in the mirror. Slowly, and with new appreciation, she walked to the mirror and stared at herself. Her expression told the story. This was the first time she'd seen her body as an asset, a tool that might lift her from the doldrums of the life she shared with her parents.

Gradually, sensually, she pulled the sweater over her head and tossed it on the bed. Standing there in just her tank top and jeans, she studied herself once more. She ran her hands over her arms and shoulders, down the lines of her sides and toward her narrow waist. She allowed a smoldering feeling to build inside her, a feeling that came easily. Then slowly she peeled her tank top off and stood there, her chest heaving, her body breathless as she imagined the possibilities. Andi could no longer tell where the character ended and she began. It was like she was truly seeing herself for the first time. She stared at the mirror, waiting.

"Cut." Taz breathed a quick laugh as he came to her side. He touched her arm—awkward since she was still in her bra. "That was amazing. Really, Andi. You're a natural. I have a feeling you won't have time for many more student films. Not with that talent."

His words spoke straight to her heart, to the place her parents had failed to recognize. If Taz saw the talent in her, then Hollywood agents and directors would see it. Taz moved to the bed and handed Andi her clothes. "Get dressed, and let's do it again." His voice spoke straight through her, like a spell over her. "You were brilliant the first time. I can't wait to see what you give me next."

She did the entire scene a second time, and then a third, and with each one Taz grew more thrilled with her performance. Almost as if her acting were exciting him in ways Andi didn't quite understand. When she finished, he had her get dressed a final time, and he told the rest of the crew they could go. They would film the campus scenes next week.

Finally only Andi and Taz remained in the room. "I've been thinking." He gathered his things, keeping an appropriate distance between them. "I might put myself in the film, after all. Toward the end."

At the end of the screenplay, Andi's character met up with a guy from the streets, and the two of them shared a kiss. Nothing more, but still the scene was passionate. She placed her cosmetics into her backpack and faced him, trying to understand what he meant. "You mean … you'd play the guy … ?"

"The guy you kiss." He set his things down so he could approach her unencumbered. "That scene's about chemistry." He took another few steps toward her, until he was so close she could smell the mint on his breath, smell the fresh scent of his shampoo. He lightly touched her chin. "You and I, we have chemistry."

She tried to hide a quick gulp. What was it about him that captured her and rendered her unable to think straight? "We definitely have chemistry."

"Maybe … maybe we should make sure." His smile melted her and he closed the distance between them. He placed his hands tenderly on either side of her face and for the most delicious moment he kissed her—kissed her in a way that made her dizzy. Nothing Andi had experienced had felt anything like this, and she wished he would never pull away.

When Taz pulled back, his eyes smoldered with desire that was beyond intense. "Yeah." His voice was thick and smoky, his fingers still soft against her face. "We have chemistry."

She thought he was going to kiss her again, but he stepped back and grinned at her. "Let's talk between now and next week, okay?"

And with that, the session was over. Taz was a gentleman, walking her back to her dorm and giving her a quick, appropriate hug before saying good night. The kiss hadn't been a come on, any more than the scene in her bra had been some weird act to satisfy Taz's curiosity. He was simply being a filmmaker, testing the waters to see if the chemistry existed. Now the film would be stronger because of it.

She went inside and hurried down the hall to her dorm. Bailey wasn't back, but Andi wasn't surprised. She'd probably spend the weekend at home with her family. Maybe tomorrow Andi would join her. But for now she wanted to be alone so she could replay the night over and over again. So she could picture Taz's reaction to her acting and feel his kiss on her lips one more time. Her guilt from earlier was gone. The partial nudity was nothing, really, and now that part of the film was behind her. No big deal.

As she stepped into the bathroom to wash her face, she was surprised by her reflection. Not the way her hair had been slightly ratted for the scene, or even the heavy makeup around her eyes. But something in her expression. Whatever it was, Andi felt strange and a little frightened by it. Because in that moment she didn't look like Andi Ellison, daughter of missionaries, seeker of Hollywood fame, actress.

She looked like someone she no longer even recognized.

Seventeen

Bailey could hardly wait to get into the city. They'd taken a flight from Indianapolis to La Guardia first thing that morning, and now they were being driven into Manhattan. They had three hours before the eight o'clock showing of *Mary Poppins*.

"I can't believe we're here." She stared out the window and tried to get a glimpse of the New York City skyline. But the car was stuck in traffic just short of the Midtown Tunnel. The view would have to wait.

"You?" Tim had been practically speechless since they landed. "I'm blown away and we haven't even crossed the East River."

"This is always the worst part. Getting through the tunnel." Connor sat on Bailey's other side, and their mother had the front seat next to the driver.

The tunnel was always sort of weird, cars moving at a snail's pace in stop-and-go traffic, but every car crammed in so close. At one point, their car sidled up to a full-sized bus. Bailey stared at it. "That's crazy. If you stick your hand out, you can easily touch the side of that thing."

"I'll keep my window up." Tim laughed. "Let's talk about something else."

"That reminds me …" Bailey's mom handed back a copy of their itinerary. "Here's a list of the shows we're seeing. Your dad was able to connect with friends of his down here. We have the best tickets at each of these shows."

"It's like a dream." Tim looked over the list. "I never thought I'd have a chance to see one of these shows, let alone all of them. It must be nice to live like this."

Tim's comment hit Bailey in a strange way. Most of the time she didn't think about her parents' wealth. Her dad had been an NFL player and now a coach. Her family gave away a lot. She knew because they'd always believed in sharing those details with the kids. But still they clearly had plenty to live on. More than most people could ever imagine. She glanced at the guy she was dating. Tim's mom was a nurse, his dad the manager of a hotel in Bloomington. Of course Tim hadn't been on a trip like this.

But that wasn't what bothered her.

In the last week, Tim had been more attentive than usual, almost overly so. He sometimes sounded like he was in awe of the Flanigan family's money and the fact that they could take a trip like this. Bailey had mentioned it to her mom. "It's kind of weird. I mean, does he like me more now because we can take him on the trip?"

Her mom's answer was wise. "Money can be a problem in relationships, one way or another." She hadn't taken sides beyond that. "I think it's something to watch."

She was right. Tim had known them all this time and never acted so impressed by their means. This was no time to start behaving different because of it. Money was a tool, but Bailey's family didn't need trips like this to have a good time. They had as much fun playing Apples to Apples around the game table on a Saturday night.

Bailey looked over the itinerary, and Tim peered over her shoulder. They were spending all of spring break week there, and in all they would see six Broadway shows.

"This is unbelievable." Tim put his hand on Bailey's mother's shoulder. "This must've cost a fortune."

Bailey's mom looked back and smiled at Tim. "God has provided us with some wonderful times together." She exchanged a quick look with Bailey, a look that said her mom, too, had registered his comment. "I'm sure this'll be one of them." Not only that, but her dad had contacted someone from the Giants, who was friends with a Broadway casting director. "They're auditioning for a number of ensembles this summer. Dad thinks the two of you might get a look."

Bailey forgot her concerns about Tim and squealed at the news. Her mother hadn't said a word about this until now. "Are you serious?"

"Yes. I wanted to wait until it was for sure, and it is. We'll definitely be meeting the guy after the show on Thursday night."

Behind them a taxi driver laid on his horn, and still there was no light at the end of the tunnel. But none of that mattered. They were going to meet a real-life Broadway casting director. Nothing could be better than that.

When the traffic let up enough so that they got through the tunnel, the driver took them on a series of shortcuts through lower Manhattan until finally they were at Broadway and 42nd Avenue at the DoubleTree—the hotel where Bailey and her mom and brother always stayed when they came to New York City. Her mom paid the driver, and in no time they were shooting up the elevator with their luggage, headed for adjoining suites on the twenty-second floor. Both rooms had views of Times Square, and again Tim was beside himself.

"From the first time I took the stage, I've dreamed about this, about standing here over Times Square and seeing real live Broadway theater." He turned to Bailey and took her hand. Connor and their mom were still unpacking, so the two of them were alone in the living room that adjoined the two bedrooms. "Standing here, it's like I can feel our dreams coming true."

Bailey smiled, but even here on the brink of an amazing week in New York City his words fell a little flat, and she wasn't sure why. This was her dream, right? To sing and dance in a Broadway show, and to live in New York with Tim somewhere nearby. That was the dream, wasn't it? She imagined the two of them heading off for call time each night, working hard for the director and bringing audiences to their feet every performance. Of course it was the dream. There was nothing she wanted to do more than be here, performing in front of a live audience nine times a week.

Her mom and Connor finally finished getting ready, and the four of them headed down to the street level and grabbed a quick salad across the street. Afterwards, they walked a few blocks to the New Amsterdam Theater, where *Mary Poppins* had been playing for more than a year. Bailey and her mom and brother had seen it already and been blown away. She could hardly wait for Tim's reaction.

They filed into the theater, and when the lights went down and the stage came to life, she could feel Tim hanging on every word, moving forward in his seat as if he wanted to be closer to the action so he wouldn't miss a single line. Bailey smiled to herself. How great that Tim understood her passion for theater. It was something they would always share, something she couldn't share with her dad or a guy like Cody. She redirected her thoughts and leaned in close to Tim. "What do you think?"

"I'm blown away." Tim reached for her hand, but he didn't work his fingers between hers. Rather he held it sort of loosely, the way her dad might.

The sentiment was something he shared again and again that week, even while Bailey continued to feel a strange disconnect. The show performances were still unbelievable, but the rest of New York City had somehow lost a little luster since the last time they were here. She caught herself noticing the dank smell of urine and trash that lingered around the city streets, and the constant stream of honking cabs and aggressive drivers made her long for Bloomington. Even the towering buildings didn't seem as awe inspiring, but rather like walls keeping out the sky, closing in on her.

Bailey didn't tell anyone about her feelings. *This is crazy, God. I'm grateful to be here.* But in lieu of a response she only noticed other details that chipped away at her longtime belief—that this was where she wanted to live.

The highlight was a stop at Ground Zero where the Twin Towers once stood. They visited St. Paul's Chapel, and Bailey explained to Tim that Ashley's husband, Landon, had been one of the firefighters who sifted rubble and remains after the collapse of the towers. Landon still had a strange cough because of his time at Ground Zero.

"It's still hard to believe." Their mom pulled Bailey and Connor close as they studied a timeline of photos tacked to a chain-link fence surrounding the site. "I mean, no one dreamed anything like that would ever happen."

Bailey suddenly remembered a long-ago conversation she'd had with Cody about the terrorist attacks. *"If I have anything to do with it, that'll never happen again. Not ever."*

Cody had made good on his word, a fact that made Bailey proud of him still.

On another day, the group of them walked to Central Park, but again the reality fell short of Bailey's recent memories. Instead of seeing the park as living and vibrant, an oasis in the middle of the city, she noticed the vacant-eyed faces of the people on the park benches and the dirty, stagnant look of the lake.

"This lake is so famous! It's been in more movies than most actors." Tim was constantly thrilled wherever they went.

Finally it was Thursday and they attended the evening performance of *West Side Story*. The singing and dancing were enough to take Bailey's breath, and she could tell that beside her Tim felt the same way. That and the fact that they could hardly wait for the show to be over because this was where they would meet the casting director.

"Come on." Their mom led the way when the show ended. "This way to the stage door. Our names will be on a list."

A young woman at the door checked off their names and led them down a hallway to an elevator. "One floor up takes you to the wings."

Bailey could hardly contain herself. The wings? Of an actual Broadway theater.

But when they stepped off the elevator Bailey was surprised. The area was smaller than she imagined. Still, the buzz of people around them was both familiar and exhilarating. Actors turned in costumes and props, while others took off makeup in front of a long row of mirrors, or yelled out good-byes as they headed out.

A thin man with a beret and an unforgettable smile approached them, his brow raised. "Flanigans?"

"Yes." Bailey's mom stepped forward and held out her hand. "I'm Jenny." She turned and pointed to the rest of them. "These are my kids, Bailey and Connor, and our friend, Tim Reed. Bailey and Tim are in theater at Indiana University."

"Very nice. I'm Sebastian." The man nodded, politely sizing up Bailey and then Tim. "I hear good things about their musical theater department."

"We were also part of Christian Kids Theater in Bloomington. We've been doing musicals for years." Bailey held out her hand and shook Sebastian's, and Tim did the same. "Our CKT is run by Katy Hart Matthews; you might have heard about it."

The man angled his head and gave an impressive nod. "I have indeed. She's the actress who married Dayne Matthews. I read a write-up on your theater group in *People* once."

"That's us." Tim grinned.

"Tell you what." Sebastian gestured to the stage wings. "Let's give you a tour."

Sebastian clearly loved his job. He was greeted by various cast members as they moved their way along the narrow passage behind the stage toward the sets area and the different dressing rooms.

Tim whispered as they walked, "Weird how the props bring a scene to life from the stage, but back here …"

"Plain and ordinary."

"Definitely," Connor chimed in. "Also, the wings are smaller than the Bloomington Community Theater."

"Definitely smaller." Bailey whispered. She felt like Dorothy, seeing the Wizard for what he really was. Almost like it would've been better to skip the backstage and keep the magic.

Sebastian was going on about the stage being slightly slanted forward so that the audience could see everyone in the back row. "Come out and stand on it." He moved onto the wooden stage, and the rest of them followed.

"Wow." Connor bent his knees a little and found his balance. "It's more slanted than I thought."

"The cast gets used to it." Sebastian laughed. "But it takes awhile."

Bailey tried to imagine dancing in character shoes on the angled floor. No question it would be harder than it looked from the audience. Tim stood a little ahead of her, his eyes shining with excitement. He looked so caught up in the thrill of standing here that he'd forgotten she was a few feet away.

When they were finished with the tour, Sebastian took down names and contact information for Bailey and Tim, and gave Jenny his number. "We'll have open auditions in late June," he smiled. "Contact me before that and I'll get you in. You won't have to wait in line with the rest of the cattle." He laughed at his own joke. "The line can wrap around the block before ten in the morning."

Bailey felt her head spin as she tried to picture the audition. A line of actors wrapping around the building? "How many spots will you fill?"

"Two, maybe three." Sebastian made a face. "It's tough competition. We'll see a thousand dancers looking for one of those spots."

Dancers. He'd called them dancers because ensemble actors danced and provided a visual and vocal backdrop. Nothing more. Even still, the audition would be the chance of a lifetime. Especially now, before either of them actually graduated.

Jenny asked about the contract length for those who were chosen from the audition.

"Six months to a year. Depends on the dancer's schedule, and how much we like them."

Bailey knew what her mom was thinking. If they auditioned that summer, and if by some act of God they were chosen for the cast, they'd miss at least the first quarter of the next school year. Her mom looked concerned about the possibility.

When the meeting with Sebastian was over, they walked to Ellen's Stardust Diner at 51st and Broadway, in the heart of Times Square. The place was a fifties-style hamburger joint with homemade malts and the smell of fresh french fries cooking in the back. The best part was how the wait staff sang while they worked. The music to one favorite hit song after another filled the place as the waiters took turns belting out the lyrics.

They found a table near the middle of the room and were just opening their menus when one of the waiters walked by singing "Love Me Tender." The guy had dark hair and striking looks, and his voice was incredibly trained. Tim leaned in toward the others. "What's he doing here? He should be down the street at one of the theaters."

Jenny nodded. "He was. He played Danny's understudy in *Grease* last year when we were here. This is where a lot of them work between shows."

"Except him." Connor pointed to a tall, curly-haired guy flirting with a table of teenage girls. "He can sing like crazy, but he's been here every time we've come."

Bailey watched the guy and wondered about him. They'd talked to him last time they were here. He explained that he made pretty good money, enough to survive. "And I'm doing what I love. Singing on Broadway."

The thought made Bailey shudder then and now. It was one thing to perform on a stage at a famous theater in town, but to perform while serving burgers and fries? There had to be another way to stay involved with theater—teaching with Katy at CKT back home, maybe. She would never want to live here that badly.

"You know?" Tim grinned at them. "This is the first place I'll apply when I move here. If I never get a part, this would be great."

Bailey glanced at him and then lowered her gaze to her menu. Tim's comment confused her. Her main attraction to him had always been the number of views they'd shared in common. But now … Was this really how he saw his future? Here in New York City no matter what? Even if it meant waiting tables for years after he got a degree? Bailey couldn't imagine living here more than a few years. After that she'd want a place like Bloomington, where she could marry and raise a family.

They were halfway back to the hotel when her phone vibrated in her coat pocket. She checked it and her heart skipped a beat. It was a text from Cody.

JUST THINKING ABOUT YOU. YOU STILL IN NEW YORK?

His message lifted her spirits more than anything all night. She thought about not texting him back, especially because she was with Tim. Or was she? She looked at him, again walking a little ahead of her, taking in the barrage of sights and sounds and barely aware of her. He wouldn't notice if she turned and walked the other way, let alone if she texted Cody back. She kept up with her mom and Connor and turned her attention to her phone.

YES. BUT IT'S NOT LIKE I REMEMBER IT. I'D RATHER BE THERE WITH YOU.

She sent the text and then felt her cheeks grow hot. There were a couple of ways he could take her message. She meant she'd rather not be in New York City at the moment. Not that she'd literally rather be with Cody. Right? She pushed back her guilt and lowered her phone to her side just as another text came in.

LET'S HANG OUT WHEN YOU GET BACK. I MISS YOU. I STILL WANT TO TALK.

Her mom slowed her pace a little so she was right next to Bailey. "Who're you texting?"

Another wave of guilt washed over her. Tim was still up ahead, talking to Connor. Even so, Bailey spoke barely loud enough for her mom to hear. "Cody."

Her mom didn't ask anything else. She only gave an understanding nod and slipped her arm around Bailey's shoulders, and the two of them kept walking.

Bailey thought about Cody's invitation. If she texted him back, he'd for sure think she meant she'd rather be with him. She pictured him, his phone in his hands, thinking about her and in as much time as it took her heart to skip a beat she knew exactly what she'd meant by her text. She swallowed hard. Again she lifted her phone so she could see it and she texted him one more time.

I'D LIKE THAT. I MISS YOU TOO.

She sent it before she could change her mind. Then she slipped her phone back in her purse. This was wrong, texting Cody while she was with Tim, and she ordered herself not to text him again tonight. But she felt lighthearted and giddy, unaware of the city sounds around her. Her guilt didn't come close to the thrill of what those few texts meant to her. Suddenly she couldn't wait for what lay ahead for her. Something she never thought would happen again.

The chance to hang out with Cody one more time.

Eighteen

The NTM meeting had been postponed five times, and now at the end of April they were finally being ushered down an impressive hallway to the office of Ace L. Rustin, VP in charge of theatrical development for the studio. Keith tried to maintain a calm exterior, but everything about the afternoon had been surreal—from the private parking that had been arranged for them ahead of time to the walk down the studio's Brandon Paul Avenue to the framed posters of one hit movie after another. All that and the actual meeting hadn't even started yet.

A secretary held open a door and led them into a boardroom with a table longer than any Keith had ever seen. *Give us peace, God. You opened this door. Let us walk through with Your confidence.* He felt himself relax a little.

Besides him, their group was made up of Chase, Kendall, Stephanie Fitzgerald, and Luke Baxter, the lawyer Dayne Matthews had suggested. The five of them took seats across from each other at the front end of the table.

"I can't believe we're here." Chase folded his hands and kept his voice to a whisper.

"Don't talk like that." Stephanie wagged a finger at him, chastising him even while her eyes sparkled. "God did this. You're a child of the King!"

Keith wanted to add his own disbelief. This was NTM Studios, which meant he and Chase were doing well to breathe, let alone sit upright. But he kept his comments to himself. It was important that they stay on their game. NTM executives would certainly be on theirs.

In fact, a detail bothered Keith—a detail he hadn't mentioned to anyone but Chase, and even then only in passing. The series of delays with NTM had raised red flags in Keith's mind. Not once had they expressed hesitation or uncertainty about meeting Keith and Chase.

"If Brandon's interested, we're interested," Ace had told Luke Baxter. "It's merely a matter of getting our schedules lined up."

If Luke had doubts, he hadn't said anything. But for Keith the whole set-up seemed a little too easy. NTM didn't need him and Chase. They had Brandon contracted for at least one more movie deal. It would be easier and more cost effective for them to find a fresh screenplay written by one of the writers in the NTM stable. In every possible way, it would be wiser for NTM to find a way around the producers, to convince Brandon to take another project, one where there were no authors or outside producers to slice up the pie with.

The door opened and Ace L. Rustin strode in. Keith had heard about the man, how he carried an aura that left people ready to agree with him. Now Keith would have to say his contacts had downplayed the reality. Ace was tailed by two assistants, men with clipboards and notebooks. They took seats on the far side of Keith and their group, while Ace moved to the head of the table.

He leaned forward and shook their hands, looking each member of their group in the eyes. Then he sat down and grinned. "Looks like we've got a lot to talk about."

"We do." Luke had a proposal in his notebook. He didn't bring it out just yet. "We have a project we want to develop, as you know."

"And Brandon wants nothing more than to star in it." Ace nodded confidently. "I'm well aware of the situation and excited to get things going." He raised his hands and let them drop back to the table. "I mean, how often does Stephanie Fitzgerald walk into your studio looking to make a movie deal?" He laughed a little too hard, a little too easily. He looked at the author. "How'd you hear about Brandon?"

"We're friends. Met on a set a while ago. Last thing I expected." Stephanie chuckled and launched into the story. Keith had heard the short version, but this time Steph drew out the details. The end result was a situation that felt nothing short of a miracle. Even to the typically jaded NTM folks.

The connection started when Stephanie was on the set of the first movie made of one of her novels. She was sitting on the tailgate of an electrical grip truck one evening, watching the crew film a scene in the driveway of the set house when she got a text from Brandon. "I like texting same as the next girl." Stephanie laughed again. "He'd already contacted me a few weeks before that and told me he loved my books. Now he was just saying hi."

I'M ON THE SET OF MY MOVIE, she texted back. THIS STUFF IS HARDER THAN IT LOOKS. MAKES ME APPRECIATE YOUR LIFE.

HEY, he responded, SOMEONE NEEDS TO MAKE *UNLOCKED* INTO A MOVIE.

"I remember smiling, because here was Brandon Paul knowing my books like they were his own." Stephanie enjoyed herself, telling the story for all it was worth. "I texted him that there was in fact a lot of interest in making *Unlocked* into a movie. His next message came almost immediately."

WHAT??? JUST REMEMBER THIS. I WANT TO STAR IN IT.

"I looked at that text and sort of shook my head. *Crazy kid*, I told myself. He probably had his future tied up to a dozen movies without starting in one of mine. But the next day Brandon's agent calls." She laughed. "Turns out he was serious. More than anything he wants to be in *Unlocked*."

Ace listened, smiling politely, engaged by the story. He looked at Keith. "Sorry, now ... How did you and Chase get involved?"

This was what Keith had feared. It was one thing that Brandon wanted to star in a movie based on a bestselling novel. But the fact that the novel was already optioned by a couple of no-name producers? What major studio would want a part of that scenario?

Chase cleared his throat. "We were contacted several months ago by Ben Adams and his daughter, Kendall." The two didn't need introducing in Hollywood. "We were told by Kendall that Stephanie wanted us to produce *Unlocked*."

"This was before Brandon came on the scene." Stephanie grinned at Chase and then Keith. "These two guys have talent and integrity beyond anything I've seen in the business. If *Unlocked* is going to be made, I want them to make it."

"I see." Ace nodded slowly, the smile still tugging at his lips. He sat taller in his seat and lay his hands palm down on the table. "So here we are. All the pieces in place."

"Right." Stephanie looked pleased with herself.

"And you'll be wanting control?" Ace looked at Chase, and then Keith. "Is that why Ben is involved?" Ace asked the question as if it was obvious Keith and Chase didn't have the money for a Brandon Paul movie.

"Yes." Kendall took the lead this time. "My dad is one of our primary investors. Because of him, we're prepared to provide half the money up front."

Luke was the only person in the room who appeared less than enthusiastic. "My clients will want creative control and a back-end deal."

"Very good." Ace allowed a slow nod and studied his notebook. When he looked up, he smiled at the group. "Well, it's pretty simple, then, straightforward. You need to produce a script everyone can sign off on—Brandon, his agent, and our team here at NTM. Then we set a date for filming and line up locations and cast. I have a few NTM actresses who would be perfect opposite Brandon. Something to think about, anyway."

"I like that." Kendall nodded at Ace and then the others. "Let's talk about which girls you have in mind."

"Great." Ace pushed back from the table. "Thank you for meeting with us." He shook hands with everyone at the table again and directed his final comments to Keith. "I'll shoot you an e-mail with some of our A-list screenwriters. I'm assuming you'll have the budget to float that until we have the okay from all parties."

Keith tried not to gulp. An A-list screenwriter would want half a million dollars to write a screenplay for a movie with Brandon Paul. The preliminary screenplay had been written by a friend of Keith's, a writer whose price tag wasn't even a tenth of that. They could talk about this detail later. Keith smiled, unwavering confidence and nerves of steel. "We're prepared for that, yes."

"Good." Ace moved to the door ahead of them. "Let's try to have a screenplay before summer. That way we can meet again and make some decisions." He waved. "Thanks again. My secretary will show you out." His two assistants stood and followed him, and like that he was gone.

Keith didn't want to comment on the meeting yet. They needed a place outside NTM's studio lot where they could talk about what had happened, and the fears tugging at him. "I'd like to meet." He looked around the room and his eyes settled on Luke's. "Not here, of course."

"There's a Starbucks down the street. Outdoor tables. Let's meet in ten."

When they were all there, Keith got right to the point. "I have a funny feeling about this."

"Why?" Chase had ordered a vanilla frappuccino and was fitting his straw through the lid. "That's the easiest meeting I've ever sat through."

"Too easy." Luke raised an eyebrow at Chase. "Your friend's right. I get the feeling NTM is stringing us along, keeping us happy so we don't take the project across town to another studio. In the meantime, I have to believe someone in creative is working on a competing project, something where NTM would write and produce the film and Brandon would be just as happy with the storyline. Why in the world would they be content to give up half their profits or half the control?"

Keith was glad their attorney was tracking with him. Chase's smile fell away and he set his drink down. "Brandon wants to do *Unlocked*. That's what matters."

"Not really." Luke frowned. "NTM has one more film with Brandon unless he renews his contract. As far as NTM is concerned, they can put him in an NTM original screenplay and force him to wait a few years before doing *Unlocked*. There's simply no financial incentive in teaming up with us."

"Other than the obvious." Kendall looked indignant. She was sitting next to Chase and she looked to him for support. "The film's going to be a huge hit. It camped out at number one on the *New York Times* list for six weeks. That has to count for something."

"She's right." Chase shrugged. "They have nothing without the book."

Luke anchored his elbows on the table. "Ace Rustin has played these games with me before. I won't let him throw us under the bus. But I can only control so much." He pulled out a sheet of notes. "Here's what we need to do." He glanced at the paper in front of him and explained his strategy.

First, they needed a signed contract from NTM stating they were—in good faith—interested in proceeding with the project. Chase and Keith couldn't spend half a million dollars on a screenplay without a commitment in writing from the studio. Second, they needed Brandon Paul and his agent to talk with Ace and the team at NTM. "There needs to be no misunderstanding that *Unlocked* is the only film Brandon's interested in doing."

They discussed other options, but at the end of the brief wrap-up, Luke gave them what seemed like the straightforward truth. "There's a risk here that NTM will steal the idea and run with it. No, it wouldn't be a movie based on the bestselling novel. But it would be a movie starring Brandon Paul. Honestly, that's enough. They could even offer *him* a back-end deal, or convince his agent that he'll make less money if he stars in *Unlocked* over something the studio comes up with."

Keith felt dizzy. They'd landed at the top of this strange Hollywood world, and now their attorney was telling them, basically, that they could be knocked back to the bottom with little recourse. Luke promised to work on it some more tomorrow and then he was on his way, headed back home to Indiana. The rest of them were still talking when Keith's phone rang. It was Lisa, and just seeing her name brought Keith a relief he hadn't felt all day.

He gave her a quick synopsis of the meeting and the concerns he and their attorney were feeling.

"I have another concern for you." Lisa's tone grew heavier than he'd heard it in a long time. "It's Kelly. She isn't doing well."

"How do you know?"

"She hasn't been to Bible study in four weeks, and every time I see her she makes some excuse about why she can't get together or talk. Even her friend Laurie hasn't gotten anywhere with her."

Keith hated this, hated the way nothing they did was easy. "What do you think's the problem?"

"Honestly? I think she's depressed. She hasn't been doing her hair or taking care of herself. It seems like she's withdrawing from everyone." Lisa hesitated. "Chase must know something's wrong."

"He's aware of it, but we're busy all the time. It's easy to forget the trouble back home." Keith massaged his brow. "We can't lose this movie deal with Brandon Paul."

"Well, he better start remembering Kelly." She sounded more worried than frustrated. "Otherwise he'll lose more than a movie deal."

"That bad?" Keith glanced over his shoulder at his friend. He was sitting next to Kendall, the two of them lost in some conversation that involved Stephanie and seemed to shut out the rest of the world.

"Yes. Talk to him, please. Maybe she needs counseling or medication. Something."

"I think she still worries about whether we can really make a living doing films."

"Of course she does. We all do." The calm was back in Lisa's voice. "It's just maybe Kelly worries more than the rest of us. She's taking care of two little girls by herself, living on a budget that's barely realistic."

Keith knew. He was worried about the movie situation too—both *The Last Letter* and *Unlocked*. But he'd walked by faith before, and he wouldn't stop now.

As he hung up with Lisa, he closed his eyes and lifted a silent prayer on behalf of Kelly Ryan. *She needs You, God. She needs a touch from You, a reminder. Because all of us need to walk by faith. It's just a matter of remembering that on a daily basis. So help her remember. In Jesus' name, amen.*

He returned to the table and the discussion, which was about supporting cast for *Unlocked*. He would pray with Chase later on—about the movie and the challenge of working with NTM, and about his home life.

Because if that fell apart, the rest would too.

Nineteen

KELLY WAS SICK AND TIRED OF feeling sick and tired. She was doing it to herself, she knew that, and still she couldn't stop. For the past ten years, every time she'd hit a low like this she could muscle her emotions around and order herself to get in line again. God would meet her in the moment and she'd wake up one morning with the strength to carry on, to right her ship before the whole thing capsized.

But none of that was true now.

She was sinking fast, taking on water at an alarming rate without any ability to find that fresh day, that new morning when she'd turn things around. She'd prayed, of course. Maybe not as often as she should have, but she prayed. And today she was doing something she should've done a month ago. She was meeting with Laurie. Four times she'd cancelled, but today was Friday and Kelly had the feeling that if she didn't meet with her friend, the weekend would be terrible. She'd slip into an even darker place, one that maybe she'd never find her way free of.

Laurie arrived after lunch, and the two hugged for a long time. "You're not okay, are you?" She searched Kelly's eyes.

"No. I'm not." She wasn't ready to admit her obsessive overeating—not that she needed to say anything. None of her old clothes fit at this point. The trouble was obvious to anyone looking. "I feel dead."

Laurie squeezed her hand and the two of them made iced tea in the kitchen. Spring was finally in the air after a long and mostly gloomy winter. Now it was late April and temperatures were already pushing eighty. Molly and Macy were practically desperate to get outside and try Molly's new bicycle, the one she'd gotten for her birthday. They'd waited until Chase was home for her to open it—partly because he'd needed to assemble it and partly because it made everyone feel like he hadn't missed Molly's birthday. But he'd missed it. Kelly was still frustrated about the fact.

They took their drinks outside to the small front porch. Macy laid a blanket out on the front yard, where she and her pink baby doll sat side by side. "Ready, Molly. Show me how!"

"'Kay, watch me!" Molly had walked her bike down to the driveway next door and now she was making her way toward them. The bike had training wheels, but they were adjusted high on the bike to give Molly as much a feel of a real ride as possible.

"The girls seem well." Laurie sat in the chair farthest from the sidewalk—in case Kelly needed to get to the girls quickly.

"They are." Kelly shrugged, hating the feeling strangling her heart. "They're doing great, completely unconcerned." She positioned her chair so the sun was on her face, and she slipped on a pair of sunglasses. "I guess this is our normal now."

"Life has a way of doing that, giving us a new normal just when we thought we had things all figured out." Laurie smiled. "The key to life isn't looking for a safe sameness with every passing season. It's learning to enjoy the ride, whatever the next turn in the road might bring. Believing that God's driving, and He'll get us home safely—however bumpy the trip."

Kelly played her friend's words over in her head again. "Hmmm. Sounds nice."

"Because it's true." Laurie took a drink of her iced tea. "Sometimes … it isn't the circumstances, but us." She winced a little. "Know what I mean?"

Of course she did. Kelly managed a sad laugh. "It's definitely me this time. I'm eating all wrong, and telling myself the wrong things about my marriage. I haven't jogged or walked or done a sit-up in months. I can barely get out of bed. Every night I promise myself it'll be different tomorrow, but morning comes and it's the same old routine." Her voice cracked and she had to swallow a few times. "I can't see my way out."

"Have you talked to Chase?"

"He's in his own world. He doesn't know what it takes to run things all alone. Besides, he doesn't want to be bogged down with my troubles."

Molly was riding faster now. She was coming from the right, picking up speed and waving as she rode. "Hi, Mommy! Look!"

"That's great, sweetie. Thataway! We'll have those training wheels off in no time." Kelly could turn on her enthusiasm for the girls. Very few people knew that she was dying inside, and even here with Laurie, she didn't want to be entirely honest.

"My turn." Macy stood, her doll forgotten. She watched her sister ride past and then turn around. This time as Molly blazed down the sidewalk toward them, Macy ran out and used her body to create a roadblock. With her legs spread, arms out, she shouted at Molly. "Stop, now! My turn!"

But as good as Molly was at picking up speed, she had far less practice at stopping. "Macy! Move!"

Kelly saw the accident coming. "Macy!"

Her younger daughter looked toward the front porch just as Molly lost control of her bike. Rather than plow straight into her sister, Molly jerked the handlebars to the left and flipped her bike on top of herself. A shrill scream followed, the kind that told everyone something was seriously wrong. Macy knew instantly that the crash was her fault. She covered her mouth with both hands and gasped loud enough for all of them to hear—even above Molly's cries. "Molly ... sorry! Sorry, Molly."

Kelly and Laurie were both on their feet running toward Molly, but Kelly reached her first. With a strength she wasn't feeling, she lifted the bike from her daughter's crumpled body and tossed it on the grass. "Molly, baby! Are you okay?"

Molly rolled onto her back and some of her injuries were immediately transparent. She had a scraped cheek and a cut on her forearm.

"Her arm doesn't look right." Laurie pointed to Molly's right forearm. "See there, how it's at an angle?"

Kelly didn't have to look very hard. No question Molly's arm bone was positioned in a way that was grotesquely abnormal. Macy started crying, her hands still over her mouth. "Sorry, Molly!"

Molly's screams quieted, but she was still crying hard, her sobs shaking her small frame. "M-m-my arm!" She held out the word *arm*, letting it fill the air like a desperate plea. "It hur-r-r-ts!"

Kelly didn't have to ask Laurie if she thought her daughter's arm was broken. But Kelly wasn't sure what to do next—whether to take Molly inside or try to wrap the arm, and how she was going to calm down Macy in the meantime. Her breathing came faster, and pain gripped her chest. *Get a grip, Kelly.* But even as she ordered herself, she felt a layer of sweat building on her forehead. Why couldn't she breathe? Panic raced through her, flooding her veins.

"Kelly?" Laurie looked hard at her. "You're okay. Breathe out."

"I . . . I can't."

"My arrrmmm!" Molly's sobs were growing loud again. "Mommy, make it stop!"

"Sorry, Molly!" Macy paced a few steps in either direction, her hands over her face.

She couldn't do this, couldn't handle it. Not another minute. "No." Kelly shook her head at Laurie. "I . . . I can't . . . breathe."

"You can." Laurie remained calm. She stared straight into Kelly's eyes and put a hand on her shoulder. "Exhale."

Another series of gasps and Kelly felt herself getting dizzy, losing consciousness. "I … can't."

Laurie rubbed her hand along Kelly's back. "Breathe out. You're going to be fine. Come on. Purse your lips and push out the air." Laurie paused. "Dear Lord, we need You here. Please, give Kelly peace. Help her breathe."

Kelly did as she was told. She exhaled through pursed lips. At first only a small amount of air slipped through, but gradually, with each breath, she felt herself grow calmer. The whole time Laurie prayed, Molly waited for someone to help her, and Macy cried out her apologies.

With her breathing more normal, the panic subsided enough that Kelly could kneel by Molly and stroke her hair. "It's okay, baby. It'll be okay."

Laurie was the first one with a plan. "Why don't you take her to Emergency. I'll stay here with Macy."

The idea was the only one that made sense. Kelly tried to concentrate, but lately her mind had been a jumble of emotions that couldn't be captured or tamed. Life happened pretty much in a fog around her.

She ran inside, grabbed a spray bottle of hydrogen peroxide and some cotton pads and hurried back to Molly, still lying on the ground crying. "Here, baby. This won't hurt too much."

"Noooo." She thrashed about, making the blood on her cheek run halfway down her face. "Please, Mommy … No more!"

In the background, Kelly could see Laurie take hold of Macy's hand and lead her into the house. Kelly stared at Molly, at the blood on her face and the strange angle of her forearm. *What am I doing? The doctor can clean up her cheek. I need to get her to the hospital.* She ran halfway to the house and then stopped and turned around again. She couldn't leave Molly here on the sidewalk. She dropped the spray bottle and cotton pads and held her hand out to Molly. "Baby, you have to get up. We need to go to the doctor's."

"My aaaarrrm." Molly was sobbing harder now. "It huurrrts."

"I know, sweetie. The doctor will help." She crouched down and took hold of Molly's left arm. Gently, carefully she eased her daughter to her feet. "Want me to carry you?"

"Y-y-y-es!"

Molly was still very light, but now Kelly wasn't sure she had the strength or energy to pick her up. She stooped down and tried her hardest to bounce Molly up onto her hip. But instead Molly slid back to the ground, still crying. Kelly's heart responded by racing into double-time. "Please, Mommy … I can't walk!"

For a few seconds, Kelly once more felt nothing but sheer panic. If Chase were here he would sweep their daughter up into his arms and they'd already be on their way. "Okay, baby. Mommy's gonna try again."

This time Kelly swung Molly onto her hip, but as she stood and took a few steps, her heart slammed around in her chest. If she carried her daughter all the way to the car, she wondered if she might have a heart attack. She stopped, out of breath, and set Molly down. "I need you to walk, baby. Mommy doesn't feel good."

Something in Kelly's tone must've convinced Molly that she needed to do her part. Together they walked to the car and Kelly buckled Molly into her booster seat. Only then did she realize she didn't have her keys. "I'll be right back."

"No … Nooooo, don't go!" Molly shrieked, straining against the belt. "My aaaarm!"

Kelly could still hear her screaming as she ran inside, grabbed her purse, and flew back out to the driver's seat. "I'm here now, baby. Mommy's back."

Molly was sobbing so hard she could barely breathe, and she didn't get any calmer the entire way to the hospital. The whole way Kelly fought from slipping into another full-blown panic attack. She parked and once they were inside a nurse met them in the lobby with a wheelchair.

"She … she fell off her bike." Kelly felt like she was hyperventilating. This sometimes happened when she ate too many sweets in one day, but never in combination with an emergency. She wondered if she would pass out and fall to the ground right here in the emergency room lobby. "She … she …"

Kelly tried to breathe, but she couldn't. Her lungs wouldn't take in a full breath, and black spots were circling on the perimeter of her vision. The nurse seemed to sense Kelly was on the verge of hysteria. She motioned to someone behind the desk. "I need an examination room for the girl." Then she put her hand on Kelly's back. "Everything's going to be okay. I want you to exhale a few times nice and slow. Then you can tell me what happened."

Kelly felt like she was going to be sick. Whatever she'd eaten that day, it wasn't helping. She was winded and heavy and unable to handle the emergency playing out around her. What if it were worse? What if Molly had hit her head? Would Kelly be so disabled that she'd slip into cardiac arrest, unable to assist her daughter? *This is it, God. I can't live like this anymore. I've got to get control again—I'm finished with this craziness. I need You to help me be finished with it. I feel like I'm dying and I can't even think clearly.*

"Breathe out …" The nurse sounded like she was losing patience. A second nurse joined them and carefully pushed Molly through the emergency room door.

"Mommmy!"

Kelly felt faint. *Help me, God … I can't do this!* The nurse's voice was very near her face, and finally Kelly did the same thing she'd done before with Laurie, pursing her lips and forcing a few breaths. After the third, she felt herself begin to calm down—just enough so she could finally inhale. As soon as she wasn't worried about passing out, she tried to shake off her own panic and she took her place next to Molly. "It's okay, baby." She sounded weak, but she wasn't leaving her daughter again. "Mommy's here."

"It hurts." Molly stuck her lip out, her little chest still convulsing from the sobs.

They hurried into a room, and a doctor made a quick decision that Molly needed a spoonful of liquid acetaminophen for her pain and an X ray. Kelly walked with her to the room, but she had to stand back with the technician during the actual picture-taking. Her absence only made Molly cry harder, and in the distant places of her mind Kelly had a random thought. What was Chase doing right now? Sitting in some meeting at some major studio, wasn't that it? He would have no idea that his family was in the middle of a crisis.

She waited until the X ray was finished and she and Molly were alone in the examining room before she took the receiver off the wall and dialed Chase's cell. It rang two times, three, and after the fourth it went to his voicemail. Kelly waited for the beep. "Chase, it's me." She sounded exhausted and still a little panicky. "Molly fell off her bike and maybe broke her arm. Call me, okay? We're at the hospital."

The diagnosis didn't take long. By then, the emergency room doctor had stabilized Molly's arm in a loose splint, and she'd fallen asleep, exhausted from the pain and the sobbing. The doctor pulled up a chair opposite Kelly and checked the chart he was holding. "Molly has a severe fracture in her forearm. It's quite bad, actually. With something like this, there's really only one way to set it, and that's through surgery."

Surgery? Kelly felt her heartbeat pick up speed again. Molly needed surgery? With Chase gone? The black spots danced into view again and she tried to remember Laurie's advice. *Exhale. Force yourself to exhale. Please, God ... get me through this.*

I am with you, daughter ... through even this I am with you.

The answer rang clear in her heart even over the sound of the doctor's voice. Kelly blinked and tried to focus. God was with her. She could do this.

The doctor explained that with breaks like this, the sooner they could set it the better. "I've called in an expert pediatric orthopedist. He can operate this afternoon." He studied her. "Can your husband be here by then?"

"No." She felt sick again. "He won't be here until late tomorrow. He's in LA."

"I see." The doctor looked concerned. "Do you think you'll be okay? I'd like someone to be here with you."

He must've heard about her near-fainting episode in the waiting room. She racked her brain, thinking about what to tell him. Laurie was staying with Macy, and she would do so as long as Kelly needed her. Then she remembered. Lisa, of course. Lisa was home this week and she would come in a heartbeat. "I ... I have someone."

"Very well, then."

She nodded, fighting the panic that breathed terrifying possibilities into her heart and mind. The doctor excused himself, and again Kelly took the phone from the wall. Her first call was to Laurie, who was more than willing to look after Macy. "I'll be here as long as you need me," she said. "And I'll keep praying."

Next Kelly called Lisa, who promised to be there in twenty minutes.

Finally she tried Chase again. This time he answered on the third ring, his voice quiet and on edge. "What is it Kelly? Is this an emergency?" He obviously hadn't checked his messages. "We're almost finished."

For a single instant, Kelly wanted to hang up, tell him never mind. That certainly whatever was happening with the studio was bound to be more important than life back home. But instead she swallowed every sarcastic thought she might've voiced and in a tone almost devoid of emotion said only, "Molly broke her arm. We're at the hospital." She sighed. "She needs surgery in the next few hours to set it."

"What?" The alarm in Chase's voice brought with it some sense of satisfaction. "How serious is it?" He was still whispering.

"Serious, Chase. She needs surgery."

He released a frustrated sound. "Let me call you after the meeting. It's almost over."

Kelly felt the room tilt. Was he really saying he'd call her back? When his daughter was lying in a hospital facing surgery? She was furious with him. "Fine." She hung up without saying good-bye and did her best not to slam the phone back onto its place on the wall.

She stood and paced to the door and back again. No wonder she'd been eating everything in sight. How else was she supposed to cope with the stress, the feeling Chase had abandoned them in a quest that had evolved over the last few months? Now his days in LA seemed less about changing the world and more about chasing fame and money. Anything to keep Brandon Paul attached to the next picture.

Molly moaned and rolled a little on the hospital bed. The doctor said he'd give her something to sleep if she woke up. He didn't want her moving around very much until after the surgery; she could do further damage to her arm. For now, though, Kelly wanted something to help *herself* calm down. When she was sure Molly wasn't going to wake up, she took a couple of one-dollar bills from her wallet. Walking quietly so Molly wouldn't hear, she left the room and went to the nurse's station. "My daughter's alone in there. I'll be right back."

"I'll check her in a moment." The nurse pointed to a monitor. "I can see her from here; don't worry."

Kelly nodded and headed out into the hall. When she reached the lobby, she turned away from the front doors and kept walking until she saw the vending machine. She stopped and stared at the food inside. Snickers ... Reese's Pieces ... Rolos ... two oversized chocolate-chip cookies. Her hands shook as she slid the first dollar into the slot. She wanted every bit of comfort she could get, and she positioned her finger over the letter and number corresponding to the Snickers. She could start there. But just as she was about to push, she felt a physical force holding her back.

She gasped and turned around, expecting to see someone standing there, stopping her from making the purchase. But she was completely alone. She blinked and stared at the machine full of junk. What had stopped her from pushing the button, and how come she was shaking so hard? Then in a rush she remembered her quick prayer, the one she'd silently uttered while trying not to faint an hour ago. What had she said? That she couldn't do this anymore, and that she was ready to stop, right? Wasn't that it? She'd even begged God to help her be finished with the craziness.

And now ... now something or someone had stopped her.

She lowered her hand and stared at the Snickers bar. She didn't need candy; she needed a Savior, a strength that went beyond herself. Not tomorrow morning or some other day, but here. Now.

She stepped back from the machine and then, at the last second, she pushed a button and heard the clank of quarters as they fell into the change dish. All four quarters. She swept them into her hand and without hesitation dropped them, one at a time, into the next machine—the one that held only bottled water.

She took her bottle and walked as quickly as she could back to Molly's room. Whatever had happened back there, she couldn't stop to analyze it. Whether the hand of God had held her back, or whether she'd subconsciously stopped herself, she wasn't sure. The only thing she knew was this: God had answered her prayer. Her marriage was on the rocks, and her little girl was about to have surgery. They owed tens of thousands of dollars because of *The Last Letter* and they'd yet to see more than the slightest bit of repayment for the funds they'd invested. But now, as she headed back to Molly's side, she had reason to smile because she had found the one thing she desperately needed, the thing she'd lost sight of these last few months.

Her determination to live.

Twenty

THE MEETING WITH THE STUDIO WAS over, and Chase stood out front of a restaurant across the street, frantic to get hold of Kelly. He tried her cell phone a dozen times before finally calling the three hospitals in the area. On the third try he found her—sitting with Molly in her room. A male nurse patched him through.

"Hello?" Kelly sounded angry, but less tired.

"Honey, it's me." His relief was an almost physical force across the phone lines. He hoped Kelly could tell how badly he wanted to talk to her. "I've been calling you for fifteen minutes."

"We can't use cell phones." She kept her eyes on Molly.

He started to say that he hadn't even known which hospital they were at, but he stopped himself. None of that mattered now. "So what happened? Start at the beginning."

In a monotone Kelly explained the bike accident. "It could've been a lot worse."

"Where's Macy?" Chase raked his fingers through his hair and leaned against the car. Keith was already inside, waiting for him.

"Laurie's with her, and Lisa is on her way here."

"Good." He racked his brain. They had come out of the meeting and gone directly to the restaurant. Kendall was on the phone with her father, and Keith had called Lisa. Chase was sitting outside on a patio chair where he'd been since he first started trying to reach Kelly. "They're sure she needs surgery?"

"The break's terrible, Chase. One of the worst the doctor's seen."

Pain sliced through Chase's gut. His little Molly suffering such a bad injury when he wasn't home to help her? The meeting had gone brilliantly, but Chase knew better than to say so now. He asked how Molly was doing, and what the time frame was. "I can be home tomorrow evening."

"Tomorrow?" Her single laugh sounded desperate. "What, Chase? What's so important that you can't get in your car and drive home now?"

He hesitated in disbelief. "I have more meetings, Kel. What do you want me to do, race home and then turn around and come back here?"

"Whatever." She didn't sound like she had the strength to fight him. "We'll be here until Sunday morning."

"I'll come straight there as soon as I'm in town."

"Okay." She didn't sound intentionally mean, just indifferent.

He settled into the white wrought iron chair. "Kelly, what's with you?"

"What's with *you*? Your daughter's had a terrible accident and you can't take my call? Are you serious?"

"I'm sorry. I was wrong. It's just … we were almost finished working out the details of an actual theatrical release with *The Last Letter*, and I didn't want to miss anything."

She took a long breath. "Look, I don't want to fight. We'll talk when you get here tomorrow."

She left him no room for further conversation. He felt his shoulders sink a few inches and he slumped over his knees, trying to focus. "If you talk to her before the surgery, will you tell her I'm praying for her?"

"Of course." She was terse and businesslike, as if she couldn't wait to get off the phone and tend to more important matters.

"I love you." He covered his free ear with his hand so he could hear the nuances of her voice, her mood. "I'm sorry I wasn't there."

"It's okay. We're used to it." She paused, maybe regretting her sarcasm. "See you tomorrow."

The phone went dead before Chase could question her again about her mood. Only then did he realize that she hadn't asked about the theatrical deal. It was what they'd been praying for with *The Last Letter*, and now they had it. But Kelly hadn't even noted it. He clicked his phone off and slid it back in the pocket of his jacket. Then hung his head for a full minute trying to figure out his wife. When he'd been home lately, he'd tried not to look too deeply at the way Kelly was treating him. She probably wasn't happy with him. At least that's what he had come to believe. But at least she made an effort when he was home.

But now … now there was no question she was angry. It had come through loud and clear over the phone lines. Angry at what? That's what he wanted to know. Angry because he and Keith were following the dream God had placed in their hearts? Upset because he was gone so often? He clenched his teeth and pulled himself into a straight position again. Didn't she know this was the hardest part? One day soon they could move to LA and this phase would be something from the past. But they couldn't blame each other along the way.

He remembered the time during the filming last fall when she'd come to the set and spent a couple nights with him. She believed in him back then, but since Thanksgiving things had changed with her. Was it depression? Had she allowed herself to get so out of control that she couldn't feel anything but misery?

He was about to pray for her, to beg God to mend things between them so that tomorrow he could hold her hands and help her know how he felt about her, that he would do anything to help her. But the sound of the café door stopped him before he had the chance. "Chase?" It was Kendall.

He sighed and put on the familiar mask, the one that he wore around their new partner so she wouldn't think for a minute that

Chase's home life was anything but ideal. He flashed her a concerned smile. "Hey, sorry. It took forever to reach her."

"How's Molly?" Kendall had come outside by herself. Keith was still inside the restaurant.

"She needs surgery for sure. I guess Macy jumped in front of her. Molly didn't want to hit her with the bicycle, so she took the fall instead."

"Ahh, sweet girl." Kendall took the seat next to Chase. "Anything we can do?"

"Pray." It was what he and Kelly should've done. "I guess the operation's pretty straightforward. They've called in a specialist, but still ... It's scary stuff."

"Definitely. Plus she doesn't have the best daddy in the world there to help her through it."

Chase tried not to register the compliment. He and Kendall had only been working closely together for three months or so, and already a pattern was starting to develop. With Kelly, he could do nothing right, and with Kendall ... With Kendall he could do no wrong. He stared at the ground near his feet. "If I were that great, I guess I'd be there."

"Hey." Her voice was soft, a caress whether she intended it to be or not. "Don't beat yourself up. The reason you're here is because you care about your family's future. Not just your financial future and the welfare of your wife and girls." She waited until he looked up. "You care about the next generation of kids. That's why you want to make these movies, remember? So in the big picture, you're the best dad of all."

He looked away because he didn't want to linger on Kendall Adams' eyes. She was good and right and true, and her intentions were entirely pure—same as his. But even so, looking into her eyes was like looking into her soul. Too much of that and he'd be on dangerous ground in no time. He knew at least that much.

His mind found its way back to the studio meeting. "What's the consensus?"

"About the meeting?" She grinned and a giddy laugh sounded in her throat. "It was perfect, great that we had Luke Baxter tapped in from Indiana. His input was incredible. I mean, the studio execs offer you a theatrical deal and even agree to split the P&A budget? In this market, that's like hitting the lottery."

"I sort of figured." Chase smiled and wished he could've told Kelly the good news. Maybe it would've helped her mood a little. He gazed up at the Los Angeles sky, already hazy at the end of April. "What about Brandon?"

"Keith thinks today's meeting was good for that too. If NTM steps out of line, Brandon won't sign another deal with them. Worst-case scenario, Brandon finishes his contract with NTM—does the final film, something the studio comes up with. Then we move on and take *Unlocked* to the executives we met today. They'd pay Brandon more, and they'd understand the faith element. The studio's leading the way in that area right now, and no one's close."

Chase sort of liked the idea. "Maybe we should aim for that, since NTM's dragging its feet."

"We could." Kendall nodded thoughtfully. "My dad would be supportive no matter where *Unlocked* winds up."

Keith joined them then, carrying a bag of to-go salads. "We can eat back at the hotel room. I have to talk to Andi, and it could take a while." He didn't sit down. "Everything okay with Molly?"

"We'll know more later tonight. Her surgery's in about an hour."

"Ugh." Keith groaned and hung his head for a few seconds. "I'm sorry, man. That's terrible."

"It could've been worse." Kendall stood and reached her hand out to Chase.

Without thinking, he took it and allowed her to help him to his feet. The exchange didn't seem to draw any strange looks from Keith, and Chase told himself it was nothing out of the ordinary. A friend helping another friend up at a time when weariness ruled the moment.

They walked to Kendall's car, and Chase took the front passenger seat. The three of them talked about *The Last Letter* all the way back to the Georgian Hotel. "You know," Kendall said as she pulled up. "You guys could stay with my dad. He lives down the street from me, and he has half a dozen guestrooms. You'd be closer to the studios."

Chase had wondered that for some time, how they might approach such an idea without seeming presumptuous. Never mind the good rate they were getting, they were still spending a fortune on hotel bills.

From the back, Keith patted Kendall on her shoulder. "Tell your dad yes. We'd love that." He thanked her and stepped out of the car. When he saw that Chase wasn't making the same hurried move, he waved. "See you inside."

Chase nodded. He wasn't sure why he wasn't jumping out of the car too. It was a valet area, and in a minute or so one of the uniformed parking attendants would hurry Kendall on her way. But Chase wanted to thank her first. "About earlier, what you said. How I'm a good dad for trying to get these films done." He opened the car door and set one foot on the ground. For the slightest moment he allowed his eyes to look into hers. "Thanks for that. I needed to hear it."

"I know." She put her hand on his knee, but only briefly. "It can't be easy, being gone so much. I'm sure your wife misses you like crazy."

"She does." His answer was quick, the only answer he could give. "Anyway…" He couldn't look away. "Just wanted to thank you."

She smiled. "It's the truth. Oh, and I'll be praying for Molly this afternoon. Let me know how it goes."

"I will." He hesitated one last time before stepping out of her car. "You'll meet us here for breakfast tomorrow?"

"Of course. We have the meeting with Brandon's agent, and then lunch with Brandon. Lots to talk about now that we have a theatrical deal. Everyone in Brandon's camp should feel a lot better about you and Keith producing *Unlocked.*"

"Good." His smile was the easiest thing that had happened that day. "I'll see you then."

The moment seemed to call for a hug—especially since she had lifted his spirits when he was at such a low point earlier that day. But with the two of them in the car, a hug would be awkward. Besides, hugging hadn't really been part of their working relationship. Instead he waved once more and thanked her for the ride, then stepped out and headed up the front steps of the Georgian and into the open-air lobby. He needed to find a quiet place where he could pray about Molly. Not just Molly, but Kelly and whatever struggles she faced. But for now, he was glad that at least one part of his life was going right.

And that God had been kind enough to pair them up with a young woman as wonderful as Kendall Adams.

KENDALL DROVE DOWN OCEAN AVENUE WITH one thought on her mind: the safety and complete healing of little Molly Ryan. She opened her car windows and breathed in the ocean breeze. The farther north she went, the less traffic, and the more easily she could concentrate on her prayer.

She begged God for wisdom on the part of the surgeon, and for complete healing for the child's arm. Beyond that she prayed for Chase's home life. Not because he'd mentioned that anything was wrong, but because she sensed trouble. Maybe he was just tense about not being home when he was needed. Whatever it was, she prayed, and when she was finished she thanked God for the answers that were certainly coming.

Before she reached the turnoff for her home, she added one last plea to God. She'd loved and lost once a long time ago, and since then no one had come along. No one with faith in Christ or the integrity she needed in a relationship centered in Hollywood. That was okay, she had told herself a thousand times. She could be single and alone and still serve God by helping make movies with a message.

But spending time with Chase had increased her longing for a guy, for a man she might marry and share her life with. Before connecting with Chase and Keith, she'd wondered if there were any men left who would meet her high standards. If not, then she would stick by her determination. She'd rather be single. But since meeting the young producers—especially Chase—she knew differently. There were good guys out there, and she finished her prayer asking God to send one her way. One who was handsome and kind, humble and loyal, a guy who loved his family more than life and who would be guided each day by his faith in God. "Please, Lord … send me a guy like that."

She rested her head against the seat back and smiled at the late-afternoon sunshine. Somewhere out there her guy existed, a guy who wasn't already married. She concentrated on the road ahead and felt no shame in the way she'd prayed. God understood what she meant. She wasn't attracted to Chase, though she still wanted to be careful around him. His wedding ring almost always stopped her from feeling an attraction toward him. But it didn't stop her from praying that the guy she married wouldn't be some Hollywood phony, some high-ranking executive with money and power and prestige. She wasn't looking for that in a man, not anymore.

She was looking for a guy like Chase Ryan.

Twenty-One

Bailey walked into the Cru meeting and wondered if she'd see Cody. Tim wasn't with her tonight. They'd been home from New York less than a week, and since they'd missed a day of classes, Tim didn't want to fall behind on homework. Andi hadn't come either. She was hanging out with Taz again.

Bailey was about to head down the aisle to her place near the front when she spotted Cody sitting by himself in a seat near the back row. He smiled at her with his usual enthusiasm and motioned for her. Bailey felt her heart leap. His text while she was in New York had said they should hang out some time. Now at least maybe they could talk about it.

She walked down the empty row of seats and took the one beside him. "Hey."

"Hey." He stood and hesitated. Then, as if he didn't want things to be awkward between them, he gave her a quick hug. "Where's Tim?"

"Studying."

They sat down next to each other, and the sound of his voice felt wonderful beside her. "What about you?"

"I'm caught up. I didn't do the spring play, so I guess I had more time."

They had five minutes before Cru began. Cody shifted so he could see her better. In the process, his knee brushed against hers. Bailey didn't shift away from him.

"I stopped by your parents' house a few times."

Once a week, Bailey wanted to say, because her family shared with her each time Cody came by. But she stopped herself. Her brothers loved seeing Cody, and her dad said he'd been talking to him about coaching. She felt her smile light her eyes, the way it so easily did when she was with him. "They love when you come over. You're part of the family."

"I feel that way."

Cody seemed uncomfortable with silence between them, so he told her about his mom, how she was doing better and staying sober. "I take her to church every weekend, and each time she's getting a little closer to God. It's amazing." He chuckled. "For the first time in my life I have a mom, only now it's more like the tables are turned and I'm the one taking care of her."

Bailey could picture that. Cody had walked away from alcohol and escaped a prisoner-of-war situation in Iraq. Back in the U.S., he'd learned how to walk on a prosthetic leg without any limp whatsoever. He even competed in local triathlons. Of course he could take care of his mother. He could take care of anyone.

"So you wanna coach? That's what my dad said." She looked at him, let herself get lost in his eyes. Not because she wanted to have feelings for him again, but because she missed the connection between them. Missed it more than she realized.

"Yeah, I think I'm made for it. I want to help kids and teach them football. It's an important time in a kid's life. Without your dad, I would've drunk myself to death by now. So that's my new goal. Be a guy like your dad for some kid like me. For a hundred kids like me."

The picture warmed Bailey's heart. "You'll be wonderful at it."

"I hope so. It means an extra year of schooling to get my teaching credential, but I don't mind. I'm taking a few summer classes, so I might finish early, anyway."

She nodded, and without meaning to she thought about Tim. The trip had changed something in Bailey. She still wanted to perform on Broadway, but the city had lost some of its glamour. Even if she won a starring role, she couldn't picture herself living in Manhattan for long. But Tim … Tim could hardly wait to pack his bags and find an apartment.

Her mother's voice came to mind, something she'd said the afternoon of Bailey's eighth-grade graduation. All the other girls had boys who liked them, but Bailey had only friends. She had wondered if maybe something was wrong with her, since none of the boys had wanted to go out with her.

"You're too mature for them," her mom had told her. "They think you're pretty, but they don't dare say so. Because they know none of them is what you'll be looking for someday."

"What'll I be looking for when I'm ready?"

Her mother had smiled, a knowing look warming her eyes. "For someone like your daddy."

Bailey had never forgotten that conversation, and along the way she could look back and realize why guys she'd had crushes on in high school had never worked out, and why a guy like Bryan Smythe from CKT would never have been a match for her. Those guys were nothing like her dad. But then, more often lately, neither was Tim.

"What're you thinking about?" Cody nudged his knee against hers.

"Nothing." She didn't dare say. Especially not in the wake of their discussion about Cody's coaching dreams.

The Cru leader, Daniel, took his spot at the front of the classroom. He started by reading from Psalm 139 about how God had known them since before they were born, and how He'd knit them together inside their mothers' bodies, and how His plans for them had been destined since before the beginning of time.

When he finished taking questions about the Scripture passage, he moved onto the year-end events. First, they were planning a retreat on the far side of Lake Monroe. A church camp had been there for decades. A cluster of cabins and a mess hall, located in a place secluded from the rest of the lake. Perfect for time away, time to reflect.

The weekend sounded perfect to Bailey. She listened intently as Daniel continued.

"We'll be there the third weekend in May. There are no classes that Friday, so we'll have three days." He held up an orange flyer. "The details are here."

Finally he told them about a mission trip to Costa Rica set for August. Cody leaned close to her. "I think I'm going. What about you?"

Bailey wanted to go in the worst way, but she needed to talk to Tim. The two of them were planning a weekend trip to New York in June so they could audition for the opening ensemble roles. If they won parts, then the mission trip would have to wait. "I don't know," she whispered. "Maybe."

"What about the lake retreat?"

"Definitely."

After signing up for the May weekend and after Bailey connected with the girls in her Bible study, she and Cody walked out into the night. The week had been the warmest since winter, and now, after nine o'clock, the air still felt fairly warm.

They walked slowly, side by side, until they came to the place where a couple of main paths intersected. "Can I walk you back to the dorm?"

As much as Bailey worried about her heart, she was glad for his offer. She didn't want to walk alone, but even more she didn't want to say good night yet. Cody kept his pace slow and easy, and Bailey fell into his rhythm.

"Okay …" Cody's voice rang with subtle teasing. "Is this my lucky day?"

"Your what?" She smiled at him. "Why do you say that?"

"Because here we are hanging out, and I keep thinking if get lucky—I mean, really lucky—maybe you'll tell me why you pulled so far away. I mean, I apologized for my stupidity in staying away from you last fall, right?"

She stifled a giggle. "Okay. Right."

He made a funny face. "So maybe you think I have bubonic plague? Or maybe you're so blinded with love for Tim you forgot I'm alive." His eyes lit up and he pointed at her. "Or you fell and hit your head and now you have amnesia and you can't remember where you know me from." He shrugged. "Or if you know me."

She laughed again. "Cody ..." They were walking more slowly now, and once in awhile Bailey felt his arm brush against hers. She had missed this so much, this camaraderie with Cody. "You're crazy." She grinned at him. "I don't think you have the plague."

"You saw my picture in a post office on a Most Wanted poster, and you've convinced yourself I'm a felon?"

"Come on ..."

Cody was laughing now too. "Or you've got it in your mind that I'm not Cody Coleman at all, but some evil twin, and now you're afraid to talk to me?"

Bailey laughed harder, so much that she slowed to catch her breath. How long had it been since she'd felt this way? Her feelings took her back and made her long for another time. She poked her elbow at him. "You're ridiculous."

"Actually ..." He gradually came to a stop and faced her. "I don't want to be too serious, Bailey, but really, for the life of me, I can't understand it."

They were at a part of the path that lay out in the open, no seclusion whatsoever. Even still, Bailey felt like they were the only two people on campus. She wanted to look away, but she couldn't. She'd avoided him this long, so maybe he was right. Maybe it was time she gave him an answer. "Really, Cody?" Her voice was soft, the laughter gone for her too. "You want the truth?"

"I do." He looked so good in his gray Colts sweatshirt and jeans. For a moment he looked like he might hug her, or touch her face. But instead he slipped his hands in his back pockets and waited. His eyes never left hers for a single second. "Why do you stay away from me? I miss you more each day."

"Because …" She didn't want to cry, not now and not ever around him. But her heart didn't know the rules, and tears built up anyway. "I know you're sorry. But you cut me out of your life for nearly three months. Like you didn't care at all, and something happened to me during that time." She raised the zipper on her sweater, but the extra warmth didn't touch the chill inside her.

"What?" He studied her eyes, her expression. "What happened, Bailey?"

A hot tear slid down her cheek, and she caught it with her shoulder. "It's like I told you before. I still can't trust you. I almost deleted your texts last week too."

He couldn't have looked more hurt if she'd told him she'd forgotten his name. "Then you don't understand me at all."

"Of course I do. When you came back from war you told me you weren't interested in me as more than a friend. You wanted me to date Tim Reed, and that's what I'm doing." She wished she sounded more enthusiastic about the fact. "But you promised me I'd at least have your friendship. Only then …" Another tear fell. "Then school started and you started going after my roommate." Her voice was slightly louder than before. "How did you think I was going to take that?"

He exhaled hard and rubbed the back of his neck. Without saying anything, he turned and stared at the empty campus lawn. After a few seconds he looked at her again, his eyes full of a hurt deeper than any she'd seen in him before. "You really think I could replace you with Andi Ellison?" The sound that came from him was more a frustrated cry than a laugh. "She's nothing like you."

"But that's what you did." Bailey pressed her knuckles beneath her eyes and willed herself to find control. "You became her friend instead of mine."

"Because you had Tim."

"Of course I had Tim." She caught her voice this time, and dropped it to a frustrated whisper. "You wanted me to. Wasn't that what you said? He had more in common with me, and he was better for me. All to distract me from the real issue. Why *you* weren't interested. But I didn't think you'd turn your back on me."

He looked completely defeated, and for a long time he only stared at her. Then finally he allowed a sad laugh and a shake of his head. "You'll never understand. You were already with Tim when I came home. You were happy, I could see that. It wouldn't have been cool to call you and text you all the time when you already had Tim."

She wanted to tell him that they weren't all that serious, even now, and that Tim's dreams were starting to feel very different from hers. But that would feel like a betrayal to Tim. She loved Tim, and however long they stayed together, she could never talk bad about him behind his back. Not now or ever. He'd done nothing to deserve that.

Instead she swallowed hard and lifted her eyes to the trees up ahead. New leaves showed on their branches, proof that once more winter wouldn't have the final say.

"Tim and I are still serious." She gave him a conflicted look. "So why the effort these past few months, Cody? Why the texting and calling?"

"Because God made it clear to me that I was an idiot. I never should've backed off just because of Tim. I wasn't a threat to him, and by backing off I only confused you." He looked intently at her, past the surface and straight to her soul. "I never stopped thinking about you."

"So that's it, huh? You want to be my friend."

"Exactly." His eyes gradually took on the light they'd lost in the heat of their discussion. "Because really, Bailey, I don't have the plague. I promise you."

Her cheeks were dry, and she laughed even though she hadn't intended to. Maybe things hadn't changed as much between them as she'd thought. Not if he could still make her laugh at will. "Brat." She kicked at his feet, then paused for a long while, lost in his eyes. "So you're saying I can trust you this time, that you'll be a real friend."

"As long as Tim doesn't care."

"He doesn't." Her answer came quickly. "He trusts me."

The joy in Cody's eyes was enough to make her laugh again, and once she started, he joined in. "You're not worried I'm an evil twin?"

"A little. But I'll stop erasing your messages." They started walking once more and she felt her eyes dance as she gave him a side glance. "How would that be?"

"Wow. I feel like the luckiest guy on campus." He leaned his head back and shouted. "Bailey Flanigan's going to stop deleting my messages!" He took a long breath and grinned at her. "Definitely the luckiest guy."

She kept laughing. "Shhh. People will wonder."

"Yeah, well, that's not always a bad thing." His laugh fell to a quiet chuckle. They were almost back at her dorm. "Now here's what'll happen. You'll go into your dorm and put away your backpack and before you can even think about washing your face you'll get a text message." He held out his elbow and touched it lightly to hers. "It'll be from me, and then … instead of erasing it or ignoring it or banning it from your phone the way you're used to doing, you'll sit down on the edge of your bed and text me back."

They were at her dorm now, and they stopped at the bottom of the steps. "That's what's going to happen?"

"Yes." His eyes glimmered. "Okay?"

"Mm-hmm." She lowered her chin, feeling a little sheepish. "I guess I've been sort of rude."

"No, no." He punctuated the night air with his forefinger. "The plague can be very contagious, and you had to look out for your health."

She allowed herself to get serious one more time. "Not for my health. For my heart. In my book, friends don't just stop talking to each other."

A long breath slid between his lips. "I know. It was my fault. I'm asking you again to forgive me, Bailey. So we can try one more time."

"Okay." Her heart hung on every word he said. "I forgive you." They were standing so close she could feel the warmth from his body. "And I need you to forgive me too."

He tapped his foot against hers. "For what?"

"For not talking about this with you sooner."

This time they needed no words. Slowly Cody wrapped his arms around her. The hug lasted a long time, and Bailey wished it would've gone on longer. Because against all the odds, she and Cody had finally done the impossible.

They'd found their way back to each other.

They whispered good-byes, and when Bailey was inside her dorm, before she had time to wash her face, her phone alerted her to a text message. She smiled and picked it up.

I'M TRYING TO FEEL THE GROUND BENEATH ME, BUT IT ISN'T EASY.

Bailey grinned and texted back her answer. ME TOO.

ACTUALLY, I'M THANKING GOD WITH EVERY STEP BECAUSE I WASN'T SURE WE'D EVER HAVE THIS AGAIN, AND NOW WE DO.

MORE THAN THAT, she tapped out her response, WE ALWAYS WILL.

It was the one thought that kept her company as she fell asleep. She and Cody had found their way back to each other, back to the friendship they'd almost lost. No matter what Andi was out doing tonight, or how her feelings for Tim were shifting, that was all that mattered.

She had Cody again, and all was right with the world.

Twenty-Two

ANDI WAS GLAD THE SPRING SHOW was over. She'd received much praise for her role as Maid Marian, but deep inside she knew she could've done better. Her focus was off—the way it had been off since she and Taz began spending time together. For the past month, ever since they'd shot the first scenes of Taz's movie, the two of them had been nearly inseparable. When they weren't together, they were texting or talking on the phone.

Taz told her she was his kindred spirit, his soul mate. In the past words like that would've seemed cliché or trite, but with Taz they took on new meaning, the way all of life did with him.

"What is it with this Taz guy?" Bailey asked every few days. "Come on, Andi. Be honest."

But Andi would only smile and shrug. "He's nice. We're not dating or anything." She was telling the truth, even if she was purposefully evasive. "Just getting to know each other."

Even so, Taz had become an obsession. Andi was grateful she was a strong student and that her grades hadn't suffered. Because when she wasn't in class, she was all about Taz.

I CAN FEEL US IN THE TREES, he'd told her yesterday over a text. NEW LIFE BURSTING THROUGH EVERY BRANCH AND PUSHING THROUGH OUR HEARTS AND SOULS. CAN YOU FEEL IT?

The crazy thing was she could. Even if she wasn't always sure exactly what he meant. With Taz she felt free and full of potential, not stuck in a box the way she'd felt before. Their talks never stalled in the bog of Christianity or the Bible or the existence of

God—topics Andi had spent a lifetime exhausting. Instead she and Taz laughed and talked about the pulse of a person's soul and the beauty in a blade of grass. The topics were endless with Taz, and once in a while they even dreamed about the future.

Taz had been careful not to kiss her again. He'd wound up playing the role of her character's love interest, but the kiss they shared on screen was purely professional, art at its best. When they'd finished filming it, he let his eyes hold hers a few seconds more. "Definite chemistry," he said. And that was all—then or since then.

There were times when she wanted to beg him to kiss her the way she was dying to be kissed. Other times she wanted to scream at him, "Okay, so are you falling for me or what?"

But always the question seemed pushy or forced. "We are like wind and rain," he'd told her last week. "Dancing over the earth the way two people are supposed to dance." Another time he touched her cheek and whispered, "We enjoy each other—hearts, minds, and souls." His eyes shone with a mesmerizing depth. "One day, maybe, we will enjoy more than that."

In the past she'd feared a physical relationship with a guy. She had promised God, herself, and her parents she'd stay pure until she was married. So when guys made moves on her earlier this year, the attempts felt like an affront. Something to stay away from.

But everything was different with Taz. Each time they were together, her desire and curiosity grew. The more he seemed almost uninterested in kissing her, the more she wanted to be kissed. Her wanting him only added to the other heightened sensations she felt whenever Taz was around.

Andi tuned out her psych professor, clicked a button on her phone, and smiled. Another text from him.

HEY, BEAUTIFUL, I NEED TO RESHOOT A FEW SCENES FOR THE MOVIE. I REALLY WANT AN A ON THIS THING,

AND I'M NOT SURE THE STUFF WE DID IN THE BEGINNING IS STRONG ENOUGH.

Andi's mind raced.

THE BEDROOM SCENES?

YES. I DON'T WANT TO TALK ABOUT IT OVER TEXT. LET'S MEET AFTER YOUR LAST CLASS TODAY.

She wasn't sure what he had in mind, but the idea of meeting him sounded wonderful. They had several places on campus where they often stole a few minutes together and she gave in to the dizzy way he made her feel. When class was over, she met him on a hilly path overlooking an ancient chapel, one of the few religious buildings on campus. Andi tried not to think about how long it had been since she'd set foot in a church.

He took her hand in his, eased his fingers between hers, and led her to the top of the hill, to a bench set back from the path and shaded by two enormous maple trees. "Your skin feels good." His pace was slow so he could look at her as they walked. "Enchanting. Like everything about you." He slid his fingers deeper between hers. "Can you feel it?"

Kiss me, she wanted to scream. But instead she focused her attention on the place where their fingers connected. "Mmm." She smiled at him. "I can."

"People are meant to experience physical connection. You and I—" His smile touched the center of her soul. "—we're all about real love."

"We are." It was back. The dizzy lightheadedness that always came when Taz neared her. She swallowed and tried to clear her mind. What were they supposed to be talking about? "The movie," she said out loud. "You wanted to talk about the bedroom scenes?"

Taz seemed careful not to break the bond between them. His hand, his eyes, remained connected to hers. "What we have on screen is good. You're a talented actress, because you allow yourself the privilege of feeling. I watched the bedroom scenes ten times yesterday and I feel everything about your character. But I wonder something."

She reminded herself to breathe. "What?"

"The character is a very bad girl. And you, Andi ..." He let his eyes caress her for a moment. "You are very good. So innocent."

Andi wasn't sure where he was going.

"I was too careful when I wrote that scene, too worried that if I pushed too far, you'd run, you'd tell me no and I'd lose you as an actress." He ran his thumbs along the tops of her hands. "I'd lose all this."

Time seemed to stop, and with everything in her Andi wanted only to fall into his arms and kiss him, a kiss that would last half an hour or longer or forever, even. She blinked and tried to understand what he was getting at. "My character wasn't bad enough?"

"Not really." He furrowed his eyebrows, intent on his explanation. "She's a girl about to do the unthinkable. She'll model, sure. But she'd sell herself if that's what it takes for freedom." He didn't blink. "In that bedroom scene she's making a decision to run away and use her body as a means of survival." He angled his head, his tone thoughtful. "If I'm realistic and honest to the storyline, the character wouldn't stop at her bra. She would take off everything standing in the way of her old self and her body. So that she could fully realize the power of her nakedness."

Why hadn't Andi thought of that? Of course her character wouldn't have stopped at her bra. She wouldn't have been afraid to completely strip in front of a mirror. She would've taken everything off and studied herself, aware that from that point on she would use her body to rescue herself from her parents' control and captivity. "So, you want to reshoot that part?"

"I do." His look implored her to understand. "Like I said, I should've written the script that way from the beginning. But I didn't want to ask you to do anything you'd be uncomfortable with." He paused. "I wrote the script for you, Andi."

She tried to remember who she'd been back then, how she might've reacted if there'd been full nudity in the original screenplay. Taz was right. She would've run from the idea, turned him down flat. Now, though, a strange excitement began working through her and she practically buzzed with the thrill of redoing the scene. The film demanded honesty, and nudity was as honest as a person could get. She didn't need to fear her body. Taz had taught her that. He saw the body as art, which meant Andi had a pretty good idea he would be particularly taken with hers.

"When can we film it?"

"This afternoon, if that works for you." Taz was always gentle, never forcing anything. He cared about her as a person, the beauty of her from the inside out, as he'd often told her.

They made a plan, and Taz checked his phone calendar. "I have to go. Do me a favor." His voice deepened, his head near hers, the two of them swimming in a private sea of feelings and emotions. "Until then, be the character. Be the girl trying to break free and find independence from her controlling parents. I expect what you'll give me on film today will be some of your strongest work yet."

He didn't kiss her, but he didn't have to. His presence left a physical impression on her, and as she walked to the library, it was several minutes before her heartbeat returned to normal. "*Be the character,*" she told herself. And in her mind she allowed a deep and powerful resentment to build against her parents. How dare they tell her what to do and how to handle her life? They didn't understand art or real love or the desires of a young girl like herself. Their old-fashioned views would only keep her from experiencing life and emotion. It was time she broke free, whatever way she knew how.

She played the thoughts over and over in her mind, allowing herself to freefall into the psyche of the character. But as she did, she could feel the lines blur between fiction and reality. Her life wasn't much different from that of the character's, was it? Her father had called earlier, and all he'd done was ask questions. Who was she seeing? What was Taz's background? Was the guy a Christian? Maybe she should get more involved in Campus Crusade or a local church. She hung up after ten minutes, exhausted.

She walked faster. *"Be the character ... Be the character."* How dare they tell her what to do, and how to handle her life ... Their old-fashioned views would only keep her from experiencing life and emotion. It was time she ... How dare they ...

Over and over and over again she immersed herself in the character. By the time she finished with the library and walked back to her dorm, she could no longer tell for sure who she was talking about—the character in Taz's film or herself.

She met up with Taz in the same classroom fifteen minutes earlier than he'd requested. This time they were the only people in the room, and Taz explained that he'd operate the camera. So she'd have privacy. She could hardly wait to reshoot the scene, to show him that she was capable of using her body, capable of cutting-edge acting. He went over the blocking, the timing of the scene, and the feel of it. The first part would be the same as before, but as she stared at herself in her bra, the idea would take root in her heart and then filter through her eyes. Why wear a bra? She might have to dance topless or strip to make money. She couldn't find the true power of her body with a bra in the way.

"The scene will be more shadowy than last time. Better to show curves and silhouettes than too much nakedness," Taz told her. Even here he was nothing but professional, caring only for the integrity of the film. "You're okay with this?"

Andi didn't want to sound overly anxious, but with all the buildup throughout the day, she could hardly wait to shoot the scene. "Yes." She felt her heart beating hard against her chest. "I think you're right. The honesty of the film demands it."

He smiled, grateful for her understanding and proud of her at the same time. "Let's get going."

They ran the scene twice through to the place where she was supposed to take off her bra, and each time he cut it there. "More emotion, Andi. More anger and defiance." His voice was smooth against her soul, leading her, guiding her. "Let go of everything you've ever held onto or believed. Here there is only the character and her emotions. Let's try it again."

Finally, on the fourth time, when she reached the climactic moment, she was no longer Andi Ellison, missionary daughter. She was the character, body and soul. The emotions came like springs of muddied water, pushing through her hands and fingers, emanating from her eyes. In the distance, she thought she heard Taz's breathing change, faster maybe, more intense. Good. Let him see what she could do, what she had to offer. Slowly, and with raw defiance, she unhooked her bra and one at a time, she eased the shoulder straps down. Then with little effort, she let the bra fall to the floor.

Taz had told her the truth: the lighting was dark and shadowy. But now that she had done it—now that she was naked from the waist up—she had the strangest compulsion to keep going, to take the rest of her clothes off too. But Taz hadn't asked for that, not yet, anyway. She was still the character, still a living breathing creation of Taz's imagination. So instead she turned slowly one way and then the other, admiring herself in the mirror, imagining how she would use her body as a key to freedom.

Taz let her go, let the character take on a life of its own, acting from the organic place of character embodiment, as Taz called it. Finally, after a minute or so, he called out, "Cut!" and he was at her side. "That was beautiful. I believed every second." His eyes were wide with excitement, his breathing still faster than usual. "I could feel you, Andi. You're so very talented."

She was still without her bra or her top, but she didn't mind. It almost seemed like Taz had a right to see her this way, like he'd created this part of her and now she had nothing to hide. There was something else going on inside her, a sense of power she'd never felt around him. Taz's expression, his jagged breathing—all of it was a sign that her body hadn't only been a tool for the character, but for herself as well. She'd seemed to have gotten to him deeply, physically, and the truth in that was electrifying. Sure, Taz was touched by her acting ability. But was also clearly affected by her body, by the way she looked without clothes and the way she moved in front of the mirror.

When he was finished praising her, he stepped back so she could get dressed, and she did so without any sense of modesty or embarrassment. "You think you got what you were looking for?"

"Definitely. More than I ever imagined."

Andi smiled. She slipped into a light jacket and sized him up. Always in their friendship, Taz had seemed like the one in control, the one perfectly willing to wait for things to reach a more intense level. He was clearly attracted to her, but he was in no hurry to take it further. Drawn to her, but in no rush to date.

But here the tables felt dramatically turned. His cool confidence had been shaken and he seemed like a high school boy crushing on a college woman.

He walked her back to her dorm, and halfway there he took her hand in his again, his fingers between hers. His breathing was back to normal now, and most of his control was in place. "Andi, I was wondering." An easy laugh came from him and he stopped, facing her. "There's a jazz concert on campus next Saturday, and then afterwards, I should have my film edited by then. Maybe you can come back to my place and watch it."

Andi's heart soared, but she'd learned from him. So she refused to seem overly anxious. "I'd like that." She drew a long breath and let her eyes find his.

As she did, he put his free hand on his chest and looked suddenly startled. "Hey … I felt that." His eyes danced with that familiar teasing she'd come to love.

"What?" She held back a ripple of laughter, playing up the mock drama of the moment. "You're having chest pains, Taz? Is that it?"

"No." He touched his fingers to her throat and then laid them again on his chest. "You breathed in." The laughter faded into sheer, unfiltered desire. "And I felt the air."

Her body trembled with the depth of his flattery. In all her life, she'd never known anyone like Taz, never imagined anyone like him. Night shadows hovered around them, and they were alone on the path. It was a moment when her body practically screamed for his touch, his kiss. But he took a step back and finished walking her to the dorm. Before he left, he complimented her again on her acting. Then he told her good-bye. "I'll be on Facebook later."

"Okay." The increasing distance between them felt like a physical blow. But she wouldn't make the first move, so she backed up to the steps of her dorm building. It was Friday and Bailey was spending the weekend at home again. Facebook would take the edge off Andi's loneliness. "See you there."

As she walked back into her dorm, a picture came to mind. A scene from her favorite musical, *Phantom of the Opera*. Midway through the play, the Phantom has seduced Christine so completely she no longer has a choice in the matter. She belongs to the Phantom, heart and mind, body and soul. In the past, Andi couldn't relate to the dark connection between the two, but that was no longer the case. Taz had that sort of control over her, and

Andi had given it to him willingly. She was not his angel of music, she was his angel of acting.

Never mind the promises she'd made as a young girl; she belonged to Taz now. Whatever he asked of her, she would give because like he said, love needed to be shared. Emotionally, intellectually, and physically. Especially physically.

She i-chatted with Taz for an hour before turning in and fell asleep dreaming of his kiss.

She could hardly wait for Saturday.

Twenty-Three

Keith finished packing early and followed the smell of fresh-brewed Kenyan roast into the kitchen. Lisa was filling two tall mugs, and she glanced at him as he entered the room. "Two more weeks. I can't wait."

"Me either." Keith took one of the cups and held it under his chin. The hot steam felt good on his face. "We have a dozen meetings between now and then, but the festival has everyone talking. The guys at the studio think we could take top honors."

"I want a front-row seat." Lisa held her cup in both hands and leaned against the kitchen counter. "Have you talked to Andi? I'd like us all to be there."

"She wants to go." He slid up onto the kitchen island and let his legs dangle over the side. It was impossible to be entirely excited about their movie when the topic of Andi came up. "I'm worried about her."

"The boyfriend?"

"Whatever he is." Keith took a quick sip from his coffee. It was still too hot to drink. "His name comes up, but she gets defensive. She won't admit they're seeing each other."

"They're still working on his student film." Lisa's forehead lined with concern. "I got that much out of her. She dodges the question when I ask if he's a Christian. She said he's a spiritual person. Whatever that means."

"I don't like it. She's talking about staying on campus for the summer, working at the library and taking a few classes."

"Her grades are good. She said she'll get all *A*s and one *B* for this last quarter." Lisa lifted the mug to her face and blew at the wisps of steam. "But I'm worried too. She seems different. She used to tell me everything, even her doubts. Now it's more of a 'Good, great, fine' sort of existence."

Good, great, fine. It was the way Keith and Lisa would describe most high school kids in their relationships with their parents. *How are you? Good. What about your friends? Great. And your classes? Fine. Good, great, fine.* They'd always been grateful that they shared a deeper connection with Andi, that she felt compelled to tell Lisa every detail of her high school life. But now … Keith lowered his coffee cup and stared out the window into the gathering darkness. "What if this is worse than it seems?"

"I've been on her Facebook. She doesn't have a single picture of this Taz guy anywhere. And all the comments on her wall are from high school friends or Bailey Flanigan."

"I'm not sure that's proof." Keith still had a strong feeling something wasn't right. "She knows we're on her Facebook."

"True." Lisa looked more worried than before. "Maybe we should fly out and talk to her?"

Keith thought about that. "I'm not sure if she'd open up to both of us. Maybe you and she can take a day together before the film festival, take the car and go to the beach. You know, create an environment for conversation."

Lisa nodded. "I like that. We have to make time to talk." She thought for a few seconds. "I'm really not that worried. Andi knows the truth as well as anyone on that campus."

"That's what I keep telling myself." Keith pushed back his fears and concerns. Andi was a good girl. She knew the Bible, and right from wrong. Whoever this guy was, it couldn't be too serious. Andi was way too smart and levelheaded to fall that fast for a boy who didn't share her beliefs. At least that's what Keith had convinced himself. He let the subject pass. "I told you about NTM, right? We still haven't got anything in writing with them."

"Doesn't that worry Luke?"

"He's suspicious, same as me. But for now we're pressing ahead with *The Last Letter*. The studio agreed to a four-hundred-screen theatrical release, but they're willing to triple that if the movie does well at the festival."

"That's a miracle, really." She set her mug down on the counter and folded her arms. "Has Chase got a commitment from Kelly yet about the festival?"

"Last time I talked to him, she was planning to stay home. Same as before." The past month had been rocky for their friends, but Chase was committed to talking with Kelly, getting her to open up about her feelings. "She's seeing a doctor next week, a therapist. In case she's dealing with depression."

Lisa made a frustrated sound. "She doesn't need a doctor to tell her she's depressed. That's been obvious since Christmas." She threw her hands into the air, then dropped them. "Her husband's gone half the time, their finances are shaky, and Molly's still struggling to recover from her broken arm. That's enough to make the happiest person on earth depressed."

"She needs more time with God."

"Definitely." Lisa sounded defensive for her friend. "That's true with most of us, and especially for people battling depression. But she might need some kind of bridge between where she's at and where she needs to be with God."

"Bridge?"

"Right. Like an antidepressant." Lisa softened her tone. "Depression is truly a chemical imbalance in the brain. Sometimes medicine is the only way to set life right again."

Keith didn't want to argue about the issue. "Kelly needs help, we can agree on that."

They were quiet for a long moment, drinking their coffee, lost in their own thoughts. "A reviewer from *Variety* screened *The Last Letter* this past week. Loved it, absolutely raved about it. The story will run in a few weeks."

"Really?" Lisa's face lit up. "I'm so proud of you, Keith. I love you so much. Have I told you that lately?"

He slid back down to the floor, set his mug in the sink, and crossed to her. "All the time." He put his arms around her waist and pulled her close. "That's why I'm the most blessed man ever."

"I don't know about that. But I'm proud of you because you deserve it. You and Chase have worked hard, and now it's all about to pay off." She kissed him, clearly enjoying their closeness. "Tell me about the review."

"They compared the screenplay to something from Arthur Miller." He raised a brow and couldn't resist a single amazed chuckle. "Not only that, but they likened Jake Olson to a young Marlon Brando."

Lisa stared at him. Then she brought her hand to her mouth, a joyous laugh escaping through her fingers. "Are you serious? *Variety* hates everyone."

"Not us." Keith caught her face in his hands and kissed her — a kiss of joy and celebration despite the concerns they shared about Andi or Chase and Kelly. They were making movies for God, and if they were going to change the world with the power of film, they first needed to convince the gatekeepers.

The *Variety* review was proof the Lord had gone before them.

That would hopefully remain true in the week ahead. He and Chase were flying out first thing in the morning. They wouldn't need their car for this next round of meetings. Ben Adams had arranged for a driver to take them around in his Bentley. "At this level, it's better to make an impression," Ben had told them. In addition, they were staying at his place. Their car would only be in the way.

"I'm going to check our airline reservations. Make sure everything's in place."

"It is." Lisa's words held a deeper meaning. "It's more in place than either of us could begin to understand."

Keith was still smiling when he rounded the corner to the computer. He sat down, moved the mouse, and waited for the screen to come to life. It took just seconds to find their reservation and make sure there'd been no changes or scheduled delays. Weather was great. Keith didn't expect any trouble. He was about to sign off when he realized he hadn't checked the news—not in several days. It was always good to be aware of the issues as they headed into studio meetings.

He typed "Foxnews.com" in the search line and hit the enter button. The connection was quick, and almost instantly a list of stories appeared on his screen. One held the name of Brandon Paul.

"What?" he whispered to himself. Panic grabbed hold of his throat and tightened its grip. He desperately scanned the words, trying to make sense of them.

"Brandon Paul Agrees to NTM Movie Deal," the headline read.

Keith wanted to believe it was their movie the story was referring to, but it couldn't be. Luke would've told them if the studio had reached an agreement, if they were ready to make an announcement like this. He clicked the headline and the story came to life. Keith could barely focus as he read.

> Executives at NTM Studios announced today that Brandon Paul will star in an NTM original movie about a mentally challenged boy whose love for music gives him wings. The story comes from an NTM original screenplay, and is ex-

> pected to be filmed later this year. "We are committed to maintaining and building our relationship with Brandon," said Ace L. Rustin, NTM VP of Development. "We're in the process of negotiating a new five-year deal and doing everything we can to keep him in the NTM family."

That was it, just a news brief. For anyone else checking the headlines at this hour, the story would be nothing more than a bleep on the screen of Hollywood life. Brandon Paul in another movie. Ho-hum. But for Keith and Chase—for them it meant that everything they'd worked on for the past six months was finished. Gone for good.

A fine layer of perspiration broke out across Keith's brow and he hung his head, trying to catch his breath.

So that was it? Brandon had signed a deal to make a movie almost exactly like *Unlocked*, without telling them or their attorney or Stephanie? This was Luke Baxter's worst nightmare coming true.

Keith gripped his knees. Were there no ethics in Hollywood whatsoever? He fought the desire to shout at the screen, to demand that Fox News pull the story because it couldn't be true. Brandon had promised them this movie.

But there it was in black and white. He lifted his eyes and let himself read the details one more time.

God, what's happening? What does this mean? We were so close to making a name for us and for You.

He wanted to run outside and raise his voice to the heavens, begging God for some kind of understanding. Despite their lawyer's fears, Keith had told himself this couldn't happen. Not with God on their side. But here they were.

He checked the time on the computer and saw it was after eight o'clock. Still early enough to call someone, but who? Should his first contact be with Chase or Luke? He was reaching for the phone, still figuring out what to do and who to call, when the phone rang.

He answered it on the first ring. "Hello?"

"Keith." The voice on the other end was serious. Dire, even. "Ben Adams here."

"Ben." Keith stood and paced from the computer to the far wall of windows that overlooked the backyard. Had Ben seen the news already? He decided to play ignorant, at least at first. "Our flight's set for tomorrow. The meetings are all still in order."

"I'm not calling about that." Ben exhaled, and the sound rattled across the phone lines. "Have you seen the news?"

"Actually, I was just checking it. The NTM story was a complete shock."

"For us too. I've got a call in to Luke Baxter. But the timing couldn't be worse."

Keith waited, his heart racing.

"I met with my financial team today, and my accounts aren't what they used to be." His voice sounded tired, deeply discouraged. "The whole market thing isn't of interest to me, not on a day-to-day basis. I've tried to look the other way. But the market crash has cost me half my net worth."

Half? Keith felt the floor beneath him shift. He gripped the windowsill and closed his eyes. Ben Adams was supposed to be worth a billion dollars. That meant the change in the market had cost him, what? Five hundred million? Keith couldn't begin to understand what losing that kind of money might mean to a guy like Ben. "I'm ... I'm sorry."

"We all are. The fact is I planned to sell a portion of my stock portfolio to finance *Unlocked*. Now I can't do that. No one would sell in this market." He drew a steady breath. "For that reason, my advisor is warning me not to invest in the film—and I guess that's especially true now, since it looks like you've lost your star and your studio."

Keith blinked his eyes open and stared at the still-darkening sky. Was this really happening? Was he really having this conversation with the man who had seemed so financially stable? "I guess I need to talk to Luke. The NTM announcement doesn't make sense."

"Either way, I have to pull out. Try to understand." Ben seemed to gather himself somewhat. "I told my advisor I still wanted to provide half the P&A budget for *The Last Letter*. He wasn't happy about it, but he agreed." There was a considerable silence. "These are the times that make a man, Keith. Especially a man of God. You'll be all right, and so will I. The markets will bounce back; I've seen it all before. But we must cling to the Lord, otherwise we'll lose more than our financial security. We'll lose hope. And we can't lose that."

They talked for a few more minutes, though later Keith wouldn't remember a word of it—nothing but the part about God and His direction. When they hung up, Keith returned to the computer and dropped, entranced, to the chair. They'd lost the Brandon Paul movie. They'd done everything they could. They had the actor and the author, the funding and the best lawyer in town. But they'd still lost it.

He needed to talk to Luke and Chase and Stephanie Fitzgerald. He needed to know whether Brandon was behind this. And if so, why he'd turned his back on them. But more than that, he needed to talk to the Lord.

With his face buried in his hands, he cried out to God about what had gone wrong and asked the Lord for wisdom and direction. With no hint of an answer, he asked anyway. He begged for peace and clarity, and most of all he asked God how it was even possible that they could lose everything they'd worked for—the promise the future held and the ability to influence a generation.

All in five crazy minutes.

Twenty-Four

The girls were both in bed when the phone rang at Chase's house. He was packing again, something he always seemed to be doing, but before he could answer it Kelly must've picked it up in the kitchen. The call was probably for her anyway. Laurie Weeks had been in touch a lot lately, making plans for a women's conference coming to town in a few days.

But after a minute or so, he heard her footsteps. Not until the last few months had he understood how discouraged a person's footsteps could sound. He could've picked out Kelly's in a room full of people.

"Chase." Her voice held a flicker of concern. "It's Keith. He doesn't sound right."

Chase frowned. Life in Hollywood and their roles as producers couldn't have been any better. He couldn't imagine why Keith would call—unless a problem had come up with their flights. He took the phone and turned toward the bedroom window. "Hey, what's up?"

A long pause filled the phone line before Keith finally spoke. "It's over, buddy."

Chase's heart hesitated, and then slammed into double time. "What do you mean, it's over?"

"It's over. We lost the Brandon Paul movie."

Chase sucked in a quick breath, overcome by disbelief. "That's crazy. Nothing's changed. If NTM doesn't want it we'll take it somewhere else. That's what the meetings are for this week."

"Get to your computer. Fox News will help you understand." Keith sounded weary, defeated. There wasn't even the hint of possibility in his voice.

Kelly still watched from the doorway. Now as he passed her, she whispered to him. "What is it? What happened?"

He held up his hand and gave her a look that implored her to be patient. With the receiver covered, he mouthed in her direction, "I'll tell you in a minute."

She hesitated, but then she returned to the kitchen, her body language proof she wasn't happy about being put off. Chase had no choice.

He went to the den, pulled out his laptop, and powered it up. He was on the Internet in seconds, tapping out the address to Fox News. All the while, Keith remained silent. Completely silent—as if there was nothing he could say that wouldn't be absolutely clear once the news page loaded.

Chase saw the headline about NTM and immediately called up the story. It took less than a minute for him to understand what had happened. "This is crazy! They can't steal our story!" Fury ripped through him and he clenched his fist. "Are you kidding, Keith? Nothing's over. Stephanie's agent won't stand for this, and neither will Luke. This is a bunch of garbage."

"I talked to Ben Adams. He says NTM can do pretty much what they want. They have teams of lawyers to cover their tracks." If Keith had been angry earlier, he wasn't now. "There's more."

A sick feeling grabbed hold of Chase. Had everyone lost their minds? Of course NTM couldn't do this. They'd sat down at six different meetings with Ace Rustin and his cronies. The proposal, the storyline, everything about the movie was already in place. They couldn't just recreate the plotline and go their own way now. He directed himself to focus, to listen to whatever else Keith had to tell him. "Go ahead."

"Ben talked to his accountants today, and his people have convinced him not to sell stocks in order to finance a movie. Not until the market improves."

The air seemed to leave the room. "That's not possible." Chase was on his feet again, his head hanging, knees trembling. He tried to grasp at the first question to surface. "He's still with us, right? He still wants to invest in our movies?"

"He can cover half the P&A, but that's it. Even if by some miracle we wind up with the Brandon Paul movie, he can't help us out."

The reality was immediately clear. Without investor money, what did Chase and Keith really bring to the table? Producers had to have money to work with, otherwise they weren't producers. Chase began to shake, shivering as if overtaken with a high fever. "So that's it; we have no movie."

"It doesn't look that way." Keith hadn't sounded this down in a long time, maybe ever. "We have *The Last Letter*, of course. But even if it does well, we won't have profits to reinvest for at least a year or eighteen months. By then *Unlocked* will be a thing of the past. One more movie that's already been done."

They talked for a few minutes, and Keith explained that they would still fly to LA in the morning, still take meetings around town. They still had rights to the novel, so if not NTM, other studios would still be interested. Even without Brandon Paul.

"What if the studios cancel? I mean, we no longer have the star."

"We have the book." Keith's tone showed some sense of rebounding. "Either way we need to meet with Luke and Kendall, then Stephanie and Brandon. We need to find out how this crazy announcement happened, and move on."

"That's it? We find out what's behind it and give up?"

"Of course not." Keith's intensity was back. "We're missionaries first, remember that?"

Chase felt the chastisement straight to the depths of his soul. It was the first time since the phone rang that he'd even thought about God. He sank into the living room sofa chair and stared at the ground. "I remember."

"Okay, so we pray. We remind ourselves that no ground is ever gained for Christ without great effort. It's a battle, not a land grab. The world owns the movie industry, so what makes us think anything about this job will be easy?"

Slowly Chase began to nod. "You're right." He wanted to cry out to Jesus, apologize for having such a human response instead of immediately turning to his faith. "You've already prayed about this, I take it?"

"For the past half hour. But I want to pray together. Back in the jungles of Indonesia, we prayed as often as we breathed. We would rather miss a meal than a chance to pray together for the people we were preaching to."

Chase could picture that old life, and suddenly he longed for it, for the simplicity of knowing that his job was clearly spelled out: tell people about Jesus, one after another, as long as he drew breath. This world, the world of Hollywood, was much more complicated. Especially in moments like this. In the back of his mind he wondered what he would tell Kelly. An anxious sigh filtered between his teeth. "You start."

Keith took a quick breath and began. "Lord, we are Your witnesses here on earth, Your missionaries. We left Indonesia to take the message of hope and faith to the world of Hollywood. We've felt Your presence every step of this journey, back when our actress was threatening to run and our food truck burned down, back when we were out of money and not sure how we would finish one film, let alone more. But we stood firm, believing in You then, and we stand firm, believing now. You know all things, and You know why NTM would make such an announcement, and how things with Brandon Paul fell apart. We ask You now for clarity and vision, for wisdom and direction. Without You, we don't know where to turn."

A moment of silence separated their cries for help, and then Chase began. "I'm sorry, Father. I heard this terrible news and all I could think about was myself. The work I've invested, the money and hope. All of it lost. But You're a God of miracles. We can only follow where You lead. So lead us now, dear God ... Lead us now. We ask this in Jesus' name, amen."

There wasn't much more to say. They made last-minute plans for the morning drive to the airport and ended the call. Chase could hear Kelly in the kitchen, putting away dishes. He wondered if there were visible weights on his shoulders, or if they just felt that way.

Be with me, God. Help her understand. Keith is right. There must be something great on the other side of this mountain, or the battle wouldn't be so fierce.

I am with you, Son ... I am your strong tower.

The verse was from something Chase had read the day before. He clung to it as he walked to the kitchen.

Kelly turned around, her eyes anxious. "Well? That didn't sound very good."

"It isn't." He leaned on the refrigerator, and the old machine groaned in response. He shifted his weight away from it and made himself look into Kelly's eyes. "We lost the Brandon Paul movie." He didn't wait for her questions, but rattled off everything he knew about the Fox News story and the similarities between *Unlocked* and the movie NTM was calling an original. Then, barely taking time for a breath, he told her about Ben Adams and the funding crisis.

Slowly she dried her hands on a nearby towel, never once even blinking as she stared at him. "Without funding, there's no movie anyway. Isn't that right?"

"I'm not sure which piece matters most—the NTM announcement or the realization by Ben that he could no longer invest in our film." Chase tried to sound as positive as possible, but his voice failed him. "Either way, we have to accept the obvious. We no longer have a Brandon Paul movie."

Chase expected Kelly to fall apart. She would start crying and rail on Chase for ever believing that God had called him and Keith to the mission field of Hollywood. Of all things. But none of that happened. Instead she straightened and for the first time in a long time, a tender smile tugged at her lips. "Everything's going to be okay. We still have our faith." She held her hands out to him. "We still have each other."

He went to her, trying to figure out where she was coming from. All along she'd been doubtful of their movie ventures. So then why now was she so calm, so sure that things would work out? He pulled her close and stroked her back. "You're not mad?" His voice was a tentative whisper. This Kelly was the one he'd fallen in love with, the one who had all but disappeared these past months.

"I'm heartbroken. But I'm not mad." She ran her hands over the back of his head and whispered close to his ear. "This means you can stop traveling and be home with us. You tried your best, Chase. What more could God ask of you?"

Gradually, he began to realize what was happening. Kelly wasn't mad because she thought he was giving up, wholly and completely. With this single closed door, she figured the game was over. No more movie-making, no more traveling. No more wondering whether they'd be in financial ruin a year from now. He could get a real job and they could find their way to normalcy.

He drew back, feeling the shock in his eyes as he studied her. But before he could set her straight, she brushed her fingertips against his face. "My dad called yesterday. He knows someone at the post office. Most branches are laying off, but this one's hiring.

Just a few miles from our house." The enthusiasm in her voice was new, something she hadn't allowed for a long time. "His friend promised to put in a good word for you. If you're interested."

Chase felt like he was being ripped apart, like the floor had become a deadly sea of knives. "Are you serious?" He pushed back from her, not wanting a single minute more of her pity or easy answers. "I'm not looking for a job at the post office." He spat the words like they were laced with poison. "Keith and I are flying to LA tomorrow, where we're taking meetings on *Unlocked.* Without Brandon Paul. We're moving ahead, believing with everything we are that God will clear up the details."

Kelly's calm, collected veneer shattered like a cheap piece of glass. "But you just said it was finished. There's no Brandon Paul movie, right? So that means you come home and get a real job." Her tone grew intense, her voice louder than before. "That's what fathers do—they provide for their families."

"And wives support their husbands." He scowled at her for a long moment and then rolled his eyes. "We're not finished making movies. If God closes this door, He'll open another one somewhere. It's our job to find it."

"What if the door is right here in your own house? Huh, Chase? What you're doing scares me to death. Did you ever think about that?"

"There's nothing to be afraid of, Kelly. I won't let you down." He stared at her, alternately hating her and longing for her understanding. Finally he brushed his hand in her direction. "Never mind." He turned around and headed back to his laptop.

The headline still screamed at him from his computer screen. *Brandon Paul Agrees to NTM Movie Deal.*

For almost an entire minute he stared at the words as doubts began to crowd in around him. What if Kelly was right? At what point did they wave the white flag and surrender their dreams of making movies in lieu of earning a regular living? If he was honest, this news scared him too. The announcement was strange and unexpected, and for that reason maybe it *was* a sign. Maybe God could use him better as a mail carrier.

He felt angry tears in his eyes and he slammed his laptop shut. No! Kelly was wrong. This wasn't a sign. It was a mountain. Nothing more, nothing less. If this were a sign to quit making movies, Keith would've felt that way, too, right? He would've said something about having a meeting, just the two of them, and deciding whether they should call it quits.

But that wasn't how Keith felt. During their conversation he had even reminded Chase of Jeremiah 29:11. Jeremiah Productions. God knew the plans He had for them, to give them a hope and a future. If they felt led to Hollywood, convinced God wanted them to make movies that mattered, then they would follow that dream until every door was closed and locked. He would mention Kelly's fears to Keith, but he could almost hear his friend's response.

Trust God. We have to trust.

The Brandon Paul movie was just one door. Keith had even said they should feel excited, that the battle was only fierce because God has something better for them in the long run. So why couldn't Kelly see that?

He clenched his fists again and released them. A mail carrier? Was she serious? He'd rather go back to Indonesia.

He needed to talk to someone—Luke or Stephanie, someone who believed in their projects. Certainly Stephanie would be furious when she saw the NTM announcement. She was an early riser who turned in each night around eight o'clock. Otherwise he'd call her right now. NTM could put Brandon in an original film, but the screenplay would have to, indeed, be original. A story about a mentally challenged boy finding freedom in music? It was almost exactly the same plot as *Unlocked*. NTM or not, they'd never get away with it.

Even so, he needed to talk. He thought about calling Keith back, but his friend was clearly exhausted, and they still had their early flight in the morning. He racked his brain, wondering if he could reach Luke at this hour, and then deciding against the idea of even trying. It was much later in Indiana, and Luke was a professional. They would talk at length tomorrow, Chase had no doubts. But tonight …

The idea hit him in a rush. He could call Kendall. She would know about her father's financial trouble, and she'd have a sense of how things would go tomorrow at their first meeting. She was used to the highs and lows of Hollywood.

He pulled his cell phone from his pocket and dialed her number without stopping for a minute to consider whether doing so was right or wrong. She was their business partner, their teammate. They needed to talk now more than ever.

The call almost went to her voice recorder, but at the last moment she answered. "Chase …" Her voice held compassion and understanding. "You saw the news?"

"That and the situation with your dad."

"I know. I talked to him." She sounded down, but not out. "I hate this part of movie-making, how quickly things can fall apart. But I know this—" Determination rang in her voice. "God is still on His throne, and He's still working miracles. He didn't bring us this far to let us down."

Chase closed his eyes and breathed in deeply through his nose. This was what he needed, a confident, trusting voice on the other end assuring him that they might have lost a round, but they were still in the fight. "What's the deal with NTM? Any ideas?"

"Some. I put a call into Brandon, but he must be out. I've seen a few recent paparazzi photos of him clubbing it up with Hollywood's wild-child crowd. I've been meaning to talk to him about it, but we've played phone tag." She exhaled. "Now this."

"So you think ..." Chase grabbed at straws, desperate for more of her positive spin on things. "You think maybe it's all a mistake?"

"That's possible. Brandon was dead-set on starring in *Unlocked*. I can't believe he'd sell out to NTM like that. Not for any kind of money." She went on to explain that even if NTM offered him more money for ditching the author and producers, to take their offer would be shortsighted. "We have studios lined up who will pay him more than NTM, with all of us involved. This can't be about money."

He nodded, grateful for any hope she could offer. "Keith and I want to press on, but I don't know. I mean, do you think maybe God's closing the door on all of it?"

"Not at all." She sounded outraged by the idea. "Chase, you listen to me. You and Keith are two of the most talented producers I've ever come across. Combined with your talent as a director, I believe with all my being you're about to break into this business with a vengeance. Brandon's lucky to work with you, and I think Stephanie's told him so."

In the wake of her words, hope suddenly had a heartbeat again. Brandon Paul wanted to work with them. Which meant they could most likely attract other investors. A single announcement by NTM didn't change that, no matter what the explanation. "We'll meet for lunch tomorrow after you fly in," she said as the conversation wound down. "Between now and then I'll talk to Luke and Brandon, and we can figure out where things really stand."

"Okay." Chase felt much better. The weights on his shoulders were gone, at least for now. "God's brought us this far, right?"

"Exactly." There was a smile in her voice, and it was contagious.

He felt his own weary smile fall into place. "We need to believe, that's all."

"Right. God wins, remember that. You and Chase are God's filmmakers. You keep on, and He'll meet you. Seriously, Chase. You have to keep believing."

He let her words roll around his heart for a minute, soothing the wounded edges. "Thank you."

"We're a team. When I'm down, you can remind me. This time it's my turn."

As the call ended, Chase returned to his packing. Calling Kendall had been just what he needed. She was right. Even with the disappointments from tonight, their movie-making was headed in the right direction. Ahead of them they had this week's meetings for *Unlocked* and *The Last Letter's* appearances at the film festivals. And there was the theatrical release. *The Last Letter* might be a huge box-office hit. It was all suddenly possible.

He reached the bedroom and stared at his wife. Kelly had apparently brushed her teeth in record time, because she was under the covers, softly snoring, not concerned whatsoever about the state of his heart or his confidence. *Fine*, he thought as he looked at her. *At least I have Kendall to believe in me*.

He finished packing and set his suitcase near the front door. Then he brushed his teeth, set his alarm, and turned in, careful to stay to his side of the bed so he wouldn't wake Kelly. So he wouldn't have to deal with her. He'd be gone before she woke up, which meant one more time of parting ways without finding common ground. One more time of leaving home feeling her disappointment like a chain around his ankles. But that couldn't be helped. He would press on without her and when they climbed over this mountain he would spend time on his marriage. Until then, he could survive without Kelly's support, the way he'd survived these past several months. He didn't need her praise and encouragement.

God had given him Keith and Kendall for that.

Twenty-Five

Andi understood there was a battle going on — a battle for her heart and soul. But she didn't care. If the world was on one side and God and her faith on the other, Andi was cheering for the dizzying, intoxicating world. Everything about her life had grown more intense, more exciting, since she'd fallen for Taz. And if that meant stepping over the edge, she would do it. For now, at least. While she still had so much about life to experience, so many emotions to discover. She could always go back if things got too deep. What was the worst that could happen?

Her date with Taz to the jazz concert had been like a journey of brilliant reds and oranges, all the colors of a sunrise and sunset combined into one amazing night. They sat next to each other, the heat from the nearness of his body filling her senses. But even then, he didn't kiss her. They talked about physical love as they walked back to her dorm, and Taz said he wasn't a fan of free love. "Our bodies are instruments of art and love, all tied into one. If we share them too freely, we cheapen the art."

Andi loved that, the way he saw physical love as simply one more form of art. Until that night, she'd wondered why he was waiting to kiss her, why he hadn't acted when he was clearly taken by her, the same way she was taken by him. But after their talk on the way back to her dorm that night, she understood better. If physical love was art, then this time of waiting was a prelude, a way to heighten the beauty of whatever lay ahead.

It was the second week of May and finals were over. Andi had studied hard, and she had a good feeling about her grades. Taz hadn't been a distraction in that sense whatsoever. She filed out of her psych class, and across the campus she spotted Cody Coleman. He was walking with a group of guys, and for a moment she stopped and watched him.

How different she might feel about her faith if God had allowed her to have a relationship with a guy like Cody. Whatever his rocky past, he was completely sold out to Christ now, and Andi guessed he always would be.

She started walking again, making sure her path wouldn't cross his. Their friendship had fizzled, and she could live with that. She didn't need a lecture from Cody about how she spent her time. She had Bailey for that. Also, she was in a hurry. Taz planned to make her dinner at his apartment tonight. She didn't need an awkward conversation with Cody to make her feel guilty.

She remembered a time a few weeks ago when she'd run into him between classes. "Why so quiet?" she'd asked him. She kept her tone light, not wanting to sound like the poor victim in their friendship.

"School has me pretty busy." He raised an eyebrow. "And you seem busy with Taz Bazzi."

Andi had been surprised. "You know him?"

"He went to Clear Creek High. Hung out with the music types." Cody shrugged. "Had quite a reputation with the girls."

Something about Cody's tone offended Andi that day. She wanted to defend Taz and his beautiful heart, his unique way of looking at life. "That doesn't surprise me. He's very special."

Cody laughed. "Be careful, Andi. He had that 'special' thing going on back in high school too. Most of the girls figured him out pretty quick. He could say what he wanted to get his way with one of them, and then he moved on." He let his laughter fade. "If you were my sister, I'd forbid you from seeing him. Seriously."

If she were his sister ... Andi hated the way he said that. As if she could never be good for anything other than a close friendship. She wanted to scream at him and ask him what was wrong with her. What did Bailey Flanigan have that Andi didn't? But she wouldn't give him the chance to hurt her any more than he already had. She held her head high. "We must know different guys, then. The Taz I know is nothing like that."

The conversation ended, and Andi hadn't seen or heard from Cody since. But now his warning came back to her, and she was frustrated at herself for remembering it. Today was a perfect day, otherwise. The sun was out and the leaves and flowers were coming to life across campus. The temperature was already in the mid–eighties. Finals were behind her, and tonight she and Taz were going to celebrate. She didn't need Cody or anyone else putting a damper on her excitement.

She walked back to her dorm and caught Bailey just as she was leaving. "I'm having dinner with my parents and Tim." She beamed with happiness. "Doesn't it feel good to have finals over?" She let out a victory cry. "And all of summer stretched out before us."

"Yeah, it's amazing." Andi had been so busy with Taz and her classes that she and Bailey had grown somewhat distant. "Did you decide what you're doing? For the summer, I mean?"

"I've got the Cru retreat at Lake Monroe. But after that I'm definitely going to New York next week with Tim and my mom. We're auditioning for ensemble roles in three shows—sort of an open casting call. After that, I'm not sure. If I don't get a part, I'll be in Bloomington." She set her bag down on her bed and looked at Andi, her interest genuine. "What about you?"

"I'm not going on the retreat, and I'm not going home. I know that much." She laughed at the idea. "My parents would have me signed up as a church camp counselor in no time." Andi realized how she sounded, but it was too late. She managed a sad smile. "You know what I mean."

Bailey hesitated, as if there was much she wanted to say. But she only held Andi's gaze for a long while. "You can stay with my family any time over the summer. We have the apartment. If your parents don't want to pay for the dorm ..."

"Thanks." Andi imagined the freedom she'd have with Taz if she had their dorm room to herself. Taz had three roommates. It was a rare night when—like tonight—he had the place to himself. "Actually, I'll probably stay in the dorm. I'm taking a few classes. Nine units, maybe. I'd like to get ahead a little, so that means making up the time somewhere."

"Acting still, right?"

"Definitely. My dad's struggling with the Brandon Paul movie, but there'll be others. I wanna be ready next time the chance comes up."

Andi felt strange, the way the conversation with Bailey was going. When they started out as roommates last fall they were so much alike—two girls with a love for God and a determination to be pure. But now ... their differences made even a talk like this feel strained. Like there was far more they weren't saying. "I talked to the librarian. Looks like she has a part-time job for me over the summer recataloging the books."

"Sounds tedious." Bailey wrinkled her nose.

"I can listen to my iPod while I work." Andi gave a light shrug. "Sounds like a paycheck to me. And my parents won't let me stay unless I'm earning money."

Again Bailey seemed like she wanted to say something, and this time she dropped the chitchat about their summer plans. "How are things with Taz?"

"He's wonderful." Andi felt her whole face light up. "I wish you knew him better, Bailey."

"I knew him a little at Clear Creek. He was a year older, so I'd forgotten until Cody reminded me." She frowned with worry. "He didn't have the best reputation."

"He's changed. I've never met anyone like him."

"Hmmm." Bailey fiddled with her bedspread. She'd packed up most of her things, so her side of the room was pretty bare. "What do your parents think?"

"They don't know that much, really. Just that I'm seeing someone."

"But it's more than that, right?" Bailey didn't sound judgmental, just concerned. "You can be honest with me. You're falling for him, huh?"

"I guess." Andi walked over and sat on the bed next to Bailey. "He talks about love and then he talks about art and film and music, and the lines blur between all of it. I've never met anyone so romantic."

"What about … what about the physical stuff. He's kissed you, right?"

"That's the weird thing." Andi was dying for someone to talk to about Taz. Until now she and Bailey had only said a few words in passing, both of them too busy to discuss in depth their lives outside school. And of course Andi didn't want to be reprimanded. "We spend all our free time together, but every time I think he's going to kiss me, he backs away. I mean, I feel like we're kissing every time because, I don't know, we're just that close. But he's a gentleman, Bailey. He doesn't want to do anything I'm not comfortable with."

Bailey looked relieved. "That's good." She bit her lip. "What about the movie? The film you made?"

"It's finished. He turned it in last week as part of his final. I guess the department gave out awards and his film took the top prize." There was something else, something Taz wanted to tell her tonight. But for now that's all Andi knew. Except that the short movie was the talk of the Indiana University film department. "I think it really grew me as an actress."

Bailey nodded. "You took off your shirt, right? Down to your bra?"

The conversation was going too well for Andi to ruin it now with the whole truth. She nodded. "Yes. The scene called for it."

"You'd better hope it doesn't get out on the Internet." Bailey put her hand on Andi's knee. "You know how easy it is to put things on YouTube or Facebook. If your parents saw it, they'd be freaked out for sure."

"For sure." Andi's stomach twisted at the thought. She hadn't considered the possibility, and now it was too late. She would talk to Taz about it later.

"And what about God?" Bailey seemed more relaxed now. Less worried about hitting a taboo topic. "How are things with you and Him?"

"Well ..." She winced. "I haven't exactly been a good little Cru girl this quarter. Too busy with *Robin Hood* and my grades."

"And Taz."

"Yes, and Taz." She took a quick breath and tried to sound upbeat. "But there's always the fall quarter. It's easier to get involved then, anyway."

"Yeah, but I wasn't talking about Cru." Bailey's voice softened. She cared; Andi could feel her sincerity in a way she'd forgotten until now. "I was talking about God."

"God." Andi stood and wandered back to her side of the room. She opened her dresser drawer and glanced at Rachel's journal, tucked in near the back. She shut the drawer and leaned against the wall near her bed. "I still believe, if that's what you mean. I guess I just have to find my own way. You know, because God will always be there for me."

"But we won't always be here for God." Bailey lowered her eyes to the dresser where she must've known Rachel's journal was. "Your friend Rachel's life told us that much."

Andi understood the message. There was risk for the people who walked away from God, who believed that He'd be there waiting in the tomorrows of their lives, when they were tired of exploring the world, when they wanted the safety of His narrow path once again. What if tomorrow never came, the way it hadn't come for Rachel Baugher? "I don't know," Andi sighed. "I have to find my own way. That's all."

"Okay." Bailey's smile was sad. "But remember what the Bible says about life. Real life."

"That only God can give it?" Andi knew her Scriptures. That much hadn't changed.

"Exactly. And apart from Him, there is no life at all." Bailey stood and checked the time on her phone. "I have to get going. Wanna join us for dinner?"

"No, thanks." Andi met Bailey near the middle of the room. "Taz is taking me out. We're celebrating his film and the fact that finals are over. I get to see the finished movie for the first time tonight."

Bailey nodded slowly, her eyes never leaving Andi's. "Be careful, girl. And call me if you need me." The two of them hugged. "Let's get together early next week."

"Okay." Andi was glad they'd talked. It had been too long without a heart-to-heart, and even though they disagreed about life and the way to true happiness, they were still close. Closer than Andi had thought. Bailey wasn't going to write her off just because of her decisions. Andi was grateful, because someday—some very far-off day—she might want to be like Bailey again. And when that day came, if it came, Bailey would be her best friend ever. The way she couldn't really be right now, when they were so different.

Bailey left, and a few hours later Andi arrived at Taz's doorstep.

He stepped out onto the small landing and looked at her for a long time, his eyes taking in the length of her. "You're the most beautiful girl on campus, Andi. In person, and in front of the camera." He led her in, and she caught the smell of incense burning in another room. It was sweet and spicy, but not overpowering, and it mixed with something cooking in the oven. A Mexican dish of some kind. Andi took off her sweater and laid it over the back of the first chair they walked past. She wore skinny jeans and boots, a form-fitting navy-blue T-shirt and her best perfume. She hoped it would be enough to finally convince him to make a move and kiss her.

She looked around his apartment, at the way it felt like him. She'd only been here one other time, and then only to meet up with him before a movie.

Now, with his roommates gone and the place cleaned up, she took time to appreciate the place. Photos of partially nude women hung on the walls, each of them shot in dramatic black and white, a collection of art the way only Taz could appreciate it. He watched her. "I look at those photos, at the way they use their bodies to make a statement about love and nature." He gazed at a row of portraits, and then back at her. "And all I see is you, Andi. The way you would look in every picture. Every pose."

Her head spun, and her mouth went dry. He was falling for her, he had to be. If he didn't kiss her tonight, she would find a way to kiss him. She couldn't go another night without feeling his touch.

They moved into his living room, which consisted of an old leather sofa topped with a number of warm, fuzzy blankets. He came close to her, so close she could smell the freshness of his skin.

With the lightest brush of his fingers, he framed her face. "I thought we'd start with the film."

"Great." She felt a thrill of excitement run through her. "I can't wait."

He clicked on the TV and turned off the lights. But before he pushed the Play button, he sat on the sofa beside her and faced her. "You won best actress, Andi. I didn't want to tell you until now, so I could see your eyes."

Hope surged through her. "You're serious?" She wanted to get up and run around the room, but she threw her arms around his neck instead. "You know what this means?"

A soft chuckle came from him. "It means I was right." He pulled back and looked deeply into her eyes. "You have a gift."

"It means I can act! I can do this for a living, I know it!"

They looked at each other for a long time, and Andi wanted him to kiss her in the worst way. But just when it seemed like he might, he put his arm around her shoulders instead and eased her close against his side. "The film is amazing, and it's all you." He hit the Play button, and the movie began.

When they reached the scene where she strips down, Andi held her breath. But Taz had stayed true to his word. The scene was shadowy and sensual, and other than the moment when she looked at herself in the mirror, it would've been impossible to tell she was the actress.

"Beautiful," Taz whispered near her ear. His breath came faster again, the way it had when he filmed the scene. "You take my breath away, Andi."

He whispered to her again and again throughout the film, and when it was finished, when he hit the Stop button and powered down the television, Andi could feel his desire like a physical presence. Taz turned to her and lightly touched her forehead, her cheeks. "You're mine. You know that, right?"

"Yes." Andi didn't hesitate. Her whisper was breathy, revealing her own heightened sensuality. "I've belonged to you for a long time."

That was all he needed to hear. In a move that felt almost scripted, Taz kissed her. The feeling was like every wonderful thing Andi had ever experienced, all rolled into one brilliant rainbow of emotions. She wasn't sure when he eased her onto her back or how he moved from kissing her to touching her, to peeling away her clothing. But whatever was happening, Andi didn't want it to stop. She'd never felt like this in all her life.

Thirty minutes later, when she had given Taz everything she had to give and was getting dressed, she felt a flickering pang of regret. Her father's face flashed in her mind, and she imagined for an instant how disappointed he'd be, how this was a promise that could never be lived out after tonight. But even if her father knew, and if she were forced to defend herself and her actions, Andi would do so. Because nothing in all her life had ever made her feel the way Taz had this past half hour.

She wasn't just another college girl sleeping with any other college guy. She was in love, and Taz was everything she'd dreamed of. She would remind herself as often as the doubts might come. So what if she wasn't the sweet and innocent virgin she'd hoped to be. She was a grown woman, mature enough to make her own decisions. Never mind everything she'd been taught or the narrow path she'd read about in the Bible. Everything would be just fine. What she and Taz had shared wasn't sex or sin or anything of the sort.

It was art.

Breathtaking and beautiful.

LISA SAT STRAIGHT UP IN BED, gasping for air and clutching at the covers. A feeling of utter doom surrounded her like thick fog and she could do nothing to get away from it. It was Andi! Her daughter was in trouble.

Lisa shot a look at the bedside clock. Just after midnight, three in the morning in Bloomington. Keith was in LA so it was too late to call him, too late to call Andi. But that didn't change how she felt. She sat up straighter and realized her heart was pounding. Faster, louder, faster, louder.

God, what's happening?

Pray, my daughter. You must pray continually.

The answer came quickly and with it a vivid picture of Andi the way she'd looked in the jungles, wide-eyed and happy, telling the women about Jesus. Something had changed that, she was suddenly certain. Never mind if Andi's Facebook didn't give clues, and if Andi kept convincing her and Keith that everything was okay. It didn't matter that Andi had never given them a reason to doubt her. This was an emergency. The intensity of Lisa's fear and panic couldn't have been worse if she were watching her daughter fall off a cliff.

Andi was in deep, desperate trouble.

Pray. She had to pray. That's what God wanted and that's what she would do. She climbed out of bed, trembling, shivering. *Please, God ... be with her. Save her from whatever's happening. Please.*

Lisa fell to the floor, to her knees and then flat on her face, her nose and mouth pressed against the rough carpet fibers.

God, she's our girl, our only child. Please, help her. Give me a window to her life so I'll know how to intervene. Open the lines of communication and clear the deception. Please, God ...

Lisa prayed that way for twenty minutes, battling the darkness and fear, the certainty that Andi was in dire trouble. Finally the panic eased and she stood, weary, exhausted from the fight. Even then she prayed, because that's what God wanted from her. She could hardly wait for morning because this time she would press until she received real answers from her daughter. She would accept nothing less. Because if the intensity of her strange and sudden certainty was accurate, her precious daughter didn't face the sort of trouble that could be quickly fixed.

But the sort that could destroy her.

Twenty-Six

Kelly agreed to the women's conference for one reason. She had never felt further from God and Chase in all her life, and she was scared to death. Scared about the road she was on and terrified about where it might lead. Besides, Laurie had raved about the speakers and the music, and she'd done something else that pushed Kelly over the edge.

She'd arranged a babysitter for Molly and Macy.

When the teenage leader of the church's youth group showed up at her house just after eight that Saturday morning, Kelly was ready. She showed the girl around the house and explained the meals for the day. "You don't mind cooking?"

"Not at all." The girl smiled easily. "I cook all the time for my little sisters."

Finally, when Kelly had introduced Molly and Macy to the teenager and when she was certain she'd left every possible emergency number, she set out for Laurie's house. She was running early, so she stopped at McDonald's and bought two orders of hotcakes and a sausage biscuit. That way she wouldn't be hungry for lunch. She ate on the way to Laurie's and carefully wadded up the wrappers and reached back to stick them in the pocket behind her seat.

Not that Laurie would be looking. Kelly was leaving her car at her friend's house so they could ride to the conference together. Besides, she'd told her friend she was doing better. Which she was. Most days. Especially since her appointment with the therapist. Sure enough, he'd diagnosed her with a moderate to severe case of depression. More severe now that Chase was refusing to give up his crumbling movie dreams and come home. The doctor had prescribed Prozac, which was supposed to help not only elevate her mood, but also cut her appetite. Kelly wasn't sure if it was working yet, but she did feel a little better.

Laurie lived just a few miles away, and soon the two were hugging before getting into Laurie's car. "I have a feeling about today," Laurie told her as they climbed inside. "God's up to something big."

Kelly hoped so, but she certainly didn't feel it. She'd spent less than an hour talking to God the entire month of May, and now she felt like a hypocrite wasting a day at a Christian women's conference when she could be home cleaning or reading to her girls.

The event was in downtown San Jose at the HP Pavilion. Once they found a parking place and filed in with thousands of other women, Kelly's doubts returned.

"It'll take a half hour to get out of here," she told Laurie. "I mean, if something goes wrong with the girls."

"It's raining outside." Laurie put her arm around Kelly's shoulders. "They'll be inside watching movies and coloring all day. Nothing's going to go wrong."

Kelly had to agree. The rainy weather did limit the possibility of injuries. But maybe that wasn't why she felt uneasy. Maybe it was because Chase had flown down to LA that day and now he was meeting with his Hollywood friends and trying to figure out what to do next. He wanted nothing to do with Kelly's more practical response, which was fine. He was bound to see soon that the optimism from his Hollywood friends wouldn't pay their bills.

All around them seats were filling up fast. "There have to be eight thousand people here." Laurie leaned close, in awe over the gathering. "Can you imagine, this many women in one place praising God? Like a glimpse of heaven."

Kelly felt completely and utterly detached from the reality happening around her. What had happened that she wasn't caught up in the excitement? Back in her Indonesian days, she would've loved nothing more than a day like this, surrounded by women worshiping the Creator. But here … she had no right to be excited about worship. She was at odds with her husband and she could barely get up each morning. What good would worship do except remind her of her failings?

The music started, and a sharp, professional praise band started in with "Blessed Be Your Name," a beautiful number by Matt Redman. The music and words were familiar, but Kelly hadn't heard them in so long that the memory of them almost seemed to belong to someone else. Even still, there was power in the sound of thousands of women's voices singing the same song, believing the same message.

"Blessed be Your name, in the land that is plentiful ..."

Kelly was familiar with the first verse, the picture of joy and prosperity during times when it was relatively easy to worship God. She let herself be drawn by the music, by the ebb and flow of it. By the time the song reached the first chorus, ladies all around her were rising to their feet, hands raised in praise. Kelly moved her mouth, singing along even if she didn't feel the words.

The second verse kicked in and Kelly finally felt her heart engage.

The words seemed to hang on the screen longer than usual, and Kelly read over them again and again. Words about her being in the desert place. Wasn't that exactly where she was now? She and Chase barely spoke to each other, and she couldn't stop her cravings for more than a day or two, no matter how hard she prayed.

Suddenly it hit her that maybe there was a connection. It was times like this—when she was in a desert, in a wilderness—that she most needed to bless the name of the Lord.

She stood as the song played on, and she clasped her hands near her chest. Next to her, Laurie was already on her feet. God was here; Kelly could feel His presence. But what could He possibly want with her? She had no right to stand here with these other women, women who were better believers, more faithful followers.

The song built to a crescendo and Kelly was surprised to feel tears on her cheeks. She dabbed at them and remained standing as the next song blended with the last. It was a Hillsong praise number called "Mighty to Save," and in the stronger days of last fall it had been one of her favorites. *"Everyone needs compassion ... love that's never failing ..."* The music grew and built to the chorus and Kelly had the strong sense that the words, the melody, were for her alone.

After another few songs, the morning worship ended and a speaker took the stage. She talked about the battle of life and how in the end Christians had the privilege of knowing for certain that they win.

Kelly was knocked back in her seat by that simple truth. She hadn't thought about that realization for far too long. No matter how tiresome and weary she felt today, with Christ she was on the winning team. She wasn't supposed to grovel along, discouraged and depressed. She was supposed to draw strength from that one fact. Her team was going to win. Why couldn't she just believe God would take care of them when they had so much to look forward to? She felt terrible, like the worst possible wife, the worst Christian ever. If only she'd heard this six months ago, before things had gotten so out of control.

More music followed but Kelly couldn't sing along. She stared at her lap and let the tears fall. The second speaker talked about the struggles and disappointments of life and how wrong it was to drag them through each day when God called all people to trade them in.

"Give Him your ashes, and He'll give you a crown of beauty," the woman declared.

The entire auditorium burst into applause.

Kelly thought about that. How long had she walked around dragging a bag of ashes? And wasn't there a point in time when it was too late to trade it in for beauty? Certainly God had to be tired of her weak attempts at living a Christian life. Maybe ashes were all that was left for her now.

The next speaker talked how each of them needed to accept their place in life, because God was the One who had done the placing. When she was finished, the speaker invited ladies to the front if they wanted to ask Jesus into their lives for the first time. "He's calling you, my friends, calling you to a life of freedom and strength, peace and purpose. Come now; don't let anything hold you back."

Kelly fidgeted in her seat. She had fresh tears on her cheeks, but this wasn't the time to go up front. Besides, she already had Jesus. She'd believed in Him, and she'd been baptized. What more was there? Someone might see her and wonder why she was going up when she'd been a Christian all her life. She'd served as a missionary, after all.

But when the first wave of women reached the front, the speaker invited another group of people.

"Maybe you've been stuck in your faith, unable to hear God or feel His strength in your life. If that's you, then this is your day, your moment. Come and give Him your situation. Feel His loving arms holding you up, leading you to the front of the room where people can pray for you."

There was no one holding onto her, no one pulling her to her feet, and no one keeping her stuck to her chair. But Kelly felt the struggle as surely as she felt her next heartbeat. A tug-of-war was going on between the life she'd been living and the life God was calling her to. A tug-of-war where she, Kelly Ryan, was the rope.

She watched as one woman and then another, and then dozens of women made their way to the front. Emotions and heartache flowed freely and the floor of the HP Pavilion became wet with the tears of the women strong enough to accept the call.

But still Kelly sat. She hadn't come here to make a decision or find renewal in her walk with Christ. She was simply taking a break for herself, spending time with Laurie. She needed more time before making a decision like the one the women around her were making. If she went up front, that meant she was willing to give up her resentment of Chase's determination to make movies and find strength in Scripture—the way she used to find it.

Maybe tomorrow or next week, but not now. She remained seated, watching countless women find freedom. Next to her, Laurie leaned close and patted her knee. "Like I said, God's doing something here today."

No question. But it would take longer for Him to do something with Kelly. No amount of emotion or tears could change her life or the facts as they were. Chase had no patience for her concerns and he seemed to rush to get out the door and back to LA. She was overwhelmed most of the time and she would most likely remain so—even with the Prozac. If she went forward here and now, then what? That wouldn't make her into the nice, supportive wife or clear away the work she had in running their home by herself.

Not now, God. I can't surrender now ... I'm not sure about anything.

The pressure on the rope grew greater. She could feel it, feel the battle raging. But still she sat.

During lunch, Kelly excused herself to the restroom. But afterward, she stepped outside and sat on the edge of a cement block wall under an overhang, one of the few places outdoors that was still dry. She didn't care about eating; a boxed lunch wasn't interesting to her on a day like this, and there was no candy for sale inside—she'd checked.

"Okay, God ... What are You doing?"

She'd had her phone off all morning, but now she turned it on. She felt a sudden urge to talk to Chase. Even for a few minutes. She clicked his name and immediately the phone began to ring. She waited—two rings, three, but on the fourth the call went to his voicemail. Her mouth opened to leave him a message, an apology or a plea that he call her later so they could talk. But nothing seemed right, and she hung up. Better to talk to him in person.

The rain had let up, but still the sky remained a dark gray. In a moment like this it was hard to believe the sky would ever clear again, same as it was hard to believe that for her life.

Why, God? Why am I fighting You?

She pictured the prayer lifting all the way to heaven, but there was no answer. No sign that God cared about her sitting here, lost in her own little world of ashes and self-pity.

Inside the music started up again. Laurie would wonder where she'd gone and how come she'd passed on lunch. Kelly pulled herself up and worked her way through the crowd back to her seat. The song was another Hillsong number, "From the Inside Out," and they were halfway through the first verse when Kelly took her seat.

"Everything okay?" Laurie looked into her eyes, clearly trying to see the truth.

"Fine." Kelly covered with a quick smile. "I went out to call Chase."

"Oh." Her friend nodded. "Good."

She turned her attention to the praise band. No point telling Laurie she hadn't even gotten through to her husband. She'd needed time alone—even in this massive crowd. The music filled the air around them. "*Everlasting, Your light will shine when all else fades ... never ending, Your glory goes beyond all fame ...*"

The line seemed custom-made for Kelly. No matter what lay ahead, Christ's light would remain, beyond the darkness and valleys, beyond the deserts and wilderness. Beyond any fame—whether their future involved a movie deal with Brandon Paul or not. God was King of all, Lord of all.

Kelly could still feel something holding her back from breaking completely, from giving in to the Lord's calling. But the wall was crumbling.

Each word of the song seemed written for her, and she stood with the other women, joining her voice with the throng.

She wanted to believe the lyrics, wanted to let God have His way with her, but her shame and guilt were too great. What reason would the Lord have for wanting her? How many times had she given God control only to take it back the next morning—overwhelmed by worry and discouragement? She was stuck, but still she sang, and as she did she could feel her vision growing clearer, feel the Lord's love nearer than before.

Finally, at the end of the day, came a concert by Nicole C. Mullen. Back in the days when Kelly listened to Christian music morning to night, Nicole had been one of her favorites. Her songs "Redeemer" and "Call on Jesus" were songs that marked eras in her life, times when she was a new mom and doubting her ability to stay strong for everyone who needed her. Kelly hadn't known Nicole was closing out the day, and now her time here seemed ordained from God. As if the Lord Himself had arranged for this performance.

"*I need a brainwash from my head to my soul ... I need a brainwash, bring it down to my toes ...*" Nicole's voice rang out across the auditorium. She was young and fit, and she easily danced as well as any of the teenage dancers behind her on the stage, including her fourteen-year-old daughter. The audience was on its feet singing along, enjoying the call to be of pure mind. Kelly swayed to the music, startled by the message.

The battle she was losing was in her mind. Each day she woke up overwhelmed only to wallow in self-pity the whole day—feeding the emptiness in her soul with comfort food. Only if she changed her mind, only if she gave God control over her thoughts, would she find freedom from her depression and mindless eating.

Nicole moved on to her hit songs, and all around her Kelly could hear the sniffling of women giving in to God's gentle prodding. "*I know ... my Redeemer lives ... I know, my Redeemer lives ...*" Kelly sang along, and for the first time that day she felt herself meaning every word. She was a failure, yes, and a sinner at the worst level. She'd ignored God and walked purposefully in a direction opposite the one He called her to. But still He lived, and He was hers. Her very own Redeemer. Even if she were the only one left on the face of earth.

The concert flew by, and toward the end, Kelly could feel tears on her cheeks again. She couldn't fight God much longer. It was a losing battle. No matter how much she'd let Him down, He wasn't giving up on her. She could feel the rope of her soul sliding in His direction.

Nicole ended her performance by introducing her last song with a brief story. "There was a woman in the Bible, desperate for healing. A woman who had been suffering for more than a decade. No one and nothing could heal her, but Jesus was passing by that day. There would be crowds of people, and hundreds more worthy of His attention than she could ever be." Nicole walked slowly to the edge of the stage. "But she knew. She absolutely knew that if she could only reach out and touch the hem of His garment, she would be healed. Her belief in Him and His power was that strong." She paused, letting the truth of the story sink in around the enormous room. "This song is called 'One Touch.'"

The music was pretty and lyrical, and Nicole started in with the first verse.

Then, as she sang, something dramatic began to happen. First her daughter, and then the other dancers moved stealthily out onto the stage. The girls wore flowing white dresses and black sweatshirts. On the back of each sweatshirt was a single, simple word: Shame ... Guilt ... Loneliness ... Doubt ... Addiction.

Nicole reached the chorus as her dancers formed an ominous half circle around her. Then with every bit of her energy, she clutched desperately at the air in front of her. *"If I could just touch the hem of His garment, I know I'd be made whole."* But as she reached out, the girls with Shame and Guilt and Addiction on their sweatshirts used all their energy to hold her back.

Nicole pushed against them.

The harder Nicole tried to press forward toward Jesus, the more Shame and Guilt, Loneliness and Doubt and Addiction held her back. The image was overwhelming and for the first time—the very first time—Kelly could see an actual picture of her life, the way Jesus saw her. She could try to touch the hem of His garment, she could beg Him for the scraps of His kindness, but something was holding her back. Something she had felt deep inside her for all these months.

Shame, guilt, loneliness, doubt, addiction.

The second verse began, and the story followed the one in the Bible. A crowd of people, a desperate attempt to press through to Jesus. Nicole's clear voice rang out. As she reached that part where Jesus looked back, every obstacle fighting for her soul stopped and stared.

Kelly began to cry, struck by the picture. That was how the battle went, wasn't it? If she would only get close enough to Jesus to touch the hem of His garment, she could hear His voice, and the things holding her back would hear it too.

One by one, the dancers representing Shame and Guilt and Loneliness and the rest fell in a heap to the floor. The message was as clear as it was powerful. No barrier could stand in the presence of Christ. *"If I could just touch the hem of His garment, I know I'd be made whole."*

As the song built, Kelly's tears came harder. That was her, reaching out to Jesus and letting her shame and addiction hold her back. But not anymore. *"Somehow He pressed His way through my madness,"* Nicole sang out, *"and His love has healed my soul."*

That was it, Kelly understood now. She needed to get close enough to Jesus to hear His voice, to touch the hem of His garment so she could be made whole again.

Laurie seemed to understand that something was happening with Kelly. She put her hand on Kelly's shoulder. "It's okay," she whispered. "Let God have His way."

Kelly nodded as the tears ran down her face and into her mouth. Salty and hot. *I'm sorry, Jesus. I don't want to fight anymore. I surrender. I surrender completely.* She didn't need more convincing. The picture of Nicole straining for Jesus and being held back was one that would stay with her forever. A picture of the battle. But the victory would also stay with her. She didn't need to fight against shame and guilt and depression. She only needed to stay close to Jesus, where the things that warred against her soul didn't stand a chance. Close enough to touch the hem of His garment.

The way she was standing now.

A Note from Karen

Dear Reader Friends,

More than any other book I've written, I was amazed at how life imitated art while I was writing *Take Two*. Midway through the book, and even after I'd written my outline, I had the privilege of attending the Palm Springs Film Festival, where my movie *Like Dandelion Dust* was one of the featured films. *Like Dandelion Dust* was selected as Best of the Festival and received much praise from local news and even a stunning review in *Variety*. In addition, it won Best Picture at a number of other film festivals.

But that is pretty much where the similarities ended.

The brothers who produced *Like Dandelion Dust* experienced some of the logistical distractions detailed in *Take One*, but here in *Take Two* fiction took over. There was no Kendall Adams or Ben Adams in the lives of the real producers. Even so, I believe the storyline of the fictional producers represents an important truth. In today's market, there is a great hunger for Christian films, for movies with a message and not merely a couple hours of mindless entertainment. That said, the struggle remains. The task of putting a movie onto the big screen is still daunting. I encourage you to pray for the many real-life producers like Chase Ryan and Keith Ellison who sacrifice much for the sake of changing the world with the power of film.

Also, I love that this series gives me the chance to follow Bailey and Cody and their group of friends. College life is very difficult for today's young people, with many distractions to faith and family and all that is right. It's important to see how differently a young Christian girl can meet those challenges and tests. Certainly as Andi goes her own way, the consequences will become clear. Likewise, as Bailey chooses God's will, though she may have heartache at times, she will find the plans God has for her.

In the books ahead Tim and Bailey and Cody, Andi and her parents, Chase and Kelly, and Kendall Adams all will face great temptations and trials, and at the same time brilliant, tearful triumphs. As always, I'm grateful you're continuing this new journey with me, and I look forward to hearing your feedback.

Take a minute and visit my website at www.KarenKingsbury.com, where you can get to know other readers and become part of a community that agrees there is life-changing power in something as simple as a story. On my website you can post prayer requests or pray for those in need. You can send in a photo of your loved one serving our country or let us know of a fallen soldier we can honor on our Fallen Heroes page.

My website will also tell you about my ongoing contests, including "Shared a Book," which encourages you to let me know when you've shared one of my books with someone in your life. Each time you let me know, you're entered for the chance to spend a summer weekend with my family. In addition, everyone signed up for my monthly newsletter is automatically entered into an ongoing once-a-month drawing for a free, signed copy of my latest novel.

Also on my website you can find out which women's conferences I'll speak at next and whether you might live close enough so we'll have the chance to meet, to share a hug, or take a picture together. In addition there are links that will help you with matters that are important to you—faith and family, adoption, and ways to help others.

Of course, on my site you can find out a little more about me and my family, my Facebook and YouTube channel, and my Karen's Movie Monday—where I release a YouTube clip each

Monday dealing with some aspect of my family and faith and the wonderful world of Life-Changing Fiction™.

Finally, if you gave your life over to God during the reading of this book, or if you found your way back to a faith you'd let grow cold, send me a letter at Office@KarenKingsbury.com and write "New Life" in the subject line. I would encourage you to connect with a Bible-believing church in your area, and to get hold of a Bible. If you can't afford a Bible—include your address in your e-mail and I'll send you one.

One more thing: I've started a program where I will donate a book to any high school or middle school librarian who makes a request. Check out my website for details.

Again, thanks for traveling with me through the pages of this book. I can't wait to see you next time. My next book will be a stand-alone called *Shades of Blue*. It's a book I've been longing to write for three years. After that, look for *Take Three*!

Until then, keep reaching for the hem of His garment.

In His light and love,
Karen Kingsbury

www.KarenKingsbury.com

Reader Study Guide

Please use the following questions for your book club, small group, or for personal reflection.

1. The editing process was long and tedious for Keith and Chase. What do you think drove them to put in such long hours? What have you been a part of in the past that required an amazing effort? What drove you in that effort?

2. What led to Kelly's discouragement and depression? Share about a time when you or someone you know was taken into a dark time because of a series of events.

3. Kelly struggled with mindless eating. Discuss what you know about this type of problem. What do you think led Kelly to struggle with this?

4. Thanksgiving Day at Katy and Dayne's was a chance for the Baxter family to be back together again. Tell about the times during the year when you and your family get together. What made this time special for the Baxters? What makes these times special for you and your family?

5. Discuss the importance of being thankful. What were the things Keith and Chase and their wives were thankful for? What are ten things you are thankful for?

6. What led Andi to be interested in the offer from the student filmmaker—Taz? Why is flattery from worldly sources such a dangerous thing in our walk with the Lord? Talk about a time when flattery led you to make a decision you regret.

7. Bailey felt a strain in her friendship with Cody through much of this story. What caused this strain? Share about a time when you experienced a strain with a close friend. What caused the strain, and what brought the friendship back around again?

8. For Keith and Chase, the first part of *Take Two* has them at a time in their professional careers when everything seems to be going right. What did the producers learn during this time? Have you learned more about your faith in good times, or in difficult times? Explain.

9. Cody wants desperately to help his mom stay on the right path, but still he worries about her. What does Cody do to show his mother he's there for her? What have you done to be supportive of someone you love? How has that support made a difference?

10. Explain Andi's series of compromises where Taz's movie was concerned. How did Taz convince her that these compromises were acceptable?

11. Talk about a time when you or someone you know made a series of compromises. How were those compromises justified?

12. Midway through the book, Keith began to experience red flags where the smooth and easy details of moviemaking were concerned. Why is it important to look closer when the details of life seem too easy? Talk about a time when the easy life suddenly became very difficult.

13. Bailey found much strength in her involvement with Campus Crusade. Why is it important for youth to be involved in a faith group of some kind? Why is it important for all Christians to belong to some sort of group of believers?

14. In what ways did Kelly make things worse in her relationship with her husband? What about her relationship with God? Talk about a time when you or someone you know made choices that harmed their relationships.

15. How could Kelly have helped her situation? Talk about how you or someone you know might find help in a troubling situation.

16. Kelly had the chance to attend a women's conference. Talk about a Christian conference you attended. Did you come away stronger because of it? Why or why not?

17. In what ways did God soften Kelly's heart during her day at the women's conference? Why was she reluctant to allow herself to be changed? Discuss Kelly's emotions that day.

18. Discuss how Nicole C. Mullen's song "One Touch" made a difference for Kelly. Explain how the visual illustration of the song connected with Kelly.

19. Have you ever imagined a spiritual battle as a literal force holding you back from Jesus? Talk about a time like that.

20. Cody and Taz are very different college guys. Talk about the differences, and what motivates each of these young men.

Read an excerpt from the next book in the Above the Line Series: *Take Three*

Bailey arrived at the Lake Monroe retreat center lost in thoughts about her roommate. Their recent conversation had been good—for the first time in awhile. Maybe if they had more time together, Taz wouldn't be such an obsession in Andi's life. No matter what Andi thought about him, he was trouble. Bailey could feel it in her spirit. God didn't want Andi anywhere near the guy.

Still, convincing her would take a miracle at this point.

Bailey climbed out of her car and was met by a group of her Cru Bible study girls. Tim had had to cancel at the last minute—a case of strep throat—and Cody was spending the weekend with his mom, because of her birthday. At least that was the plan. But when she and the girls walked with their sleeping bags and pillows to their cabin, she heard Cody's voice.

She waited until she had her bed made before finding him with a few other guys near the fire pit. She caught his attention and he smiled. "I didn't think you were coming."

This wasn't the time for a serious conversation. But she had to know what had changed his mind.

"My mom had other plans." He grabbed an armful of wood and stacked it near the pit. "I'll tell you later."

While they ate, she could feel Cody's presence the way she could feel the presence of her family when they were in a crowd. A couple times she looked over her shoulder at him, and once she caught him looking too. He still hadn't explained what had happened with his mother, but there would be time for that later. Right now she needed to give her attention to the girls in her cabin. She'd asked God for closer friendships with them as a result of this retreat.

So far He was answering her prayers beyond anything she could've dreamed.

One of the guy cabins had cleanup that night, and Daniel dismissed the rest of the group for an hour of free time. A few of the girls wanted to make calls home, just to check in. Bailey waited until she was sure none of them were looking to talk to her, and then she wandered out the door and down the path toward Cody's cabin. She saw him long before she reached it, sitting outside on a tree stump, staring at the lake.

She stopped and watched him, the familiar way he held his head, the way the fading sun cast light over his shoulders. What was he thinking, sitting there like that? Was he worried about his mom, or a new girl in his life? Or maybe he was taking in God's beauty. She almost didn't want to disturb him, but then—as if he could read her mind—he looked her way and smiled. "Hey."

The path was smooth, but she watched her step anyway. Just in case some critter crossed in front of her. She was much more of a hotel girl, more comfortable at the Doubletree with samples of lotion and shampoo, than here in the woods. But she could appreciate both, and she was glad to be here. Especially now, with Cody a part of the retreat.

She reached him and grinned. "You looked lost in thought. I didn't want to interrupt."

For a second she thought he might tell her what he was thinking, but then he set his jaw, his smile guarded. "I'm glad you did."

He pointed at a path that led closer to the lake. "Wanna take a walk?"

"Sure." They set out side by side, and suddenly Bailey laughed out loud. "I just remembered something funny."

He slipped his hands into the pockets of his jeans and laughed a little too. The way he always did around her. "Which thing? There's lots to laugh at with you around."

"Hey." She pretended to be hurt. "I'm not sure that's a compliment."

"It is." His eyes danced. "Believe me, it is."

"Okay, well, remember when we were at the beach that time, on the other side of the lake? We took a walk and you challenged me to a race."

"Me?" He stopped and pointed to himself. "That was you, missy. You're the one who wanted to race."

"Anyway …" She kept walking, undaunted. "I got about ten steps and I twisted my ankle. You had to practically carry me back to the picnic tables."

"That was the summer before I shipped out."

"Yeah, it was." She allowed her laughter to fade softly, mingling with the early summer breeze. They turned a corner and lost view of the campsite. The lake spread out before them, but still they walked on. Up ahead was a bench, and when they reached it, they sat together. Cody seemed careful to allow space between them.

"So what happened? I thought you were going to be with your mom this weekend."

"She met some guy." He frowned. "I'm not sure how good he is for her. I was sort of hoping she'd meet someone at church, but she met this one at the health club."

"She made plans with him?"

"Yeah. She said she didn't want me to miss a retreat on her account."

"That was nice."

"I guess." He breathed in slowly, deeply. "I still worry about her."

"I know. I can tell." She lifted her chin and filled her lungs with the sweet-smelling air. "I forget how great it feels to be out here, just us and God."

"That's why I came. I need time with God. To really think about this coaching idea and whatever else my future holds."

Despite the cool bench beneath her Bailey felt her heart warm inside her. Cody, whose life might've turned out so different, was doing better than any of them had dreamed. His life was a living miracle, every aspect of it. "I'm glad. I still pray for you all the time."

His expression grew deeper, the connection between them as close as she shared with any of her brothers. "The way I still pray for you." He faced the water again. "Speaking of which, what happened to Tim? I thought he was taking this trip for sure."

"He got sick. Strep throat."

"Oooh." Cody frowned. "That's too bad."

"Yeah. I told him I'd give him details when we get back on Monday."

Cody was quiet for a long moment. In the distance trilled the haunting sound of a blue heron, swooping low over the water. The sun had already set, and dusk was settling across the lake. "You and Tim," Cody said finally. "You're still very serious, aren't you?"

She sighed. He'd never quite understood that she had loved him first, that if he'd come back from Iraq and declared his love for her, she and Tim would've been nothing more than a passing fling. But Cody didn't have those feelings for her, and now she wished he wouldn't ask questions about Tim.

"Sorry." Cody faced her. "You don't have to answer."

"No, it's fine." She folded her arms in front of her and pulled one foot up onto the bench. "Things are the same."

"Your dad said you and Tim are auditioning in New York next week."

"We are." She shrugged. "It's something I've always wanted to do. But last time I was in the city it didn't have the same appeal as before. I don't know." She stared at the water, at the light reflecting across the center of the lake. "New York's crazy. All sorts of noise and smells and cramped living. You have to look straight up on some streets just to see the sky."

Cody made a face. "Not my style."

"Definitely not." She gave him a sad smile. If she wound up in New York, that would be the end for her and Cody. Distance would have the final say. "My dad can't stand it either."

The conversation flowed easily, without the walls she'd kept up around herself for so much of the last school year. It felt wonderful, being close to him again. "I guess I realized something this last time. When we go to New York, we stay at this nice hotel and see the top shows, sitting in the best seats. We stay three days and then we're out of there. But that's not how it would be if I lived there." She hugged her knee to her chest and looked at him. "I'd be commuting in on a bridge or a subway, walking fast and trying not to get accosted. I'd pay high rent to share a small apartment and have almost no fresh air."

The sky grew dusky, but in the dim light that remained an eagle floated in the distance and landed in a towering pine. A breeze brushed against her face and for a few seconds she closed her eyes. When she opened them, she smiled again. "No moments like this."

"What about Tim?" Cody seemed guarded when he talked about Tim. "How does he feel about the city?"

"He loves it. I think he could live there for the next five years and feel great about it. He really wants to perform."

"What about finding a church? Do they have anything like that in New York?"

"They do." She uttered a sad laugh. "But Broadway's a long way from the Bible Belt."

They talked for a few minutes about a church she'd heard about not far from Times Square. "If I lived there, I guess I'd become a part of that."

Again Cody was quiet. Their hour was almost up, and they would need to get back soon. Neither of them had brought a flashlight. "So you really think it could happen, huh? You and Tim, performing on Broadway, living in New York City?" He smiled. "I guess that would be a dream come true for both of you."

"I guess." Everything about the possibility sounded right, like something she'd longed for since her early days with Christian Kids Theater. But right now, with the fresh lake air all around them and Cody by her side, her dreams were no longer as clear as they'd once been. "What about you?" She hadn't asked for a long time, and now she wanted to know. Even if she was afraid of his answer. "You seeing anyone?"

"Me?" A quiet laugh rattled his chest. "Definitely not. God's still making me into the guy I need to be. I want that before I want a girlfriend."

His answer made her feel starry eyed. "She's a lucky girl, Cody."

"I'm saving my heart for her. Any sort of casual dating at this point in my life would only cheapen what I have to offer." He looked out at the water again. "Whoever she is."

For the craziest moment, Bailey wanted to tell him that he didn't need to wonder, that no other girl would ever love him the way she could love him. But she stopped herself before she said something and sounded like a crazy person. She had a boyfriend, after all. She could hardly confess her love to the friend beside her when she had just finished talking about building a life with Tim in New York City.

"What are you thinking?" Again Cody seemed to read her mind.

"Nothing." Her smile was shyer than before. "Nothing I can tell *you*, anyway." She put both her feet down on the ground and kicked at his tennis shoe. "I'd say let's race back, but I can't afford another sprained ankle. Not with my audition next week."

Again he laughed. "That's just one of the things I love about you, Bailey. You make me laugh."

"Same with you."

"Can I tell you something?" His knee brushed against hers, and just as quickly he eased back, keeping things between them appropriate and on the level.

"Yes. That's the deal now. We're friends." She tapped his foot again. "You can tell me anything."

"Okay, now, don't weird out on me or think I'm trying to get between you and Tim or anything."

She giggled. "Go on. At this rate you'll never spit it out."

"The truth is I thank God every day for you, Bailey. For your family and your friendship. For the way we've found each other again."

"Ahhh." She tilted her head and let her eyes get lost in his. The last remainder of daylight shone on his face and she knew without a doubt she'd remember this moment as long as she lived. Without wondering whether it was right or wrong, she put her arms around his neck and hugged him. "That means the world, Cody." The hug was quick, nothing she wouldn't give one of her brothers. "I'm glad you told me." She pulled back and felt her eyes start to dance. "Now it's my turn."

"Go on."

"I thank God for you too. I was so mad at you back in the fall, when you wouldn't talk to me." She made a face and wagged her fist at him. "I thought we'd never have a day like this again in all our lives."

"I was worried about it."

"But here we are." She held up her hands and let them fall lightly to her knees. "That's why God's so amazing. He knows how to fix things, even after we make a mess of them."

"Exactly." He stood and reached out his hand. "Come on, it'll be pitch dark in a few minutes."

She took his hand and felt the thrill of his touch all the way to her toes. Once she was standing she drew her fingers from his and kept the conversation light. She could hardly hold hands with Cody. First, it would only confuse things. And second, holding hands with Tim never sent a chill through her. And she wasn't ready to analyze what that meant or what it said about her relationship with Tim. Better to keep her distance where Cody was concerned. Besides, he was holding out body and soul for the girl of his dreams. She didn't want to get in the way of that, even if a part of her desperately wished she were that girl.

On the way back, Cody told her about a bear sighting in the woods not far from the campsite.

"Great." She was about to tell him the story of her little brother BJ and a northern copperhead he'd nearly stepped on when her foot settled on something soft and slithery. She screamed and fell all at the same time, her ankle giving way beneath her as she dropped. She had no idea how Cody moved so fast or how in the dark he was able to catch her, but the next thing she knew she was in his arms, clinging to his neck. She pointed down at the ground. "There's a snake, Cody! Be careful."

He set her down a few feet away and went back to the spot where she'd felt the snake. Using the toe of his shoe, he pressed around and came up with something long and bendable. "This, you mean?"

He brought it closer and she stifled another scream. "Don't, Cody! It could be poisonous. Shawn says there's copperheads all around this lake."

"Well ..." He held his hands out so she could see exactly what had frightened her. "This branch is definitely not part of the copperhead family, I can promise you that much."

Bailey straightened and stared at the thing Cody was holding. "A branch? You've gotta be kidding. I could feel it moving."

"It's a young branch. A little more flexible than some." He tossed it off the path and grinned at her. "You probably scared it to death."

She tested her ankle, but it was fine, and suddenly she pictured herself stepping on the branch and practically jumping into Cody's arms. She burst into laughter again and had to hold onto Cody's waist as they walked. Otherwise she would've fallen to the ground, unable to breathe because she was giggling so hard.

The others already had flashlights out, and as they reached base camp, everyone wanted to know what was so funny. Bailey told her snake story, but when she reached the part about stepping on the branch, she cracked up once again. Cody had to finish the story.

It was like that throughout the weekend. She had hours of solitude with the Lord, times when she could pray about the direction God had for her life, and whether New York City was something she really wanted. Other hours she and the girls talked together, or she and Cody took long walks together. Always their time ended up in laughter, except for once—the last night of the retreat.

That night, with the moon little more than a thumbnail of light overhead, they sat by the fire until everyone else had turned in. They talked about Cody's mother and Bailey's wonderful family and Cody's dream to help kids the way Bailey's parents had helped him. They sat close together, neither of them seeming to mind when their knees touched a time or two.

Before they turned in, Cody held out his hands to her. "Pray with me, Bailey. Can you do that?"

She wasn't sure how smart it was, but she didn't hesitate. She slipped her fingers in his and together they bowed their heads. She started the prayer, the way she'd seen her mom and dad pray together so many times over the years. "Dear Lord, this time away has been so good for us, for the friendships that have grown stronger and for the way You feel closer than ever. Right now I want to thank You for Cody and his friendship. Please, Lord, keep him close to You always. And let him know how much he means to me."

It was Cody's turn, and he gave her fingers a subtle squeeze as he started. "God, You know how I feel about Bailey." He hesitated for a moment, as if his feelings for her weren't something he was willing to actually put into words. "I begged You for a second chance at her friendship, and now here we are. Copperhead snake branches and all." They both shared a couple seconds of quiet laughter, the sound of the fire crackling a few feet away. When he had control again, he finished. "Lord, I ask that You protect what we've found on the far side of Lake Monroe this weekend. I feel closer to Bailey than ever before, and I'm blessed for that fact.

"People could live all their lives and never have a friend like Bailey Flanigan. So thank You, Lord. And I pray for her audition coming up. If You want her to live in New York, to perform there and be part of a revival taking place in that city, then throw open the doors for her this next week. Let her stand out and let her get a role in a Broadway play." He paused, and there was no hiding the sadness that had crept into his voice. "But only if it's Your will, Father. Otherwise, shut the door. Then she'll know which way You're leading her."

He took a steadying breath. "Be with Tim, too, dear God. If these two are meant to be together, make that clear. Life is too short to waste on half-hearted connections and meaningless run-throughs. So let them know whether what they have is something that will last." He paused once more. "Most of all, let Bailey know how much I love her. How much I've always loved her. In Jesus' name, amen."

Bailey didn't want to let go of his hands, but slowly he let go first. She had lost her breath somewhere around the part about half-hearted connections and meaningless run-throughs, and when he asked God to let her know how much he loved her she felt her heart go into a rhythm she didn't recognize. She swallowed hard, trying to find a way to right her world back on its axis. He didn't mean the sort of love she'd always wanted from him. *It's only a friendship love*, she told herself. *Nothing more.*

But still, as they stood and shared a long hug, and as he walked her to her cabin and they said good night, Bailey had to remember to exhale. She lay in her bed in her sleeping bag for a long time, looking out the window at a brilliant spread of stars and replaying every word of Cody's prayer. He really did love her. That much was evident by the way he'd asked God to bless her audition, and in the way he'd prayed for her and Tim. When was the last time she and Tim had prayed like this, with such intensity about serious matters? She couldn't remember the last time they'd prayed together about anything.

She fell asleep certain that the one thing she didn't want was an existence of half-hearted connections and meaningless run-throughs. Never mind that Cody didn't see her as the girl of his dreams, the girl he was saving his love for. They had this between them, a wonderful bond that some people could spend their whole lives seeking.

Before she was fully asleep, she made up her mind about something: she would rather be alone than have a love that was less intimate than what she still shared with Cody Coleman. They had found something special these past few days. A deep friendship-love that had come to life once more amidst the presence of northern copperhead snake branches and laughter and God.

Most of all, God.